PRAISE FOR FLOTSAM
PERIDOT SHIFT BOOK ONE

"Combining the best elements of steampunk and space opera, placed in a lavishly detailed and imagined world, *FLOTSAM* will hold you firmly till the final page."

—Cat Rambo, author of *Beasts of Tabat*

"*FLOTSAM* tosses you headfirst into a fast-paced world of noir swashbuckling and intrigue. Airships, renegades, and plenty of action await within."

—Scott Warren, author of the *Union Earth Privateers* series

"*FLOTSAM* sucked me in and wouldn't let me go. R J Theodore is a fresh voice who will soon be on your must-read list!"

—Jennifer Foehner Wells, author of the *Confluence* series

"This author can paint a picture as vividly as if she had acrylics and a brush in hand and she isn't afraid to use a cutting sense of humour . . . I can't wait to find out where the story goes next."

—Tracey Stuart, Goodreads

"A powerfully imagined world which sucks you in, and a cast of characters that make the journey enjoyable."

—Alan Brenik, NetGalley Review

PERIDOT SHIFT

FLOTSAM

BOOK ONE

R J THEODORE

PARVUS
fantasy + science fiction

Parvus Press, LLC
PO Box 224
Yardley, PA 19067-8224
ParvusPress.com

Parvus Press supports our authors and encourages creatives of all stripes. If you have questions about fair use, duplication, or how to obtain donated copies of Parvus books, please visit our website. Thank you for purchasing this title and supporting the numerous people who worked to bring it together for your enjoyment.

[lawyerly catawumpus]

ISBN 13 978-0-9976613-7-8
Ebook ISBN 978-0-9976613-6-1
Cover art by Julie Dillon
Cover typography and interior illustrations by R J Theodore
Print design and typeset by Catspaw DTP Services
Digital Design by Parvus Press
Author photo credit Riley J Esposito

For my grandfather.
Ted, you never doubted me.

CHAPTER 1

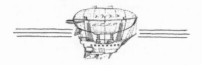

THE LAYER OF TRASH BELOW Talis's feet sparkled as she descended toward it. Frost coated the generations of detritus and caught the light as it slowly shifted. She hung in open skies, a tiny dark figure on an impossibly thin thread. Her airship lurked in the shadow of a small island above her. Around her, the shrapnel of Peridot's tectonic crust peppered the skies, tiny islands not big enough to park a chair on.

A soft click sounded in the comm of her helmet, and Dug's voice cut through the quiet sounds of her heartbeat and steady breathing. The voice tube transmission made him sound small and far away. "Progressing well, Captain. How much farther do you need?"

Talis unclenched her jaw to answer. "I'd guess I'm just about halfway down. Can't make out any details yet."

"Understood. There is plenty of length on the winch." Her first mate's voice was low and even, though he clipped his consonants the way he often did when he was tense. Dug was worried about her.

The bulky descent suit didn't make it any easier to see the view below her. It was a one-size-fits-all antique, big enough to wear over her clothes. Big enough that Dug could have worn it, if he was so worried. It was designed to keep her body heat in, and it was certainly doing that. The musty wool lining felt moist after the short time she'd had it on. Her breath fogged the glass dome that protected her from the thin air, even though she wore a scarf over her mouth. At the same time, her fingers were still getting stiff with the cold. She could have worn thicker gloves if she was just going down to strap up a large object to tow out. But this time her quarry was smaller than that, and thinner gloves provided better dexterity.

From this distance, the garbage below her looked deceptively beautiful. A lazy flow of icy shapes caught the green light from Nexus, and their reflected light sparkled through the fogging on her helmet. It wasn't hard to imagine why there were so many stories about treasure down below.

And there *was* treasure down there. Or she wouldn't be dropping into it. The flotsam layer was where the dead went to be forgotten. Dead people. Dead ships. Dead technologies. Gravity trapped it all there. Kept it from dropping out of Peridot's atmosphere on the bottom side and drifting off into the stars.

If things went wrong, Talis would be trapped, too. But the contract for this salvage made it worth the risk. She could make a lot of overdue repairs on *Wind Sabre* with the payoff. Her crew—Dug, Tisker, and Sophie—had been enthusiastic about the operation when she proposed it, knowing what kind of money a salvage might bring in. Better than the jobs they'd scrounged up recently. None of them had volunteered to make the descent, though.

"You're the reckless one, Cap," Tisker told her at the time, his eyes sparkling. The cheeky helmsman got away with the comment. He always did. His infectious grin made every gibe seem like a morale boost.

Details emerged, just a couple lengths away. Large shapes

at first. Broken hulls of ships tangled in their own lift canvasses. A roof, a wagon. An old tree trunk. Anything organic or burnable should have been composted or used for fuel, not pitched over island edge. But those hadn't always been the rules. Seventy-something generations back to the Cataclysm that fractured Peridot and the Recreation that made it what it was now, for better or worse. Seventy-something generations of garbage and waste swirled in the gravity trap. And nothing ever decayed down here.

Evidence of that: she got close enough where she could see the faces. Glittering frosted skin with closed eyes. Dead open eyes on others. Mostly Cutter folk. Some Vein. Even a Rakkar. The Bone fed their dead to the ravens and kept the bones, but still, she saw some here and there. Likely lost with their ships. No Breakers, of course.

"Almost there. Slow it down." She didn't want to end up waist-deep in the flotsam. There was always the danger of her descent line catching on something sharp.

"Aye, Cap." That was Tisker's voice on the other end now. He relayed her orders to Dug somewhere out of range of the mouthpiece. Talis felt the feed of her line slow.

Thick as the trash was gathered, she could still see through it in spots. Dark beyond, with pinpricks of light, before the garbage would shift and close the view off again.

There. The bow of an airship. The familiar pointed shape jutted up from the mass around it, its aft sinking into the accumulated garbage. The hull's dark green paint looked faded under a velvet coat of ice. But her name had been painted in white, nice and stark against the dark background. Talis held her breath, and after a moment the glass sphere of her helmet cleared enough to make out *M-P-R-E-S-S* above the shape of an old sofa that had cozied up against the hull.

"Spotted it. *The Emerald Empress.*" She pointed a finger, in case any of them had a scope on her.

"How much line do you need?"

Talis sighed, and the glass fogged again. She spared herself a small curse.

"Afraid it's more complicated. The wreck's ahead of us. We came in a little late, looks like. You'll need to reposition *Wind Sabre*."

"Wanna come back up? I just put some coffee on."

She could barely feel her fingers. Of course she wanted to go back up.

"No, just keep it steady as you can, please."

"Aye, Cap."

"And Tisker?"

"Aye, Cap?"

"Make sure you save me a cup."

She could just about hear his grin as he signed off the horn and returned to the helm. If the ship's engines could run on coffee it would nicely complete the crew's dependence on the brewed beverage. Some of her strictest policies were on the matter of proper coffee etiquette. Topping the list: If you take the last of it before the glow pumpkins were full-on orange, you'd better be damned sure there was another pot put on to brew with haste.

The descent line tugged her sideways as *Wind Sabre* began to move. She leaned back to watch her ship, and to move her neck against the crick that was settling in above her shoulder. The enormous pumpkins above, cultivated on stations spaced out across Horizon, glowed the deep purple of night. The auras around the pumpkins shifted softly as their gaseous bodies bobbed on the vines, their light reflected off swirls of mica hanging in motes around the stations' cliffs. Though not as bright as the golden candescence of their day cycle, it was still enough to highlight the edges of nearby islands. And the edges of her airship's contours.

Gliding in gentle loops through the shimmering motes, mantas fed off the duskfey that flitted in sparse clouds around the islands' edges. Against the shadow of the island, their bodies imitated the purple glow. Against the brighter shape of the pumpkins, they were a barely visible flock of shadows darting after mites that nibbled the delicate flesh of the vines and fruit. Innocent activity, no danger to her ship, but every movement in her periphery looped another knot of worry in her chest.

"Skies still clear up there?" she asked, not for the first time.

Dug's voice came back, "Yes, Captain. Sophie is on watch. No ships moving in the area, Imperial or otherwise."

Talis watched the slender shape of *Wind Sabre* emerge from beneath the shadow of her hiding spot. The faded canvas of the ship's lift envelope, stretched over the light framing ribs beneath, was black, as were its numerous patches. The smooth carrack hull was stained black. Shutters closed over the glass expanses of the great cabin and even the ventral observation deck to avoid reflecting light from any angle and all shipboard lanterns were doused. An observer looking from the Horizon altitude might only see a slight shadow pass against the glitter of flotsam below. But from where Talis hung, their ship stood out from the skies, conspicuous against the aquamarine and lavender pre-dawn light and the field of unmoving islands. Their forward and pectoral sails were furled tightly, and the only propulsion came from a pair of steel-sheathed turbines mounted to either side of the rudder. Talis caught herself holding her breath again, certain that if she could hear the hiss of the ship's steam and the hot breath of her engines, someone else would, too. But the only sound in her suit was the creak of its leather as she craned her head and adjusted her grip on the line. *Wind Sabre* was mute at this distance.

As Tisker navigated around the islands above, the impetus traveled down the line and caused Talis to spin slightly. She turned her attention back to *The Emerald Empress*. Kept her eyes on it.

"How is our course?" Dug again.

"Catching up nicely. Move a point or two anti-Nexus and I should get my toe on it in a minute."

"Captain."

Talis felt the course correction and saw her angle was good.

"Speed on the wreck's less than a half degree. Slow us down to match . . ." Her toe touched the railing. "*Now.*"

Delay from message to action was just right. Her movement synchronized with the dextral spin of the flotsam layer as she lowered the last meter to settle on the derelict galleon's forward section. She unclipped the pin in her lead line.

"Okay, good speed. I'm moving."

"Be safe, Captain."

"Aye, Dug. Talk to you in a bit." She unclipped the voice tube from her helmet and hopped down from the descent line.

Her boot slipped in the frost, and she grabbed for the railing. If she landed on her backside, the deck's steep angle would send her sliding into the flotsam that covered the aft end of the ship. She detached the grapple from her tool belt, fixed it to her lead, and hooked it around a decking brace. A couple hard tugs, and it stayed attached. She was thankful for the thinner gloves as she fed out her line slowly.

Half-walking, half-sliding, she let herself down to the deck hatch that would lead to the forecastle. The latch indicator dial read 'UNSEALED,' but the frost had done the job as well as if it had been battened from within. Talis pulled the sally bar free of her heavy tool belt and chipped both wood and ice away at the frame edge with its flat end. She gritted her teeth and strained against the ice's grip on its hinges. Nothing.

Frowning, she surveyed the layer of flotsam just below the forecastle's railing. Twisted bits of the ship's collapsed lift balloon, the trailing reinforced lines, and jagged edges of other ruined trash. Hazardous to try and push through in her suit, and likely to tangle up in her own line. Worse, something sharp and unseen in that mess might sever it entirely.

Imagining worst-case scenarios triggered her captain's paranoia, and she looked up. Nothing felt good about being this far from her ship and crew, and without comms. But the skies were clear. *Wind Sabre* was still alone up there.

She flipped the bar around in her grip and gave the iced hinges an angry whack with the sally bar's hammer end. Frost flew off in chips, but the metal itself only dented. Flattened hinges wouldn't rotate any better than frozen ones. She put the bar away and cursed its failure under her breath. There was also a portable blowtorch on her belt, but it didn't have a large paraffin tank. She'd meant to save it in case she ran into a vault door below, but if she couldn't get that far, there was no use in having it.

A small jet of blue flame popped to life as she opened the torch's valve and hit the striker. With the line wrapped around her elbow to keep it out of the way, she worked the torch back and forth over the frozen hinges with one hand and pulled on the stubborn hatch with the other.

The ice gave up its hold quickly, and Talis pushed the hatch open all the way. Darkness below. The lamp on her shoulder came to life at a flick of a toggle switch on her belt. To reduce the height of the drop, she sat with her legs dangling into the forecastle cabin. Took a big inhale, as though about to drop into a pool of water, then let herself down into *The Emerald Empress*'s dark interior.

There were a couple of possible ship designs that would have placed the great cabin at the bow, but she wasn't that lucky. From the multitude of hammocks, this was clearly crew quarters. Something crunched under her boot, and she looked down. Her light fell across the brittle frozen wrist she had stepped on. She shuddered. Instinctively tried to kick the body away, but frost had sealed it to the deck. She closed her eyes for a moment, tried to pretend she was anywhere else. Her breathing slowed.

Assuming the ring was with *The Emerald Empress's* captain, and assuming the captain was in his quarters, Talis needed to make her way aft. After a self-indulgent look back up at the open skies above, she secured her line on a hammock cleat to keep it from rubbing on the edge of the hatch.

With a kick, the door swung out—or rather, down. The layer of loose garbage was thickest overhead, giving her clear space to rappel down the slope of the ship's middle deck. To either side, over the railing, there was more to see of open skies than if she looked up. Shadows from the shifting debris crawled across the deck, only allowing a teasing dapple of light. She left her lamp on. Her breathing, it occurred to her, sounded a little uneven. *From moving in this gods-rotted heavy suit,* she told herself.

The ship creaked as she landed against the central deckhouse, sending a ripple of noise through the air. The echoes ricocheted off the frozen field of trash above her. She stood, muscles tense, until they stopped. Nothing else moved or shifted, and she turned back to the cabin at the stern and its handsome wooden door. The great cabin.

The frost thinned and disappeared as she continued aft. The humidity was low in the thin atmo here. No chance for surfaces to collect the sparkling ice as they froze. Though her suit was even more cumbersome as it got colder, the extreme chill was a blessing in its own way. Hinges turning properly, the heavy door opened outward and fell back against the cabin wall. The impact sent echoes skittering across the ship again.

The regal wooden furniture of the great cabin was either bolted down or secured on ratcheting rails, but everything else had been rearranged by the deck's sickening tilt. Bedding and personal items piled against the cabinets along the decking. The captain lay silhouetted against the wide window built along the stern, his head turned to one side. Only the glass separated him from the twinkling stars beyond. He was laying on his right arm, with his left hand out as though he'd attempted to brace against the tumble. The fingers splayed against the thick glass.

Talis let her line out to cross to the aft window. Tried not to look beyond the windowpanes. She was as skysure as any Cutter, but the emptiness outside Peridot was something else entirely. Infinite, soulless, the vacuum beckoned to her.

She braced her feet against the frame of the window to avoid stepping on the glass, which already had a diagonal split running across it. Death pallor faded the captain's skin, as the frost had muted the paint on the hull outside. The knotted prayerlocks of Cutter religion were tangled around his head. A cream-colored ribbon still looped around a few of them at the nape of his neck. Must have come loose during whatever tragedy sunk *The Emerald Empress*.

His forehead had a blunt-force wound corresponding to the starburst center of the crack in the glass. Dark blood streaked his face.

Lucky bastard was dead before he could freeze.

Lifting him up by his torso, she turned him over. His uniform, pale cream trousers and dark green jacket, was formal but still within the realm of contemporary fashion. The ship hadn't sunk all that long ago.

His right hand was tucked into his jacket's inside breast pocket. Talis sent a silent prayer to Silus Cutter that she was nearly finished here as she fumbled with the stiff fabric to free his arm.

Frozen fingers were fixed around their prize. They'd have to be broken to reveal what the late captain regarded as precious in his final moments.

Talis wished she hadn't eaten so recently.

The brittle joints snapped and the icy digits broke off cleanly. The late captain made no complaint, but Talis felt guilt rise along with the bile in her throat. She forced them both back.

"Gods *rot* it." The curse came out with a fog of sour breath and crystallized in her scarf before it could collect on the glass of her helmet.

Pressed into the skin of his palm: an iron key. She wasn't done yet.

She lifted the key by its embroidered cord and gently lowered the captain back to the glass. Crouched on the edge of the cabinet beneath the window and looked around the cabin.

In her own quarters back on *Wind Sabre*, she had several hidden compartments. Some were easier to find; those were the decoys. The less obvious were for her real valuables. Though *The Empress* was no smuggler's vessel, chances were fair that this captain had been of a mind with her. She turned her shoulder lamp to shine it along the walls, and it went out.

The panic that gripped her throat in the dark kept her from cursing. She fumbled with the power pack on her belt, flipping up its crank and spinning it under the palm of her hand to spare her numb fingers. The bulb flickered after a moment and came back on, and she could breathe again. *Almost done,* she promised herself as she re-secured the crank. *Look sharp.*

There. A wall panel over the captain's curtained bunk. A square, unnecessary seam in the bulkhead, revealed by the tilted angle of the drapes. Cast a shadow that told her one side was raised higher than the other. She jumped for it, over a pile of the captain's belongings that would have swallowed her up to her knees. The ship lurched as she landed.

"Almost done," she said out loud this time.

The sally bar pried up the panel without a fuss. Behind it, a cast-iron door was installed in the bulkhead, unmarked except for a small keyhole. The dead captain's key made for a neat match. It resisted turning at first, but she pressed it harder and it slid a last tiny bit into the lock. If she'd had a hand free—and no helmet on—she would have tugged her own prayerlocks for luck. Instead she bit her lip and turned. She felt the barrel inside move, and inhaled a gasp of anticipation.

With a cold, harsh *tink*, the key broke off in the lock.

Talis let out a string of expletives that would have made Tisker blush and grabbed her blowtorch.

"No you don't," she informed the safe. "I'm done with this place."

The fuel tank ran out just as the frozen safe door expanded with the bang of flexing metal. She flinched as the door popped free of its casing. Nothing explosive, but her glass-faced helmet had her cautious. Bracing her knees against the angled bulkhead, she gripped the edge of the door and the stump of the broken key, and pulled the safe open.

As she tallied it, she had to be using up the last of her luck.

A neat stack of documents bound with Imperial golden ribbon topped the pile of contents within. Beneath that hid a diminutive single-shot powder pistol—a captain's last defense should he be forced to open the safe against his will. And in the safe's back corner: a small blue velvet bag cinched with a white silk cord. She was so eager to be clear of this place, she forgot to be disappointed not to find a bonus of gold coin to pad the payoff from the contract.

Loosened and upended, the velvet bag produced a masculine pewter signet ring. It was scratched and pitted. The pearls set to either side of the worn seal were chipped, the seal itself unreadable. It was beyond the ability of even a Breaker jeweler's skill to repair. By her experienced appraisal, it was worthless.

It was exactly what she was looking for.

Talis tucked the ring back into its bag and tucked the bag into one of the cargo pouches on the outside thigh of her descent suit.

Her heartbeat pulsed faster in her ears. *Time to get off this damned ship.*

Engaging the motor on her lead line to speed her climb,

Talis made her way back out of the captain's cabin, up the sloping middle deck, through the ice-glazed forecastle, and back out the hatch.

She slipped a foot into the stirrup of the descent line. Clipped the voice tube back into her helmet.

To her breathless hail, Dug replied tersely, "Got crowded up here, Captain."

Talis felt the ice reach her gut as she craned her head back. Two shadows dwarfed *Wind Sabre* in the sky above. The first was an airship similar in design to hers, but twice as large, and without any pretense of stealth. Its crisp canvas lift balloon and gold-painted hull gleamed with self-importance. A Cutter Imperial patroller. It was tied off alongside a completely foreign shape that Talis only recognized from newspaper illustrations: the round, balloon-less Yu'Nyun exploration ship.

The two vessels huddled together as if sharing a secret.

Someone knew something, for sure. No way coincidence put both those ships right there, right then.

She felt the line tighten and she began to ascend.

CHAPTER 2

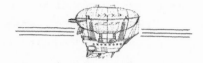

THE LINE REELED TALIS UP toward *Wind Sabre*'s curving bulk. She knew every dent and nick in the wooden airship, every scratch in the paint, like the lines of her own scars. Experience, proof of being alive.

The ship's size and shape and presence always comforted her. It wasn't the most impressive private airship in the skies—just a single lift balloon, a handful of cannons, and room for a small crew. But it was *hers*. You didn't get to have or keep much in this world. Not at the bottom where she lived. Folks at the top—or rather, at the center, on Diadem and the capital district's other larger islands at Horizon—they had whatever they wanted. More than they needed. But they didn't have freedom.

Talis didn't want estates and servants and finery. Well, maybe a little finery. But she didn't want anything that would strip her of what *Wind Sabre* provided. The skies. Just being out here. Running sometimes, well, sure. At least she was free to run.

She yanked off the helmet and let it fall to hang from its tether on the shoulder of her suit. Breathed in the cold clean air. Smelled the wood and oil and tar of her ship.

Dug, tall and dark-skinned, and Sophie, petite with a freckled honey complexion, made an odd pair as they met her at the lower transom to help her climb back aboard.

"We need to get moving," Sophie said. Her eyebrows were wrinkled under the messy fringe of short dark hair that framed her round face. The younger woman kept nervously glancing overhead as though she could see through the mass of their ship's hull to the two new arrivals up above them.

Talis put a hand on her shoulder, both for comfort and to support herself as she started to yank off the descent suit.

"Ain't that always the way," she said, and grinned.

If Talis had any sense, she'd have been frightened. And she had been at first, as the winch brought her up from flotsam. But with the ice fields safely below her and the run ahead of them, she decided she was feeling lucky. She tugged on her prayerlocks in thanks now that the helmet was out of the way, sending a silent request to Silus Cutter that their luck would hold. She had the ring. One tiny object in all that desolate mess below, and they'd found it. Easy as that. For now she ignored how 'easy' wasn't always a good sign. They had their prize. Time to trade it for a payday and keep her ship in the air for a good while longer.

"We do not believe they have seen us," Dug said. Always formal. Always on business. Or at least so long as their enemies were out of range of a fight. "The Yu'Nyun ship arrived first, but the Imperials followed behind them a short time later."

"And which one of them was following *us*, do you suppose?" Talis, free of her suit, tossed Sophie the ring in its drawstring bag. "Stow that, please."

Sophie caught the bag in cupped hands and flashed Talis a triumphant grin before gripping it tight and running off. They'd been promised a bit of a vacation once their client paid up. And this job promised the coin to make it a good one.

Talis could certainly use a vacation. And if they spent all the spare cash they made on this trip, beyond what they needed to resupply and repair, that would keep her crew content enough to stay on for the next contract. With Sophie especially, Talis did whatever she could to delay the inevitable.

A stiff breeze made Talis's damp skin prickle, and the sleeveless thermal shirt and twill cotton pants she'd worn under the suit did little to ward off the chill. She stuffed the cumbersome gear into the deck box near the descent line's winch. It would be smarter to air it out on deck before stowing it, but they needed to move, and she didn't want it flapping around in their way. She had no doubt she'd regret that the next time she smelled the thing.

"Okay, Dug," Talis said to her first mate as she yanked her boots back on, cinching the laces tight and tucking their loose ends into the tops of the calf-height leather uppers. She pulled her hair loose from the ponytail that had kept it out of her way under the helmet and felt the cool air hit her scalp. More goosebumps. She'd pay a ransom for a hot shower. Or at least for that coffee they were supposed to have saved for her.

Lines creased Dug's face, puckering the scars around his left eye. He held out her worn leather jacket, which she gladly accepted. It slipped on and settled immediately into place, matched to the contours of her strong shoulders and arms. She buttoned it up against the wind.

"Imperials," was all he said as they battened the external hatch and headed for the main deck. Both with disgust and with an almost frightening eagerness. A feral smile shone white like stars against the darkness of his skin.

The expression brought new chills. She delighted in how fearsome he was. It came in handy when she needed to make a show of force, especially considering that there were only the four of them on *Wind Sabre*. He could make just about any Cutter person think twice about whom they were dealing with. Most Cutter could go their entire lives without ever seeing one of the goddess Onaya Bone's towering people. Schoolchildren were taught about them as part of the general history of Peridot, but none were ever really prepared for the sheer intensity of the slender, muscled warriors. Even their spiritual leaders were dangerous. Beneath the wool jacket Dug wore to protect against the cool air, he was a tight coil of steely fibers, begging for combat.

Unfortunately, the Imperial airship up there outmatched their cannons five to one. She had full faith that Dug could take down every bastard on the ship if he could make it onto the railing with his knives drawn, but she wasn't looking to get the entire Cutter Imperial fleet after them. If they could sneak away without being seen, she'd like that just fine.

She clapped him on the biceps, and her icy fingers stung. Fixed him with a wry smile. "Let's see if we can't get away quietly this time, my friend. But you help Tisker get us out of here and I promise, you and me will go get into a nice brawl somewhere after this. First three rounds are my treat."

He slowly nodded, and his hungry grin hardened into something else. A brawl with Cutter civilians was a paltry trade for the chance to deal a blow to some Imperial ship. "Of course, Captain. I was referring to their presence at this particular location, at this particular moment."

"Yeah," she said, dropping the smirk. "I was thinking about that on the way up. Jasper certainly didn't mention we should expect a party."

The deck pulled under her feet and she instinctively shifted her weight to compensate for the motion. Tisker had stayed at the helm rather than greet her return, no more willing to linger than she was. He was getting them out of there, now that *Wind Sabre*'s captain was back aboard.

They reached the weather decks, and Talis held out her hand, her gaze fixed on the pair of ships hanging silent in the sky off to port. Dug, without pause, handed her the glass scope he kept in a leather pouch on his belt. Raising it to her right eye and closing the left, she examined their guests.

The silver sphere hung in the sky, silent and surreal. It looked more like the finned and glowing sirenia that grazed open atmo than a vehicle meant to convey passengers. Any other day, Talis might have been eager to finally get a true glimpse of the Yu'Nyun ship. Everything she knew about the aliens and their vessel came from newspaper illustrations and scuttlebutt in the ports where they stopped for trade. She hadn't gotten a clear idea of what the visitors looked like, just heard unsettling descriptions that had to be half fiction.

The aliens came from somewhere far beyond the thinnest edges of Peridot's atmosphere, and their ship's hull was sealed tight to keep the air in. There was only a small line of translucent portholes on the top half of the round hull, at the wrong angle to allow Talis a view inside. Instead, the bubble windows were silhouetted against the skies, lit from within, like the glowing eyes of some amphibious cave dweller.

The airship—only that wasn't right; the papers called it a 'starship'—had no external markings. No flags or banners. No lift balloon, sails, or rigging. No propellers or turbines. Talis wanted to ask Sophie how she figured the thing could stay aloft, but there was no time to get her engineer started. Get that girl close enough, and give her a screwdriver, and Sophie'd have the ship in pieces. Then maybe she could tell Talis how it worked, if Talis could follow what the young woman offered in the way of explanation.

The sight of the starship was unsettling and mesmerizing at the same time, but the Yu'Nyun weren't the real threat here. Despite the long, thin ventral cannon mounted on the starship's bow below its nose, Talis had never heard of it actually attacking, or even posturing. Enormous, yes. Sent shivers up Talis's back, for certain. Still, the aliens were only a potential nuisance, not the prime threat.

Talis pursed her lips as she fixed the scope on the Imperial ship. It was one specimen of the enormous fleet deployed across this half of the world by the Cutter government, and a far more immediate concern. Patrol ships, hunter ships, service ships, and war ships peppered the skies like acne. Ostensibly their presence protected the Cutter folk, aided stranded airships, assisted in civil emergencies, and guarded the borders of the Cutter territory.

But it wasn't just because Talis was perpetually on the wrong side of the law that seeing them up close put a knot in her gut. The Imperials were bullies. Guardians of the status quo. They kept rich bureaucrats rich and paupers poor by enforcing not only judicial law, but moral and trade laws as well. Taxes, tolls, and tariffs. Fines for indecency or disturbing the peace. All of them excessive unless you knew the right bureaucrat. The Cutter folk who couldn't eke out a living for themselves and their families got overtaxed on the barest profit and fined when they couldn't pay. Bankrupt, they'd be compelled into mandatory labor (or *civil service*, as it was called by those who'd never have to serve it) to pay their debts.

The alien starship blocked enough of the view that Talis couldn't see the Imperial ship's designation, but she wouldn't know the airship by name anyway. The design of the hull and rigging was unfamiliar. Something new. It was larger than most patrol vessels she'd encountered since she left the service. Gun ports were packed tightly in neat rows across five decks, almost enough for a warship twice its size.

Dozens of small maneuvering and stunsails were rigged along the equator of the airship's twin lift balloons. Six turbines crowded around its rudder—more than enough power to rip their own ship apart if they gave her all she had. Add the excessive propulsion to the size of that lift system, and it was a safe bet that the wooden hull was reinforced with iron, and strong enough to take any beating that *Wind Sabre's* nine-pound cannons could dole out. It had twice as many securing lines leading from the hull to the lift balloon, and so many sets of ratlines leading up to it, that the deck reminded

Talis of a cage for some flighted animal.

The Imperial ship was outfitted for a fight, not a patrol. It could easily staff seventy hands, maybe a hundred, plus rifles enough to arm them. And from the silence that hung in the short distance between it and the Yu'Nyun, it was clear that it wasn't the starship they were looking to engage.

Both ships sat motionless a few lengths above and several hundred lengths toward Nexus from where *Wind Sabre* was positioned. There was a fairly good chance their small black hull hadn't been sighted yet. Then again, the fact that the Imperial ship was out here in the nothing reaches at all, and lingering close to where Jasper had told Talis she would find the ring, meant nothing good.

"Much as I itch to be away from those ships," she said, handing the scope back to Dug, "better we don't move any faster than the flotsam. Stay a shadow against it. No sudden movements. Those Imperials sight us, they'll run us down without effort."

"And the Yu'Nyun?" He snapped the scope back into its pouch and tucked his hands under his arms. Dug's tribe came from humid jungles and warm breezes, and he did not enjoy the biting gusts of open air. When they got their cargo back to Subrosa to exchange it for money, she'd tell him to spend some of his cut on a pair of gloves. "If they see us?"

Talis leaned her head back to try to relieve some of the tightness in her neck, which ached from her time in the descent suit. Coming back up to two unwelcome guests hadn't helped the tension. The aliens had a reputation for being curious, and something about Peridot fascinated them. Since they'd arrived months ago, they'd been exploring the ruins, libraries, and cities across all four territories. They could be a nuisance when they interrupted business or got invasively interested in someone who would prefer to be left alone. All the races had tried to be friendly and cooperative, warned against seeming rude by their governments. But if the aliens got in the middle of *Wind Sabre*'s escape . . . Talis made an attempt to massage her own shoulders.

"They worry me less than that Imperial ship." She frowned and chewed the inside of her lip. "But it's like you said. All of us together, over this one patch of garbage? This breeze carries rot. I want to get our featherweight cargo to its buyer before this job blows up like a senile Rakkar's laboratory."

Dug handed her the scope again and moved off toward the wheelhouse to convey her orders to Tisker.

She stood in silence at *Wind Sabre*'s railing, scope locked on the pair of ships as they grew smaller. Trying to control the bounce in the viewfinder, she forced herself to breathe slowly. Out in the skies, the pumpkins were lavender, tinted with gold at the vines and along the ribs. Their glow would be at full strength in a couple of hours.

Flotsam didn't spin fast enough to get them away from the area with any haste. At some point before golden dawn, *Wind Sabre* would have to make her escape or be spotted.

The lines creaked above her, tethering the buoyant lift balloon to the weight of the hull beneath it. Wood creaked. The steam engines at mid-deck hissed and hummed within their housings, puffing hot air up into the envelope and feeding pressure to the pair of turbine thrusters mounted to either side of the rudder. Through the soles of her boots, she could feel the rumble of Sophie's belt-driven stoker rig as it tumbled dark bricks into the firebox two decks down. Talis fingered her prayerlocks, this time asking for their luck to hold. She loved the little songs her ship sang as it was under way, but now she wished the old girl knew how to whisper.

Paranoia. At this distance the noises should be lost before they reached that Imperial ship. She'd invested a dozen contracts' worth of earnings to insulate the hull and the engine compartments, and knew her ship was as quiet as they came.

She laced her fingers into her 'locks and gave them another tug. Begged Silus Cutter that finding the ring would be the start of a lucky run, not the end of one.

The Imperial ship began to move. It peeled away from the Yu'Nyun starship and angled its bow to a trajectory that would intercept *Wind Sabre*'s current course.

Silus must have been too busy to perceive her wish.

Talis clapped the scope shut, yelling orders as she ran aft toward the wheelhouse.

"Kick those boilers and shift it to the thrusters!" she bellowed. "We've been spotted!"

CHAPTER 3

THE IMPERIAL SHIP WAS CALLED *The Serpent Rose*. Talis got a look at its designation as it pulled away from the Yu'Nyun. Lighter than a warship, but with twice as much ammunition relative to its size. The smaller dimensions gave the ship speed, and the delicately sweeping line of its hull cut through wind resistance. This ship was meant for the chase. A hunter.

And *Wind Sabre* was her prey.

Their position was bad. If Talis and her crew wanted to get away, pinched against the far reaches of breathable atmosphere and a barrier of garbage was no place to find themselves with a hunter ship on their Nexus-side. The Imperials were between them and just about anywhere they'd rather be.

Tisker was at the helm, though, Talis reminded herself. He'd negotiated them out of a career's worth of tight spots. It wasn't just his skill. Talis had skill enough on her own. It was his instinct with the ship that had sealed his place on her crew. His left hand danced across the levers on the control board while he deftly managed the wheel with his right. She saw him shift his body to starboard and felt *Wind Sabre* angle to catch the wind, their motions synchronized. The ship handled as though they shared a bond, as though it was an extension of him. Some Cutters had that. Understood the wind, natural as breathing.

So Talis was a spectator. In good conditions, the ship could be run by one person if it had to be. A crew of four had no slack, so she'd made the right upgrades to ensure that. With Sophie aloft to watch their clearance and Dug supervising the engine output, Talis would only get in the way in the tight spaces around the engine compartments. The crew knew where to go and what was at stake.

All the same, *The Serpent Rose* gained on them. It seemed as though *Wind Sabre* was frozen in place, despite the bitter air buffeting her face.

Then movement from the Yu'Nyun ship caught her eye, the reflections of purple light sliding across its burnished surface as it changed direction. Once again envious of its closed hull, she watched as it descended in a straight line, down into the flotsam layer. The trash stirred around it, disturbed and displaced, sending shivers of movement in its wake. Good thing she'd already found the ring, or that little dip would have destroyed any accuracy in the coordinates she'd gotten from Jasper. The garbage would skitter and swirl around for days from that disturbance.

The starship's arching dorsal fin cut through the wrecks and castoffs, the only thing visible as the ship became submerged in the detritus. Whatever business the aliens had with the Imperial ship, it had apparently been satisfied. Talis let out a breath. No doubt in her mind now. The aliens were looking for the ring, too.

Tisker navigated *Wind Sabre* through clusters of tiny islands that weren't worthy of being mapped on the sky charts.

He's hoping the Imperials catch one in the hull, she thought, amused. *Or, better, in the lift envelopes.*

But *The Serpent Rose* did not answer the challenge.

She kept to her higher elevation, where the islands were big enough to spot, where she didn't have to restrain her engines. Up where *Wind Sabre* needed to be if they wanted to take full advantage of their small ship's handling and speed.

If we take the ship up at the right angle, we might not lose too much momentum, Talis thought. Just as the maneuver occurred to her, she felt the deck shift gently. Tisker was thinking on her level.

She looked back to the wheelhouse. Dug leaned out over the railing, communicating obstacles and the Imperial ship's position back to Tisker, who remained focused on his controls.

With nothing else to do, Talis went below, to the galley where that mug of coffee sat waiting for her. But one cooled cup wouldn't satisfy, and the ship's activity had spilled some of it onto the counter. She put on another pot to boil.

The percolator, clamped to the tri-gimbaled stovetop in case of turbulence or eventful flying, seemed to take longer than usual to make the bitter brew. She paced, wishing the portholes in the galley provided the proper angle to watch their pursuers. Finally, the spurting sounds from the pot subsided, and she cut the flame. She poured, then carefully carried two mugs to the wheelhouse.

"Thanks, Cap." Tisker didn't reach for the mug she placed in the holder next to the control panel. Eyes set on the skies ahead of them, his normally easy smile put aside for the moment. Hands made small adjustments to the engines and the power outputs. His usual slouch had been replaced with a relaxed alertness, from the curve of his spine to the flex in his knees. When he was in pilot mode, nothing broke his concentration.

"Where you wanna bring us up?" Keeping out of the way along the railing, she leaned out from under the lift balloons enough to locate the shape of the Imperial ship as it cruised above them. Air rippled around all six of its thrusters, but there was no sign of strain on her lines. They'd caught a wind that filled their forward sail and took the pressure off their engines. The bastards weren't even sweating.

Tisker turned on his usual careless smile long enough to respond. "I figure we give 'em an obstacle. Get us the chance to gain Horizon without being forced to come up right under them."

He pointed out a dark blotch in the distance. Talis squinted at it, though by the light it blocked she knew instantly that it was an island big enough to hide them from view of their pursuers. If they angled the approach right, *The Serpent Rose* would have to navigate around the landmass, which would cost them some speed. Not to mention the proper angle for all but their forward cannons. If Tisker could get them up to Horizon altitude before *The Serpent Rose* could recover from the course correction, they could unfurl their stunsails, catch the slip winds, and try to rabbit.

She put a hand on Tisker's shoulder and squeezed. Through the sleeve of his cotton jacket she felt the tension in his muscles. He nodded at her and put more power into the engines. Gave a lever the barest nudge, and *Wind Sabre* exhaled more steam into the lift balloon. Talis felt it pull against the shift in wind direction as the ship started to come up, and the engine hum increased its output to compensate for the resistance. Hopefully the adjustment would be smooth enough that the airship shadowing them wouldn't get wise to what they were planning.

Wind Sabre was the first and only ship Tisker had ever piloted, but he came to it like a moth to flame. Stepped onto her deck with zero deference, just walked up the plank and ran his hands along the engine compartment amidship on his way aft to the wheelhouse. Talis caught him there and chased him off five times before he had the good sense to stand his ground and ask for a job. This lanky kid, in clothes that were too short for his adolescent limbs, with no Cutter prayerlocks in his filthy hair, and not one bit of spare fat on his bones.

Against her better judgment, she cleaned him up and fed him. Polished the natural-born pilot underneath.

The morning after he arrived, Talis had worried there'd be a whole street gang of orphans with their hands in her coffers, but she found only Tisker, curled up in a blanket around the wheel's pedestal. He'd been too frightened to sleep in the crew cabin with Dug.

She hadn't trusted him to guide them clear of the docks of Subrosa that day, but out in the open skies she let him take the wheel. She stood by his side, ready to snatch back control in case he pointed them at an island at full speed. It hadn't been a necessary precaution. He was every bit as in tune with the movements of the ship that day as he was now. He might just be the best investment she'd ever made at Subrosa, and it only cost her a few meals and some hot water. She wasn't sure whether it was Tisker or she who was more proud the day he received his first crew share from a job's payout. He'd stared at the money in his hand, then tucked it away quickly, as though he were still a thief in danger of being caught. Bought himself that jacket of his with it, then showed the rest of them how to stitch hidden pockets that sly fingers couldn't easily get into.

Sophie knotted his 'locks for him, a whole bank of them across his crown, and shaved the sides and back. It was his first haircut worthy of the name, and he'd never quit the habit of rubbing his scalp to feel the shorn stubble prickle against his hand. Except at the helm, where little could distract him.

Talis still took the wheel when they were on a long haul and Tisker needed a rest, but his place under the wheelhouse was secured, and he'd never given her a reason to regret that rare act of charity.

TISKER'S COFFEE WAS COLD and Talis's was long gone when
The Serpent Rose finally made a visible course correction to
move around the island. Tisker flashed her a grin, which disappeared just as quickly. His eyes were on the craggy underside of the hovering landmass, far as he could see it before
the lift balloon blocked the view above. Jagged downward
spires of rock with scraggly brush clinging to them pointed
at the tender canvas of *Wind Sabre*'s lift envelope like dangerous clawed fingers. Tisker had allowed them plenty of room
to slip under, and Sophie was on watch atop the envelope
of course, but the sharp stone made its threats anyhow. The
mica dust that collected in drifting motes around the island
abraded her skin as Tisker accelerated through.

Dug brought them goggles, which they gratefully accepted, and the three of them stood watching the rough surface
of the island. Collective breath held, waiting to see the clear
skies open up again.

When the first stars sparkled beyond the edge of the
landmass above them, Talis couldn't help but let out a triumphant exhalation. Tisker adjusted pitch and *Wind Sabre* rose
at a steeper angle.

At the same moment that Talis dared to believe they'd
make it, Sophie yelled something from above that was swallowed by the winds. Dug moved quickly to the railing and
echoed her alarm.

Around the bulk of the lift balloon, *The Serpent Rose*'s
hull came into view before them. Directly in their path.
Sitting there, all-stop, like it had been waiting patiently for
hours. Gun ports open, and a field of cannons—eighteen-
pounders at least—stared them down.

Talis felt an icy grip on her heart.

"Silus's fragrant winds!" Tisker pulled levers and turned

the wheel to prevent them from colliding with the larger ship. *Wind Sabre* slowed, shedding that precious speed that he had worked so hard to gain.

Sophie appeared down the ratlines, sliding on the insides of her boots and controlling her descent—just barely—with her bare hands. She hit the deck and slunk back into the shadow of the deckhouse, pressing herself against the structure. Not afraid, no, but anticipating Talis's next order. Dug's fist clenched so tightly that Talis heard his knuckles pop across the length of the deck between them. They all knew what she knew.

"All right." She put her hand back on Tisker's shoulder. "Top marks for trying. Let's get ready for the boarding party."

She looked at Sophie, hidden from *The Serpent Rose*'s view by the deck house and the lift balloon above. It wasn't the first time they'd been stopped by a patrol, and they weren't out of tricks yet.

"Sophie, man down."

Sophie met the command with an impish grin—slightly feral, slightly childlike. "Man down, aye, Cap."

"Put that ring in cold storage, would you?"

Already heading for the access belowdecks, Sophie waved her understanding over her shoulder as she made for one of the many hidden compartments onboard *Wind Sabre*. They were too small for most people. Laughable for Dug. But Sophie was shorter than the average Cutter, almost as small as a Rakkar, and tiny enough to comfortably fit in all but the smallest lockers on the ship. When *The Serpent Rose*'s crew unavoidably searched the decks for all hands, Talis would still have a game piece in play.

"They'll be on our starboard," she called after Sophie, then turned back to Dug and Tisker. "All right, you two. Time to look honest."

Tisker gave her a crooked grin.

"Not even close," she said and flashed him a scowl. But

this was a practiced routine.

They stowed their expensive goggles and donned thread-bare wool jackets and fingerless gloves. Covered tattoos and downgraded their appearances. Tisker wrapped a moth-eaten gray scarf over the gold and silver finery he wore around his neck and pulled a knit cap down over his glittering earring.

Not much could be done about Dug. A Bone man on a Cutter ship wasn't a common sight, but it did happen. Best he could do was slouch and try to look less dangerous, and cover his warrior's hairstyle with a felt hat. He bit down on a battered cigar, which made him look older and less predatory, somehow, and had the added bonus of preventing him from grinding his teeth when he had to withstand the inevitable Imperial insults.

Transformations completed, they looked like nothing more than struggling merchants with too few hands to manage the rigging. Beneath notice, easy to dismiss. Hardly worth the time of a ship as fancy and important as *The Serpent Rose*. And if that failed, there were knives sheathed on the backs of their waistbands below their thigh-length coats.

Wind Sabre came to a full stop, letting the Imperials cross the final distance to them. The other ship's crew made quick work of tying off alongside their starboard railing. A gangplank painted a glossy cream slid across the gap between the two ships, and *The Serpent Rose*'s commander stepped up into view.

"Five hells," breathed Talis. Dug shot her a look. She pressed her lips into a thin line in response. It wouldn't be enough to just play innocent.

She took a deep breath and stepped forward as the Imperial captain paused at his end of the gangplank. He didn't look half as surprised as she felt.

She crossed her arms and stood, blocking his path. "Hey there, Hankirk."

CHAPTER 4

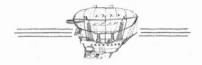

Hankirk stood at the far end of the gangway, regarding Talis with the look of disdain she remembered so well instead of the surprise which she felt. She might not be able to surprise him by being here—and why was that, she very much wanted to know—but she could at least take him down a few notches in front of his crew by ignoring his rank.

"It's Captain Hankirk, currently," he said, his eyes narrowing. Sounded like he was counting on a promotion soon. "Some careers progress further than others."

His connections had clearly served him well. He was well-polished, trim, healthy. Still handsome, though the smirk of entitlement on his face always ruined his good looks. He had no Cutter prayerlocks knotted into his hair. She recalled that he never seemed to think he needed any help from, or favor with, The Five. It wasn't surprising to hear him boast, though his cadence was a bit formal compared to their last conversation. He was showing off—either for her, or for the crew that was waiting behind him to board her ship.

"Hey now, she's a captain, too." Tisker, even without knowing the history Talis and Hankirk shared, couldn't let the implied insult go unanswered.

"That's right," Talis said, giving the Imperial captain the most insincere smile she could muster. "Look at that, we're both captains now."

At a nod from Hankirk, two of his men moved forward and crossed their rifles in Talis's face. She was forced back a step so he could board.

He stepped onto the deck of *Wind Sabre* as if it were his ship. He had more personnel on board to command than she did, at that point, as his crew spilled onto her deck and began the expected sweep of the ship. Talis knew the pale coats would find everything tidy. She made a practice of stowing what the Empire felt she shouldn't have where a cursory search wouldn't disturb it.

Hankirk glanced around and took in her trappings, her weathered black paint and tarnished brass fittings. Glanced up, at a lift balloon patched in several places. Talis kept her eyes fixed on him. Willed him to make some remark and see what happened. She was as proud as a mother of her ship. And no ship with a crew small as hers wasted their days polishing brass.

"Been, what, about ten years?" She kept her voice amiable. But not too much so. They had been less than friendly last time they spoke. Not much reason to pretend to be old pals now.

"I'd have thought it would be far longer before we met again," he said, with a cocked eyebrow and a matched tone in his voice. "Once I heard you'd quit the service."

She smiled instead of speaking. The only response that came to mind was a quip about how relieved he must have been that, with her gone, he'd have finally been at the top of his graduating class. Could be satisfying to take him down another rung, but it wouldn't get him off her deck any faster.

With the pleasantries out of the way, he held out an open hand, and one of his crew appeared to place a dossier into it.

"You are under arrest, charged with illegal salvage operations, evading Imperial forces, and"—he looked around the ship again—"I'm certain a search of your vessel will only reveal material for additional charges."

She'd talked her way out of plenty of situations by playing dumb and weak, but that wouldn't fly with Hankirk. He knew her as well as she him. Fortunately, their cover story didn't hinge on her acting the role of bumpkin. She'd stick to what they'd planned, because she honestly didn't know what else to do. And, if her crew was separated for questioning, they all knew their lines.

"Salvage?" She played a little laugh into the statement. A touch of relief. But not too much. "There's been a mistake. It wasn't a salvage."

She had to sound mournful, too. She let her eyes go big, hoping he still found them as pretty as he once told her he did.

"We lost one of our crew. A line came loose on the lift balloon, and she fell. We hoped if we got down after her fast enough, we could get to her in time."

"Crew overboard, then?" There was a glint in his brown eyes. He was on to her.

She nodded anyway, not ready to give up on the plan until she had something better.

"Safety violations can be added to the list, then," he said, curtly. "Perhaps we might have aided you, but you attempted to ghost from the area as though you had something to hide from an Imperial ship."

Talis shook her head. "I found her. It was too late to help her." She gestured over her shoulder at the direction from which they'd come. "And as for running—did you *see* that alien ship? We've never been so close to it before. Spooky thing. We know the stories. They're all curious and nosy, right? Might come aboard and get too friendly."

"The aliens."

"Right, Captain. Wasn't *your* ship we were running from."

She hadn't meant for it to sound like a dig at the enormity of his presence, but the twitch at the corner of his eye told her that's how he'd taken it. She had no problem insulting him, but right now she needed him to lose interest in her, real quick.

"We're just a transport," she said, a little too urgently. This was all falling apart. Their ruses depended on the officiating Imperial captain being uninterested in anything more than properly filling out his reports before moving on again. Hankirk was all sorts of interested.

And Dug was barely content to go along with the act as it was. He always argued that it saved time to open necks and send bodies headfirst over the railing. Talis sensed him, still as a stone behind her, growing impatient.

"Freelance? With a black hull and canvas." Hankirk's tone was full of opinion. One of the officers who had been sent off to search *Wind Sabre* returned and whispered in Hankirk's ear. He nodded stiffly to the officer, and the search party returned to *The Serpent Rose*. The look of disappointment was obvious. They hadn't found anything, or anyone.

That left eight Imperials plus Hankirk on Talis's ship.

"That's right," she said, running a hand through her hair. The guards, still holding her back with their rifles, pushed aggressively at her motion. She shot them a scalding look before continuing. "Just not as fond of the gold trim as you are. Licenses are in order, as you'll no doubt want to see."

Hankirk spared a glance at Dug. "And does your refugee have the official paperwork to be on this side of the border?"

Talis tensed. Hankirk's men chuckled, not so animated that they lost their disciplined demeanor, but to her it was as loud as tearing canvas. Heat pulsed off Dug like someone had opened a furnace door. Talis shifted her weight into one hip, moving subtly in front of him to warn against any action he might be considering.

"He's got his license stamped for all four territories, if that's what you mean."

Not *quite* true. Dug was unwelcome in his own people's skies, but Hankirk had no right to that information. Or to know how close the word 'refugee' was to the truth.

Hankirk wrinkled his nose, then opened the dossier. He feigned scanning the page, but when he spoke he glared at her directly. He'd memorized the contents. The motions seemed rehearsed.

"You accepted a contract for an unlicensed salvage in this sector, and you are acting as the agent of one Jasper, a Breaker goods receiver operating out of the Corrugated District of Subrosa. Under this contract, you agreed to salvage an ancient pewter and pearl ring from the flotsam and return it to the Breaker man for the promised sum of thirty-five thousand silver presscoins."

She felt her face contort with surprise, and quickly tried to guide it into a look of confusion. Her mind raced. Superstitious, she hadn't even told her *crew* how big the payoff was, much less blabbed about it to anyone in Subrosa. Sure, she visited the bars after taking the deal, but no matter how deep in her cups she got there was never any doubt that she didn't trust a single bastard in that bottom-hanged black-market city. So how'd Hankirk know? Jasper wasn't likely to be intimidated into divulging client information by any show of force or authority. His business depended on it.

If Hankirk noted her reaction, he didn't say. He continued, "Of course I don't have to remind you that any items in the flotsam layer are the exclusive property of the Empire, from the moment they cross into Cutter skies, until such a time as they orbit into another territory."

There was only one way Talis could think of that Hankirk might know about the deal.

Tisker stepped forward, protesting. "Look, clearly we have some sort of misunderstanding."

Imperial hands moved forward to intercept him, rifles raised. Tisker put his palms up and stopped talking.

"What you clearly *misunderstand*," Hankirk said, still addressing Talis, "is that I have you tightly pegged, and nothing is going to prevent me from searching your ship plank-by-plank, finding the contraband, and bringing you all to hang for your crimes in the capital province."

Talis sensed Dug's tension like a physical force pushing against her back. He hadn't moved, but she knew he was thinking about the knives tucked up his coat sleeves. She had to figure a way to defuse this situation and get away clean, or it was going to come to violence. Fun as that might be, and satisfying, attacking an Imperial crew was no way to untangle themselves from consequence.

Where's Sophie?

She manifested what she hoped was a charming and not venomous smile. "Okay, fair enough. It's like you said. We have a ring."

Now Tisker tensed, too. *Trust me*, she willed him silently.

"You want the ring. We want our thirty-five thousand silver." She took a casual step forward and found confidence in the fact that no one pushed at her with their weapons again. "The deal can still be made. Surely you were going to be paying Jasper more than that. His commission rate still the highest in Subrosa?"

Hankirk chuckled and shut the file.

So. She was right. The job *had* been a setup.

Knowing that didn't make her feel any better.

Hankirk closed the gap between them, and the two riflemen moved aside. Shorter than her by half a hand, he had to look up a bit to meet her gaze.

"Look at my ship, Talis. First of its class. I *told* you I'd be taken care of. Look at the strength of my crew. I will *take* the ring, and I will bring you to face the only reward that you deserve." He looked at Dug over her shoulder and said, "Justice."

Knuckles popped, this time her own. Her arm tensed to swing a hook at his pompous face. If they were going to get in a fight, let her please, *please,* at least break that pretty nose of his.

But an outcry from his crew snatched his face out of her reach, as he turned to see flames climbing the lines of his ship.

Talis resisted the urge to laugh. Felt a bit of the tension lift like steam evaporating off the deck. *Thank you, Sophie.*

Deckhands on *The Serpent Rose* ran for the suppressant tanks, their academy-drilled discipline requiring no order. If enough of those lines burned through, the weight of the ship's hull would do the rest of the work. Of course, they'd get the fire put out before it got to that. This was just the distraction.

"Oh, I'm looking at your ship, Captain," Talis said, unable to resist. "Not sure I'm seeing what you want me to, though."

"Search *The Rose*," he barked to his crew as he turned back to glare at Talis. "They've got a man aboard!"

Dug moved, taking advantage of the break in their attention. His knives flashed purple and gold, reflecting the morning skies. Talis cursed him for it. She had been holding out hope that Sophie's distraction would get Hankirk and his crew off her deck long enough for them to escape cleanly, without spilling blood and without ending up on the top of the Imperials' warrant pile.

That was no longer an option she could consider.

A few steps from the gangway, Dug wiped bloodied knives against his moleskin pant legs. Two officers and their rifles lay in a heap on *Wind Sabre's* deck. The two Imperial guards nearest Talis turned to challenge Dug next. That was that, then. Not much reason to be polite anymore. The instant that Hankirk's men left his side, Talis took a swing.

CHAPTER 5

HANKIRK SAW THE PUNCH coming and leaned back far enough to dodge it. Talis felt his breath on her knuckles as they swept through the empty air in front of his face. But her elbow was in pursuit, and she slammed it into his jaw. He staggered, momentarily dazed. She brought up the opposite knee and struck him hard in the ribs. He tumbled to the deck, grunting. Off balance, she went down after him, but rolled and came up on the balls of her feet, ready for more.

The four remaining officers circled Tisker, who stood unmoving in the middle of their group. The spring-loaded blade he'd hidden up his sleeve had found its way to his hand. It was gripped casually at his side, ready to come up and answer the first move any of them might make.

Talis wanted to help, but Hankirk wasn't done with her. His guards were finished, though, at Dug's feet. So Dug and his knives went to Tisker's aid.

Hankirk climbed up on one knee, the arch of his cheekbone already bruising. His arm was across his chest, tenderly holding his ribcage. He struggled to catch his breath, but looked as pleased as if he was the one who'd landed the blows.

"You could *never* take me down in a fight."

Rot him and his boasting. It was true, though. In their academy days, their matches had always ended in his favor. About the only thing he did better than her. He'd broken her arm once. But she'd broken his wrist, collarbone, and several fingers in the same match. His advantage was that he could always ignore his injuries and keep going. He was tenacious, fighting like a demon to best her, even earlier on, when the sparring was meant to be friendly.

"That was ten years ago. Bet I've had more practice than you since then." Talis twisted her head around to relieve a pressure on her neck. The vertebrae popped as they realigned.

Dug liked to spar with her twice daily to keep his skills honed. And when a Bone warrior insisted on full-contact sparring, you learned fast or wasted precious supplies in the med cabin.

Hankirk pretended to stumble as he stood, then kicked one leg out in an attempt to sweep her feet out from under her. But she knew the trick and was ready. That fake had never worked on Dug when she tried it. She put her knee down on his back to pin him as he kicked, then got her hand under his arm and up. Hankirk twisted loose from her grip as she tried to lock her hand behind his neck. He threw his head back, and just missed her nose. Got her in the mouth, though. She tasted blood as she blinked back the flash in her vision. She rarely went unscathed sparring with Dug, either.

Talis and Hankirk scrabbled clumsily for advantage. He bent her fingers back and twisted around to face her, throwing her off balance. She swung her left arm with that momentum, finally got a good crack in on his nose. But he swept her other arm and wrenched her shoulder. His arms couldn't reach her throat, but he yanked on her hair and managed to get a boot up under her jaw. She used the side of her forearm to strike his knee so that it twisted out of place. The hit didn't land hard enough to tear anything, but the pressure removed itself from her throat and Talis coughed away the feel of the boot heel against her windpipe.

She heard a deep laugh as she tried to torque his arms into submission, and then Dug cracked Hankirk across the back of his skull with the pommel of his knife. Dazed, Hankirk fell backward, his head hitting the deck with a thud. Talis shoved him away, untangling her legs from his. She blinked against the blood that had gotten into her eyes.

"You fight like siblings." Dug held out a hand to help her up, lifting her an inch into the air with the strength of his pull.

Tisker, wearing as much blood as Dug, grabbed Hankirk by the short hair of his crown and held his knife against the reddened flesh of Hankirk's neck.

"Hold on a second, leave him," Talis said to Tisker.

It would be hard to keep their heads down and her ship in the air if the entire Imperial fleet was after them for killing one of its prized and privileged commanders. She needed a better way out of this knot.

"Unhand the captain!" The shout came from the opposite end of the gangway.

Sophie, one eye swollen shut and her lip bloodied, stood on the deck of *The Serpent Rose*. Her hands were bound in front of her. An Imperial gripped her by the shoulder on each side. An officer held his service flintlock to the side of her head, half-cocked with his finger hovering over the trigger.

Sophie's face was blank. Either they'd rung her bell hard, or she was masking her thoughts and putting on a brave face for everyone.

Dug stepped forward to help Tisker get Hankirk up off the deck. He teetered a little as they got him to his feet, but tugged the hem of his coat to straighten it and stood proudly, chin lifted. No doubt certain he'd won the day already.

"Send ours over and you'll get yours," Talis called across.

The crew of *The Serpent Rose* had gotten the last of the

flames doused, and some were already working to replace the worst of the damaged lines. There was an arm's length of deck railing that had caught fire as well. Some poor crewmen would be refinishing and painting that tonight. Tomorrow you'd never know the ship had suffered the indignity of Sophie's arson.

They just needed to get Sophie back and get themselves away before the crew figured out what else the freckled imp had been up to. No doubt the *Rose*'s crew would find a way to answer *that* insult. No doubt Hankirk knew how to file the paperwork to make it look like sinking them was the appropriate and just response.

Hankirk's first mate called over, her alto voice carrying easily over the distance, "Send the Captain over and after, we'll return your woman."

"Bad idea," Talis called back, noticing with annoyance that her own, rougher voice didn't sound half as commanding. "He got a good knock just a moment ago. Might take a tumble off that plank into open air. Come get him, if you still want him."

They weren't expecting that. There was some hesitation among the officers, until finally one motioned to Sophie's guards and they made for the gangplank, grabbing rifles on their way.

Sophie was pushed roughly across and stumbled once. Only the firm grip of her escorts kept her from falling off the narrow walkway herself, and they let her lean a little too long before pulling her upright again. Talis added another mark against them to her mental tally.

Tisker met Sophie at the railing, and put an arm around her, drawing her away from the other crew. She sagged against his side, slack with relief. Tisker walked her backward, his eyes never leaving the Imperial crew members on the deck. Sophie's eye was going to need a close look, her jaw was bruised, and her lip was split. But she was in one piece.

Her eyes flashed, and Talis didn't miss the tiny smirk tugging at the corner of her bloodied mouth. It had been done proper, and no one yet the wiser.

Hankirk took a step forward, and his officers moved to sling their rifles over their shoulders in order to help him back to their ship, but he waved a stop to that motion, and rolled his shoulders to square them before stepping up onto the plank with his dignity intact. He eyed Talis as he passed her, but she had no interest in provoking them further. She'd gotten her crack in on Hankirk's face. A trail of blood ran from his broken nose to his chin, and dripped onto the pale blue of his formerly pristine uniform jacket. She probably would live to regret that. Now she just wanted to get her crew out of range of *The Rose*'s rifles before Sophie's work was discovered.

As Hankirk stepped down onto his own deck, he turned back to face her. She stood firm, expecting another insult against her and her ship. Expecting him to point out she hadn't bested him without help.

She didn't expect him to say, "Fire on their hull."

Talis marched forward and kicked the board free of her railing as Hankirk's crew were spurred into action. The carefully painted board with narrow sand-textured grip rails tilted, scuttling the pair of officers still stepping down on the other side. Then it dropped off the railing of *The Serpent Rose* and tumbled out of sight below their ships.

Tisker ran for the wheelhouse. Dug cut through the bindings on Sophie's wrists and handed her his blade since she'd returned from *The Rose* with empty sheaths. Dug always wore more than one. He ran forward along the starboard railing, severing the lines that tethered them to the Imperial ship. Sophie slipped the blade beneath her belt and dug in the large pocket over her thigh as she approached her captain.

Talis tried not to think about how close they might have come to losing Sophie. Her shoulders knotted up and she felt the burn of anger in her cheeks. She wanted to lash out, as if a swing of her arms could bat *The Serpent Rose* out of the skies.

The deck moved under her feet. A small shift. She knew Tisker wanted to be out of there as fast as she did, but he made it look casual. Good man. Don't let them see you sweat. She wiped her brow on the back of her jacket sleeve. Try not to, anyway.

She cuffed Sophie on her uninjured cheek.

"Took your time," Talis said.

"Had to pace it for effect, you know," Sophie said, and slipped two objects into Talis's hand.

Talis lifted the prizes up and grinned wide enough to expose her gold-capped canine tooth. A heavy bolt, as big around as her wrist, and a cannon fuse. Souvenirs from *The Serpent Rose*. Then the little imp hurried aft to help Dug cast off the last of the lines tethering *Wind Sabre* to the Imperial ship.

Talis strode back to the starboard railing, enjoying the moment. The consequences were coming, she knew. A man like Hankirk didn't let an insult like that stand without an answer. But for now she could breathe again. Even if she couldn't quite get the muscles of her jaw to unlock.

Wind Sabre leaned away from her would-be captor, her turbines chuffing, her engine purring, and her lift system hissing.

Across the widening distance, Hankirk's order to pursue them sounded small and hollow.

Talis finally unclenched her teeth. "Push 'em, Tisker. They're about to move."

"They'll try to, anyway," Sophie said, and adjusted the navline while she watched the other ship with interest.

There was a coughing rumble. *The Serpent Rose* lurched. Then the hull shuddered. Talis winced involuntarily as the engine screeched a death rattle that would give a ship's mechanic nightmares. Sophie pressed her lips together, leaning forward over the rail. *The Rose's* aft port engine puffed gray smoke, and then it began to bleed oil from its joins.

Talis saw Hankirk turn to yell at his crew, and saw a confused gunman report their missing fuses. Then the Imperial captain pushed past the man in a pantomime of irritation, pulled the rifle out of someone's hands and brought it to bear on *Wind Sabre*. The other riflemen did the same.

Wind Sabre was pulling ahead, but they still weren't out of range. Talis ducked as she saw the rifle pull in Hankirk's hands, saw the puff of smoke the same instant a bullet cracked the wood of the great cabin's door behind her. Another mark on the tally. He could afford to buy her a new door.

The impulse to return fire was strong, but with the four of them on deck they'd be out of range before they could bring their cannons to bear.

The whizz and *thwup* sounded as Hankirk's men started their volley. One bullet pierced the lower half of their lift envelope, and Talis grit her teeth.

"Push it," she said to Tisker. Never mind a confident casual retreat; she hated patching canvas.

"Hankirk's ordering them to cease fire," Dug said, the scope to his eye.

The timbre of Hankirk's voice was barely audible as he shouted at his crew, and the words were too tousled by the wind to hear.

Sophie squinted across the distance. "Why?"

"Save bullets? I don't know. You prefer they shoot us and hit the top of the envelope, or the turbines?" Talis asked.

"I prefer they behave like I expect them to behave, Captain."

"For good reason. But let's say we take the only victory the day gave us, Soph."

Talis stood at the stern railing as *Wind Sabre* lifted up and slid away. She knuckled her brow cheerfully at Hankirk, who turned away in disgust. She didn't feel that cheer, but she wasn't going to let him know that. And it wasn't like being humble would stop him from hunting her down at this point. When *Wind Sabre*'s sails were unfurled to catch the slip winds, and *The Serpent Rose* still hadn't made any progress toward pursuing them, she went below to reheat the rest of that pot of coffee.

CHAPTER 6

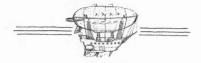

THE SLIPS CARRIED THEM WELL away from where they'd left *The Serpent Rose* with hobbled props, impotent cannons, and toasted lift lines.

That evening, they grappled *Wind Sabre* behind a small island with the stars to their back so they could get a meal in and maybe let their hearts slow their pounding. They might have stayed on the move and rotated duty at the wheel, but as a group they'd decided their little ordeal called for a sit-down meal and a platter of Tisker's famous glazed beef. It was a true bachelor's recipe: rehydrated strips of jerky drenched in a bourbon reduction and served with spicy sautéed peppers. He steamed shredded cabbage and added the last of the ship's butter, with Talis's blessing. Comforting, quick, and satisfying. They ate at the table in Talis's cabin, with a brass cylinder spinning cheerful pipe music from the alcove opposite her bunk. They'd all but licked their plates clean and were leaning back in the worn wooden chairs. Talis had relaxed enough to join in the laughter over Hankirk's last furious expression as they made way.

But as Tisker brought in a round of coffees to finish off

the meal, Dug brought up the topic that had been lurking in their minds all evening. "So there was no contract, then," he said.

They'd kept the discussion off it until now. Sophie had recounted her solo adventure sneaking aboard *The Serpent Rose* to sabotage their engines and, after, they got her going on the subject of how the alien ship propelled itself or stayed aloft. But the contract had been peeking between the pauses of conversation all through dinner. Their bruises, and the wince from Sophie as each careful bite of her food crossed her split lip, were persistent reminders.

Everyone shifted in their chairs as Tisker distributed the hot mugs, and it seemed as though the heaviness of their predicament settled as extra weight on the protesting furniture.

Talis upended the velvet bag, retrieved from the hidden compartment in the back of the galley's ice box, dumping the ring out onto the table. It spun, wobbling on the rough edges of its chipped surface, then settled to a stop with one of the pearl cabochons facing her. Glowing softly under the half-lit chandelier, its milky white surface stared up like a blind eye. Talis had the uncomfortable sensation that it was waiting for an answer as much as her crew was.

She leaned forward with her chin cupped in her hands and stared back at it.

"No contract," she agreed. "So much for your captain's business instincts."

"You trusted Jasper on his word," said Tisker, quick to defend her. Even from herself. "Normally that's good as guaranteed."

She gave him a brief, unconvinced smile.

"It will be guaranteed again after I've had a word with him," she said, brooding into her coffee.

"We should move on." Dug sat just outside the halo of the chandelier's soft candlelight. His height forced him back from the table to avoid tangling his legs with everyone else's.

"It was a waste of resources to go down there."

Talis took a deep breath. Dug was a fighter, not a trader. And now he was slipping into one of his moods. She didn't appreciate the comment, but knew he'd eventually lapse into silence. It was easier to argue with him while he was still talking.

"I'm not so quick to abandon the ring," she said. "He might not be planning to pay, but it's clear Hankirk still wants it. Likelier than not, someone else will buy it. If not at Subrosa, then in other undercities."

Across the table, Sophie tucked one arm under the other, and used her knife to trace a pattern in the sauce remaining on her plate. "We can't get much farther than Subrosa, Captain. That worn bi-clutch is going to leave us stranded if we push it more than that. Might not even get us that far. You promised me we'd replace it next stop."

"We've gotta sell the ring, Soph, if we're going to buy any new—"

"Then we'd better hope it sells at Subrosa." Sophie's chin went up, defiant. Her look was rebellious, made even more so by the angry purple bruise across the arch of her cheek. The imp didn't back down when it came to the airship's two steam-powered engines and their needs. "You put off this repair too long already."

"To buy that descent gear, which opened up all kinds of new business for us." Talis had already had this argument once with Sophie, and that had been back when the salvage job seemed like it would be a clean break. She hadn't forgotten what she promised. There were, in fact, a number of promises riding on this job. She didn't welcome having it shoved back in her face paired with a 'told you so.'

"Not if we can't sell what we dredge up." Sophie still leaned back in her chair, but what had been a relaxed gesture before was now stiff and sullen. "*Captain.*"

Talis looked at her, hard. Her lips pressed into a thin line.

She appreciated the care Sophie gave to her duties, but there had always been those moments that made it clear Sophie's respect for Talis's commands came in second, behind what the young girl thought was best for the ship. That was a good thing, most days. Didn't have to worry if the engines might need a new gasket or a viscfluid change because, sure as salt, Sophie would tell her. Not something Talis was in the mood to deal with now, though. Not when she knew she was already on unsteady standing with the crew for the failure of the 'sure thing' contract that had nearly gotten them blown out of the skies.

That was another thing prickling her skull. Dug had gotten them deep in the blood of Hankirk's men, but *The Serpent Rose* hadn't perforated their lift envelope when they had the chance. Nothing about the day felt right. She took a sip from her coffee but kept her eyes on Sophie.

"We'll sell it," Tisker said with a confident smile, trying to cut the tension.

Sophie dropped the knife on her plate, letting it clatter, and re-crossed her arms. She glared back at Talis. Tisker's charm wasn't wearing down her arguments. She gave no indication that she had even heard him.

Talis turned to Dug, wanting to say something about the interaction with Hankirk. The prickle overrode her concerns about Sophie's tired objections. The situation was upside-down, or at least sideways. She was missing something, something that should be obvious, like a familiar word that fails to come to the tongue when summoned.

But Dug thought she was still looking for an answer on whether to pursue the ring's sale. "They hired a ship outfitted with the descent gear for the job. The number on that contract could have been anything, so long as it was high enough to tempt the risk on the salvage. They intended to capture us the moment the ring was pulled up on deck."

Talis felt a pressure behind her brow as her temper flared.

They had a treasure on the table in front of them. Nothing that ugly got so much attention for being worthless.

Before she measured the words, she said, "Like you intended to *kill imperial officers* as soon as you saw their bow point our way?"

Dug stared at her now, too. His defiant gaze joined Sophie's on the opposite side of the table from Talis and Tisker. Like a wall going up in the middle of her cabin.

The cylinder ran out of music and everything went quiet, save for the rhythmic thrumming of *Wind Sabre's* engines, and the creak of the lines tethering them to the lift balloon above. Those were the heartbeats of the ship, omnipresent when underway. Talis stopped herself from saying anything else. Tisker sensed the quiet power struggle and had the sense to keep his mouth shut. The silence formed into something solid enough that she felt it press in on her eardrums and her temples. Before her first mate stopped arguing, she could usually figure a way to placate him, soothe his anger and restore peace. Not this time.

He wasn't getting away with ignoring her orders, whether stated or implied. Sure, she may have twitched as Hankirk provoked her, and the reckless part of her mind had been glad of the chance to smash his self-righteous smirk into the deck. But it was Dug who'd dropped his decorum and plunged them into a bloody fricassee with the gods-rotted Imperial service. He was her best friend, but he still called her Captain often as not, and she'd make him mark that title.

If she could browbeat Dug, Sophie might back down, too. Talis let her vision tunnel on him, watching the muscles move at the side of his jaw. Clenched, like he was clamping down on his own temper. A vein pulsed on his high forehead. The edges of her vision went dark and a headache started above her eyes, as though the willpower she was directing at him was a living thing trying to hatch from an egg. No chick—not a bird at all. A raptor, born with clawed talons and a hungry mouth ringed with pointed teeth.

Finally, Dug's nostrils flared with a deep inhale. Something in his posture softened, and her friend was back. He nodded—a slight twitch in the angle of his neck—and finished his coffee, tilting back his head to break eye contact. The insolence was gone out of him. For the moment, anyhow.

"Besides," she said, satisfied, returning to the point Dug had been trying to make as though they'd only paused to sip from their cups. "A setup doesn't mean the ring isn't worth having."

CHAPTER 7

Talis didn't press the issue of Dug's violent care-lessness any further. It was done. She knew they'd have to balance that scale with Hankirk and his crew someday. For her own crew and ship affairs, all she'd needed was to point out his own misjudgments. Looked like the message was received.

Blood still up, Talis was tempted to go to the cabinet for something stronger than coffee, but while they were still on the subject of the ring, she wasn't about to have her wits addled. This was an argument that she intended to win. Sure, she had the same doubts as Dug about their ability to sell the thing. But that was something she couldn't afford to admit, even to herself. Their cargo hold was empty, and their ship *did* need that blasted engine component before they could take another contract. Sophie didn't have to remind her; it had been on her mind. She needed to make this a quick sale, and without too much loss. Maybe half price would be enough to get the ugly thing off her ship and let them move on with their lives. Placate the crew, put this behind them.

Tisker tucked a toothpick into the side of his mouth and

spoke around it. "Right, why bother sending us after the ring at all if it's worthless? There are other ways to entrap us that are faster and less involved. Maybe they wanted to make an arrest, but I agree with Cap. They wanted that trinket in the bargain. We'll find a buyer."

Sophie frowned. With Dug off the hunt, she was alone in her defiance of their captain. She was a smart girl. She knew those odds for what they were. "Not flashy enough to sell just anywhere, is it?"

The signet ring's pewter surface was scratched and abused, but Talis could see raised motifs swirling around the bezel and halfway down the shanks of the band. It had probably been a handsome thing when it was made, but it was old enough that those days were long forgotten. The pearl cabochons to either side of the raised seal were chipped and wobbled in their settings like loose teeth. The center was worn at the edges, obscured by a dent in its surface that made it look like it had been assaulted with a chisel, so that the design was illegible. Sized for a large hand, the band was wide and solid. In contrast, its inside surface was barely damaged at all. As though it had been handled roughly but almost never worn.

The ring sat, silent, between them, refusing to divulge its secrets. Talis still felt like it was watching her.

She leaned both elbows on the table and cradled her forehead against the heels of her palms. No doubt the ring was ancient. Maybe pre-Cataclysm. On the other hand, *The Emerald Empress* was nowhere near that old. From her captain's uniform and the style of her winches, fittings, and lift system, Talis would wager the airship sank only a decade ago, no more than two. So maybe that captain had found the ring, and it had gotten lost again when they went down. But who sent them down? And how did Talis keep her own ship from sharing that fate?

"How did Hankirk come to know of it?" Dug produced a knife from one of the folds of his loose pants, and pushed its tip against the pads of his fingers. The skin paled at the pressure, but he knew what he was doing, and the flesh didn't break.

Talis's mind took a moment to come back to the conversation, and for a moment she thought Dug was asking about *The Emerald Empress*. She frowned, dredging up half-forgotten memories for the second time since Hankirk stepped onto her deck. He had been in her graduating class at the Imperial academy before she'd decided on a different career path. He was smart. Quick, mentally and physically. They might have been friends if they'd had a touch more in common, or if they hadn't both been so competitive. They had dabbled in dating, but that relationship quickly reached its nadir. He always triggered her alarm bells when he'd talk about—

"Oh *hells*." Talis sat up straight in her chair.

"What?" Sophie stiffened as though Talis's curse had been a gunshot.

All three of them looked at her in confusion.

"That absolute *bastard*."

"You're just figuring this?" Tisker cocked a smile at her. "Thought you said you knew him."

She ignored him as her mind furiously worked it out. "I've been sitting here feeling like I was missing something all night, and *by The Five*, I've got it now. Our man Hankirk grew up in the capital, privilege-fluffed, his career all rolled out for him like a carpet before the empress. Look at him. He's already an Imperial captain, and *The Serpent Rose* is no insignificant ship. It's barely been in the skies long enough to require a polish."

"Okay, so?" Tisker prompted, still looking more amused than alarmed.

Sophie shushed him and turned her eyes back to Talis, her sour mood over the engine part forgotten for the moment.

Talis drummed her fingers lightly on the table. "Wager you don't know about the Veritors of the Lost Codex."

Tisker shook his head, while Sophie looked at her expectantly.

Dug growled low in his throat. Talis already knew that *he* knew about the Veritors.

"We should have killed him," he muttered. "If that is the adders' nest we have kicked over, we should turn around and sink them before they can make their repairs."

Partly, Talis agreed with Dug. Partly. Though her inclination was more along the lines of tossing that ring over their railing and putting Cutter skies behind them for good. But that would leave them having to avoid the two largest territories of Peridot, and she was in no rush to narrow their market.

Something stronger than coffee was definitely in order. She went to the liquor cabinet built into the starboard bulkhead, pinched the rims of four glasses with one hand, and grabbed a mostly full bottle of dark spiced rum by its neck with the other.

"Who are the . . . Varistors of the Lost Codex?" Sophie looked to Talis for an explanation as Dug's humor worsened.

"Veritors." Talis returned to the table and placed the glasses down, then unstoppered the rum and poured herself two fingers. Tisker and Sophie filled their glasses in turn while she seated herself again, putting her feet up on the trestle of the table and sliding into a slouch against the back of her chair.

Staring at the dark brown liquid in the bottle as if he was watching a scene play out in its distorted highlights and shadows, Dug slipped into a gloomy silence.

Talis took a sip of rum to delay the explanation. It burned her tongue and throat, and she gave it a moment, feeling the fire trace a path down her gullet, ignoring how Tisker and Sophie leaned forward as if to drag the story out of her. The threads of her suspicions were braiding into a cord, still too fragile to tug.

She made them wait while she drank the rest of the glass.

Tisker poured her another, an offering in exchange for finally getting to the damned tale. She sighed and crossed her ankle over the opposite knee. Ran her thumb over the well-worn texture of her leather boot and traced the hammered pattern in the brass clips as she began to talk again.

"They're a secret society of Cutters—well, they're a cult, really. Far from the first mortals to figure out how the gods' alchemy works, but they *are* the first to want to wield it like a weapon."

Tisker chuckled, still not taking in the gravity of the situation. "What, like Fens Yarrow? Those idiots will get caught like he was, and be cinders before they even figure out which incantation to use."

"Would I waste worry over that?" Talis rested the glass on her knee and turned it with her thumb and forefinger, staring at the signet ring on the table again. "Half-cocked fools running around trying to set themselves upon a throne? The gods can deal with that; we've all heard those stories. The Veritors are different. They've been around a *long* time. Ages ago, like the name implies, they read some Pre-Cataclysm text and got the notion that Cutter folk are the only natural race on Peridot. They want to kill the gods, and the other four races with them. What makes me worry is that they've got connections, and smarts to make up for lacking sense. Plus they're bankrolled by fatcrats and can recruit with the promise of elevating anyone to such circles. Anyone who's Cutter. You hear anything about some new Imperial decree to suspend foreign work licenses, or to push Cutter territories around Nexus even farther despite our standing border agreements with the Bone and Rakkar, and I'll bet their influences are behind it. My guess is—and Hankirk made it all but explicit—they've implanted themselves in the top levels of Imperial fleet command, too."

"You must be joking, Cap. That's a nice conspiracy." Tisker's eyebrows were way up, and he looked ready to laugh the support beams down from the overhead. He'd reached the bottom of his first glass of rum, so really it was a wonder he hadn't laughed yet. She knew how it sounded.

But she pressed on. "There's more than one reason I left the academy before I committed to five years indentured."

"Thought you said all the rules didn't suit you?" Sophie asked.

"Well, sure, I said that." Talis smirked. She could still remember that conversation from two years back when Sophie had joined them. She and Dug had discovered the young imp aboard a colony ship where she was apprenticed to the engine master, lost amid a gaggle of other young wrenches-in-training and bored out of her freckled skull shoveling coal, waiting for a chance to really get her hands into an airship's engine. Talis had been competing with another interested captain to win Sophie over, both of them in dire need of a wrench with her kind of natural talent. Talis had just bought *Wind Sabre* and couldn't match the pay the other captain was offering, but tales of her adventures outside Cutter skies had given her the edge. The financial security of a ponderous water trawler couldn't compete with the exploration and excitement that Sophie craved. "The theory that the Empire is in thrall to occult fiends who want to kill the gods and commit quadruple genocide didn't seem entirely relevant at the time."

Tisker laughed again, but it was uneasy. "Aye, and I might've snuck onto another ship had you warmed *me* up with that line."

"But if they're a secret cult or whatever, how'd you find out about them?" Sophie looked at Dug. She wanted his part of the history, too.

But Dug remained silent, staring at that bottle. Talis knew well which memory had snagged his thoughts, so she continued before Sophie could ask him again.

"Hankirk was always trying to best me or impress me, back in training. I should probably mention that I had a brief fling with the pompous button shiner."

She braced herself, knowing how that would go over. As she feared, Sophie started to giggle and Tisker guffawed.

"Go ahead and laugh." She refilled her drink, noticing that her arm was a little unsteady. The brown liquid splashed up the side of the glass and a droplet hit the table. "I said 'brief.' He's not ugly. Seemed worth a romp until I got to know him."

Dug's eyes came back into focus when the bottle was moved. Talis poured some into his empty glass, whether he wanted it or not. After a moment he took the glass and swallowed its entire contents in one smooth motion. He set the cup back down, placing it right in an old stain that some past moisture had left in the table's surface. His eyes were darker than ever in the low light.

Talis continued, "Funny, Tisker, that you should bring up Fens Yarrow earlier. As it happened, Hankirk thought he'd dazzle me by saying he was the man's great-great-great-grandson, or some such. That he was entitled to a comfortable life among *worthy* peers because of his lineage."

Tisker scoffed, a loud half-snort. Paternity was a vaporous concept for Cutters. Colony airships traded passengers at such a rate that it was far easier to keep track of maternal lines. Cutter folk were far from being matriarchal, as the Bone tribes were, but in determining heritage, one could only say for certain which woman birthed them.

Sophie shot him a look. "But *Fens Yarrow*? Why would he claim something like that?"

She was raised on the same lessons as most colonials. *Don't be like Fens Yarrow. If you're naughty, Onaya Bone will fry you, too.* The actual parable went into more detail, which was far more gruesome. It was effective at keeping Cutter folk, both children and adults, in line. Only maybe Hankirk hadn't been told the same stories as a babe.

"Imagine it, Soph. If there's a portion of society—*high*

society—that values Yarrow's flavor of ambition? They might consider his progeny to be heir to that legacy." Talis finished her drink while that sank in.

Her mind drifted through the memories, and she had to force herself back to the present. "Anyway I didn't believe him, of course." Talis set her empty cup on the table, watching Dug's expression. "I didn't learn the Veritors' actual name until years later. Never connected the two until just now."

Tisker nodded his chin at the ring between them. "So we sell the ring to the Veritors?"

"Well that would be tricky, don't you think?" Sophie finished her drink and put the glass down. "Hankirk's already proven that they don't expect to part with coin for the thing."

Dug twitched, like a sleeping man having nightmares. Talis refilled his cup, and the bottle clinked against the rim of his glass.

"Sell the ring to anyone *but*," she said. She chafed that the conversation had circled back to the crew's pessimism about the bloody ring, and she still didn't know what to make of the Veritors' interest in it. "There will be other buyers. I've got a list of folks who like to dabble in alchemy, if that's what this thing is. Couple of them might even be able to afford it."

Sophie pulled her hands off the table with a sharp gasp, as though the ring could burn her across the wooden surface. She glanced out at the clear skies beyond the portholes and gave a tug on the set of short prayerlocks at the nape of her neck. Almost immediately, she caught herself, and lowered her hands sheepishly to the table. "Secret cults *and* alchemy? Hells, Captain, what did you get us tangled up in?"

The Divine Alchemists had torn Peridot apart with their elemental manipulation. When they created new peoples to populate the planet's scattered islands, they enforced one rule above all others: Don't mess around with alchemy.

Of course not everyone listened. Even *Wind Sabre* had a few illegal trinkets and devices in her lockers. Sometimes the benefits were worth the risk, for a particularly clever widget, and Onaya Bone didn't *always* appear to destroy transgressors with her swift punishment, as warned in the tales of Fens Yarrow.

Hells, Talis knew that Arthel Rak, Lord of Fire and Creator of the Rakkar, even *encouraged* his people to dabble in it. Or at least he rewarded the most notable accomplishments with a personal congratulatory visit.

Maybe they could find a Rakkar buyer. Then at least she wouldn't have to worry that she'd sold the ring to the same people who'd funded Hankirk's shiny new ship. Any buyer except a Cutter would do, really.

But she put a clumsy hand out to calm Sophie. "*Could* also just be some historical treasure. If it's pre-Cataclysm, maybe some Vein researcher wants to put it in a museum with the rest of their old 'tronics."

The word 'cataclysm' was challenging for her rum-soaked tongue. This conversation needed to end. Soon.

Sophie's eyes widened. Between the parables, eight siblings, overprotective aunts, and her youth, she hadn't seen as much of the world as the rest of the crew. Dug and Jasper were probably the only non-Cutters Sophie knew by name. She looked far less worried now. Eager was a better term.

"So we're going to Subrosa," said Dug, surprising Talis by speaking. The visions that had clouded his eyes moments before had cleared and his expression was focused. "Despite the fact that Hankirk placed the contract with Jasper there."

"What?" Talis picked up the ring and returned it to its pouch. "Aren't you curious to hear that big bastard explain why he sold us out?"

Dug's grin, as he raised his glass to her in a toast, was frightening.

CHAPTER 8

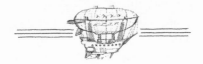

AFTER DINNER, TISKER SHOOED Dug and Sophie away from the great cabin, offering to clear the table himself. Talis could see that he had something on his mind, though he started to gather up the dishes without a word, loading them onto their trays. He was waiting to be sure the others were out of earshot. She thought about ordering him to return to the wheelhouse so she could sleep off the rum before she had to deal with anything else.

His faith in her had been steady since the day he showed up on the docks of Subrosa, a scraggly kid looking for more than the usual handout. His starry eyes made her think, at first, that he was as interested in her as in *Wind Sabre,* but over time it became clear she lacked the preferred interactive body parts to be his type, and that the helm was the only thing he wanted to get his hands on. Didn't mean he wasn't enamored with her, though. He'd staunchly defend her any time he was given the opportunity. Started more than one bar brawl before even Dug could on account of someone saying the wrong thing to, or about, his captain.

Everyone onboard needed *Wind Sabre* for their own

reasons. For Tisker, the ship was his salvation. His way out. The only way an orphan who had grown too old for the urchin gangs could escape Subrosa. Well, not the *only* way, but she certainly could see why he wouldn't have chosen the usual, less savory options.

He stood at the table, looking down but not seeing the cup in his hand. "If it makes a difference, I can wait for my back shares."

Well. There it was. Too late to send him off and avoid this conversation.

Talis pushed herself straight up in her seat and pulled on the hem of her jacket to smooth the wrinkles that had formed against the chair back.

"First, I don't intend for my crew to suffer for this situation."

He nodded, as if he'd been expecting that answer. "And second?"

She gathered her utensils onto her plate and pushed it toward him so he could clear her spot without having to come around the corner of the table. "Second, deferring your shares only helps us buy Sophie's engine part if we have the money to dole shares out in the first place."

She owed them for this job and the last one. She didn't like running the ship on her crew's credit, but the contract from Jasper seemed like such a sure thing, even with the luck needed to drop into flotsam for an object as small as he wanted. With one hand the ancient Breaker man had pushed across the payment for their previous job, a shallow tray of Imperial presscoins. The royal family's faces had glittered there, smiling up at her. The stack was a little thin, but after ship's costs and captain's share, it would have netted her crew just over a thousand each. And then Jasper, his great serene face belying nothing of what was to come, mentioned a new contract. Mentioned how the payment sitting solid as stone on his desk before her would neatly cover the cost of refurbished descent gear and its installation. How the coin could be multiplied in only a few days. Reminded her that the descent gear would broaden their skill set for even more contracts later, and opportunity to prospect for more valuables on the side.

She wasn't a tyrant, didn't take the contract on her own say-so. She ran it by her crew. Their money in her hand, right in front of them. They could have taken it if they wanted. If they chose the payment they could count with their hands instead of their imaginations, fine. Talis could have found them some other job. Something smaller, no doubt, but that wouldn't require negatives in their logbook. Gods rot it, she could've bought that bi-clutch right then.

But they trusted her. Took her enthusiasm up as their own.

As Tisker opened his mouth to speak again, she saw his chest rise with an unsteady breath. "You think Sophie's gonna leave us?"

Sighing, Talis stood up, and grabbed the rum bottle off the table. It was nearly empty. One more thing on the list of purchases she couldn't afford to make at their next stop. She fumbled to re-cork it, then stowed the bottle away.

"What Sophie does is up to Sophie. But one day, yeah, she's going to want to follow through on those plans she's always scratching at."

Sophie wanted her own airship. More than that, and more expensive, she wanted to *commission* her own ship, from her own designs. Talis knew that someday, when the prize from a contract topped off what it would take to make that happen, Sophie would leave *Wind Sabre* and go be her own captain. Then maybe she'd learn what kind of hard decisions it took to keep a ship and crew together.

"But . . . soon?" Tisker was still just a kid. Didn't know that a pain barreling down at you in the here and now was sometimes easier to deal with than one you could only anticipate. One haunting the distances beyond your prow, too far out to get a bead on.

"Not as soon as maybe she'd like," Talis said. Her voice sounded bitter. She hadn't meant for it to come out like that. The rum had made her too honest. "Don't know what she's managed to put aside for it, but it can't be enough for the marvel of engineering she's no doubt got going."

Not that Sophie was keeping the plans a secret. Probably the girl wanted Talis to show some interest in them. No doubt, as first mate and liaison to the crew, Dug knew a lot more about the workings of Sophie's dream ship than he did about *Wind Sabre*'s. Talis had really only let Sophie tell her about any upgrades she could imagine for the ship she was on now. They'd made a number of them over the years. It was how they ran a ship built for twenty hands with a crew of four, with shift rotations. Sophie could plan upgrades for the ship for the rest of her career, and Talis would be quite satisfied with that.

But Sophie wouldn't.

"It really is an impressive design, Cap." Tisker wiped down the table with a cotton cloth, soaking up the droplets spilled from their drinks and using the dampness to get any sauce from the food that had dripped on the polished surface. "It would mean a lot to her if you'd look at it. She's real proud."

Pride. Yeah.

"She's gonna come smack up against a real surprise when she finds out what it takes to captain a ship. It's more than the paperwork saying the deck under your feet belongs to you."

"She knows that." Tisker loaded the full tray into the dumbwaiter in the aft bulkhead, cranked the handle to tighten its springs, and flipped the toggle to send it all rattling to the deck below. While it jostled and clanked, he turned back to her and buried his hands in his pockets. It only made him look younger.

"Seems to conveniently forget it whenever I gotta make a decision between keeping the engines polished or keeping us going."

As soon as the words left her mouth, Talis knew how inane they sounded. If she let the engines fail, she wasn't keeping them going at all. Poor phrasing. Gods-rotted rum. Maybe she shouldn't worry so much about restocking the treacherous amber liquid.

She got up, pushed her chair back under the table, and stood with her hands on the back of it. Keeping her steady. Her head was starting to swim.

"Not something you have to worry about today," she said to Tisker. And to herself.

He gave her a small smile. Nothing convincing, though, as he said goodnight and left her cabin.

CHAPTER 9

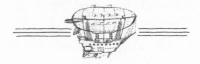

SUBROSA WAS NOT A SAFE PLACE.

Forget for a moment the cutpurses, gangs, and dark alleys—even the questionable food. The black-market city itself was held together with little more than willpower, descending in hastily constructed layers from the underbelly of Rosa, the island proper.

The proximity of Rosa to Bone skies at the seventy-third-degree border made it a convenient place to conduct trade between the two peoples. As a result, the population of Rosa had boomed. The original city had grown up, then out, and then finally over the cliffs and under. Once the undercity was formed, citizens of all five of Peridot's races found their way there, settling into their own businesses for their own reasons. Cutter folk, no matter how prejudiced, made up the most populous customer base on the planet. And they wanted all sorts of goods and services.

The first layer of Subrosa anchored to the rocks jutting out beneath the island, and each subsequent layer clung desperately to the one above. Cobbled together from whatever building material was available: corrugated metal, polyboard, concrete reinforced with metal mesh, wooden planks, old cargo crates, and other things less identifiable due to their age and condition. Materials were cannibalized from other structures when nothing new was available. Shops and offices grew like tumors, entrepreneurs always building new kiosks that blocked the flow of traffic and forced detours and reroutes. At every intersection, graffiti and handwritten signs were updated daily, attempting to lead customers along the best route to any location. Coded symbols and glyphs did the same for the subcity's gangs. With the map's ever-changing arrangement, the layers of paint and posted bills encroached more and more upon the already narrow and claustrophobic passages.

The chaos became the spirit of the city. It was a haven for unsanctioned business in all its varying categories. Shops proffered a vast array of items with the potential to get their new owners in trouble. Assassins mingled with smugglers in the bars and brothels. Orphans and beggars worked for crime lords, or for merchants. Sometimes both. Anyone who would feed them more than they could steal for themselves (which they also continued to do). Talented buskers were forced to hone new skills to build up their worth in this place.

And *then* there were the cutpurses, gangs, and dark alleys. Not to mention the questionable food.

After mulling the decision into a spiral, Talis scraped the bottom of the ship's coffers and paid extra for an enclosed docking berth. It would earn *Wind Sabre* unwanted attention from within the city. Only those who were worth a bounty or carrying a fortune bothered to pay the extra to have their presence at the docks hidden from those vessels circling outside. But she didn't want their nose tied in and their tail-end exposed if *The Serpent Rose* made quick work of their repairs and caught up to them. Talis hoped the fact that she didn't pay the optional bribe to the dock manager for his silence—sometimes silence was louder than rumors—would be enough to counter the news that a familiar ship had arrived seeking an uncharacteristic level of privacy.

The arching frame of the dock's outer gate slid past their lift balloon, and the yellow-green glow from the station's interior lighting bathed them in a jaundiced hue that could make even a brand new ship look poorly maintained. The sounds and smells of Subrosa enveloped them. The lively pulse of drums and wailing from brass instruments played with more enthusiasm than skill clamored out from the restaurants that lined the docking levels. The breath of stale alcohol mingled with the aroma of fresh, hot anything and everything. The walls thrummed as thousands of feet moved along the many levels above and below, all sending their vibrations through the layers of the city. Dust and loose debris pattered down to bounce on the docks or fall past into the depths of the enclosed bay. Voices carried from every direction, a range of dialects arguing over prices, quality, schedules, or other contested terms. Dockside machinery complained of overuse with minimal maintenance as it loaded and unloaded cargo to slowly tow it through the crowds to its destination. Beneath that, the sound of the dock's central furnace lungs, squeezed by regular pumps of steel bellows, was an ever-present pulse, sending puffs of hot air through sealed canvas tubes across the gantries at each occupied berth, keeping the lift balloons of transient ships inflated while they refueled or repaired. Grease, tar, and oil from the docking apparatus mingled with the smell of food. The latter was probably fried in something near the same as the former.

Sophie waited by the railing while Tisker and the dock workers cooperated to secure *Wind Sabre* to their berth via windlass and bracers. She was dressed for the outing, following Talis's example. A cropped long-sleeved jacket of blue and green satin displayed only a small expanse of skin above her halter-necked dark leather corset. Though the corset accentuated the line of her waist and darted toward the buckle on her belt, mostly its line drew the eye to the pair of mercyblades in metal clasps beneath her ribs. A pair of shotguns crossed Sophie's shoulders. That was in addition to the two pistols at her hips, the brass-knuckled knife at her thigh, and three or four other weapons that Talis knew were hidden out of sight. She wore gold rings in her ears, a thick golden torque around her throat, and a gold chain with quartz and citrine beads looped between the toggles of her vest. All the gold played nicely off the bruise that sat darkly across her cheekbone. Just the right effect.

In a city where many interactions happened without the benefit of introduction, visiting crews needed to communicate to Subrosans of every vocation that they were capable of handling themselves. It was a balance between dissuading thieves and instilling confidence in potential customers. To look both ready for a fight and worthy of the effort.

The captain donned her weathered jacket, each scuff and patch a testament to a hardship she had walked away from. Beneath it, a simple three-button long-sleeve black cotton shirt. Under that, the ring's pouch was tied to a leather thong around her neck and tucked into her undershirt, between her breasts where it would make no visible lump. Her boots were buckled over a pair of soft pants with reinforced knees and no shortage of pockets. Double gun holsters at her hips. Shoulder holster beneath the jacket. Knife sheathed in its case on the back of her belt. Tool wrist cuff on her left arm. Her hair was braided with strands of turquoise beads, a gift from Dug many years ago, exotic and rare among Cutters. She capped her prayerlocks in more beads of gold and brass and let them fall over her left shoulder. Beneath her belt, she wore a scarf of pale green silk, doubled around her waist to disguise the shape of her money belt. The scarf's gold floss tassels brushed the backs of her knees.

Dug, on the other hand, lost layers. He bared his tattooed chest and scarred back. A pair of loose twill cotton pants gave him complete range of movement, and he squared his shoulders under the familiar weight of a half dozen sheathed knives and daggers. He had washed up, and shaved his scalp higher on the sides, so only the very top of his head sprouted purple-black hair and feathers. The style lengthened the bone structure of his face, the pointed tips of his ears, and the angles of his cheek hollows. To increase the effect, gold powder highlighted his sharp features.

It was yet to be decided whether Talis needed Jasper to see the jewelry or the weaponry. The swagger or the danger. The Breaker giant was unlike many of his kind in that he had just enough greed to do well in business. Most Breakers who opened shops still suffered from philanthropic tendencies, which almost inevitably bankrupted them. Jasper instead focused the experience of his age to be a nearly infallible judge of character, and his innate craftsman's eye to recognize the market values of items that passed through his shop. Add to that his massive size, accompanying stubbornness, and thick hide, and he had cut out quite a respectable place in Subrosa. One of the few thieves to be trusted, or Talis had liked to think.

But now, what to think? Either he'd misjudged the agent who brought him the salvage contract or he had knowingly given Talis a job likely to turn sour. She didn't like the implications either way.

Talis, Sophie, and Dug left *Wind Sabre* in Tisker's care. He was at home, though somewhat reluctantly, in Subrosa. He read the stale air currents like pheromones. Any anomalous behavior on the docks, and he'd spot it and be ready before it turned into something treacherous. Talis would have loved to have his instincts at her side, but she wanted Dug with her more. If the ship was to only have one crew member as guard, she wanted it to be Tisker. Sophie could hold her own in a fight but wasn't suspicious enough to be left alone with the ship in a port where everyone—down to the dock manager—was going to steal from them at the first opportunity.

There was no direct route to where they were going. Talis marched them through the corridors and access ways, up loosely bolted ladders from one level and up rickety spiral staircases on the next. Through a noisy bar that stank of body odor and grain alcohol and out the back, into a cluttered alley where uncollected garbage mixed with puddles of condensed moisture that dripped from the concrete walls. Sophie made a small noise as the smell of fermenting garbage reached her, and held her sleeve over her nose and mouth. Talis didn't enjoy it any more than her mechanic did, but she refused to look like there was any Subrosan offense she couldn't take in stride. Sophie picked up on the silent rebuke and dropped her hands back to rest on her pistols.

Talis led them through another back door, into the red lighting and smoke-filled halls of a pleasure house. Simpering music oozed from a dark corner of the foyer, enhancing rather than covering the carnal noises coming from the curtained-off rooms along the hallways that led deeper into the establishment. Their noses were accosted with perfumes, oils, and incense. Talis was thankful that was all they could smell.

They exited through the front door and found themselves in a wider corridor with high ceilings. The traffic was heavier here but there was room for it, and in the slightly more open space, Talis felt like she could breathe again. From somewhere the benign and inviting scent of fried dough reached her, and her stomach rumbled.

A young child, bony and barely covered by rags, dashed out of the brothel behind them and ran ahead into the street. Talis pursed her lips. Likely the madam inside sent the street rat ahead to warn Jasper of their approach. That was to be expected in Subrosa, but today it added to the prickling sensation on her neck. She didn't let it slow their steps, but she did cast a glance at Dug. He nodded slightly. She sensed Sophie move in closer behind her.

The façade of Jasper's shop was a masterpiece of Breaker artisan wood carving, crafted by the proprietor himself. Abstract twisting cords, trailing ivy, and gracefully sweeping reeds were a testament to the planning and care that had gone into the design. That the whole thing hadn't been pried off by thieves and relocated to the illicit art markets was a testament to the respect Jasper commanded within the community. Then again, Talis noted that there were a few recent chisel marks around the frame of the door, bright pocks against the dark-stained wood, made since her last visit. Someone was always willing to try.

A cart overloaded with rugs and pulled by two ailing goats forced them to pause before they could cross the street. A short, sour-faced man with a switch shouted obscenities at the animals, whacking their rumps to urge them along. The goats trundled on without seeming to pay him any mind.

When that obstacle moved out of the way, five new ones stood between Talis's group and the entrance to Jasper's shop. Cutter men. Lean and mean, combat-ready.

They were dressed well enough for the city in cotton and leather. Their clothing was free of any patches, or at least had been patched by someone who knew what they were doing. Three of the five brandished blunt weapons: a bat, an iron bar, and a well-notched fighting staff. The fourth had a large flat blade, designed for utility but certainly well suited to damaging flesh. The fifth, front and center of the group, wore a gray felt hat with a rounded crown and a golden grosgrain ribbon. He held a pair of barreled six-shot revolvers leveled at them. An expensive set of guns, well above the station he otherwise represented.

Dug's knives were in his hands with the barest twitch. Sophie tensed, elbows bent and hands neutral, ready to draw any of her weapons.

"Trust you had a prosperous voyage, Captain," said the

man with the pair of sixes. His hungry gaze lingered on the pouches at her hips.

Talis crossed one arm over her stomach and rested the other elbow on its hand, then made a show of examining her fingernails. "Sorry, boys. Haven't got time for fun today."

He hadn't addressed her by name. It was possible this robbery was of the standard Subrosan variety, innocent in its way. If so, the place and timing were an unholy coincidence.

But he only brought four men with him. Dug had a reputation here, and not just for throwing punches in the bars. If they knew who they were fighting, if they were Subrosan natives, there would have been twice as many of them.

"Market values being what they are," the man said, pulling back the hammer on his guns, "you won't find anyone willing to pay more than we're offering for that little item."

CHAPTER 10

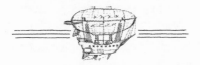

TALIS FELT HER EYELID TWITCH. They *were* here for the ring.

She let her hand fall to rest on the butt of her holstered gun. Casual, largely posturing. The real threat was Dug. "And who can I thank for the courtesy?"

The man chuckled. "Got so many friends in Subrosa, haven't you?"

Could be Talbot. Could be Cormack. Could be Ellanis. Perish the thought, it could be Jasper.

"Always happy to make a few more."

Then she rushed him.

When guns are leveled at someone's head, generally the expected response is that the target will be subdued, act slowly, avoid any sudden movements. Those who do the leveling, as a result, tend to get a little overconfident. This man's hands were relaxed, his eyes still scanning her person for the most likely hiding place of the trinket in question. Talis had wagered on his inattention. The hammers were cocked but, in response to her unexpected advance, the man actually brought his hands up a smidge. By the time he thought to pull the triggers, he was pointing high. And Talis had dropped low. She aimed a shoulder at the tender space beneath his sternum as she barreled him over.

Dug and Sophie were right behind her, and Talis could hear the grunts of the other men as they clashed with her crew.

She had enough concern left for Jasper to feel a brief twinge of remorse as the wood of his shopfront cracked under the impact of their two bodies. Then she was wrestling the man for his revolvers. They'd landed hard, him crumpled against the wall and her on top. She got her knee up and onto his right forearm. She worked the gun in that hand loose as he fought for breath against his malfunctioning diaphragm.

He got off a second shot from the other gun, which went high over her shoulder again, but it was close enough to her ear that all sound was replaced with ringing. In the brief instant when light flared in her eyes, he got his empty right hand up and pushed it up under her jaw, forcing her head back.

They were still a tangle of limbs, so aiming for his chest with the appropriated six-shooter was no issue, even as he switched his grip to her larynx. She had just inhaled, so she held her breath. The crushing pressure on her windpipe was temporary, she told herself. No time for panic. He squeezed her throat, and she squeezed the trigger.

Nothing.

The hammer!

She didn't have a limb free to stop him from bringing up his left hand. She saw the grime on that thumb as it came up for the hammer. She involuntarily swallowed as he pressed the warm barrel against the soft flesh under her jaw.

He squeezed her throat harder. Her lungs protested against the held breath. In slow motion she saw the cylinder of his gun rotate to a fresh chamber and the shadowy dimples in the points of the glistening copper-cased bullets. He'd spent a shot before she arrived. The barrel had three empty chambers, and she was reminded of the day-night dials in the workings of a clock face. His finger moved toward the trigger.

The report from a single shot rang in her ears. Scorched cotton and gunpowder clawed at her throat, and she gratefully inhaled it. Wiped the blood spray on her hand across the man's jacket. Blood soaked his shirt in a blossom that seeped outward from the bullet wound in his chest. Blood bubbled from his mouth and nose as he worked his jaw, forming a wordless final protest. His eyes were unfocused. She untangled her leg from his and stood.

"A gun can always be taken and used against its owner," Dug said from behind her. His distaste for the weapons was made clear at any opportunity.

A glance over her shoulder showed Talis that he and Sophie had dispatched the other men neatly. There was barely any blood on her crew, and not much of it their own. Good. There would be fresh bruises, though. She swallowed hard against her battered throat.

She claimed the other revolver from her would-be assassin. The custom holsters, too. Figured she'd earned them. She found his pouch of ammunition and took that, along with his purse. What honor she had was not wasted on such decisions.

"Same's true for knives," said Sophie, her chest heaving as she stood over the last man to fall. There was a dark-tinged slice in one of her satin sleeves, a light kiss from the machete that was now protruding from its owner's chest.

"Not these knives," said Dug, and he absently squeezed the grips on his two blades like he might the shoulder of a friend. There wasn't a drop of blood to be wiped off their lethal edges. The same could not be said for the corridor flooring beneath the three men who had danced with *Wind Sabre*'s first mate.

A TINY BELL RANG as the door opened into the dimly lit shop, a cheerful sound that pretended the morning was normal and benign. The cacophony of Subrosa faded to a murmur inside the carefully kept shop.

From a low display table in the center of the shop, polished brass and copper reflected the flickering of simple candelabras which swung in small circles with the vibrations of the city beyond the shop's walls and ceiling. Lining the walls to either side, varnished boxes with framed paper labels were stacked in neat rows on shelves, giving the impression that this was more of an archive than a store. A waist-high glass cabinet stood just within the door, with a selection of hand-carved pipes and knife handles on its lowest two shelves, and a selection of jewelry, pocket watches, and small silver trinket boxes featured below the cabinet's glass top.

Beside the cabinet stood a tall, narrow time piece with complicated workings, pull chains and weights of hammered copper and pewter, and a pendulum shaped to look like a glow pumpkin. The back of the cabinet was painted black and shone with inlaid chips of quartz which twinkled like a field of stars. The day-night dial placed Peridot's sun in the late morning position over Bone skies. The disk behind the sun's movement piece was intricately etched, but from the door and without better lighting, Talis could not make out the details. A clock that fine was a rare sight, but she could look at it on her way out, after she'd gotten satisfaction from Jasper. In the form of explanation or, better, compensation.

Talis shouted for the proprietor, louder than necessary. The space was not large and Jasper had keen hearing. She hardly cared. Her throat objected to the burst of sound she forced through it, but she enjoyed the way the rasping bark punctuated the quiet shopfront.

She'd nearly decided to give Jasper the benefit of the doubt, but that party outside had changed her mind. Too many people knew about the ring. Too many people for

Jasper not to have some responsibility in the matter. Either he'd badly misjudged someone, or he'd told someone. He owed Talis an explanation, either way.

But there was no response to her shout. No shuffle in the back room to indicate that he'd heard her and was moving his enormous person toward the curtained door. She crossed to the shop counter and tapped a fingernail on the brass bell that hung over the well-polished wood. A clear, sonorous tone rang out. She shouted again, then winced as her throat made her regret it.

Still nothing.

She looked at Dug. If Jasper had gone out, there would be a clerk left in charge, or the door would have been secured. There was too much of value in his storerooms to leave unattended, parcels inbound and outbound, and none of them strictly legal.

She glanced around the showroom, trying to measure for a sense of trouble. The floors were swept clean, the shelves without dust, and the glass cases free of fingerprints or the haze of neglect. Nothing was out of place. Except Jasper.

Talis and Dug drew their weapons again.

Dug lifted the hinged portion of the countertop and moved behind it. He used the point of one knife to push back the heavy curtain to the room beyond. All was dark.

Talis had been in the private area of Jasper's shop a handful of times, but only passing through on the way to his office. She felt the wall inside the doorframe for a switch but found none. A pull-chain then, perhaps.

Sophie rescued them, striking one of her matches on the doorframe, cupping her hand around it to protect the tender flame until she could get through the door and raise it above her head.

The tiny bit of fire could do little but cast dancing shadows about them, indicating only bouncing lumps of darkness or the glint off a metal or glass item. But Talis spotted the swaying shape of a pull-chain a few feet beyond Sophie and made for it, even when the match burned down and Sophie cursed on behalf of her singed fingertips. In the final two steps through darkness to where the pull-chain hung, Talis caught her shin on a step stool or some such she hadn't noticed, but her hand found the chain and pulled.

The room was bathed in red as fluorescent lights buzzed, strobed a few times, then held steady. They were not the room's main lights, but a pair over the table that had been darkened with thick red film over the bulb housing.

"Cheery," commented Sophie. She struck another match and used it to light a cigarette. Its cherry glow was right at home in the red-lit space. She puffed out a cloud and the sharp tobacco and clove flavors hung in the still air.

The lights weren't the back room's main lights, but meant for Jasper's hobby. The man was fond of daguerreotype. On several occasions Talis brought him silver plate, amberlith, and chemical solutions from photographers in inner radii cities as a personal favor. But the red illumination, however innocent, made Talis's skin prickle. She looked for, but failed to find, another light switch. The aisles of the stockroom were filled with shadows deeper than reason allowed for. Everything the color of blood.

By the feeble light, they saw that the room was in disarray. Items tossed from shelves littered the floor. A chair was pushed up against one set of shelves. The step stool she'd knocked herself on was under the shelves on the other side of the main aisle. Items had been swept off the table and scattered. Even Jasper's framed daguerreotypes were askew on the walls.

The narrow door to his private office, its frame half as wide as a Breaker might comfortably fit through, was unlocked. Bad sign. Anything that could be locked, in Subrosa, generally was.

"Sophie, bolt the front door." Talis kept her voice low.

Jasper probably had a rear exit. Probably, but she didn't have the first clue where and she didn't want them pinned down if more menace was on its way.

Dug came up behind to cover her in the narrow doorway. She inhaled, held it, and pushed the door inward.

It stopped after a few inches, blocked on the other side.

She exchanged a look with Dug, then pushed harder. Something heavy slid on the floor within, but she gained the room.

This time she found a pushbutton switch next to the doorframe and pressed it. She blinked for a moment against the brightness of standard lighting. She heard the hiss of Dug's breath taken in through teeth, and squinted her eyes to see what he could.

Jasper was dead, slumped against the door.

His face was battered, his forearms bloodied. Defensive wounds. One of his silver-tipped tusks was broken, and the lip around it had bled. His eyes were still clear, though the sparkle of his humor was gone. The giant's forehead sported the entry wound of the bullet that had killed him. His skin was still warm under Talis's hand as she searched for his pulse.

She remembered the missing bullet in the cylinder of one of her new guns.

Her anger at Jasper was forgotten, and she felt shame flood in to replace it. The five men outside hadn't come for her. A Breaker might be stronger than a horse, but they were passive. Defend themselves, sure, but not attack. Not even in return. Not even to protect what's theirs. Five thugs with bats and knives were more than enough for *that* job. Breakers were ancient. Their population were the originals created by Helsim Breaker, gifted with the long life that made them so excruciatingly patient, and so far the only dead ones Talis knew of were ended by violence. That didn't happen often. Shouldn't need to happen, ever.

"We could have stopped this." She had trouble saying the

words, and they came out in a croak that had nothing to do with the recent abuse to her throat.

Dug did not argue, but put a hand on her shoulder and squeezed. She leaned her cheek against his forearm, closed her eyes, and felt the burning behind her lids that threatened tears. She'd been so ready to hang the blame for Hankirk's appearance around Jasper's large shoulders, but he was as thick in it as she was. Dug's grip on her shoulder remained firm, and he gently pulled her backward toward the exit. Nothing left but to sort out those who had done this. The shame went red, forged into vengefulness.

A small gasp sounded from behind them, as Sophie returned from securing the shop's entrance. Her hands went to her mouth and her eyebrows arched high in surprise. She'd seen her fair share of bodies before, and had been responsible for half of them at least, but they'd all been Cutter folk and unremarkable. A living Breaker was a rare enough sight, let alone a dead one. And this one had always been kind to her.

"I thought he took off," she said. "A frightened Breaker would have been bad enough. It didn't cross my mind that anyone would actually *kill* him."

Sophie's emotions tipped the balance of her own, and Talis felt tears finally appear. She blinked them away. Tried to breathe deeply to steady herself, but the office smelled like faint musk, clove, and allspice. Like Jasper.

"Do we search his office?"

Sophie looked around the small room. It may have once been a broom closet. Or maybe it was just the size of the furniture, made by Jasper to his own dimensions, that dwarfed the small square space around them. There was barely room for anything but the desk, two chairs, and a built-in case of shelves. They were empty now, their contents spilled onto the floor. The desk drawers were pulled all the way out, on their sides. Papers, pens, and ink bottles were emptied out into the mess on the floor.

Talis swallowed. Sniffed. Ran her palm over Jasper's eyes to close them—for his size she had to do one at a time.

"No point," she said, standing. "Those stinking woodrots outside weren't carrying anything but their weapons. We know what they were here for."

She patted the lump under her shirt where the ring nestled in its velvet bag. Beneath it, her heart beat against her ribcage.

A SIDE DOOR TO JASPER'S SHOP led out into Assessor's Hall, which was little more than a dimly lit maze of pawn kiosks. The kiosks were little more than makeshift chicken coops stuffed to bursting with collateral and sale items and guarded by their attending shopkeepers. A brighter corridor opened up ahead, spanning two levels with catwalks that crossed and looped the space above their heads. Talis eyed the balcony, feeling like a fish in shallow water at the bottom of a barrel. Crowds pressed around them as they merged into the flow of traffic. She became hyper-aware of any movement in her purse, now perceptibly weighted by their attackers' coins.

"And now, Captain?" Dug asked it quietly, but she bristled that he had asked her at all. Here, in the open, on the promenades of Subrosa where everyone was listening for a hint at weakness. And he knew it. He wanted to know she had a plan, and that it was a good one. And he'd make her think hard about her answer before she spoke it.

"Curse your hide, Dukkhat Kheri," she hissed, using his full name for effect. She was surprised at the volume of her own voice. No heads had turned their way at the outburst, which pretty much guaranteed everyone was listening.

Sophie certainly was, though she kept her mouth shut and watched the streets for ambush and mischief.

That question had been bouncing around Talis's own skull since they'd found Jasper. Sad as she was to see the gentle old dealer murdered on her account, it left her with that question echoing louder with each pulse of the headache gathering in her temples.

She stopped short and turned to face them both. "You two head back to the ship," she said.

A purple-capped dandy walking behind them, who had been looking down at papers in his hands, ran up against Dug's back. He looked up in surprise and irritation, opening his mouth to brandish insults at whatever lug had stopped in the middle of traffic. But upon observing the multitude of knives sheathed across Dug's back like rail ties, he closed his mouth with a snap and ducked away, losing himself in the crowd as quickly as possible.

Sophie started to protest, but Talis held up a hand. Breathed deep and popped them a smile. Made sure it was broad enough to flash light off her gold canine.

"I'm going to knock on a few doors and set up some appointments. See who's around that we can deal with. You go back, give Tisker a break on watch. Both of you—four eyes, four ears. Make sure the gentlefolk of Subrosa don't give us any more trouble than they've already done."

Dug hesitated. She hadn't exactly answered his question. Because she didn't have the answer he wanted. She'd pawn the ring if she had to, but she'd rather find a respectable Subrosan fence to get her what Jasper's death had convinced her it was worth. With the Breaker gone, she had to go down her list of contacts here. See who was still around. See who might already have the wind up their backs about her blasted little cargo. Someone's lips had been to the ears of more people than she cared for, and she was now convinced it hadn't been Jasper's. Which left someone still living out there, making trouble for her.

She could fix that, if she could find them.

CHAPTER 11

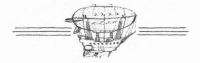

THE DOCKED TAIL WAS AS disreputable a place as any establishment in Subrosa that dared to call itself a restaurant. 'Restaurant'—as though the food were not an afterthought to the watered-down ale served to sullen patrons at the long, ring-stained bar. One could, and did, count on poor service and little attention if they sat in the dimly lit booths along the far wall, across the expanse of wobbly-legged tables that customers ignored entirely. You either came for the drink and wallowed at the bar, or came for the relative privacy and wallowed in the shadows. You certainly did not come for the cuisine.

The walk there had calmed her jangled nerves to some degree. She still felt the chill of horror at Jasper's death, but her heartbeat steadied and her mind cleared a bit with each step. This was not, she told herself, entirely unexpected. All the islands had their industries. Subrosa's primary export was trouble, and there was little reason to be as nonplussed by it as she'd allowed herself to become. Trouble was a long-standing partner of hers. It was not her master.

Talis slid into one of the booths, opposite a lanky Cutter

man with a too-well-considered goatee and mustache. He was dressed down in a blue twill cotton jacket, the primary feature of which was an oversized hood, which he now wore pushed back, freeing carefully groomed hair that fell in loose curls to his shoulders along with five of the smoothest prayer-locks Talis had ever seen. Fingerless kidskin gloves revealed a series of tattoos down each finger. Enough to show they were tattooed, not enough to see what the designs were. But Talis already knew.

"I see you got your set finished, Talbot," she said, signaling to the bartender to bring them a round.

There was already a full mug of the pitifully pale ale in front of Talbot. The refill was a courtesy.

He held up his hands between them and splayed the fingers, as if admiring the ink work through the gloves. He had invested a small fortune on the alchemical sigils that strategically marked the backs of his hands, down to just above the bed of each fingernail.

"Aye, I did. Just got back yesterday, matter of fact. You would've missed me had you come any earlier, you know."

"Lucky me. You try them out yet?"

Talbot wiggled his fingers, connecting first his thumb and forefinger, then thumb and middle, and so on to his pinky.

"Aye, I gave it a go."

She raised her eyebrows as he raised the mug of ale to his lips to draw out his tale.

"Hard to say, really," he admitted, when he replaced the mug into its condensation ring on the discolored table. "When your fingers are as light as mine to start."

She laughed. "You were had."

His amiable smile soured at her jest. "I'll cut that Rakkar ink-slinger's throat if that's the case."

"Try something tougher, then?" she suggested, not wanting to put his mood off before she got what she came for. "Maybe the dock officer's safes?"

"Nah, I've done them." He looked thoughtful for a moment. "You're right, though. Need me a challenge to know properly. Wait until they're right healed. Fingers swelled up like corpses under the needle, and they still sting."

She nodded, though the corner of her eye twitched in sympathy. "You'll have plenty of chances, no doubt. Somehow folks keep walking around with heavy purses, however often you keep relieving them of the weight."

He grinned, crooked smile flashing white teeth. Drinking overpriced half-watered ale at least didn't stain like the stout Talis would have preferred. Sparkling green emeralds winked in the centers of Talbot's incisors, even in the low light. Talis knew he'd spent as much money on his looks as his tattoos. Everyone had their money pits, she figured, and couldn't help but wonder if he'd skipped any necessary maintenance on *his* ship in pursuit of beauty.

With Talbot's mood restored and a fresh pair of ales delivered to the table, Talis leaned forward to get to business. The bar was quiet this morning and, with no music, she felt as though her voice carried farther than she'd like. Probably her nerves. But Subrosa was never what she'd call quiet. This afternoon it was eerily so.

Talbot held up a hand before she could speak, though. His grin had lost some luster.

"I know what you're here to propose," he said.

He cast a glance around the barroom at the other patrons. One other booth, its occupant slumped and asleep. Three heavy-lidded and overweight men at the bar, noses inches from the tops of their steins. The bartender, studiously wiping glasses with a discolored cotton rag, eyes trained on his work. All inattentive demeanors either sincere or practiced.

Talbot leaned forward. Their foreheads nearly touched over the center of the table.

"Word's around, you're trying to sell something the wrong people want."

He didn't ask to see it, or about it. Just knew. All she'd said was that he should meet her at the bar, but he knew everything, like she'd proposed it all right there in her message to him.

"That's a bad item you got." He licked his lips and polished off the first mug of ale. "Anyone pays you for that, and it's going to end up taken from them, and them out the price. Lucky if that's all they're short at the end of it."

Talis put her hands up, a non-threatening gesture. "Hey now, since when do we take things other people *aren't* trying to relieve us of? That's the business. That's the meat of it."

Talbot shook his head.

"What do you mean, 'no'? You want to test that ink work, but here you won't cargo a stolen item. Out of *Subrosa*?" She laughed in disbelief. "I'd find more nerve in Silver Isles than I'm finding here. You even know what I'm asking you to carry? A tiny bit of *nothing*, except to the right buyer."

"I don't want to know what it is. I know it's drenched in problems. The authority that'd chase me down for it isn't one I'm going out of my way to invite aboard."

Talis couldn't believe what she was hearing. Didn't like the feeling that settled into the bottom of her stomach. Here she was, *so close* to what ought to be a payday she could roll around in properly, but coming up with nothing but dead ends. She couldn't afford dead ends.

"The original contract I had to fetch this thing was a half-fortune. I can't walk away from that. I spent money and time—risked my neck—on fetching it. Made promises to my crew. Put off repairs on my ship to fund the salvage. I need a buyer."

Talbot thumbed one side of his thin mustache. Looked contrite, even. But refused to say what she wanted to hear.

"You and me, we have a long-standing business history. But as a *friend*, Talis, I'm telling you to shed that thing. Put it in the nearest bin, or dump it out in the skies, whatever.

But you wanna be done with it. Go and scrape up some more honest contraband."

She pursed her lips at him, then blew a short blast of disgusted air. "Subrosa's thieves have gone coward."

Talbot put a hand on hers, looked like he wanted to say more. But she pulled her hand away and stood.

She should stay. Get another cargo from him, get some news from around; there was always something to talk about here. But between the daggerpoint feeling in her gut and the panic in her mind, she needed to move. Wanted to be far away. Alone.

"Thanks for the drink," she said, giving him one last angry stare, childishly putting her problems on him for the moment. Willing him to change his mind.

"Hey now, I thought you were buying."

"Can't spare the coin. I'm broke 'til I sell this thing."

He made a face at her but didn't say another word as she turned and stalked out of the dingy pub.

THREE BLOCKS FROM THE DOCKED TAIL, Talis dipped into an alley to escape the press of the crowd. She leaned back against the wall of a restaurant. From deeper in the shadows, the fermented smell of spiced food caked on the filth-encrusted garbage chute found its way to her nostrils. It was almost as overwhelming as her own thoughts, which swirled, berating her for being a fool.

She needed to put this ring and the trouble it wanted as firmly behind her as she could, as soon as she could. Didn't dare toss it, no matter the unanimous counsel she'd been getting. It was worth something. The more they told her to be done with it, the more people showed up to relieve her of it, the more she was convinced of that. It *had* to be, and somewhere there *had* to be a buyer.

Talbot had been her best bet. He had the fewest scruples and the warmest feelings toward her now that Jasper was dead. Every other buyer she could think to line up was a long shot, and word was out that she was selling a bad deal.

The fallback was Assessor's Hall. Would the pawnshop clerks know, too? Whatever she could get for it, she'd have to take. There was a small bonus of the coin from the assassin's wallet, and Sophie and Dug had each taken their own prizes from that fight as well. It hadn't been a lot, but it was more than they'd started with. And the new revolvers weren't a bad take.

Pawns would do, she decided. Best to be done with this quickly.

She took a breath. Nearly choked on the garbage stench but made herself hold it. Pushed it out again, forcefully, a moment later.

Feeling better, the rank alley no longer seemed like such a haven. It was a corner, and there were eyes on her. It was no place to be caught.

She slipped back into the traffic of the main corridor and almost instantly was nudged at the elbow and hip. Felt the barest tug at her belt, and then a small child ran ahead into the crowd, clutching the assassin's coin purse she had tucked into her belt pouch.

"Little bastard," she snarled under her breath, and pushed after him.

If anyone had a mastery of Subrosa's mazes and secrets, it was the pint-sized populace of malnourished children. They fended for themselves, formed small gangs, or worked for the shopkeepers and crime bosses. Sometimes all of the above. They were the perfect army of thieves: abundant, hungry, and, with the proper tutelage, could be quite heartless. That's how Tisker had been raised, before he joined her crew. His skills had been developed by escaping punishment and staying alive in the urchin pits of Subrosan slums, until he was too old to hide from authorities under a mask of dirt in the crowd of other children. At that point, many former subcity children would move into business for themselves, turn around and guide the next generation of children on their dubious career paths. But Tisker wanted out, and saw his chance in the black-stained hull of *Wind Sabre*. Talis had needed some convincing. She definitely had preconceived notions about just how far she should trust a scum-dwelling, bottom-feeding former child of the alleys. She still believed, to this day, that Tisker was an exception to the rule.

The reed-thin Cutter boy with her purse managed to stay just ahead of her. Traffic seemed to part for him and then close back in to block her path. It was probably only half her imagination. A couple times she thought she'd lost him but then saw his twig-thin form just ahead of her, forced to dodge a cart or a burdened courier. She closed the distance and made a grab for his collar, nearly on him, but he dove at that moment into the dark shadow of an open doorway.

Pursuit took her through a bar, choked with pipe smoke, decidedly not tobacco. The door on the other side opened into the streets of the next Subrosan district, with polyboard walls and floors, a patchwork of colors taken from previous installations elsewhere. The mismatched panels bounced beneath her feet as she ran.

The boy slipped through a space between boards, so narrow she saw the edges scrape his shoulder. Undeterred, she kicked the board with her foot. It broke off, falling into a cramped alley lit with black-smoking tallow candles. The ground beneath her feet was littered with dingy blankets and coats, and beneath the candle smoke, the air was surprisingly unflavored by the smell of garbage. Though it did smell of other things.

There were more children here, and they pressed in at her, making a show of panhandling, grabbing at her arms and, in the case of the smaller children, her legs, to slow her down and aid in their compatriot's escape. There were too many of them to move through, though it was more like being swarmed by wake moths than held back by a mob. She kept her eyes on the bouncing gait of her quarry and pushed through the throng of dirty arms and faces. She felt small feet beneath her boots and shoved the bodies to the side, back into the press, until they gave up ground to avoid being stepped on.

At the far end of the alley was a blank wall. Talis cursed, almost out of breath. She toed at the edges of the board, but it was not loose as the last one had been. She slammed both hands, in frustration, against the dead end.

A small scuff of sound made her look up. A foot disappeared over the top of a ledge above her. The wall to her left had a narrow vertical strip of panel missing, revealing the wooden studs beneath. Just enough to use as a narrow ladder. If she'd not heard the movement she'd never have considered it. As she tested the strength of the support against her weight, she wondered how many of these catwalks and ladders hid in plain sight across Subrosa.

The ledge led into a plenum space less than half an arm's length tall. Better suited to urchins and vermin than a grown woman. She slid along in the near darkness, lit from the outside wherever the polyboard was not evenly adjoined.

This is an incredibly bad idea. The thought repeated itself with every elbowed inch she gained in the tight passage. She could feel dirt and the dried husks of dead insects beneath her palms, and her hair snagged on the underside of the boards above her. The thief moved easily ahead of her, not quite able to crawl on all fours but certainly having an easier time of it than she was.

Her breathing quickened and an invisible hand clamped around the base of her throat. She was not made for cramped spaces. Only her rage and frustration moved her forward after the child. Everything else inside her clawed to go back. She half hoped that the boards beneath her would collapse under her weight, dump her through into the shop below, and give her an escape from the darkness.

There were children who were pickpockets and children who were assassins. Others just did whatever it took to survive. Talis shimmied after the child, wondering which variety it was she followed. And what she was following him into.

At the far end of the plenum space she saw the child crouch, then disappear upward again. Talis rolled after him, not keen on being left behind with only her claustrophobia for company.

The ascent was a narrow shaft at the corner of whatever levels they were scrabbling between, and the crawlspace she left behind was a ballroom compared to the tight vertical climb.

There was a brief increase in the light level as the child pushed through a hatch above. Then it was dark again, and Talis was alone.

Awkward in the narrow space, she managed to climb in tiny steps, squeezing her arms tight against her sides so she didn't end up wedged against the opposite wall of the shaft.

At the top, she found the hatch locked from the other side. Not really surprising, though she was no less panicked by it. She pounded against it. She tried to run back over the route from the streets in her mind, to hazard a guess as to where the boy had led her.

She'd been reckless. And now she was lost, crushed into a tiny space barely big enough for the bony child she'd chased after, faced with retracing the squeezing path back to somewhere familiar. Faced with returning to *Wind Sabre* penniless and outsmarted by a child. *And* without a buyer for the ring. She gave the hatch one last half-hearted pound with the side of her fist.

Defeated, she let the back of her head drop against the

wall behind her. Only the panel swung outward before her head could thud against it. She stumbled out backward, falling without grace. Someone caught her and gently propped her back on her feet. The hands that supported her were pale and three-fingered.

"Ah, good," said a melodic voice. "We have been expecting you, Captain Talis."

CHAPTER 12

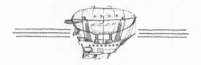

Talis had never met Zeela, the Vein merchant woman from the Platform District, but without question that was who stood calmly to one side as a younger Vein woman helped Talis out from the crawlspace behind the wall in the corner of a softly lit shop.

The businesswoman, in contrast to her plainly-dressed assistant, was an exotic and elegant vision. Almost nothing utilitarian about her appearance. She was dressed like a queen among the starving thieves of Subrosa, radiating the confidence of someone who could do so without fear of being mugged or otherwise harassed. The tales of her people's sixth sense undoubtedly augmented the air of mystique she wore as openly as the silks of her gown.

Zeela was slender, her frame delicate. Her nose was narrow and long, with a petite button tip. Her eyes were large shining moonstones in a pale cream face shadowed with purple undertones. Her thin eyebrows arched like the antennae of a moth. Small gemstones sparkled from where they had been glued to the skin around her eyes. Amethyst, topaz, and citrine spilled across her temples, down across the arches of her cheekbones. Her thick, shining, colorless hair was elaborately styled: first braided into tiny individual strands, then gathered together and piled about her head like a pale corona. Silver bells, strands of pearls, and shimmering sheer ribbons in lavender and orange threaded in and out of the braids, shifting as she moved. A single fall of straight unadorned hair, dyed in a gradient from pink to lavender, fell from the nape of her neck down her back to end in a perfectly straight line at her hips.

Layered in sheer tones that mixed their own colors, her clothing appeared weightless, a remarkable feat considering how much she wore. A full skirt tied beneath her bust fell to sweep the floor. It was embroidered with patterns of colored silk thread hand-stitched into the delicate silk fabric. Swirling colors conveyed no image or pattern that Talis could see, though from what she knew of Vein fashion, she was sure there was a design to its texture that the wearer would feel when brushing a hand across it. A short jacket covered Zeela's bust, shoulders, and two longer arms, with full sleeves that enveloped the limbs in shining silk. The sleeves fell beyond her hands, not to hide them from sight, but to convey that Zeela was so completely at ease in her space, and so well-served by her maiden clerks, that she did not require the manual labor or spatial guidance for which the outer pair of arms were intended.

Her second, smaller pair of hands, clasped gently over a delicate silk apron, were stained with herbal dyes in elaborate dotted designs from fingertip to just past the elbows. More gemstones were adhered in a two-finger-wide stripe from the back of her hands up her forearms. The flickering candlelight of the shop played across the faceted gems, their reflections dancing across the walls and ceiling and lending Zeela a celestial beauty.

Her appearance was carefully crafted to impress the other races. The sighted races, that is, who made judgments based on such things.

The entire Vein race was born blind. Created in the image of their Divine Alchemist, Lindent Vein, who regarded vision as a lie. He and his people relied on more physical sensations for situational awareness, along with a sense of perception that bordered on telepathic. Their blindness was the primary gift that Lindent Vein had bestowed upon his people during Recreation.

A young Cutter child learning about the Vein for the first time might not understand how the absence of vision was a gift, but Lindent Vein's people were preternaturally sensitive to sound, touch, and scent. Lindent Vein had made for himself, even before the Cataclysm, two pairs of arms. The outer, attached at the shoulder, were stronger and made for broad tasks, such as lifting and aiding in navigation of an unfamiliar place. The smaller, attached at the sides of the ribs, beneath the pectoral muscles, were long-fingered and sensitive, as much antenna as tool. With these they performed the most intricate of circuitry or jewelry design, with fine motor control that the most steady-handed Rakkar would envy.

Talis was pretty sure there was even more to it than that. She suspected the Vein could perceive electrical impulses as easily as the sighted races could see color. They had an industry based on backward-engineering pieces of arcane 'tronics that others, like Talis, lifted out of the flotsam, and they had a particular fondness for anything predating the Cataclysm. No doubt they had a knack for alchemy as well, but their economy was based on the technological advances they made and the patents they immediately filed.

Zeela's House of Antiquities offered apothecarial concoctions, collectibles ranging from vintage to arcane, and mechanical device repair. It was a sensible business model for a Vein entrepreneur. The shop displays were full of such fragile, irreplaceable, and expensive items that Talis had always assumed she couldn't afford to walk in the front door. It hadn't been on her list of possibilities, but it *was* a sensible stop for someone trying to sell an ancient and mysterious item.

Talis instinctively checked for the pouch she wore over her heart. Confirmed that it hadn't been dislodged in all her crawling.

She inhaled, opening her mouth to speak, but Zeela inclined her head in a barely perceptible tilt toward a customer at the counter who had yet to complete her purchase.

Understanding the warning, Talis closed her mouth again. As the young clerk who had helped her out of the crawlspace picked cobwebs and insulation out of her hair and off her shirtsleeves, Talis scanned Zeela's showroom.

The shop had no widespread lighting. Scented candles were lit, casting their minimal illumination across the narrow space—just enough to keep a sighted person from bumping into anything. The candles were more for atmosphere and communication, however, than for lighting. Talis inhaled deeply. Lavender and sage. Relaxing, calming. If she remembered correctly, that scent signaled to customers that a fresh delivery of healing herbs had arrived. As the scented air hit her sinuses, warmth spread through her upper body. The panic melted from around her heart.

Banks of tiny drawers lined the shop's walls, in black lacquered cabinets carved with unique Vein language marker code. It wasn't the mathematical and systematic marks of their written alphabet, but more arcane symbols, able to communicate an elaborate idea with a single character carved into the drawer and painted over in black. Only the shopkeepers would understand what each drawer held.

The parquet floor swirled with more elaborate patterns, formed from veneers of wood in varying thicknesses, giving both sighted and unsighted customers a level of craftwork to enjoy. Not enough to trip over, but enough to feel through the sole of a thin leather slipper.

A second young assistant parceled up the purchase of the

customer, a petite Rakkar woman who wore an open brown cotton jacket over a well-used leather apron and ankle-length skirts. The girl folded a sheet of parchment neatly around the bundle of individually wrapped items, no doubt ingredients meant for some dangerous alchemical process, or medicines to treat the damage thereof. She cut a piece of string the length of her larger arms' span—a quarter again longer than Talis's own—and webbed the package in a complicated series of crossovers. Then she strung a tiny copper bell onto the end and secured it with a bow.

As she handed it across the counter to the woman, Talis noted that the young clerk's smile was more deliberate than natural. The Vein did not smile as a matter of instinct. They relied on audible expressions of happiness and pleasure. The smile was meant for their sighted customers and needed practice. The veil of simulation dropped as soon as the customer, whose own chitin-plated face was half expressionless itself, uttered a brisk 'thank you' and turned to leave.

The woman passed through the shop's archway, which was hung with two layers of beaded curtains. The interior curtain was strung with what looked like pearls, which shuffled softly as she departed. The exterior curtain clinked more noisily, made of dark beads that might have been metal.

"Welcome, please, Captain," Zeela said, more animated now that they were alone in the shop. "We have a fresh tincture that has just finished fermenting. It would be of great use on that scrape."

Talis looked down and rubbed the outside of her left hand. She hadn't noticed it was bleeding. "Bit of a rough route to get here."

"You must pardon the deception," said the businesswoman. She produced Talis's stolen purse from beneath a fold in her sleeve and gestured to it with one of her hands.

"The nature of your visit, and of what I would like to speak to you about, necessitated caution. I did not wish to have your approach to my shop observed by the less savory denizens of this port."

Zeela's assistant removed a shallow glass jar from a shelf and transferred a translucent yellow paste from a larger container with a flat spatula, coordinating all four hands in her task. She placed the jar on a scale, ran her delicate fingers across the spring-loaded needle that indicated its weight, and twisted a lid into place.

"Your shop is being watched?" Talis felt foolish as soon as she asked. Of course it was. The real question was why that should change their behavior at all.

"There have been offers made, a price set for your death. It seemed prudent, in order to have you arrive all together."

Zeela accepted the jar from her assistant and placed it in Talis's hands, along with the reclaimed purse. The smell of rosemary and mint moved with her. Talis couldn't help but take another deep breath. She felt the tension leaving her aching shoulders.

"A gift for you," Zeela said. "My apology for the inconvenience."

Fortunate, as Talis was certain the little jar cost as much as that bi-clutch Sophie wanted. Too bad the thief hadn't led her to as generous a mechanic.

"Thank you," she said as she accepted the items. "You no doubt know of my other, less dismissible, inconvenience."

"Inconvenience, perhaps, but quite a prize all the same." Zeela contracted her nostrils and made a small series of exhaled chuffs. Laughter.

Talis untied the cord on her neck and placed the ring in its bag onto the counter between them. "Apparently so valuable that none of this city's entrepreneurs have the connections necessary to find a qualified buyer."

Zeela's hands moved over the pouch without touching it. "The cost is about more than just currency, as you know, Captain Talis. *Pressures* have been applied to prevent you from making an exchange."

Talis desperately needed this visit to go well, but the prick of a suspicion planted itself in her head. Zeela might be a ruthless enough businesswoman to have sent those thugs to Jasper to intercept her. The child that led Talis there was proof that Subrosan orphans acted as Zeela's eyes and ears on the streets. It was common practice for anyone with power in Subrosa. Assassination less so, but it was a technique employed with regularity among Vein competitors. Talis hoped Zeela's outward grace reflected a preference for more delicate handling of such situations. And that her appreciation for ancient things would extend to one of Helsim Breaker's people.

"As is its *value*." Talis bargained with the suspicions she had about the ring's history, and on the actions of those who had been after it thus far.

"Indeed. You have a reputation, but not the sort that attracts such dramatic threats."

Talis crossed her arms and wished she'd had a couple more drinks on Talbot's credit back at The Docked Tail.

"Maybe I'm losing my touch."

Zeela pursed her lips but picked up the ring in its pouch, resting it on her open palm.

"You are correct, however, about the value. I have found you a buyer."

Talis almost felt dizzy with relief. This was it, then. After what had quickly escalated into the worst day she could remember in a long time, after her crew's barely contained mutinous thoughts, after worrying how her ship was going to stay in the sky. Just like that, she'd found her fence. Stumbled onto her, really. She wouldn't have to pawn the thing off for a pocketful of change on her way back down to the docks after all.

Zeela disappeared through a silk and velvet curtain into the shop's private area, taking the ring with her. Talis expected her to reemerge with appraisal tools or paperwork, but one of the clerks lifted the hinged countertop for Talis to follow.

The twisting hallway behind the shop was pitch black in comparison to the low candlelight of the shopfront. Talis paused, completely lost as the curtain closed behind them and the blackness swelled around her. After a minimal pause in which Talis still found time to feel the panic rising to clutch at her, a golden glow emanated from the carpet and grew brighter until she could see Zeela adjusting a round dial on the wall to her side. The walls were wainscoted to the level of Zeela's lower elbows, and wallpapered above that with decadent golden damask. She gestured with one arm in its flowing sleeve, and Talis followed the shopkeeper down the hall and around two turns.

At the end of the passage, a strip of bright light showed at the bottom edge of a door. The buyer was sighted, then, Talis surmised. Possibly another Rakkar, Talis figured. Likely not Breaker, Bone, or Cutter.

Hopefully not Cutter. A Cutter buyer could prove to be a member of The Veritors of the Lost Codex. An agent for Hankirk. As desperate as she was to sell the ring, she wasn't sure what she'd do if that was where this was headed. She swallowed and her fingers found their way up to clasp at her prayerlocks. Hoped the Veritors wouldn't lower themselves to dealing through a Vein acquisitions agent.

She needn't have worried about the Veritors. Zeela pressed the unlatched door in on its hinges, and as it swung into the room, four Yu'Nyun turned to greet them.

CHAPTER 13

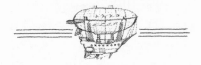

WHATEVER GUESSES TALIS might have made about Zeela's connections, she had not anticipated the aliens.

Her mind blanked. Forgot to tell her feet to stop moving. Momentum carried her into the room, and one of the aliens stepped forward to meet her. That sudden movement finally got her to brake before she walked right into it.

From descriptions, rumors started by those who claimed to have seen them, she expected the Yu'Nyun to be tall, lanky, and bony. They were that. Except for the bony part. Exoskeletons are made of chitin, after all, not bone. The Rakkar had chitin armor on their arms and plating over a portion of their faces, but the aliens were fully sheathed in the protective hard casing. Their waists were narrow. Narrower than the corsets Talis had suffered in a former life as a proper young lady. Talis wondered how they had room for vital organs, for her own had once been crowded from such tight cinching. The protrusion of alien ribs and hips harshly accentuated the tiny stomach between.

She also recalled some mention about body paint.

Another inaccuracy. It wasn't paint. The surfaces of their bodies were engraved.

Carved.

Chiseled.

Lurid blue tissue showed through where some cuts were so deep they became perforations. The alternating white and blue shades formed delicate, graceful, horrific patterns.

Talis had heard the aliens wore headdresses or elaborate hats. Wrong again. The sweeping crests that rose up and curved back *were* their heads. Carved, just like their bodies.

She struggled to find a comparison for them. The closest she could come up with was wasps. Enormous, cadaverous, ghostly wasps.

Three of them wore nothing but blue leather loincloths, belts with pouches, and some superficial metal adornments across their collars and around their arms, jewelry as rigid as they were. The fourth, who was still seated, might have been dressed straight out of Zeela's wardrobe. She—he? *it?*—wore silks, threaded with silver and beaded with what looked like sapphires. Its head was veiled in diaphanous tulle. Glints of the blue tissue, the flesh beneath the carapace, were visible through the veil. So much of the outer shell was carved away that it must have been more delicate than even that impractical anatomy would ever have intended.

The resemblance between the Vein and the Yu'Nyun went beyond the unnecessarily fancy garment, though the Yu'Nyun had only two arms. But both were tall, slender, and graceful. And pale.

Talis's mind was still coping. Must be. To compare the Vein to the Yu'Nyun . . . It was like comparing a butterfly to a walking stick.

Something yelled in her brain that first impressions were in order. Cultural understanding, the governments had called for. Business to deal with, Zeela had promised. *Business.* That got her mind moving. The only way out. Hopefully at least the rumors had gotten the aliens' wealth right.

Sell the ring, take the money, disappear back into the skies. A darker coat of black paint on *Wind Sabre*'s hull, maybe. Never mind repairs. *Upgrade* the engines. Cannons. All the things money could buy that she'd need next time *The Serpent Rose* appeared in their long-range.

So the aliens would be her salvation. All right. She took a deep breath. She could work with this. Little choice, anyway.

Zeela waited with tilted head beside the open door. Left open, if Talis felt the need to retreat. No doubt watching closely to see if she could deal with the situation that presented itself. A less worldly Cutter might balk at such clientele and remove herself as abruptly as she'd come. Talis imagined what might have happened if Sophie had come with her. Wished Dug had. Would they even believe her when she returned to *Wind Sabre* with the tale?

Business, she reminded herself.

Talis inclined her head slightly and tried to look important. While her alien counterpart stood with perfect posture on its—*Five Hells* . . . It stood digitigrade, each long leg balanced atop three arching toes. Still carved, right down to the floor. She absently wondered if any of them had ever carved away so much that their bodies just crumpled beneath them.

Business, woman. Talis put her weight into one hip, a cocky lean to one side. Let her right arm fall, forearm brushing the pistol on her belt. The other hand rested on the jutted hip.

The obvious leader of the alien party had representatives with it. Once again she wished she had Dug with her, if for nothing else than to act as her spokesperson.

She heard the coarse grating of gravel being scraped with a bamboo rake. As the sound modulated in speed and rhythm, Talis noticed the slithering hiss of a secondary sound weaving in and around the percussive noises.

It was the Yu'Nyun language.

Lindent's Wisdom guide me, she thought, only half as sacrilegiously as she might normally mean it.

But the sound soon faded, reduced to a humming drone, and a new voice began. Speaking the Common Trade, though not well and not pleasantly. The interpretation was coming from a flat device held in the speaker's hands. Points of light danced across its smooth glass surface, modulating curves moving across the screen in response to its vocalization.

"Our pleasure," came the voice from the pad, "to make introduce with you. To mutual benefit, with trade for wealth and items."

Zeela made the tiniest strained sound, a high-pitched sigh that came from somewhere in her sinuses.

She doesn't care to hear it, either. Talis's teeth ached, listening to the multi-pitched rasping and hissing of the alien language, overlaid with the monotonous tone as it made a mockery of grammar. She didn't know which sound was worse.

Zeela responded for her. "Captain Talis would be most happy to sell to you. Shall we negotiate the item's value?"

Bless her, Talis thought. *She's acting as my agent.*

Now Talis only had to hope Zeela was acting in her best interest.

Sell my ring, get me out of here. I'd give you a full three-quarter commission if it means I'm gone before all my jaw clenching cracks a molar.

Zeela stepped forward and gestured to the bolstered seat cushions that surrounded a lacquered table. Another young girl appeared, dressed in a thin silk robe, finer than the cotton worn in the front of the shop. She carried a tray of aromatic tea, which she placed on the low tabletop. It wasn't until the smell of the tea leaves reached Talis's nose that she became aware of the other smell in the room. Like dust, and sand, and old metal.

It's them, she realized as Zeela poured everyone a diminutive porcelain cup of tea.

Once, in a Bone village, Talis had met an old priestess, so arcane and primeval in her methods of practice that she was rumored to be more witch than worshipper. Outside the woman's abode were strung the bones of animals she had hunted, or sacrificed—Talis hadn't asked—and in the wind they clapped together, making soft percussive music. It had chilled her to the core. These aliens evoked an uncannily similar feeling. She attempted to relax her jaw and moved to a seat opposite the apparent leader of the Yu'Nyun group.

She could not get through this, and away from these aliens, fast enough.

Zeela sat back down between Talis and the spokesalien, produced the ring, now free of its pouch, from one of her long sleeves, and placed it on a ceramic stand on the table. She gestured to it with one of her smaller hands.

"I stand in witness to the authenticity of the item," she said.

The aliens leaned forward. Curiosity was universal, it seemed. Talis saw the hand of their veiled leader twitch in its lap, but it did not reach out. She remembered how the alien ship had plunged into the flotsam. Couldn't help but imagine a full ship's crew of these bony devils. She had a moment to appreciate that they were here to buy the ring and not outright take it.

In Talis's mind, the price for the ring was going up in direct proportion to the amount of time she had to spend in this unsettling company.

Get a grip, she told herself. *Business, business. Breathe. This meeting won't last forever.*

The alien representative spoke again.

"With a price for the item," the alien's translator relayed after a moment. "Prepared with precious metal and stone in value like seventy-five thousand your coin."

Talis looked at Zeela, head turning so quickly she felt something pop in her neck, and the sensation of icy fire traced the tendons up to the base of her skull. Vein were one thing. Vein left you in awe. Vein didn't make your skin feel like it wanted to pull free from your body and leave you behind if you didn't have the sense to run. The deep breath Talis had been taking seemed lost somewhere on its way to her lungs.

And now the translator made mockery of their currency conversions.

"Could they rephrase that?" Her voice was calm, level. Detached from the part of her mind that begged to vault the colorful upholstered cushions and be gone from the room.

"I believe," said Zeela calmly, slow as pouring syrup, "the honorable representative from the Yu'Nyun ship is offering you the trade equivalent of seventy-five thousand silver press-coins, in the form of silver bullion and precious gemstones."

The alien listened as Zeela's words were converted to painful hisses and clicks. Then it looked to Talis, and waited.

It was a good thing the aliens didn't expect Talis to speak on her own behalf. She was on the verge of panicked laughter. It threatened to break through her outward calm.

The aliens wanted to pay almost double what the ring was worth. Though *worth* was becoming more and more difficult to peg when it came to this item. To her, it was rubbish. Rubbish she had hinged her future on. Rubbish that had cost the world a Breaker life. Perhaps the aliens had no concept of fair value, or of exchange rates, for the translator to muck up.

She opened her mouth to tell Zeela she accepted the offer. Or should she counter it? Did the aliens barter?

"Also," the alien appended to its statement before Talis could speak. "Request wise lady captain sell additional service."

Damn. And there it is.

Built into that generous sum of money, which she'd surely regret to walk away from, was going to be another item. Another service. Something she suspected she wasn't going to like. How would she signal her refusal to Zeela? Cough?

Kick her in the leg?

Zeela spoke. Her tone was level as before, but the words were clipped and her accent heavier. "What does the Yu'Nyun representative require of the esteemed captain?"

"Take us to meet your gods."

The translator made a valiant effort on the grammar. Best sentence so far. Too bad it had completely flubbed the message. Talis looked to Zeela.

"I think that was mistranslated again."

"Not," droned the alien through its device. "We take many tries, since arrive. Approach four government. All religion spokespersons. Learn many topics surround your deities. Very curious your planet structure. Very curious your planet history. Buy many your artifacts from many times. Information is missing. Your gods witness missing information, complete our research. Exploration we seek knowledge. Interview with gods serve last information to complete our mission."

It was well known that the aliens had been curious about Peridot. Poring over libraries, excavating ruins, collecting whatever information they could. It was even rumored that the aliens had visited the Rakkar alchemists in their subterranean laboratories. Unlocking Peridot's secrets, apparently. The gods would certainly be able to provide any of the missing pieces of information.

This time the laugh really did almost escape from Talis's mouth. The Divine Alchemists barely communicated with their own followers. They definitely didn't conduct interviews.

She felt that seventy-five thousand evaporate before she even got to touch it.

How do you know The Five's interests? something in her head asked. *Maybe they'd like to meet the alien visitors.*

If they wanted to meet the aliens, she argued with herself, *they'd have done it. Gods don't wait for an invitation.*

Everyone in the room was looking at her, she realized. Waiting for her reply.

"If the governments of our planet each refused to sponsor an audience request with The Five," said Talis, carefully, "what makes you think that I have the ability to provide such access?"

The alien in finery moved then. It lifted its veil, then reached out with a spindly finger and ran the tip along the edge of the battered ring.

"You already do more what your government cannot."

It turned its head to look at Talis directly. She shrank, inwardly, from the strange sapphire eyes, wide as Zeela's own sightless ones, but all darkness. No pupil, no cornea. In the rigid skeletal face, they had no expression except what the fixed carvings across the brow ridge implied. Something glittered deep within those eyes, though. Not any sort of personality, Talis didn't sense, but a definite vastness of intelligence.

"Lady captain makes stories." The first speaker took over again as the leader replaced its veil and sat back. "Repu-ta-tion." It spoke the last word for itself, and the translator sputtered it back to the room in the alien language.

Talis wouldn't have recognized the word, as the alien struggled with the softer consonants and the vowels disappeared almost entirely. Except she held that particular word dear. Her reputation had gotten her good deals in the past. Big contracts. Because she'd get the work done, whatever it took.

Curse my reputation now, she thought, *to all five hells and what's left to flotsam.*

But they'd appealed to the right element of her personality. And Zeela must have known what Talis knew: She *could* take them to talk to The Five. Or one of them, anyway.

So then. She was going to do it, wasn't she?

"It will be very expensive to escort your ship on a venture like that."

The alien gestured, and the other two rose, moved behind the bolsters on their side of the room, and lifted a crate between them. They carefully stepped back over the cushions and placed it before Talis. One of them flitted its hand across the alien latch, and it popped open just slightly. Then the pair stepped back, pulling the lid open on silent metal tracks as they retreated.

Somewhere far away, Talis heard herself make a tiny sound. The room spun, sparkling with silver, gold, and a rainbow of twinkling gemstones. Her mind took several heartbeats longer than the communication pad to process the alien's next words.

"For second request we make first payment of five hundred thousand coin equivalent. Second same payment after."

CHAPTER 14

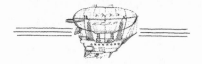

Talis left Zeela's House of Antiquities by the front door.

The wooden porches and suspension bridges of the Platform District were kept freshly sanded by sighted custodians paid for from the coffers of the district's shopkeeper co-op. No paint marks made along the walls here would remain for more than a few hours. The golden boards reflected the tawny warmth of delicate lights strung along railings and overhead. Around each glass bulb, duskfey flew in spheroid circuits, their luminescence competing with that of the electric and gas street lights. The cheer of the setting belied the chill of the cold winds below Rosa's dark mass, and the danger of the undercity.

In the Platform District, where the Vein who came to live in Subrosa kept their shops and offices, wind chimes replaced the painted signs and graffiti that visually cluttered the rest of the black markets. The shopkeepers' delicate hangings—tinkling metal, glass, and ceramics—competed for attention with the gangs' makeshift cups, pins, and thin metal takeout trays as they danced in the open spaces just past the archway that led from the Tined Spoon District.

Talis's hands trembled like those chimes. All the adrenaline that flooded her system during the meeting had abandoned her in its aftermath. She paused to lean against the railing of one open bridge. Her head spun as she stared into the skies beneath her. She was lightheaded, chilled. She hugged herself for warmth.

Gods. Dealings with the aliens now? How am I going to tell the crew?

The multi-octave sounds of the chimes announced a gust of wind before it reached her, and she braced her legs as best she could on the swaybacked bridge that would take her back to the docks.

Show them the money. Worked on you, didn't it?

The trunk and its glittering contents would soon be on its own way to *Wind Sabre*, repacked into a cargo crate bearing customs forms for tea and herbs. Lighter, of course, by Zeela's eighteen percent. Talis didn't begrudge her the generous amount. She would have given Zeela an even bigger commission. The woman had saved her. Saved *Wind Sabre*. But for Talis, haggling was like breathing, and Talis talked her down because the initial amount Zeela requested would have been higher than she'd hoped for. If Zeela had pressed, Talis would have given up ground. She'd still come out well ahead thanks to the antiquarian and her clients.

Paranoid that the aliens might exit Zeela's shop and catch her alone on the bridge, she pushed off, heading back to the docks. She still felt odd for not having haggled with the aliens, but what they'd offered was beyond her ability to properly appreciate. The mind stopped understanding numbers above a certain count.

Her feet bounced on the wooden planks strung between platforms, and her spirits bounced higher with each step. It was done. The troublesome ring was out of her hands and the money was forthcoming. Barely an hour after her dark moment in the alley outside The Docked Tail, the engine repair was a non-issue. Bills could be paid, overdue shares balanced for her crew, and luxuries still afforded beyond that. And all before they accepted the second payment at the other end of this. Her mind turned fanciful and the numbers turned to vapor. The math still made sense, but only in terms of abstracts. Everyone aboard *Wind Sabre* could afford their own ship after the shares were distributed.

A knot formed in her stomach at that thought, and she slowed her pace.

But why shouldn't they all go on with their own careers? Or retire, buy an island? Hells, an *inner* island! Plague the aristocracy with their presence.

Gods, woman, don't get ahead of yourself.

The money wasn't aboard the ship yet. She could be anxious over that at the right time, which wasn't now.

What Zeela gained in the bargain went beyond wealth. Beyond eighteen percent of one million seventy-five thousand presscoins. She could now declare herself the official trade representative to the aliens. Wouldn't *that* be something to put on her shop sign? 'Herbal Remedies, Antiques, Alien Trade.' The Yu'Nyun had provided her with a communication tablet and as Talis left the shop, they were in the midst of arranging some sort of exclusivity contract.

Zeela would probably backward-engineer the translator and have a corner on that market, too. Good position to be in, if the aliens didn't conclude their exploration too soon and return to wherever it was that they came from. Whatever kind of world would birth beings such as those.

Too soon? Laughable thought. Talis might have accepted their money, but if they returned home yesterday it wouldn't be too soon in her mind.

She didn't reckon that Onaya Bone was going to give the aliens the information they wanted. There was a fair chance they wouldn't even get the audience with her that they sought.

She rarely spoke to her own people. Other races of Peridot even less frequently. And here were these outsiders, skulking around, behaving like cosmic stalkers. Acting as though Peridot was a public archive, forgetting it was people's *home*.

Talis considered herself worldly. Believed she stood apart from the rest of Cutter folk, who were ignorant and isolationist. They stared at and avoided the other four races, spreading rumors and folklore to amplify their differences. She was proud that she darted here and there across the territories, and that she considered anyone who could be trusted beyond the edge of her eyesight as a potential friend. That she could drink firewater with the Rakkar, play skill games with the Vein, consider a Breaker man her closest business partner, or share her deepest secrets with a Bone warrior. So it came as an unsettling surprise to her—and an unsettling blow to her ego—that she felt so much discomfort around the Yu'Nyun.

All the same, Talis was not as annoyed at their presence as she had been before. Her skin prickled a little less in picturing the gaunt forms of her new clients. Her instinct to run had settled back down in her stomach. Which resumed its normal operations, reminding her she hadn't had anything to eat all day.

The vision of sparkling precious metal and gems was now mated in her mind with the thought of the aliens. The flesh beneath their carved, bony husks might as well be polished sapphire.

Not that she thought she'd ever get used to seeing them. But at least she wouldn't have to spend much time in their company. They were going to stay on their own ship. *Wind Sabre* would escort them to Fall Island, a day and a half's cruise on the other side of the Bone border.

Hells, customs crossing is gonna be fun.

Talis entered the Tined Spoon District, where the biting fresh air of the open platforms was replaced with the hot spiced breath of Subrosa's eateries. They were clustered together in one mostly fireproof concrete construction, centrally located and anchored directly to the inverted pyramid-shaped mass of Rosa above. All cultures were represented in the food stalls and restaurants, their smells mingling in the still air and the heat from the ovens and cooktops ensuring healthy sales of cold drink.

Her stomach rumbled and she changed course. She'd taken a scoop of the money from the coffers before departing Zeela's back room. Tried not to look desperate. But now that her money belt was full and overdue expenses weren't flowing in an endless list behind her eyes, it seemed reasonable to indulge in a tray of her favorite takeout. She had yet to figure out just how to tell her crew about their new contract, but a hot meal might help warm them to the idea.

Talis passed by stands of peppered sausages, kiosks where folded grain pockets were filled with crumbled mince and corn, and restaurants where thin cuts of meat and vegetables were served in bowls of fragrant broths. Past steaming stalls where batter-dipped indeterminate shapes were fried crispy and golden on the ends of wooden sticks. Headed for a tiny shop on the edge of the district, hiding in a back alley. Unnamed, the food stand mostly served the residents of Subrosa rather than trying to attract docked visitors. No pretense of friendly service, clean facilities, or tables that didn't wobble. It was one of the best-kept secrets of Subrosa, and that was saying something. Either you knew the food was fantastic, and how to get there, or you stuck to the main thoroughfare, living on in ignorance.

At ease for the first time in months, Talis was rounding the last turn before reaching the food stall she sought when Hankirk nearly collided with her. He froze in surprise, a skewer of roasted poultry half-bitten between his teeth. One hand holding said skewer, the other supporting a tray containing the rest of his order. His face was something to see. Probably mirrored her own shock, though his eyes sparkled with something like delight. Well, sure. About to finally make that arrest, wasn't he?

Her new revolvers were free of their holsters and leveled at him, with the food still half in his mouth. Their weight was strange in her hands, but she was thankful to have the advantage.

"No witnesses," she said, pulling back the hammers with audible clicks. "I could save myself a lot of trouble right now."

In truth, there were plenty of witnesses. There was a line snaking out of the door of the restaurant. But this was Subrosa. They had looked up when she drew the weapons but now turned uninterested eyes back to the menu boards in front of them. Shots fired, throats cut, inert bodies left in busy streets; these were all part of the place's charm. She thought of the assassins. Of Jasper's cooling body, and gripped the guns tighter.

Hankirk wasn't even wearing his Imperial uniform. Of course he wouldn't declare his allegiance in this place. Bad enough his ship was in full regalia. It was likely he'd anchored at some smaller island nearby, and come in on a local transport. No one would know to report the death of an Imperial captain, if they cared to report the death at all. He had two days' scruff of growth on his cheeks. He almost looked the part, almost fit in with the brigands. In her experience, he was the worst of them.

But she stayed still. Wasn't a murderer. Killer, sure, when given provocation. The guns were testament to that. Survivor. She liked the sound of that better.

Hankirk recovered, finished the bite and dropped the skewer back on his tray. Held the now-empty hand up in the air in surrender while he chewed and swallowed. There was no gun at his hip, but that didn't mean he wasn't dangerous.

"I see you met my friend Geram." He nodded at her guns.

"Briefly," was all she said.

But she could have kissed him. A huge weight was

removed from her shoulders. The men outside Jasper's shop hadn't been in Zeela's employ, and there was no anonymous third party at play here. Just more of Hankirk's tangled work, and that much she was already handling. Veritors wouldn't hesitate to murder a Breaker. It made so much sense, and largely cleared up the rest of her questions.

This was turning out to be a fine day.

"Talis," he said calmly. Addressing her like a friend, though she knew his raised hand could grab for her wrist at any moment. "You don't know what you have."

"Getting a better idea every time you make an attempt on my life, you motherless bastard."

"Are you hurt? They were only supposed to rob you." His confusion was almost convincing. "Just take the ring and put you off of it."

She scoffed, leaning her weight into one hip. The guns were heavy. "*You* were going to put us off a hangman's platform. *They* were going to put us off the docks. You'll have to try harder if you want to fool me."

"Just give it to me, Talis. This is a bigger thing than your little ship can carry."

She stared at him but didn't reply. Her nose itched, but no way was she moving the revolvers.

"Give it to me and I'll drop the charges. I'll even let your Bone man live." He retained that self-assured tilt to his shoulders, but she'd almost swear he was begging. Far cry from the elitist disdain he'd put off back in front of his crew. "Or come with me, and we can finish this thing together."

"What thing? What's the course you're plotting here, Hankirk? You want the ring for what? You can't get much richer, can you?"

She squeezed her elbows against her rib cage to keep her hands steady. This conversation was lasting too long. She wondered if she could safely holster one of the guns without appearing to back down. His eyes flicked momentarily to the movement of her hands. She abandoned the idea.

"You remember what I told you, back at the academy?" He looked as though he wanted to take a step toward her, but had the sense not to.

"Oh, I remember. You remember I removed myself from your company after?"

"Just give me the ring, Talis. Please."

She delighted in disappointing him. "I don't have it."

His eyes dilated. Contracted. Dilated again. He opened his mouth. Closed it again. Shock and anger battled for control of his face.

She enjoyed the show. He was desperate for it.

"What'll it get you? Another promotion? An even bigger ship with even more brass to polish?"

He started to take that step forward, but she motioned with the gun in her right hand. He put his foot back.

"Where is it?"

She wished she'd pulled a knife instead of the guns. These things easily weighed twice as much as her usual pistols, and she'd already climbed half across the width of Subrosa since breakfast. Hankirk's desire for the ring went beyond orders and laws, she realized. What did he have to prove? He was Fens Yarrow's heir, wasn't he? He'd told her so.

Or maybe that was just it. Prove he was up to the legacy? Do something more dramatic and foolhardy than his forebear had? Try to kill a god and actually succeed this time? The ring must be at the center of that. She had no proof, but the look on his face made her certain. She was suddenly very glad it was out of his reach.

"Sold it. Got myself a buyer, no thanks to you or the flags you sent up. Ought to thank you, though, for forcing me to hold out for the right price. Made a nice tidy profit after all."

Tidy was hardly the word. She wanted to pour that coffer out on the deck of her ship and look at the bright shiny mess it would make, then enjoy picking up every gem and gold bullion rod again to stow it. She decided she was feeling generous. She holstered the guns, put her hands on her hips instead. The muscles in her arms and shoulders nearly shook with relief, and she didn't need her arms trembling just now.

Hankirk barely noticed that she'd put down the weapons. He almost dropped his tray of food, and had to catch it in a spasm of movement. "Who was your buyer? That ring is the key to everything. Talis, what have you done?"

He took a brazen step forward, looked ready to grab at her, maybe shake her for an answer. Then he focused on something over her shoulder, and his eyes went so wide that the whites showed all around the red-brown of his irises.

There was a clacking sound. An undercurrent brushing of dry grass in a stiff wind.

A translator pad said, behind her, "Does this one make personal bother you, Talis Captain?"

"No, it's not possible . . ." Hankirk's voice was barely a whisper.

Talis empathized with his panic. It took every bit of self-control she had to look casually over her shoulder rather than whirl around to face the Yu'Nyun party.

They were armed, or so it appeared. Their weapons were not the down-to-business guns that Talis was used to. They were beautiful, more sculptural than practical, like something that belonged on a pedestal. Instead they were slung from shoulder straps across the aliens' pale thoraxes—and they were leveled at Hankirk.

There was a ripple of motion from the crowd, and some dropped their guise of disinterest to stare openly at the aliens. More specifically, at their weapons.

Talis put a hand out. A shoot-out between Cutter folk was one thing. But the aliens hadn't attacked anyone since they arrived, and she didn't want them to start on her account. "He was just leaving, friends."

She turned back to Hankirk. Nodded her chin quickly at

the passage behind him.

"We'll see you later, won't we?"

Hankirk's eyes flashed with a sequence of silent reactions like the slides of a flicker show. His face twisted and he looked as anxious as he did angry. He backed up a few steps, turned, and stalked off. Tossed his tray of uneaten food atop an overflowing bin before he rounded the corner. The score she'd have to settle with him, one of these days, was growing.

Talis took a deep breath and turned back to the Yu'Nyun. What did it say about her that she would rather be alone in the recesses of Subrosa with four aliens than with Hankirk?

"All is as discussed," said one of them, speaking through its flat device.

Talis listened as much to the alien's vocalizations as she did the message its device passed along. The language structure was bizarre. But where it had been barely recognizable as speech earlier, she was starting to get a feeling for its patterns. It wouldn't be as easily learned as the native Peridot languages she had picked up as a matter of professional courtesy, but those languages came from throats far more like her own than that of the Yu'Nyun. But given time. . . .

She blinked that idea free of its footing. No point in chasing a rabbit of a thought like spending enough time with the Yu'Nyun to learn their language, let alone to speak it. If she did her job right, they could leave Peridot's thinnest atmo in a few weeks. Maybe less.

The alien was looking at her expectantly. Talis realized its last comment had been a question.

She pasted a smile on her face, not even sure if that would mean anything to them, and clapped her hands together. Made a point of speaking plainly. Last thing she wanted was for a misconstrued idiom to blow the whole deal.

"Yes, of course. That man is an old acquaintance of mine."

"Ours as well."

That was news to her. Had they spent more time together

than the brief meeting of their two ships over the flotsam, before *Wind Sabre*'s hasty exit? The alien's face was rigid, and the mechanical interpreter added no inflection to its translation.

"Previous, he agree audience what we seek. He delay, speak false words."

She nodded. Kept up the smile, for what it was worth, though she felt one corner of her mouth twist wryly. "Ah, I see you *do* know him. As I said, he's an old acquaintance. Not anyone I do any dealing with currently. We only met by accident in the alley."

"Coincidence."

She chuckled. "Not really. The food stall at the end of this passage has some of the best roasted meat you'll ever taste. Not to be missed when visiting this port. Perhaps you'll allow me to buy you dinner? My treat, in thanks."

The aliens turned their heads to exchange looks. Talis wondered how that message got through. The guns moved. She twitched, but they were only being shouldered.

"Not eat food this," said the veiled alien. The diplomat. It touched the side of its mandible with long fingers. She realized she probably didn't *want* to see how they chewed their food. "But with gratitude."

The first spoke again. "Company to your ship, Talis Captain. Safety for you."

Anyone who was watching her already knew she was dealing with the aliens. The person she would least want to know had already run off, undoubtedly to start whatever trouble he could with that information. And wouldn't it get the fools of Subrosa talking, to see her with an entourage of extraplanetary foreigners? Gods, the word might get back to *Wind Sabre* before she could.

"My gratitude to you," she replied, bowing her head slightly. "If you'll just be patient with me, while I buy dinner for my crew and myself?"

Her unusual company stood back a bit from the kiosk

as she made her purchase. The herbs and spices wafting from the cooktop seemed to be making their eyes water.

She paid for enough food to feed a small army, and the restaurant owner pushed an open cardboard box into her arms. The scented steam enveloped her and she breathed deep. The carton was heavy, hot, and no doubt would soon be leaking grease out of the bottom flaps.

CHAPTER 15

T RUE TO THEIR POORLY translated words, the four
Yu'Nyun saw Talis all the way to the berth where *Wind
Sabre* was docked. She walked beside the veiled alien, with
one of their entourage walking in front and the other two at
their backs. The last time Talis had been escorted so formally,
she'd been under arrest.

Attempting small talk with her new business partner
didn't go far. The translator pad worked well enough, but
either a compulsive need to fill dead air with conversation
was not a universal trait, or the alien didn't relish their time
together any more than she did. Somewhat relieved, Talis
dropped the pretense and they walked the rest of the way in
silence. She did her best not to seem too curious about her
companions, keeping alert to the pulses of Subrosa instead
of staring at the lead alien's back and the fascinating pattern
of carvings across the segmented plates of its neck and shoulders. In return, her escorts seemed to try not to be offended
by the smells wafting from the dinner carton. Anyway, the
rest of Subrosa had the staring amply covered.

Within sight of *Wind Sabre,* she saw Sophie gaping

openly at them from the top of the gangway, a cigarette in danger of dropping from her parted lips. Talis felt an involuntary grin trying to split her face. She struggled to keep her expression under control as she turned to say goodbye to the veiled alien.

"I thank you, again," she said to her Yu'Nyun counterpart. "For your assistance, and for your company."

"We most eager to begin," came the response. Foreign words spoken by the alien who faced her, but interpreted to her right-hand side by the pad in another alien's hands.

"As am I," Talis said. "On that note, and due to the presence of our mutual acquaintance, Captain Hankirk, I suggest we avoid any unnecessary delay. Would you be amenable to meeting at the agreed location early tomorrow morning?"

"Most reasonable, Talis Captain. Wise and reasonable."

Normally she'd shake hands with a business partner, but a glance at the skeletal fingers obscured beneath the long veil, and Talis awkwardly decided a small bow was more appropriate. The aliens, in a single synchronous movement, touched the notches at the base of their throats, then their foreheads, and turned to leave.

"Can't say I've ever heard anyone call you 'reasonable,' Captain."

Talis looked up at Sophie, who had recovered from her shock. She leaned one elbow on the railing of the ship, looking down as she stubbed her cigarette against the metal disk sewn into her leather wrist band. She was still wearing her finery from before, though she had shed the weight of the shoulder holsters. No, Sophie certainly hadn't called her reasonable lately. But the girl was grinning. Hadn't meant anything by it, just the usual smuggler's gibe. Talis took a breath through her nose and tried to let her nerves settle.

"Oh, I am *most* reasonable," she assured Sophie, hefting up the box which had, as she predicted, soaked through at the bottom. "Now take this gods-rotted heavy thing before I reason I ought not to share."

Dug met them on deck, and Sophie unloaded the box into his arms. She eagerly cleared a space on one of the engine houses, pushing aside a coil of line so he could put it down, then ran off to get plates and utensils.

"We'll eat in the galley," Talis called to Sophie before she could disappear below. "Got news. Don't want to share it with everyone on the docks. Where's Tisker? Sleeping?"

Sophie came up short of the access below and her demeanor shifted. Her hand went to the leather pouch on her waist as if to fetch another cigarette from the brass case inside, but only fiddled with the flap instead. She was headed to the lower decks, after all. "Oh, he, uh . . . had a personal errand to run. Said he'd be back by dinner, Captain, but it's a bit early yet."

Talis eyed her. Sophie was a better liar than that.

"We accepted a delivery," Dug said, "only a short while before you returned."

Talis turned her head to Dug. In her peripheral she saw Sophie use the distraction to make her escape.

"Tea and herbs from Zeela's House of Antiquities?" she asked, and enjoyed the way his eyes narrowed at her. He only liked when she was unpredictable in combat.

"Yes, Captain. What is it really? Herbs don't weigh that much, or clink when their carton is shifted." He reached out and plucked something out of her hair, holding it up between them. A dead sackbug, which she must have picked up in her chase after the pickpocket.

Talis grinned at him. She shouldn't be grinning. Dug certainly wasn't grinning.

Between Hankirk, the aliens, and the route ahead, there was so little to smile about. Little, but enough to fill that crate from Zeela and put some of the raucous voices in her mind to rest. She couldn't help it. It had been a long day, and at the start of it, things hadn't looked like they'd work out half so well as they had.

"You procured a new contract?"

"It's a longer answer than 'Yes,' my friend. Where's the delivery? I'll need to verify the contents. Then you'll see what I've procured."

She clapped him on the shoulder. He stood firm, in her way. Polite. Deferential. Her best friend, dearest advisor, and very concerned first mate.

"Come on, Dug." She screwed up her face in a feigned pout. "At least hear what I have to say before you decide to mutiny."

"Aye, Captain."

It wasn't always easy to tell when he was joking. She pushed him playfully toward the hatch that led below, following behind. Tried not to let his hesitation color her mood. She already felt guilty enough, dropping the news that she'd taken a contract like this. Contracts were a captain's prerogative and she owed no explanation. But this was the Yu'Nyun. This, even more, was Dug's own goddess.

"Where is Tisker really, Dug?"

Dug's shoulders tensed. He'd washed off the gold dust, but in the still air of the docking bay, had not bothered to put his shirt back on. Talis could see the muscles ripple under his bare skin and the scars on his back shift with the motion.

"Right here, Cap. No worries."

Talis jumped, and was thankful she managed to control the yelp that had threatened to burst from her throat. She turned toward the sound of Tisker's voice and saw him heading down the access behind them, one hand on the railing installed over the steps. His other arm was tucked around an odd-shaped parcel wrapped in old newsprint. From the lean in his shoulder, it was heavy for its size.

"Good," Talis said. "I don't think Sophie was going to hold dinner for you."

She let her gaze slide up from the mystery object to his

face, so he'd know she was asking. "Anyone out there give you trouble?"

But Tisker's nostrils flared and his chin rose to follow the scent of food coming out of the galley. "Is that what I think it is?"

Their feast was laid out on the drop-leaf table in the galley, and Sophie'd turned on only half the cabin lighting. The cramped dining compartment was warm and cozy and smelled amazing. The trays of food sat unwrapped with a serving spoon thrust into each. Talis's mouth watered, and her stomach rumbled in empathy with the bare plates laid out at each setting. Tisker sidled around her to his end of the table as Dug headed past the galley on route to the cargo hold.

Sophie scooped a hefty portion of rice as Tisker examined the different meats Talis had brought back. He placed the paper-wrapped parcel down on the table beside his setting with a solid clunk, then nibbled a small crisp end that had fallen loose of one skewer, with his help.

He closed his eyes and savored the bite. "Haven't had this in ages. Gods, I missed that place."

It would be fair to say that Talis had gone a little overboard. Usually the four of them would split an order of meat with a portion of rice and vegetables for each. Cheaper that way, though it wouldn't leave any leftovers. Today, in her elevated spirits, and shopping hungry, she had gotten more orders of meat than mouths to feed, and not the cheaper selections. It was enough food for twice as many people, but she trusted they'd find a way to make it disappear.

They'd been living on nonperishable ship rations, forced to skip a full grocery run on their last refuel because of the cost of the salvage overhead. So there had been food but nothing that inspired much enthusiasm: dehydrated meat and tins of boiled vegetables eaten standing at the prep counter, not even worth setting a place or pulling out a chair for. She'd taken in her belt two notches, as it happened. She planned on correcting that, easily, with this meal.

The mood in the galley was as palpable as the savory smells rising in curling tendrils of steam from the spread. Talis hated to squash it, but she couldn't let Tisker's careless outing stand unquestioned. And she had been so looking forward to revealing the contents of that crate. To silencing Sophie's complaints and Dug's questions of her judgment.

It would open up an entirely different line of questioning about her judgment, but she was braced for that already. Dug in particular was not going to be happy with her, but she planned at the very least to enjoy seeing her own surprise echoed on their faces when she flashed that alien money at them.

Dug returned with an unassuming wooden crate hefted over his shoulder. He had to duck to enter the galley with it. Zeela had done her job making it look like a standard transaction. Battered recycled panels formed the crate, old labels covered with the new customs forms, locked with a padlock, and nailed shut with enough tacks to make even the most by-the-books custom agent think twice about putting forth the effort to open it. As long as no one jostled it, it wouldn't seem worth the trouble.

Swinging the load off his shoulder and down, Dug placed it before her chair. It hit the deck between her and her plate with a thud and a faint jingle from within. Dug laid a sally bar on top. The meaning there was clear enough. Answers first.

Exactly her thought. First answer she wanted, though, was what Tisker had run off for, and why Sophie had lied about it.

She put a foot up on the edge of the crate. Looked hard at Tisker. "Where'd you go? Ship's on high watch and you gotta run off into the thick of Subrosa?"

Tisker's gaze darted to the parcel on the table. Looked like he wished he'd put it somewhere else. "You know I'm fine out there, Cap."

"Nothing's fine out there today. You hear we were attacked before you run off? That Jasper's dead? Spill it."

Sophie cleared her throat and took a big bite of food. Dug still hadn't parked himself in his seat. He stood over them, arms crossed. Tisker shifted, moved his utensils on the napkin. Then picked up a set of tapered nimblesticks from the pile that came with the take-out.

"Yeah, I knew. Sophie told me what happened to Jasper and how there wasn't going to be a payout for the ring if you—we—couldn't find someone else. Wanted to help," he said. His words sounded small, almost childish. "You know. Use my connections to find a buyer for it."

Talis felt heat under her collar and over her cheekbones. She picked up the cup of water Sophie had set at her place, suddenly too warm in the small room. "You went out there flapping about our business, with all the trouble Sophie'd just finished telling you about?"

"I grew up here," he said, a little loudly. "I still know people."

"I don't think we really know people at all, sometimes." Talis left open who she was referring to.

"Anyway," Tisker pushed on, picking up food with his nimblesticks but not eating. He moved the pieces around on his plate, but wouldn't look at her. "I didn't need to ask around about it at all. Wasn't even to the old stomps before someone's alley rat came up to me about it."

Prickles went up and down Talis's arms and legs. "Whose rat?"

"Kid wouldn't say." He looked at her then. "And I sure didn't. I'm not careless, Cap. They ask about something, directly, before you get a chance to offer it? I battened down and dropped all notions of telling anyone about it. Seemed like the news was all out, anyway. But it wasn't on my account, Cap. I tell you that."

His grin had flatlined. He looked downtrodden all over,

like that kid who begged his way onto her ship. More like that kid than she'd seen in Tisker for a long time, in fact. She squinted at him.

"You went out without your flash?"

Tisker's hand shot to his earlobe, the empty piercing where the ever-present twinkle of a diamond earring should have been. More than that, Talis noticed. The torque at his throat, the bronze wrist cuff, a couple silver rings.

"*Tisker?*"

He pushed the parcel across the table and the weight of it scraped against the wood. Only the paper wrapping protected the table against what sounded like it might have been a right easy scratch to its surface.

Sophie was staring at him as hard as Talis figured she was herself. The girl reached out a tentative hand and pulled at a loose corner of the paper.

"Aw, no, Tisker," Sophie said. Her voice cracked. "You didn't . . ."

"Need it, don't we?" He stuffed a piece of meat in his mouth, and chewed too long. It looked like he was having trouble swallowing.

Dug sat down then, lifted up the parcel, and finished unwrapping it. Nested in the paper, thick with old oil but otherwise in good condition, a double steam engine bi-clutch glistened like a polished gemstone in the half-lit cabin.

"It's the right part, isn't it, Soph?"

"Yeah," she said. Voice cracked again, and she repeated, "Yeah, it's the right part, Tisker."

"Helsim strike you down himself." Talis said. She put her cup back down on the table and leaned back, her hands resting heavy on her thighs. "You're one hell-bound scoundrel, Tisker."

He practically glowed under the compliment.

"Wasn't necessary," Talis said. Tried to say it gently, but she was struggling just to get the words out. She'd bought him some of that jewelry he'd pawned, when he first earned his spot behind *Wind Sabre*'s helm and she wanted him to look the part. He'd been so proud of the gifts, and so fearful of owning something of value after he'd been raised by thieves, that he'd worn them to sleep. And while she was out getting them tangled in business with the aliens, he was pawning every shiny thing he owned to buy a cheap refurb part. Guilt bit at her, and she couldn't help but feel that the smatter of coin he'd managed to get for his prized possessions was worth double the contract she'd gotten. Talis felt her eyes burn, and turned on Sophie to avoid a spill of emotion over Tisker's sacrifice.

"So why'd you lie about it, Sophie?"

Sophie swallowed the food she was chewing and looked from the engine part in Dug's hand, to Tisker's face, then down to her plate. "Well, I knew you'd be mad he went out, didn't I?"

"Damned right," Talis said. But what was Sophie going to do about it? "Dug, you let him walk off this ship, knowing his intention?"

"I only told Sophie," Tisker said, jumping back in. "If Dug knew, he got it out of her."

Dug opened his mouth to say something to Talis, but Sophie spoke again before Dug could confirm or deny any knowledge.

"It's done, though," Sophie said. "Isn't it? He did good. Kept quiet when things seemed off, and found another way." She reached out with both hands, and Dug handed her the engine part. She cast the paper aside, letting it fall to the floor away from their meal, and turned the part over. The dark grease got on her perpetually engine-stained fingers, and in the low light it looked like blood. "We needed this, no argument from anyone on that, and he got it for us."

Talis chewed the inside corner of her lip. Mutiny, that's what it was. Crew slipping off on business she was already about, and lying to cover for each other.

Dug took her silence as a chance to get his word in. "You have your own story to tell, Captain, do you not?"

Talis stared at him from beneath her furrowed brows for a minute, then gave up on getting a bite in while her food was still hot.

"All right." She sat, pulling her chair back a foot and leaning forward. She rested her elbows on her knees. "Fair enough you should see what new business bought this dinner that's going cold on us."

CHAPTER 16

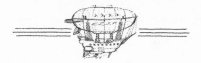

Dug and Tisker leaned toward Talis, and Sophie rose to come around to Tisker's side of the table.

"So." Talis said, sitting with the crate before her. "Talbot told me—and it panned out true enough—that word was out to scare off any buyers who might have wanted that ring. Each of you has already learned that, one way or another."

Sophie and Dug exchanged glances at the shared memory. Talis closed her eyes against the vision of Jasper's body, but it was waiting in the darkness behind her lids in full detail. She opened them again quickly, shifted her feet, and continued.

"So, Talbot didn't want any piece of it, and I left our meeting thinking that was the end of the trail in Subrosa. With Jasper's murder went any hopes of someone taking a chance on buying the thing. Even the pawnshops were looking unlikely, but that was my last shot in this port. Failing that, I figured maybe we could make for another territory on what fuel we had and find an archivist or collector who might buy it. Someone Hankirk couldn't intimidate. Probably wouldn't get much for it that way, but at least there was a chance we'd get *something*." She put up a hand before Sophie could interject. "I know. That engine part. It wasn't a good plan, but at the time it seemed like our only way forward.

"But the collectors found me first. They hired Zeela as an intermediary for the deal, and they bought the ring for seventy-five thousand."

The room was silent for a moment. Then Sophie whistled low. "And the buyers . . . Your new friends out there?"

Talis nodded. "That'd be them."

"Who are we talking about . . . ?" Tisker had missed her return.

"The Yu'Nyun."

Tisker's jaw worked up and down, but no sound came out.

"Do you think it wise, Captain, to sell them something apparently so high in value?"

She shot Dug a look for his cynicism. "So high in value as to prove completely *untouchable*? *Now* you think the ring has value? It was either sell it to them or let Hankirk badger us until we had no choice but to hand it over to him or drop out of the skies. So yeah, I chose the course that finally got us a payday."

She held out her hand, open palm up. Dug considered her for a moment, then dropped the crate key into it before his hesitation could lengthen into insubordination.

Tacks popped loose, skittering on the deck as she worked the sally bar around three edges of the lid. It was secured with a scuffed four-panel puzzle clasp, too, which released with a turn of the key. The crate's sides fell away, clattering against the deck to reveal the foreign design of the Yu'Nyun coffer within.

"Hells, Cap, I thought maybe you and Soph were joking," Tisker said. "You really sold the ring to the aliens?"

The coffer's gleaming white contours were like nothing else on Peridot. She pressed the seal on the side, a smooth black panel the aliens had shown her how to operate, and the lid lifted, moving up and back on its rails. The overhead lights reflected the shining contents into her eyes, so she sat back.

Her crew leaned forward.

"That's worth a coin or two more than seventy-five thousand, Captain!" Sophie squinted and turned her head slightly to the side, as though trying to see through a mirage.

"Aye, it is." Talis looked to Dug, who sat back with arms crossed. "Hope you saved some of that anger, my friend. This is the part you're *really* not going to like."

Putting a boot up on the side of the coffer, she straightened in her seat. Despite her own doubts about this job, she'd have to apply some swagger to make them love the idea, or else she'd have to force it through on captain's prerogative.

"So you all know our alien friends have been poking about for a while now. Libraries, ruins, museums. Whatever archives of knowledge they can find."

Sophie nodded, drawn into the setup. Tisker and Dug were sharper eyed, waiting for the catch. But the glint of bullion and precious gems was reflected in all their eyes.

"Apparently they've never seen a world like Peridot before, and they want to learn as much as they can about it."

"Fair enough," said Tisker. "They picking up souvenirs then?"

"I'm thinking maybe they don't have alchemy where they come from. No way to understand how The Five did it, kept the planet together, created new peoples. That much hasn't really been told, on account of them not wanting any of us trying anything similar. And we have The Divine Alchemists to manage that, so not many have really pressed.

"But to the Yu'Nyun's measure of it, there's a page missing from our history. Their curiosity will keep them here until they have their answers. But they've run through Rakkar libraries and Vein universities and probably even some Wind Monk archives, and they still haven't found whatever they're after."

Dug shifted, his back stiffening. "And you promised to

lead them to a new resource."

Tisker and Sophie saw the anxiety in his movement and turned back to Talis. Sophie's eyebrows rose to hide beneath the fringe of her hair. Tisker bit one side of his lip, forming half a smirk, but his eyes reflected none of his usual humor.

"That's it, summed up," she said, and kicked the side of the coffer with the toe of her boot, and the contents jumped in response, jingling for emphasis. "What we've got here is seventy-five thousand for the ring, plus five hundred thousand for an escort job. Minus Zeela's fees. Tisker, you can go buy back your things from the pawn alleys before we go, if you hurry."

Sophie craned her neck to look at the glittering contents of the crate around the table top. "I've never seen so much altogether at once."

Talis grinned at her, grateful for a chance to make the impact she wanted. Soon as they got to imagining what they'd spend their cuts on, it would be harder for them to turn down the job. Not that she *could* turn it down at this point. Even if she had to go on alone.

"This is just half. There's another five hundred thousand on the other end of a little trip. A long week's travel, at the most."

Tisker reached forward and grabbed a piece of gold from the crate. "To Nexus?"

Talis didn't stop him. It was *Wind Sabre's* money, not just hers. And if they held it, they'd want to keep it.

Tisker hefted the yellow metal in the palm of his hand, then ran his thumb along the indented eighth-marks down its length. Grabbed a knife from the table and pressed it into a notch, which dented and pinched until he'd easily cut off a quarter-piece of gold. He grinned at her. She saw him inventing ways to spend it.

Dug, however. . . .

"Not Nexus," Talis said. "I don't see the need to take

them for an audience in person."

"You're taking them to Illiya." Dug was not asking. Knew Talis well enough.

She nodded. "That's right. Look, if they wanted to go to Nexus, we don't have an advantage over any other ship out there. But if all they want to do is *talk* to one of The Five? That, we can do."

"Illiya?" Sophie looked at Dug. A Bone name, so no blaming her for confusion. But Dug only knew of the Bone priestess from Talis's stories, so she answered the open question.

"Old friend from my mercenary days. Now she's high priestess at the Temple of the Feathered Stone on Fall Island."

"*Tangled lines*, Cap. You owe us a story. Where'd you meet a Bone priestess?"

"I always have more stories than I tell you." She grinned at Tisker. "That's why I'm captain."

Sophie looked like she was fit to burst with questions. Bone priestesses were not just spiritual guides for their congregations. They were also highly skilled intelligence operatives. And their methods bordered on—then crossed defiantly over into—the extreme.

"Illiya never worked *on* me. Back before I got into the shipping business, I ran with a group of mercs. We got hired by a small village to chase out a cartel that had moved in on their fields, trying to get the villagers to produce drugs for them. Illiya was our team's interrogator, helping us track down the cartel's main holdout. She was better conversation than the eye blinkers on the team. And she could drink them all under the table."

Dug was silent. The scars across his face puckered from the way he narrowed his eyes at her. The knot in her stomach twisted as tight as his frown. She tried to ignore it. Ignore the hurt she was bringing on her friend. Leading him reluctantly back to his own people, and leading the aliens into the most sacred Bone sanctum at the same time.

Swagger, she reminded herself. *Sell it*. She ignored Dug and winked at Tisker, who took that as invitation to keep on the subject.

"Your drinking buddy—and don't think I'm not coming back to your war with a drug cartel—was one of Onaya Bone's torture priestesses?"

"And now she's the high holy mother of them all."

Truth told, Illiya was as shady as anyone you'd meet in Subrosa. Her motivations were always hidden behind a smile, decorum, and hospitality. She was a spider waiting at the edge of her web for a careless moth. But she did work by a code, however peculiar it might be. There were far worse characters that Talis still considered friends. And right now, Illiya was the gatekeeper between Talis and being done with this Yu'Nyun business. It was worth plucking at the strands of her web, by Talis's account.

Tisker whistled. "I knew you had grit, Cap. Didn't realize how coarse."

She nodded at him. It was a compliment, however off-putting. She'd learned to take Tisker's words for their meaning and not judge the poetry.

Sophie shifted uncomfortably. "I dunno. What if Onaya Bone gets mad?"

"And if the aliens are planning some treachery?" Dug added to the what-ifs tainting the air. "We know nothing about them."

Talis bristled. She hadn't expected everyone to love the idea, but thought flashing the unexpected fortune would soften them.

"They probably won't even get past the priestesses," she said. "We get paid either way. I made sure that was clearly printed in ink."

They all stared at her. Dug's eyes were dark pupils in dark purple irises. They sparkled with protests in the low light of the galley. She knew what arguments were waiting there, because she'd already fought them all in her own mind.

"Look, there's nothing to worry about. Onaya Bone doesn't have to *be* there. She can disconnect when she wants to. Deny the interview before it even starts, if she likes. We're bringing the aliens to an address, and I'm making an introduction to an old friend. What happens after that isn't even our problem. We'll be flying in the other direction, set for life."

She was doing all the arguing. Dug just stared back at her. It put her on the defensive, and she didn't appreciate that it was in front of Sophie and Tisker.

"Besides," she said, trying to manifest the confidence she needed. She was their captain, and the thing was a done deal. "Sophie's never seen an Onaya Bone temple."

Sophie put her hands up. "Oh no, you don't. Don't you put that on me, Captain! I'll stay onboard the ship or restock in the port. I don't need to take one step that puts me under the eye of the Bone goddess, thank you kindly."

"Coward," Talis teased, but it came out harsher than she meant. She looked to Tisker. "You got it in you to take on the grit of the desert with me?"

"I said it before, Cap." He moved some of the food around on his plate. It seemed more for an excuse not to look at her than any interest in the meal. "You've got nerve enough for the rest of us. I'm sure you can manage."

"Superstitious nest of inner-island xenophobic finery, you lot are."

A thumb on the control panel and the alien crate shut again. Uncomfortably slow in the tense silence, and with a slight hissing of air. Talis stood from her chair and used the heel of one foot to shove the crate out from between her seat and the table. Though Dug had been able to heft it over one shoulder, she had to use all her strength to push it across the boards of the deck. And all her dignity not to grunt and fold under the effort when it was heavier than she expected.

She leaned over the table and starting spooning food onto her plate in quick angry motions. "Fine, be no more than tenants of my ship. Well, this ship is flying to Fall Island, and you all can wait on the docks of Talonpoint while I get my payday. Or you can get off here."

Sophie's eyes flickered with something, and Tisker's lips parted in a question that he wrangled back before it could be asked. But Talis heard it loud and clear. Her temper flared, and she let it loose.

"Oh, yes, I haven't forgotten. You're owed back shares, and we'll settle. You'll get your fair cut of the sale of the ring, too, since you weren't too coward to help in that. Sophie, you'll get a bonus to cover the black eye and split lip you earned aboard *The Serpent Rose*. You're all welcome to step off this deck at either end of this and go find yourself a captain who plays it safe, the way you like it."

Her gut threatened to kick back, just smelling the food, but she piled her plate high, pocketed the utensils and cotton napkin, and stormed toward the galley door. She knew she'd hurt Sophie, but she felt sure her own wounds were deeper.

"Where do you propose to cross the border?"

Talis stopped stiffly but didn't turn around. It was Dug's deep voice, using a word like *propose*. But he'd moved it forward. It wasn't a question of *if* anymore. The knot tightened. She already regretted her harsh words, the finality of what she'd said. It hung in the air like oil smoke. But her pride wouldn't settle down. It ached, burned, left her wanting nothing more than to throw her fists into anything solid she could reach. Dug wasn't just her crew. He was as much her family as she was his. But he had a limit, and she was pushing it. She knew it. She had limits, too.

Gods damn it, this contract would solve *everything*. Whatever came after, her crew would be taken care of. Even if they didn't want to be *her* crew any longer.

"Hartham to Fall Island," she told him, referring to the

point of the border on a direct path between those two. Hartham on the Cutter side, Fall Island and Illiya on the other, in Bone territory. "Border stations are far apart there, on account of the storm center. We'll pass through the cloud just to be sure."

Tisker threw his head back and laughed. Colder than his usual good humor, but it was an improvement. "And let *Wind Sabre* be struck by lightning. You *are* aimed to meet a god, aren't you?"

"It's not a problem. We've made the run before." She turned around, unwilling to let his judgment attach itself to her back. How many questions did she have to tolerate on account of the *fortune* in coin sitting right there in the room? "All comes down to the skill of the pilot, doesn't it?"

Tisker went silent.

Sophie was busy examining the wood grain of the tabletop, but she managed a coy smile. "Saw a mermaid in the clouds, once."

Tisker tossed the gold bar onto the center of the table. It landed with a single clomp against the wood, then rolled until the uneven end where he cut it stopped its momentum. "Well, Cap, you know I'm game for anything reckless. Border run sounds like a straight good laugh, and I'd like to meet your old drinking buddy."

Sure, now that their share of a million presscoins is in question, everyone's suddenly in line again. But she'd take it. She would never admit it to them, but this wasn't something she wanted to do on her own.

"Sophie?"

"Will the aliens fly with us?"

Talis shook her head. "We're escort. Them in their ship, us on ours."

"So we won't get to talk to them much, then?"

Talis laughed involuntarily, thrown off her prepared arguments by the unexpected question. "You want to get your hands on their tech, you sly imp."

The girl's freckled nose wrinkled above her smile. "It crossed my mind."

"I'll see if they'll give us one of their language pads. Or two, maybe, in case you can't put the first back together again. In the morning you can even climb aboard their ship with me."

There was only Dug left to voice actual assent. She looked to him. The vote, if there was such a thing, was three to his one if he dissented. As first mate, though, his word had more heft than an equal part. If he backed out of it, the younger Cutters would balk. He'd opened the door to making the run but hadn't formally thrown his lot in. If he refused, she didn't know if she could go through with it.

CHAPTER 17

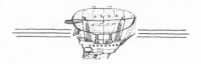

DUG TOOK A DEEP BREATH through his nose that inflated his chest, and let it out again in a slow exhale.

"You have already decided, Captain?" The words were a quiet rumble, a tone he reserved for his enemies.

She sat back down, returned the plate to her setting, and pulled her chair closer to the table so that she could lean on her elbows. "Yeah, I have."

Dug moved for the food. Scooped rice and vegetables onto his plate, topped the mound with a cluster of skewered meat. Slower than she had. But then, his anger always did burn lower and longer than hers. Then he stood, with the serving in his hands.

"Someone should keep watch up top. Captain."

He left the galley.

Talis took a deep breath. It hadn't been insubordination. Quite the opposite. He'd deferred to her judgment, even though she knew he might have argued to the point of bloody knuckles. He obeyed his captain. She felt unease settle like a chill between her shoulder blades.

Sophie spoke when Talis did not. "Should someone—"

"He'll be fine." Talis cut Sophie off. "Come on. Food's getting cold."

The three of them ate in silence until Tisker broke the tension with a wisecrack comment and Sophie joined in his banter. The atmosphere of the room brightened again as the two talked about the aliens. They made deliberately ignorant suppositions about their strange anatomy and culture, laughing until their eyes teared up. When that played out, Sophie pontificated, for a long rambling stretch, about how their ship worked.

Talis had meant to ask Sophie more about the designs, whether the planks of an airship could be similarly fitted and sealed to make safer salvage dives, but found herself unable to pay attention. She sat in her own fog. Wanted to go talk to Dug about the border crossing, about taking aliens to meet *his* goddess. But she knew her friend had walked off because he needed to be alone. So be it.

For a bit. She wouldn't let him stew too long.

DUG WAS SITTING on the starboard engine house when Talis climbed topside to find him an hour later, carrying a honeyed ginger and turmeric tea as a peace offering. She'd left Sophie and Tisker to wrap up the substantial leftovers, trusting them to stay busy long enough to allow her a private word.

He accepted the tea with a silent nod, and she hoisted herself up beside him. The space between them thrummed with potential. The right words could cut through and reach him, but she had to pick them carefully.

"I didn't take the decision lightly," she started, but winced at her voice. She sounded pitiful.

"No, the coffer was quite heavy."

She leaned against the engine house. The metal was warm,

still, in the cooling air of the docking bay. "Come on, Dug, give me a break. That money takes care of everything. Think of a life with that kind of wealth. No more of this running."

"I like this life."

That was a lie. It wasn't the life he wanted and they both knew it. He'd had a wife once, a stunning young Bone woman named Inda, as fierce as he was, and every bit as passionate. They'd started a family. One tiny, wobbling son that lit a fire in Dug's eyes like nothing else ever had.

But he was torn between the promise of settling down and the old adventuring buddy that talked him into job after job with her. Goaded him into an easy smuggling run. And while they were off transporting ridiculous harlequin rag dolls stuffed with contraband across the border into Rakkar skies, a Cutter raid left his town in smoldering ashes. Everything they'd found out since pointed to the Veritors.

He lost Inda. His son. Their home. His future. And in a drunken, grief-fueled rage, he'd destroyed much of what remained of his town. Talis had pulled him down from the stockade where they'd left him to be picked clean by the ravens, and he'd been bound to her fate ever since. That weighed hard on every decision she made.

She couldn't give him back the future he'd lost, but she never stopped trying to make a new one for him.

"Worrying about a growling stomach, busted engines, and an empty cargo hold? It isn't a life, Dug."

He didn't reply, just stared down into the swirls of spice circling in his mug.

"Cutter skies are cramped. You knew we'd go back someday."

A small nod to that.

"Oh, come on, Dug. Talk to me. Yell at me. Something."

"Captain, what do you expect me to say? The contract is taken, agreed upon. The job is good. Sure to be as simple as you say it will be. Onaya Bone won't like it, but as you pointed out, her pleasure is not one of the terms of the arrangement."

He still wouldn't look at her. Whatever he had in his sights was far away and long ago. The tea was almost out of steam.

"Say what's on your mind. Get it out. Let's have it and move on, all right?"

"You know what thoughts I have on my mind, Captain."

"Enough with the 'Captain' scrap, Dug. This is *me*. Do I have to take you drinking to get you to talk?"

He turned to her, and she saw that his eyes were reddened around the edges. His lips were parted but he had no words.

The docking bay doors rumbled into life, a complex system of chain winches and worn-tooth gears connected to a control panel outside the dock manager's office. The enormous hatch panels clattered in protest, making an obscene amount of noise as they rolled out of the way for some new arrival outside. While she waited for the din to subside, she lost herself to the same memories that were haunting her friend.

She slumped her shoulders. "Dug, I'm sorry. I'm sorry for what happened. If I hadn't—"

"That is not what this is about."

"Isn't it? Maybe going home will be good for you."

"It is no longer home for me. What might have been left for me there, I destroyed myself."

He put a hand on his knee, stretched the elbow straight, and rotated the arm. The old scars crisscrossed from forearm to shoulder, obscuring the tattoo that had been there first. The crossing scars extended down his back, too. Unlike the parallel marks over his eye, they had not been earned in combat.

He'd been tied up, flayed. Punished for the havoc he'd caused, the dishonor of it. If he'd gone off and found the actual killers, he'd have been a hero. But he was on that run with Talis, and the ashes had cooled before he even learned of the attack. The only force to fight was the entirety of the

Cutter Imperial Service, and he wasn't going to win that one all on his own.

Talis had cut him down off the scaffold in the middle of the night, half-dragged him back to their ship. She didn't give a rusted coin about letting him stay on public display to redeem his honor via a silent death. Her friend was hurting, inside and out. So she took him with her, patched him up, and now he lived among his enemies. Any Cutter might be a Veritor. Might be responsible for his family's death. Every fight was an outlet for his old pain.

After that night, he hadn't spoken for weeks. She didn't blame him for having nothing to say to her. The violence near Dug's home island had been threatening to burst for years, and she told him the war he wanted would still be waiting for him when he got home.

Gods-rotted rag dolls stuffed with gods-rotted al-chemical powders for gods-rotted Rakkar scientists in a rush to blow themselves up practicing their gods-rotted forbidden experiments.

Talis had been trying to make it up to him ever since. *How* didn't matter. She got a new ship with different contours so he'd never have to see the same bulkheads or the lift balloons that had taken him away from his family that last time. New crew. Anything she could think of was worth trying.

And now she was taking him back to that world. Fall Island was far from his old home, but he'd be among his own people for the first time in years. Those old scars were long healed but would forever mark him as a pariah. They were a death sentence among any tribe.

"You'll keep watch over *Wind Sabre* while we're at Fall Island," she said, deciding. "Anyone tries anything, you're the only one who can hold them off."

He exhaled a cold, quick breath of mirthless laughter. "True. None will approach me."

She cursed herself with an exasperated chuff. "I didn't

mean it like that."

He took a gulp of the tea, swished it in his cheeks before swallowing, then ran his tongue over his teeth to clear the undissolved spices. When he spoke, there was a strain to his voice that was unlikely to have been caused by any dregs of tea in his throat. "I know, Talis."

She nodded. Afraid to say anything else careless, she just sat with him.

She could leave it at that for now. The guilt would settle back into its usual place soon enough. One day she'd make it up to him. But today she was asking more of her friend than she had any right to.

After they'd been silent awhile, Tisker came up to collect his plate, and Sophie to take over the watch on deck. So they'd been listening from below. Talis waved a hand at Sophie's attempts to send her off to bed.

"This one's on me, Soph," she said. "We're leaving at the first touch of gold, before Hankirk decides to make a move. Take some money from the coffer. Get our refuel moved up to priority. Tisker got you that part you asked for, and don't forget what you owe him for that. Get back here fast and put it where it belongs. Tisker: prep what you can. If there's anything we haven't loaded on, get me a list and I'll see it filled by breakfast. When you're done with that, you've got my leave to go see if you can buy back any of what you sold. But don't give me time to wonder if you got lost."

The pair scurried off to carry out the orders. They'd been reasonable, after all. If one could focus on just the next step, and the next . . . Talis turned back to her brooding first mate.

"I do need you on this one, Dug."

He stayed where he was for a short while but said nothing else. A solid dark silhouette against the too-yellow light of the docks. Talis didn't try to push him. After a minute, he slipped off the engine block and went below without a word. The drafts coming in through the open bay swept in from where he'd been sitting. Shivering, she pulled up her collar and tended her watch.

As Talis monitored the activity on the docks, her mind offered up anxious thoughts. She tracked any movement. She wouldn't sleep until they were out of there. Couldn't have even if she wanted.

Across the multi-tiered levels of the bay, workers moved crates, refueled tanks, and loaded supplies. They would work through the night. Machinery hummed and clunked. The bay doors moved up and down for a few more ships, both arriving and leaving. Hydraulics whined and systems banged away at their tasks. The movements were the business of an insect hive. Everyone with a job, everyone moving, not wasting time. It was the normal pulse of Subrosa, nothing out of the ordinary. She felt the tension in her sinews start to let up.

But then there was a prickle on her neck. A lone, still figure caught her eye. Two levels above, on the promenade of a dockside bar. Hankirk sat at a small table overlooking the docks. Watching her.

CHAPTER 18

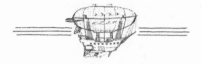

IT WAS A LONG NIGHT. Though Sophie came back to relieve Talis of her watch just after midnight, there was no rest to be had. She had supplies to restock and angry suppliers who didn't like to be rushed, even if they ran their businesses straight through the night for customers just like her. She agreed to more priority fees getting tacked onto her account than she'd have tolerated if she had the energy to argue.

All the while, Hankirk was up there. Doing nothing. The nothing was worse than an outright attack.

Talis tried to catch an hour of sleep once all the deliveries had been arranged and there was little else she could do until they arrived. The end of Sophie's watch toned on the ship-wide comms. Talis heard light conversation outside her cabin: Dug taking over, Sophie bidding him goodnight.

She spent an hour pretending there was any hope of falling asleep, but the menace of the *nothing* pervaded the quiet of her cabin until it finally drove her out of bed. She selected a new pair of pants from the drawer beneath her bunk, because the previous day's clothes were smudged with dirt and needed beating, potentially washing. She slid into a short, sleeveless shift that she could wear beneath her clothes later that day and then padded, barefoot, to the galley. The earthy scent of coffee led her to a full pot on the hob, the steel carafe still hot. Freshly brewed.

"Peace offering?"

Talis whirled around at the unexpected voice. Sophie stood in the galley access, one hand clutching the other wrist in front of her hips. Her face, streaked with coal dust, was uncomfortably formed into a questioning smile. But her eyes were still guarded. Defiant.

"Huh," said Talis. She was exhausted, stretched too thin, not sure she could be trusted to speak. Anxiety hadn't put her in any better a mood than the last time she and Sophie had faced off in the galley. She swallowed against the memory of the words they'd exchanged and the acid it brought up in her throat.

Sophie brushed past her, fetched two ceramic mugs out of the cupboard near the stove, and poured them each a cup of the steaming bitter drink. Talis lowered herself to the padded bench along the bulkhead, taking Tisker's seat rather than her own at the head of the half-folded table. Across from where Dug and Sophie usually sat. It had the second-best view of the door, which made her feel slightly less cornered.

There was no sign of the previous night's dinner. The manifests were out, a pen neatly tucked into its inkwell nearby. Talis picked up the book and skimmed the log. As she'd trusted, Tisker and Sophie had it covered. Sophie's barely legible handwriting inventoried the engine part. Tisker's tiny print recorded the fuel, water, groceries, and sundries taken on. Talis saw that a couple of the deliveries she'd arranged herself had already arrived and been put away. She took a deep breath.

Sophie sat and picked up the pen. Talis pushed the log book back over. Sophie made a couple of quick marks next to a line item, noting the locations in the hold where the crates had been stored.

Talis loved when *Wind Sabre* was fully stocked, but the weight created drag. She chewed her lip. Suddenly she was feeling as though they would need to run. With the ship's belly hanging low in the skies, she felt vulnerable. At least their only new cargo was the Yu'Nyun payment. But that only made her want to fly faster. There were no secrets in Subrosa.

Sophie finished her notations, fanned a hand over the wet ink for a moment, then pushed the book aside. Her right hand gripped her coffee mug, and she picked at the edge of the table with the thumbnail of her left.

"Listen, Captain," she started.

"Stow it," Talis said. "I've had no sleep, and I don't want to start that again."

She raised the mug to her lips. The liquid was still too hot, but she didn't want to be seen hesitating in any decisions in front of Sophie just now, so she let the coffee burn her tongue and then lowered the mug back to the table without reacting.

Sophie took the pause as leave to keep going. "I need to apologize. To you. I already did to Tisker."

Talis thought of the logbook. Entries made in two different pens. The last line Sophie had entered was the engine part; only the price was in Tisker's hand.

"Yeah, well, he was rash, too." Compulsively, Talis lifted the mug again. Burned her tongue one more time. Least of her personal injuries that night, she figured.

Sophie watched her thumb trace the edge of the hinge in the table's stowed side. "He's worried I'm gonna leave. Hoped getting the bi-clutch would smooth things over."

Talis put the mug down a few inches farther away than before, trying to keep her hands off it and spare her mouth. Her tongue had developed a bumpy texture where the hot liquid kept scalding her. She leaned back against the bulkhead behind her and crossed her arms.

"Well? Are you?"

A light thud sounded as Sophie opened her mouth to

speak. It came from somewhere along the hull. Instead of answering Talis's question, Sophie cursed the carelessness of the dock workers.

But here they were. Talis had asked the question, and she was going to get an answer.

"You know, owning your own ship isn't all open skies and cool breezes." She shifted her hips so the angle of her slouch was more comfortable. "Sometimes you have to make a decision between what's right for the long run and what you think you want in the moment. And your crew will have their own opinions."

Sophie pulled a wire-bound folio out of a cargo pocket in her pant leg and put it on the table. There was a pencil hung on a string and tucked into a makeshift loop of elastic that kept the folio closed. Unfolding it to lay open on the table in front of her, she traced the contour of a carefully folded sheet of paper inside.

Sophie's ship design. That thing went almost everywhere with her.

"It's the one thing I've always wanted." Sophie looked up at her. "You know that."

"A shiny new ship to be proud of," Talis said. "Doesn't mean you have what it takes to be the captain."

Sophie flicked one corner of the folio's back cover. "I don't want to be told how to take care of it. As long as someone else is captain, I'm always going to have to swallow my arguments about what's best for the ship and its systems."

"Don't remember you ever swallowing your arguments with me." And *that* was why Talis didn't want to be having this conversation right now.

Sophie bristled. "I hold back my opinion a lot more than you think," she said, leaning forward and snapping the folio closed. "That's why when I finally do speak up I need you to hear me. Tisker sees it. He went off and sold all his stuff so I wouldn't have to argue it with you. So you couldn't fly this ship into disrepair and leave us stranded until your old boy-friend comes by and scoops us up."

Talis pinched the bridge of her nose and closed her eyes for a moment. Was that coffee cooled off yet? She reached out, took a sip. Close enough.

"So you *are* leaving?"

Sophie absently turned the folio in a slow circle while she chewed her lip. Another thud sounded outside the hull and she glared in the direction of the sound, twitching. When she answered, her voice was small and strained. "If that's what you think is best. There was a first mate on the docks, told me *Sky Opus* needs a new wrencher."

Talis scoffed. "That sagging retrofit trawler? I don't see that as very likely to earn you your new ship anytime soon."

Sophie eyed the spot on the floor where the coffer had been laid open at dinner. "Could be nearly there with the extra share you said I'd get for the business aboard *The Serpent Rose*. Wouldn't take much more for a deposit at Jones's shipyard."

Scratching at her cheek, Talis frowned. "Okay, so you wanna go? Go. But a deposit isn't a ship. It isn't the sign-ing bonus for a crew. It isn't the cost of your first contract, or the fuel you'll need, or supplies." Sophie's shoulders were slumping. She knew this already, but Talis pressed on, feel-ing herself at her limit and backed up against a wall in this conversation. "You wanna be captain of a half-framed hull, you can show yourself to—"

The entire conversation was punctuated with small sharp thumps accosting the hull, and each one made Sophie twitch and eye the bulkhead as if she could see the culprit through the joined planks. But the next thud that hit the hull was so strong, it rattled the flatware stowed in their cabinets, and was accompanied by the sharp staccato clinking of chains gone loose. Sophie planted her hands on the table and pro-pelled herself to her feet.

"Are they rotting drunk out there?" she exclaimed, pushing away from the table and heading toward the access. "They're going to crack the hull open!"

And she was gone.

Talis sat, listening to angry footsteps stomping off toward the companionway and up to the weather deck.

Sophie's folio sat abandoned on the table in front of her, now rotated right-side up in Talis's view. She'd never once looked at the design, though Sophie had offered to show her on several occasions. But it had been a while, hadn't it? At some point she'd declined enough times that Sophie stopped asking.

Talis flipped it open and stared at the folded sheet of paper. It felt as though she was about to read Sophie's personal journal.

The paper had been folded and unfolded so many times that the pencil lines across the softened creases had faded away. It opened up to a full sheet the width of Talis's arm span. In some places the pencil lines bounced, jagged, a result of Sophie laying it out to work across the planks of the deck. It was too big for most of the ship's flat surfaces. The table in Talis's cabin would have been better for working on it. If she'd realized, she might have offered.

Talis pursed her lips, stopping herself shy of a low whistle. The design was something else.

She leaned forward to read Sophie's small notations— mechanical specs, notes on operation of the winches and articulated flaps. Comments on the ways in which it differed from the standard designs. The construction of the engine, an exploded view of custom components and a streamlined body, took up the top left quarter of the page. Every inch of the paper was covered, as though someone had spilled a box of gears and springs and it landed in a sort of inspired order.

It would take the entire sum from their new Yu'Nyun

contract to pay for something this elaborate. The shares Sophie was currently owed would make for a deposit, maybe, but she'd have to work the rest of her life to get it finished.

"Captain!"

Talis jumped, feeling guilty. But Sophie's voice was sounding on the all-ship, hollow and tinny.

She crossed the room to the polished brass intercom panel and pushed the button to reply, dial set to the same all-speaker override so wherever anyone was they'd hear it, from the lowest cargo hold to the weather station atop the lift balloon. "Here, Soph. What is it?"

"Hankirk's on the move." Tisker's voice this time. The anxiety came through the line, as clear as if *Wind Sabre*'s comms were the high-fidelity crystal and copper Vein systems that Sophie had spec'd for her next ship.

Gods rot it. She left the channel open and returned to the table to stow Sophie's drawing safely in the bulkhead cabinet so it wouldn't go sliding across the table when they started to move. And they needed to move.

"You still see him?"

"No, Cap, sorry. I didn't even see which way he went. Had my eye on someone else lurking near our berth, then I looked back up and he was gone."

In large gulps, she swallowed the contents of both coffee mugs and secured them upside-down in the sink over the prongs of the dish rack.

"Forget it, Tisker, just stay sharp 'til the ramp's up. Everyone else," she commanded, hearing her voice echo back in a wave from the various speakers beyond the galley hatch. "We're done. Up. Get some coffee in you if you need it, there's fresh in the galley. We're pushing out. *Now.*"

Subrosa's dock manager wasn't happy that they were jumping the schedule in the middle of the night after they'd already argued with him just hours before to accelerate it to early morning. His cheeks were red, and he stabbed at his clipboard with a short fat finger, so that Talis was dearly tempted to knock the docket out of his hands to illustrate how much she cared what it said. She restrained herself with valiant effort, instead trying to reason with him while her crew uncoupled *Wind Sabre*'s side of the dock connections. But reason seemed to have little effect on him, and she quickly lost her patience.

"You either get that rusting access open, or we'll blast our way through it," she told the portly man, pushing his precious clipboard back against his chest. She then turned away, hoping her bluster and her crew's activity would scare him into complying. "Prep the forward cannons," she ordered as she stalked back toward the gangway.

"Don't you dare!" he called after her. "You'll get your ship banned from this dock!"

Wind Sabre's engines chuffed in short breaths and then purred to life. There was more than one harbormaster in Subrosa, and they competed for ships. This enclosed docking bay was the largest, but beyond that, the man's threat held little sting. This was only the second time in all Talis's years at the job that she'd ever sought out an interior berth for her ship. If she had to limit herself to the floating moorings or the undercity's external scaffolding in the future, so be it.

"Fine, you number-crunching landlocked bastard," she called back over her shoulder, projecting her voice so he could pick it up over the clanks and bangs of the dock equipment as his team bustled around their corner of the bay. "I'll fasten my clamps elsewhere from here on out."

She refused to glance back at him. Didn't need to. The dock workers had hurried to help them push off. Their manager's pride was none of their business. But making sure their equipment stayed functional for the next ship heading in, so they didn't have to shut down the berth for repairs—*that* was their business.

The gantry pulled away, retracting the thick hose leading from the dock's furnace lungs, and *Wind Sabre* exhaled her own steam. There was a slight ruffle in the canvas along the length of the lift balloon as the hot air supply transitioned, then the envelope went taut again.

Dug and Tisker made a deliberate show of winding back the gangway, and Talis easily hopped the distance from the walkway onto the end of *Wind Sabre*'s ramp. As if that was how they always cast off. No panic, just business at full speed.

She heard the uneven footsteps of the manager as he rushed off, probably to log another fee against her account. There was no profit in banning her, she knew. But he could make a tidy sum leveling all appropriate fines against her.

Once her captain was aboard, Sophie left her lookout position on the catwalk that wrapped around the lift balloon above. She slid down the ratlines, padded barefoot across the deck to the companionway, and went below to monitor their engines.

The panels of the bay door trembled, then clattered into motion, the cacophony bouncing through the multi-tiered docks once again. The rolling door stretched far below them and moved so slow, Talis started pacing.

"Don't wait for clearance," she ordered Tisker. "Take us down a few levels and get us the hell out of here."

"Aye, Cap," he said.

The deck made a small lurch into motion. Fully fueled engines were far less sluggish than when the firebox was near empty. Their berth was in back and on the third level of the five-level docking bay, with at least seven ships between them and their escape. Dug crossed forward and stood his own watch upon the bowsprit.

Tisker deftly maneuvered the ship down and around the

others tied off at the berths below them. Sophie called up from her new position at the observation windows in *Wind Sabre*'s belly to help him avoid snagging their ventral rigging on someone else's gantry or lift envelope. Watch crews on the other airships' decks cried out in alarm at the unorthodox flying, but they could do little more than shake their tiny fists from the railings of their ships.

Wind Sabre slipped out beneath the edge of the rolling door into the dark purple night skies of Peridot, and Tisker palmed the brass acceleration levers forward as far as they'd go.

CHAPTER 19

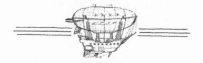

THE YU'NYUN SHIP CAST A large shadow across *Wind Sabre*'s deck. Talis took a deep breath and stepped up from the worn wooden planks of her ship onto the smooth gleaming ramp that beckoned her aboard the starship. She felt a chill rise from the metal plating, run like ice water across her bones, and settle at the nape of her neck. Sophie stepped up behind her with a light, eager hop.

The alien vessel, both inside and out, was like no airship Talis had ever seen or could ever have imagined on her own. Everything was smooth, as shiny in its guts as it was across the outside of its hull. Not beautiful though, she decided. Sterile. Its entirety was crafted of the aliens' glossy white material and gleaming silver metal. Everything reflected the glare of the harsh white lights recessed into the overhead. It stung her eyes and felt brighter than the yellow daytime glow of the pumpkins, brighter than the piercing green of Nexus.

Four aliens greeted Talis and Sophie in a small austere compartment between the multi-paned external hatch and a matching one in the opposite bulkhead. The welcome party was dressed similarly to the veiled alien's entourage from the day before, but Talis couldn't tell if any of them were the same individuals. They did not carry weapons, Talis saw, and she was surprised to realize that she had expected them to. She wore her pistol on her own hip and wondered if she ought to have left it behind, though she'd been wearing that *and* the revolvers the first time she met the aliens. At least today her clothes were clean and there were no bugs left in her hair.

"Follow," one said to them via the disembodied voice of its translator, and Talis and Sophie were folded into the middle of the group.

The interior hatch spun open, onto a corridor that curved away in both directions. Talis squinted against the overwhelming whiteness and wished for her tinted goggles. Sterile, cold light flooded from perforated panels in the overhead. Matching deck plates cast the same lighting up from narrow strips at the bottom edges of seamless curving bulkheads, to either side of a felted carpet walkway, so that no matter in which direction she looked, the eye-watering brightness pervaded her vision.

Apparently unfazed by the blinding interior, Sophie turned her head every which way, taking in every detail as they were led along. A long list of questions was clearly building up behind her lips, but all Talis cared to see was a vent or porthole, and the friendly purple-black of open skies beyond. Instead, the ice-white bulkhead stretched on, interrupted only by nondescript hatches along the interior, each with a smooth square panel beside it at approximately shoulder height for their hosts, or eye level for Talis and Sophie.

The entire way, one corridor seemed to be twin to the next. Access doors retracted into the bulkhead, opening on new concentric round corridors. Wherever the engines were installed—which was not obvious from the exterior—their guides did not bring Talis and Sophie past them.

Assuming Talis had her bearings true, they were led to the fore of the ship. Their group squeezed into a narrow compartment that carried them up, or at least the sensation felt like up, and deposited them into a short corridor, the first straight one they'd encountered. At its far end, a tall arching hatch split into three triangular sections that receded into the bulkhead as they approached. Through the doorway came such sounds and rhythms as Talis felt certain she would know anywhere: The operations bridge. Her own crew was not large enough to require formality in their shifts and watches, but the murmur of reports and commands passing back and forth, the hum and tones of systems readouts, and the particular sensation of *focus* pervading the cabin was as similar to her academy experience as the alien ship itself was foreign.

They entered onto a small platform on the second level of an airy double-high deck station. From each side of the landing, a sweeping staircase of shallow steps led down to the main deck, where more than a dozen aliens sat at various posts or moved between them. 'Companionway' was the proper aeronautical term. Stairs were for the landlocked. But she'd never seen such a grandiose set of steps, even on luxury yachts. The ornate, decorative banister made it easy to imagine she was in the foyer of a large estate rather than on a vessel, and it felt more accurate to think of the gracefully curving steps as stairs.

One of their guides gestured to starboard, then led them down to ops. The rise between each step was half the height she'd consider comfortable, and she wondered how the towering aliens had the patience not to skip two or three steps at a time as they descended.

Beneath the landing on which they'd entered, the two staircases cradled an elaborate captain's chair. Nestled into the hollow of the architecture, a wide, shallow bowl surrounded a high-backed seat. The console around the seat was host to a series of readout screens mirrored from several other stations.

Talis had assumed that the veiled individual she met the day before was the ship's captain. But the regal alien that sat upon the command seat was a different creature. Its body carvings were not as delicate as the individual whose torso and sweeping head had been perforated so dangerously. This individual's carvings looked more calculated, more efficient.

The Yu'Nyun captain wore no veil but was dressed to leave no doubt as to its superiority over the others that crewed the bridge, as if its posture did not do the job already. A rippling, shimmering blue fabric, tailored so as to appear dramatically opulent but not restrict the wearer's movement, draped over its body and one arm. The material appeared opaque at first, but then Talis realized the outline of the alien's torso could be seen when it moved. Its arms were banded in more blue, edged in silver. Silver-toned rings circled through matching eyelets in the trim. More fabric draped from the back of its head, from piercings in the sides of its exoskeleton. Talis saw others of the crew with such rings along the sides of their arching heads. Varied in number. A sign of rank? Of successful missions?

The majority of alien personnel wore blue loincloths and short waistcoats of the same color. The tops were solid only at the sides and connected in the front and back with silver leather bands, while similar straps loosely joined the sides of loincloths above the knees. Beneath those minimal pieces, they wore nothing else. On a Cutter, the clothing would have been scandalous, and definitely too cold for the chill in the air. Either their plated bodies prevented the Yu'Nyun from sensing the cold as she did, or they preferred a little bite to the air. Talis saw goosebumps on Sophie's shoulders above the neckline of her top, and the girl's exhalations swirled in the air. Her own, as well. But the aliens must have been as cold inside as their ship was, and no silver condensation appeared from their parted mouths.

Of course, Sophie's goosebumps might have been from

the thrill of getting her eyes on all this alien stuff. Her hands were curled into self-conscious fists at her sides, aching for an invitation to touch something. She turned her head every way, absorbed in the alien technological landscape. Talis could see the flame of her curiosity, rather than satisfied by the visit, had been fed enough tinder to burn wild.

"This, counterpart, ship master," said the alien to their right, sweeping its arm to indicate the being in the command seat. It spoke something else, but the translator pad stayed silent.

Was that a name? Talis wasn't sure she could ever mimic the simultaneous clicks and thumping throat noises, even with repeated practice.

Desperate to make a good impression despite her overwhelming desire to run from that place, she found herself unable to think of simple things like words and sentences. Assuming the translator pads were going to interpret them properly. Remembering the strange bow the aliens made when they parted ways the day before, she turned to the captain and touched the notch at the base of her throat and then her forehead.

The captain looked sharply to the alien with the tablet, who motioned for Talis to stop.

"That gesture: not greeting."

"My apologies, I should not have presumed."

She sincerely hoped she would not spend all her time aboard this unsettling ship being admonished for cultural missteps. At least her capacity to speak had returned.

"Do like," it replied, and then crossed its hands at the wrists, folded its elbows in a way that Talis doubted her own joints could allow, and bowed its head.

Talis began to move, expecting to completely botch the unnatural gesture, but another rustling from the alien captain stopped her again. It unfolded its limbs and rose from its bowl to walk toward their group. It was taller than the others.

"Not that one, either," it said.

In the Common Trade tongue.

The translator tablet spat it back out in the alien language. At a motion from their captain, the Yu'Nyun crew member holding the device silenced it and stepped away.

Talis's heart was in her throat, but she swallowed it back where it lodged out of place along her gullet. She focused on trying to fight the muscles in her face, to keep the surprise from being so wretchedly obvious. The alien captain's speech was accented with clicks, hisses, and other noises she didn't have words for. But it was clear.

The alien stopped an arm's length in front of them. The four aliens who had guided them through the ship stepped back as though repelled by an invisible force.

"Captain Talis," the captain said, bowing its head in a sideways tilt. "Allow me to apologize for the confusion. The gesture you were about to perform was that of subordinate, and of course as commanders each of our own ship, I consider us quite equal."

Talis swallowed again, mind racing to find something—anything—to say in a dignified response to the Yu'Nyun captain.

Sophie stepped out from behind Talis, then repeated the gesture they had been shown. Even managed the angle in her elbows. The alien inclined its head slightly at her. No objections.

Bless her five times, Talis thought, and, with some progress being made toward a proper conversation, she found her voice.

"Captain, it is a pleasure to meet you." Lie. "I am impressed by your grasp of our language." No lie there. Her formal tone surprised her, but then again, her usual smuggler's dialect could likely cause offense across cultural barriers. Something about the alien captain's grasp of the Common Tongue put her on guard, made her careful of her word choice.

"You flatter me," the alien replied. "It is a challenging language. The sounds are . . . well, you hear that they are quite different from our language."

"That's why I'm quite amazed at how well you manage it."

"Perhaps one day you will learn our language yourself. I am sure you will exceed my skill if you try."

"I would certainly give it my best," she said.

This was the most transparent lie yet. After she helped them complete their mission, they could return to the vacuum beyond Peridot's outer atmo and she'd gladly give their collective rumps a good smack to see them off.

The captain walked toward the fore of the bridge, the bulkhead of which was dominated by a large window. Talis admired the dizzying view at the top, where no lift balloon impeded their sight. It was after a slight delay that she remembered that the Yu'Nyun ship *had* no forward viewport. Certainly not of that size. The porthole was, it seemed, an enormous display screen. But unlike the grainy, monochromatic images that passed through the tiny Pre-Cataclysm devices Talis had seen in various temples, precious 'tronics used only to communicate with The Divine Alchemists, the Yu'Nyun ship had one so large and so advanced that they were looking outside the ship as clearly as though they looked through glass.

She had allowed herself to assume they were in the very forward cabin of the starship, but now realized the projection of an outside scene might come to them anywhere within the belly of the silver beast. The whole vessel made about as much sense as ballast on a boulder.

"Peridot is quite fascinating to my people," the captain said, waving one hand vaguely at the scene displayed. "There are very few fragmented planets that we have come to, and no others are home to life."

"I hear you've gathered a lot of knowledge from across the world," Talis said, not sure what else to say. "You are likely better educated on the subject than we are."

The alien made a small scraping noise in its throat, and Talis twitched involuntarily. It said, "It may well be fair to say that, though as you know we still have questions. We do wish to express our utmost appreciation for your cooperation."

"The contract price is a fair expression of your gratitude." By which she meant, *Let's not forget about that second payment with all this talk of cooperation.*

"Such trivial matters are handled by our Representative of Commerce," the commander said, almost dismissively.

Talis smiled. "Would that be the individual I met yesterday?"

The alien captain bobbed its head and wiggled its fingers as though pressing keys on an invisible piano. "You will meet that Representative again. Let us not dwell on such banalities. I am excited for the coming travel. Have you prepared our course?"

Sophie hurried to remove the tube that she wore slung over her shoulder.

Talis nodded and gestured to her. "This is Sophie, our engineer and navigator. May we spread our charts out somewhere?"

There was a shuffle of alien bodies across the deck, as several seats were cleared at the workstations along the wall. Sophie unrolled the vellum navigation charts across flat glossy control panels that had gone dark at their approach. She fished lead weights from her pockets and placed them in each corner so they didn't curl back in.

Talis and the alien captain, joined by two of the bridge crew, gathered around the hand-illustrated charts of Peridot's skies. There were vellum sheets for both the Cutter and Bone sides of the border that cut through the region, and one chart that was drawn with the current border centered. This last was on top of the pile. Talis smoothed them so that the sheets beneath showed through the top, and adjusted the alignment so they formed one continuous map. Borders from abandoned treaties showed to either side of the latest version. Shipping winds flowed in dotted light gray lines along their fixed dextral courses.

"We can sneak across the border here." She put an index finger on the point where a storm center was marked near the dashed line that defined the territory's edge, halfway between two stations indicated on the Cutter side.

"'Sneak'?" The commander tried the word out, with a heavier accent than the rest of its speech, and looked to her. "This word is new to me."

"Our territory borders are disputed," she explained. "There are stations where ships are inspected prior to moving between Cutter and Bone space."

"And you believe we would be prevented from entering?"

"Not you," said Talis. "From what's told on the docks, the authorities give you leave to go where you like. But I'm pretty certain our mutual friend, Captain Hankirk, will have sent out an alert that my crew and my ship are not to be permitted passage out of Cutter space. He will have significantly less ability to pursue us once we cross into another territory. Additionally, there is a member of my crew who might encounter trouble on the Bone side, at their crossing station. Passing at this point—traveling through the storm that forces the two nearest checkpoints farther apart—would let us 'sneak' through, as I said, without being detected or detained."

"I see," said the commander, and though its face was rigid as a fibernut shell, Talis could tell it was amused. "Sneak. We have a similar concept."

The alien said a word in its own language, which sounded like a small army of chickens tripping over each other in a patch of gravel.

It looked at her, and she realized she was being offered the word to try on her own. As if somehow she could speak from three parts of her anatomy simultaneously.

She gave it an honest effort, aware of the otherwise silent bridge, and winced at how unlike the model it sounded.

The alien repeated the word, with its guttural purrs, clacking vibrato, and overlaying hiss. Meaning clearly that she should try again. She felt a bit like a schoolchild being singled out in class for a mistake. But after a few tries they settled on a pronunciation she could handle.

That's if she could remember it.

"Admirable, Captain Talis," the alien said, quite politely.

Patronizing her. She would need at least several new bones in her jaw and an extra throat to pronounce the tri-part language, but she thanked the commander for the lesson.

Satisfied, it returned its attention to the navigation charts.

"As to the matter of the border passage, I would prefer to avoid the storm and rejoin you on the other side. As you say, no one has impeded our travels before."

"If you haven't been through a storm center yet," Talis suggested, "it's quite the experience."

"We have," said the alien, "and it was. Our ship's systems are impaired in such places. The charged ions in the cloud render our systems unreliable."

Talis tucked a stray tendril of hair behind her ear and nodded. It was no disappointment to her. If they didn't have to fly with the aliens at their backside, so much the better.

"Fair enough. All right, let's meet . . . here." She pointed to a location just off the edge of Fall Island.

"Agreed," said the commander.

At a gesture, a bridge officer nodded to the commander and entered the information on a live display nearby.

"When should we expect you to arrive?"

"About three days, assuming we don't run into trouble."

"We will meet you at your chosen location in three days, then."

Sophie caught Talis's eye and made a small tilt of her head paired with raised eyebrows. Talis remembered what she'd promised the girl.

"But say we do happen to run into a border patrol," Talis said, trying to keep it casual, "is there any way we could contact you?"

"Of course," said the commander, sounding pleased. "We ought to have provided you a means to contact us yesterday."

The commander made a gesture with its hand.

Talis saw Sophie's shoulders twitch. At least the girl didn't hop and clap her hands. *Admirable restraint.* To cover her excitement, she busied herself with rolling up her charts and stowing them.

A new Yu'Nyun approached with one of the glossy black tablets. This one was dressed at a level of simplicity on par with the four ship escorts but in fabric far more detailed than that of even the bridge crew.

The alien captain introduced the newcomer, sounding a name with a long breath's worth of hisses around a clacking consonant at its core.

Talis inclined her head, and the named alien returned the gesture. It clasped the pad to its thorax, hands crossed over it.

A suspicion occurred to Talis, and she did not like it. The captain spoke again, confirming her fears.

"Xe is a skilled interpreter, Captain Talis, as well as a scholar of linguistics. It was xe who provided my education in the local dialect. Xe has read more books from the local cultures than even I, and has interviewed many of the indigenous people during our explorations. Perhaps while you travel, xe will be able to assist in your edification of our language."

Words, in any language, drained from her. She had a tiny distracted thought that the aliens had finally made some indication of gender, though she had no idea how 'xe' might parallel to anything she was familiar with. But mostly her mind was consumed with the desire to run from the bridge before they could install any more emissaries on her ship.

She had promised her crew—promised *herself*—that the aliens would be only a shadow in their wake as they traveled. She inwardly cursed at not having been more direct with her request for a tablet.

"Forgive me, Captain, but I'm afraid our ship may not be well-suited to hosting your officer. I would be loath to insult—" She caught on the pronoun, unsure of how to shift its use. "—Yu'Nyun sensibilities with our poor accommodations."

"I appreciate your concern," spoke the alien in question. "However, I have traveled in your people's aircraft on several occasions and am accustomed to their design. I assure you, the underground cities of the Rakkar are far less accommodating, and I was delighted to be hosted even in their spaces." The words flowed with the cadence of a poem, and betrayed only a whisper of an accent. Scholar of linguistics, indeed.

No protest would pass, she realized. Ran a few more through her mind anyway.

"There is also the matter of diet," she said, grasping at an idea. "I believe our food is unpalatable to your digestive system?"

"Details." The captain turned its face away and raised an open hand. It was apparently not fond of details. "Not to worry, Captain Talis. Xe will travel with xist own food supplies, which I promise will not be an inconvenience to your personnel."

That was it. That was all she had, except the xenophobia that had inspired her protests.

These are your business partners, she reminded herself. *Make them happy—that's good business.*

She smiled at the commander and at the linguist.

"If it is truly no inconvenience, we would be honored to host you aboard *Wind Sabre* until we rendezvous in three days."

Sophie's eyes were as big as saucers, but Talis couldn't see past the girl's shock to tell if it was more of her curiosity or the same crawling revulsion that Talis felt. The commander clasped its hands lightly, as pleased an expression as it would be for a Cutter.

"Excellent, Captain Talis. You will find xin to be polite company, I am sure."

"I look forward to the opportunity to learn more about your people," she said. This wasn't actually a lie. It just wasn't the whole truth, which was that she'd much rather learn it from a book, far away from the aliens themselves. Preferably as they left Peridot and went back home to wherever they came from.

AS THE ALIEN GUIDES led them back out of the bridge and back to the ramp that would take them home, Talis chided herself for the animosity she was feeling.

The aliens were paying good money to get the last piece of their puzzle. If Talis knew the answers they were after, she would have given them herself and sent them on their way that much faster. But her part was to get them halfway there. She'd taken the job, and she'd certainly taken the money, and now the Yu'Nyun were her partners. Had they been Cutter clients, hosting a representative on their ship would have been a thoroughly reasonable part of the deal.

It seemed to Talis that Sophie was not suffering the same doubts or discomfort after all. She spoke to the alien nonstop as they walked, bubbling over with questions which Talis knew only scratched the surface of what curiosities must be brewing in the girl's mind.

The alien responded patiently, though from what Talis could hear xe was a bit obtuse in their—xist, was it?—answers. Xist accent—the clicks and hisses around the edges where vowels met consonants—was more obvious when xe spoke at lower volumes.

On the familiar landscape of *Wind Sabre*'s deck, Dug and Tisker stood waiting for them. Dug's jaw was set so tight it might take a sally bar to open it. Tisker failed to suppress a quiet exclamation of surprise when the alien ship retracted its ramp and the hatch sealed, leaving the towering slender emissary on their ship.

The sharp point of a tension headache started up in Talis's right temple. This was not going to make her crewmen think any better of this contract, or her, than they had when the aliens were going to stay on their own ship.

But Sophie had no such issues. She was obviously thrilled with their visitor, and in the presence of her exuberance, it was easy to forget that she and Talis had exchanged those heated words the day before. Sophie made quick introductions, making a far better attempt of the alien's name than Talis would have managed, and then eagerly led their guest below decks to stow xist equipment and foodstuffs.

Little Sophie, the most sheltered and colony-bred of their group, putting them all to shame with her hospitality.

Was being courteous too much to ask of herself? Talis had, after all, swallowed her feelings for any number of clients before these. Actually accepting the aliens might follow, if she let it.

CHAPTER 20

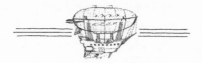

RAIN SPLATTERED ON *Wind Sabre*'s deck. Softly at first, in droplets so occasional that Talis felt like she imagined them. Then gradually, as their ship approached the cumulonimbus giant that blocked the stars like a dark smear, the rain increased in frequency and intensity until she had to pull down her goggles and cinch the hood of her foul weather gear.

The air grew turbulent and the lift balloon bounced against the lines, tiny bursts of slack rope that plunged the deck under her feet before wrenching it back up again. It was a good way to lose one's last meal.

Ahead, lightning flashes lit the cloud from within, providing strobed details of its size and shape. That information was already on her charts. It was the buoy she was watching for, marking safe entry into the storm.

The water barges that came for the storm's bounty could not easily maneuver around the active lightning zones. So the safest and most direct channels were indicated with buoy lights from the edges of the storm to the heart of it. The stormwater depot was installed on the islands amid the hardest driving rains, which collected on enormous harvester platforms anchored to the islands with heavy chains.

"Do you think we'll see any?"

Talis wondered how long Sophie had been talking to her. She had been trapped in her own thoughts, focused on the view, and Sophie had appeared at her side without her realizing it. The engineer's pale skin was rain-streaked, but rather than sharing in her captain's misery, Sophie seemed to revel in the downpour. Fat drops of cold water bounced off her bare shoulders. Her tank top and overalls clung to her skin. She wore oilcloth gaiters to keep rain out of her boots and avoid the blisters that wet socks would bring, but the rest of her gear was still stowed in her locker to the fore of the engine house.

The crew had reduced the regulator on the engines, hoisted their storm jib, and secured anything that might come loose in the wind or bounce out of its place below decks. Now they waited, with nothing to do for the moment but let Tisker guide them in. Once they spotted the buoy.

"Any . . . ?" Talis didn't take her eyes off the perimeter of the enormous cloud.

"Mermaids, Captain!"

Talis couldn't suppress a sound of disgust. "Not if I can help it. This will be enough fun without them flopping onto our deck and trying to eat us. There!"

She spotted the flashing yellow light of the buoy's lensed signal flame, and waved at Tisker to indicate the course adjustment. *Wind Sabre* shifted under their feet as the triangular sails along the lift envelope caught the wind and the airship angled toward the solitary unmanned beacon.

"I think they're lovely. In a flesh-eating-monster sort of way." Her voice was soft, trailing after thoughts that meandered ahead of them into the thick of that storm.

Talis wondered if Sophie was trying to prove she'd put their argument out of her mind for now. Talis certainly hadn't. The closer they got to Fall Island, the closer Sophie got to having the funds for that ship design.

"I prefer them at a distance," Talis said, and pushed back from the railing. With the clouds about to envelop and hide the ship, it was time.

Yawning, Sophie trailed behind her to the hidden locker tucked behind a coiled mass of rope line. "Xe's never seen one. The whole ship's instruments went dark when they tried to explore a cloud. And I don't get many chances to see them."

Talis stiffened. Never mind the mention of their alien guest, that last phrase sounded to her like another complaint about Sophie not having her own ship. But the girl leaned forward with anticipation as Talis tabbed the latch release on the locker, and retrieved a bundle from a harness mounted within. A lumpy box, wrapped in oilcloth and bound with a leather strap.

Even its buckle was an alchemical marvel. It could tell if there was line of sight to Nexus, and would refuse to release. As the cloud enveloped *Wind Sabre*, replacing aubergine sky with a soft gray that closed in around the railing, she thumbed the buckle and flipped a catch, and with a whir, the metal judged their cover. A ping indicated its approval, and its latch disengaged. The buckle smacked her hard on the thigh as it dropped away. She cursed, unwrapped the strap, and tossed it back into the locker.

It was no handicap that the device required fully obscured skies to operate. She had no intention of being caught by Onaya Bone or any other of The Five, and punished for using alchemy. Parting with the presscoins for that buckle was punishment enough.

Precisely how it worked, Talis had no idea. It required no fuel, minimal maintenance (just wipe the carbon off the metal connections before packing it away again), and if it were to ever break, even Sophie would be helpless to fix it. So she was mindful of her grip as she unwrapped the oilcloth with rain-wet hands.

It had a name, something arcane like a tripolarizing kip-arcoiled band-conducted electro-ionic … kajig. Talis couldn't remember, exactly. Alchemists tended toward flamboyance when naming their devices, and it wasn't as though she openly talked about owning one.

It was comparable in size to a small jewelry box, except that it had sliding panels to open and close it instead of a hinged lid. Behind the panels, glass bulbs were filled with cloudy liquid as a sandglass might be filled with fine grains. The bulbs were mounted inside circular metal housings, on tracks filled with ball bearings. She used a fingernail to flick one arm open and rotate a glass bulb dextral until it was upside-down, and then flicked the arm back across that housing to lock it in place. She repeated the motion for the other glass bulbs, alternating dextral and sinistral for each and then slid their covers back into place until they latched with contented clicks.

A panel on the bottom of the box released four trailing wires, each pronged at the end, equal in number to copper panels mounted in the back of the hidden locker. Each wire clipped into place, charges carefully aligned positive and negative. With that done, Talis secured the box back into its harness. She then wrapped the strap and buckle inside the oilcloth wrapping and tucked that into the bottom of the locker so it wouldn't damage the box or interrupt the current if a sudden shift in the angle of their flight sent them sliding.

"I'll consider it a good day if I disappoint you again," she said to Sophie, and thumbed a toggle switch on the top of the device.

There was a thrumming pulse from the box, which *Wind Sabre's* hull seemed to answer with a deeper tone of its own. Talis swore, as magenta light arced from the toggle's metal fitting, catching her fingertips before she could pull them away. A sharp stabbing coursed up to her wrist. She tasted copper. She shook her hand to dispel the tingling sensations and held the offended limb against her chest.

Sophie laughed. If she was hurt by Talis's unwillingness to banter, she didn't show it. She wandered off, checking the lines as she made her way forward, eager to be the first of them inside the storm.

That was a pleasure Talis would gladly cede. She secured the locker, then retreated under the cover of the wheelhouse where Dug stood with Tisker at the helm. At her approach, Dug moved away, stiffly walking past to take up a watch on the port side, making it clear he preferred to stand in the rain than share a space with her.

She had already explained herself to him. He'd already made up his mind about the soundness of her decisions. She could either wait out his anger or see him disembark with Sophie on the other end of it.

That would leave Talis with a near-empty ship. The ship she bought to be home for her and Dug. Would she even want to keep it if he left?

And if she didn't care about the particular ship as much as the bodies aboard, why not talk to Sophie about joint ownership of the next?

Her ego stepped in to elbow the sliding mess of such thoughts aside. Did she really want to have to fight with Sophie over priorities and not have the old fallback of 'it's my ship, you'll do what I say' as a last resort? Sharing a ship might be just the final tilt their friendship needed to go over the edge.

Talis shook herself. She was letting the dreariness of the rain get to her.

"Anyone check on our guest lately?"

"Scrimshaw's not exactly happy, Cap," Tisker said, squinting into the rain as it drove sideways across the deck. "Curled up below complaining of a delicate stomach. Though I think my stomach would be delicate with that food, too."

The crew had taken to calling the alien Scrimshaw as a rough approximation of xist actual name, which they all found nearly impossible to pronounce. It was an apt moniker, given the shallow, intricate carvings across xist entire body. Their guest had not objected, though Talis had no idea what xe actually thought of being renamed.

Scrimshaw had come aboard the ship with live food, a tall chrome-and-white barrel of something oily and slithering that smelled of soured milk. None of the crew had observed xin eating, as xe did not make use of the galley. In the absence of knowledge, their imaginations ran wild as to the preparation of xist meals. Talis intended to broach the subject eventually, when she learned to better gauge xist personality.

The alien had been keen to begin language lessons with Talis and anyone else who would join them. Sophie volunteered with enthusiasm, but both men declined. Tisker proclaimed that he hadn't spent a day in school in his entire life and he didn't intend to start now. Dug stayed quiet and kept his reasons to himself. Their choice. Talis didn't see the point of the lessons in the long term either, but it made for a good distraction while they sailed, and she admitted she was almost as curious about the aliens as Sophie was. The more cultural differences that emerged through conversation, the more intrigued Talis became.

The first lesson covered a dizzying number of pronoun groupings the aliens used in Yu'keem, their language. What Talis had originally taken for a gender indicator, Scrimshaw explained was related to class, not anatomy. 'Xe,' and its fifty—*dear gods, fifty*—variations, were of the 'respectful nonclass' pronoun category. Scrimshaw informed them, when Talis complained of the length of that list, it was only one of nine pronoun categories. There were honorary, noncommittal, and dismissive pronouns for Yu'Nyun premier, artisan, and drone classes, plus something Scrimshaw referred to as 'transitional.'

Talis had a knack for picking up languages, but she'd never learned one in a classroom setting. She was learning new words in her own language, as Scrimshaw threw terms around like 'prepositional object possessive indefinite' and made her head spin. She was relieved that Scrimshaw thought they could get by with just the respectful non-class category, despite xist concern that offering too much respect to the wrong subordinate would be seen as a weakness.

Sophie absorbed it all, however. She was a fast study in any subject that piqued her curiosity, and to say that included the aliens was an understatement. She hungrily ate up any morsels of information the alien would offer. Talis was almost certain Sophie had already memorized at least the singular pronouns which would come up in their conversations with and about their guest. For Talis, however, Yu'keem was demanding more of her patience than any native Peridot language ever had. It was a small grace that Peridot had several equivalent pronouns, mostly plurals, which Scrimshaw said would suffice.

While Scrimshaw did seem driven to teach them to speak Yu'keem, xe had not been as eager to discuss any topic that delved into the nature of Yu'Nyun society. Anything xe admitted seemed to be filtered through extreme trepidation and, when xe did answer a direct question, xist eyes darted side to side as though xe feared being overheard. Talis couldn't figure it. Sophie's questions were about simple things, cultural and physiological stuff. The answers to which, whatever they were, could hardly be sensitive enough to keep secret. But their alien passenger was obviously bothered by the risk, so Talis went at the issue sideways, always trying to ask Scrimshaw about xist-self rather than asking general questions about the Yu'Nyun. From that, she built the clues up into a rough profile.

Class was everything, and appearance an integral part of that. Scrimshaw admitted as much when they needed xin to explain an idiom about textiles which had no local equivalent. The social class of an individual dictated the clothing and accessories they wore. An elitist tendency that, it seemed to Talis, must span the universe. But the aliens' system was far more formalized than that of Cutter folk. All citizens, according to Scrimshaw, adhered to the strict class-based conventions. There were no variations allowed for special occasions or casual situations. No dressing up for, or attending, an opulent gathering if you were someone's housekeeper. No dressing down if you were an aristocrat. There were harsh penalties, from what Talis could gather, for those who tried to bend the boundaries of propriety.

Scrimshaw followed, xe explained, the permitted style of a skilled artisan. Xist chin lifted and xe squared xist shoulders as xe explained that all language was poetry. To xin, words were as carefully selected as the fabric of xist drapes and bands, or the designs that had been cut into xist body.

But that was all xe would say on the topic of the aliens' strange body engraving.

The previous night, Sophie spent hours sitting on Talis's bunk and wondering aloud about all the new questions raised in her mind by the first lesson. Having none of the answers to sate her curiosity, Talis eventually kicked the young woman out of her cabin as kindly as she could—though it eventually took a captain's order—so she could get some sleep.

From the persistent yawning Talis had observed throughout the day, she knew Sophie hadn't slept at all. But her mood had lifted, and the barely contained enthusiasm was preferable to the arguments Talis knew hovered just beyond the edges of their conversations. She wished the unspoken ceasefire could last.

Sophie reappeared after making a circuit of the railing, apparently having failed to spot a mermaid. She'd finally put on her coat, though her teeth chattered beneath the stiff hood.

"Want me to invite xin up top, Captain?"

Talis tried to imagine the alien in their foul weather gear, with xist long limbs hanging out of the sleeves and the extended oblong shape of xist head rendering the hood useless.

"Feel free to try," she said with a shrug, though she had to yell to be heard.

Sophie scurried off. She moved confidently across the wet deck, feet sure from a life spent on airships.

The view, already impeded by the pounding rain, became fully obscured as they reached the thickest portions of the cloud. Dug stood watch on the starboard side and Talis to port. They stared into the squall, eyes squinted against the raindrops that bounced off every surface. As they spotted each buoy marker, they called out course corrections or echoed those they heard, so Tisker could hear them over the sound of the rain pounding the outer hull and the canvas lift balloon, and the creaking of lines and wood as he fought the gusting winds.

Turbulence rocked the ship. Lightning danced within the cloud all around them. The hidden device, wired through the hull, absorbed the flashes that came near enough, and output a low regulated charge to deter the mermaids. Talis tried to ease her clenched jaw. The way was slow, but her chest pounded with excitement. There was no room for error.

CHAPTER 21

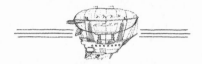

MAYBE HER IMAGINATION WAS just inspired by Sophie's comments, but Talis swore she could hear singing out in the gray murk. She placed a hand on one of the metal cleats to assure herself that the prickling charge from her alchemical device was pulsing through the ship. The mermaids wouldn't land on the ship so long as they kept the noise down and kept that device running.

"It is like nothing I have ever experienced," came the clack of Scrimshaw's accent beside her. She jumped, bracing her hands in panic against the railing of the ship. She had been so focused on watching for the signal lights that she hadn't noticed xist approach over the sound of the storm. If she was being honest with herself, she was also straining her ears for the sound of a feminine voice coming out of the driving rain. The tension was making her jumpy.

"The storms are dangerous," she said. "But damned if they aren't beautiful. A view you can't get anywhere else, close enough to rip you out of the sky."

"And a necessity of your way of life."

Talis called out another buoy as its light became visible

in the murk, then turned to xin as the ship leaned that way. Scrimshaw had not attempted the foul weather gear. Xist leather-and-silk uniform seemed to repel the water. Though the materials looked as though an unguarded sneeze could ruin them, the rain hit, beaded up, and ran off as if it was treated oilcloth.

"How do your people collect water if not from storms?"

"It was pumped from groundwater tables on our home planet," xe said. "There were also moving weather systems, mountain runoff, or glacial melt. Water would run in great rivers across our continents until it joined the salt-rich oceans. On other planets we have explored, water was trapped beneath the surface and accessible once we drilled wells. On most, however, there is no water at all. Yours is the first that we have encountered where water is sourced from fixed weather systems."

"Some islands have mountains, and rain systems," she said. "And those have their streams, but it's nowhere near enough to supply all the airships in the skies."

"Other planets' inhabitants have more access to water than here, but it is remarkable that your storm systems are infinite in their duration. While your steam-power transports you across the unnatural space between destinations, lifeforms on most planets are able to walk between any two points where the oceans do not prevent passage. We believe this was once also the case on your planet."

"Only place our ocean stops us from going is Nexus."

Scrimshaw turned xist head, as if xe could see through the cloud toward the center of the world. "Your ocean is peculiar."

"Since your ship arrived, we've heard you find a lot about our world peculiar," she said. She didn't mean to sound defensive, but the point of this conversation escaped her, and her mind was out of energy to spend imagining distant worlds and what it would be like to live on the outside of a spinning ball, as Scrimshaw told her was 'normal.'

"It is an anomaly among the stars," Scrimshaw agreed. "Most fascinating."

Talis shrugged. "It's just home."

She meant the statement to signal the end of the conversation, hoping xe'd wander off to go talk to Sophie instead. But that hint sailed past xin, and xe kept talking.

"I theorize that this is why the answers we seek do not appear in your historical records. You are not aware that some aspects of your planet are anomalous, and so you offer no commentary or explanation for them. We hope the ancient beings you worship will supply the remaining answers required to complete our understanding."

Peridot had its own explorers. Mostly among the Bone and Cutter folk. Talis understood the appeal of being somewhere where no one had been before. She tried to picture Peridot the way that aliens might. The floating rocky outcroppings of islands. Glow stations with their luminous pumpkins. The dust motes spinning off the edges of landmasses. Nexus, locking it all in place. And, of course, the massive storms.

Lightning leaped in the clouds off their port rail, and she felt her skin tingle with electricity again. She had allowed Scrimshaw to distract her, and now they were off course for the buoy. As she called out the belated adjustment, a loud wet thud hit the deck just fore of the wheelhouse, followed by the sharp smack of a slapping tail fin.

"Get back," she warned Scrimshaw. "Watch out for more of them."

She ran back, grabbing a spare belay pin from the rack on the aft steam chimney on her way.

"Mermaid!" she called as she ran. "Get me a net!"

She had no time to see whether anyone was moving to do so because the mermaid was upon her. Twice her size, counting the tail, it looked like a drowned woman half-swallowed by a fish, but it might have been male or female. It had slick scales, long claws, and fangs glinting under wet, bedraggled hair. On pale leathery wings, it lifted itself up until the end of its long tail barely touched *Wind Sabre*'s deck. Its song was no melody now, but a scream. A challenge.

It tried to dive past her, aiming at the spot where Scrimshaw pressed xist-self defensively against the deckhouse, but Talis leaped forward to head the mermaid off. Using the belay pin like a club, she struck it across the ribcage as high as she could reach. She'd meant to go for the joint at its shoulder, but the thing reared up, lifting high with a beat of its wings. Its coiling tail dragged on the deck, winding and unwinding with rage.

It hissed at Talis and swiped to push her out of its way. Claws caught in her jacket collar for a moment, then grazed her cheek as she twisted out of its grip. Let a mermaid grab you and it'll fly you out over nothing, drink your blood, and then drop the drained husk to flotsam.

Sophie came running with the net. At the sound of her boots, the mermaid turned its attention to her, wings lifted high over its head. Raindrops bounced off of them in an arcing spray that made the beast look even bigger.

No way Sophie could toss the net over it with the wings outstretched and beating. Talis would need to distract it.

She circled away from Sophie's side and went in to strike again. But the moment that she stepped out of the way leading to Scrimshaw, the mermaid was moving toward xin again. Too late, Talis swung the pin at the thing's chest, the angle too high as the mermaid slid across the slick deck on hands and hips. Talis swept the pin at it again, and managed to club it hard across a hip bone. It emitted a shriek of pain and outrage, but still ignored Talis and Sophie to lunge for Scrimshaw.

Talis grabbed at the thing's tail with both hands as it passed. "Now!" she yelled to Sophie. "Throw it!"

It dragged her across the deck, and Sophie cast the net over them both.

Wings pinioned, limbs tangled, it collapsed. Talis tripped and sprawled across its lashing tail. That and the net were finally enough to stop the mermaid from reaching Scrimshaw, and it whipped around, turning on Talis with claws and teeth. The beast thrashed violently against the net, tangling worse and worse, so that thankfully its teeth could only snap at her throat, missing it by less than a handspan. Its claws grasped at her hair, pushing her head back to bare the tender flesh. Talis bit it first, chomping the thing's arm. Her teeth sank into the waterlogged, too-soft skin, and found the wiry muscle beneath. It reared up and away from her throat in outrage. She spat, feeling like she'd bitten into a live, wriggling worm.

It rolled sideways, still desperate to reach Scrimshaw, who was cornered with no retreat that would see xin outside its reach. Talis grappled with its elbows and shoulders, trying to pull it the other way.

She had never seen a mermaid so intent on a single victim. The alien was so brittle looking, Talis feared for her contract if the mermaid got its way, but she was tangled in the net with it, and couldn't get her knees under her to push back against the deck. Instead the mermaid finally reached Scrimshaw's legs and pulled xin off xist feet. Its claws left scratches in Scrimshaw's exoskeleton that caught on and chipped the ridges of xist precisely carved patterns. Xe hit the deck on xist hip and wrist, and curled up in a fetal position, xist hands crossed protectively over the pouch on xist belt. Not over xist porcelain face, nor over the torso and vital organs. Talis narrowed her eyes.

Sophie chased after, a knife in her hand to try and free her captain. But there were legs, and wings, and tail, and net, and all moving too erratically and quickly to risk moving in with the blade. Dug was there, then, and together they pulled back on the edge of the net.

"What is going on with this thing?" Sophie asked against clenched teeth, as she and Dug hauled it back off Scrimshaw.

Talis got the mermaid's arms behind it, ducking out of the way of its frantic wings until she had the wrists pinned against each other, and she knelt over it, holding it down.

She yelled back over her shoulder to Dug. "Check xist pouches!"

Dug looped his corner of the net over a deck cleat, and dodged the mermaid's thrashing movements to reach the harassed alien. But Scrimshaw's ordeal was just beginning, Talis resolved, if xe'd somehow attracted danger to her ship.

Dug yanked Scrimshaw to xist feet, and away from the mermaid, but held xist wrists together in the grip of a single hand while he invaded the alien's belt pouch. Scrimshaw's eyes were dilated, xist head turned as xe leaned away in xist best attempt to evade the movement. Still, Talis thought xe might have resisted with more effort than that.

When Dug's hand emerged, he gripped something, and dropped Scrimshaw to the deck. The alien sank to xist knees in defeat, then edged backward farther from where Sophie was attempting to untangle the net from her captain's shoulders.

"Explain this," Dug said to Scrimshaw, holding up a small vial. Green light glowed across his hand from the contents, which pulsed and swirled like a trapped insect.

The mermaid stopped struggling beneath Talis's grip, its head lifted to watch Dug closely. Sophie used the stillness to cut her captain free.

Scrimshaw offered no explanation. Xist mouth was open, and xist chest moved with panicked breaths. Xe looked from Dug to Talis, and back again.

Sophie bound the wings and arms up behind the mermaid's back so Talis could extract herself. She hopped away quickly as she let go her hold on the mermaid's arms, but the beast was still transfixed by the object in Dug's hands.

Tisker called out to check on them from the other side of the deckhouse, where he piloted the ship through the buoys.

Without any help, Talis realized with a start. "Dug, the lanes. We've got this."

The mermaid was tied off, still tangled in the net and hooked on a cleat. Scrimshaw wasn't about to do anything to her the mermaid hadn't already managed. Dug nodded, placed the vial in Talis's waiting hand, and returned to his post, stepping on the mermaid's tail where it blocked his path up the deck. The creature barely noticed.

The glowing object cast a light that seemed to cut through the dismal air, as though there was a small piece of sunshine in the palm of her hand. But it was cool to the touch. The driving rain felt warm in comparison, though she was hot from the struggle and steam was likely gathering off her head and shoulders, as she saw it rising off of Sophie. She shook the vial, and Scrimshaw flinched, catching xist-self as xe started to reach out for it.

"Answer the question," Talis said, her voice rigid with the command. "What is this?"

Sophie began dragging the bundled mermaid toward the railing. At the movement, Scrimshaw blinked against the rain as though roused from a trance. Xe pulled xist feet under xist hips, curling up in a miserable huddle. "I am not—"

"Not supposed to say?" Talis cuffed xin, grabbed xin by the collar in her free hand, and pulled xin up. She felt xist limbs jangle like a wind chime in her grip. Xe probably wouldn't survive the throttling xe deserved, so she shoved the object in xist face instead. "I'll just bet you aren't."

She had a long list of things she wanted to say about Yu'Nyun secrets, but her words were cut off by a series of sharp thuds behind her, hitting the deck in rapid succession. She wheeled around just in time to see five new arrivals swooping toward her and Scrimshaw. Even at a distance their eyes seemed to flash with the reflection of the green light.

There were too many. Her adrenaline tried to react, to flood her veins again, but she only felt dizzy. Blood pounded in her ears and the droplets of rain around her seemed to slow. Still, the pack of mermaids crossed the deck at full speed, closing in fast on her and Scrimshaw. With only Sophie between them, struggling with the netted mermaid which had begun to thrash again at the sight of its reinforcements. It lifted and pivoted on the upper half of its tail, twisting free as Sophie's hands were pinched in the net and she let go with a cry of pain. Free again, it surged across the deck.

But not toward Talis and Scrimshaw. The first mermaid pulled against the net to growl and hiss at its own kind. They reared up in outrage, and then moved again, attacking the bound beast with claws and fangs. There was a confused muddle of flapping wings, and then the former lay in a tangled heap at the mercy of its own kind. It blinked slowly, blood bubbling from its lips, as the others descended upon it, its eyes locked on the vial in Talis's hand until they finally dimmed.

"Hide it, Captain Talis," Scrimshaw pleaded, xist voice a whisper in her ear. "They will not stop coming."

She growled at xin, raised xin up again with the impulse to rattle xist neck, then she pulled back her other arm and pitched the vial over *Wind Sabre*'s railing.

The mermaids at once and together abandoned the final insults they were visiting upon their victim, and dove after the prize. Leading their group, the largest one's blood-tipped claws picked the vial out of the air before it dropped from sight, and curled protectively around it. The other four attempted to tear the item from its grip, slashing at its forearms and face, and the tail where it curled up protectively. The wings were assaulted next, shredded with tooth and claw.

The outcome was inevitable, the danger mounting. Through the roaring wind Talis heard the song of more panicked mermaids, moving from the depths of the storm toward the commotion off their port stern. But rather than fight as viciously to defend the vial as it had to gain it, something in the large mermaid's features softened. The mad anguish that seemed a perpetual part of their bone structure dulled as it cradled its hands to its heart. It seemed to give up, for a moment, before realizing the danger it was in. It extended the tattered wings, curled the tail in a coil, then dove with the driving rain into the depths, out of sight beyond the railing.

The others, including several newcomers, flattened their wings against their shoulders and vanished in pursuit.

Panting, Talis dropped Scrimshaw's collar, giving xin a chance to settle back on xist feet.

"Help her," she told xin, tilting her head to indicate Sophie, who struggled to drag the mermaid's dead weight to the rail.

Scrimshaw hesitated, thought better of whatever xe was going to say in protest, and went to Sophie's side. Together they lifted the mermaid's body by the shoulders, yanking on the netting there, until they pushed the balance of its weight over the edge and it slid off, taking the ruined netting into the drop with it.

"Still like them?" Talis asked Sophie as she leaned against the rail, panting from the effort. The humor was forced, ruined by the treachery of Scrimshaw's little item, but she wouldn't get a chance to make the joke again, and the ironic comment had been building in her mind where she knew it would fester if left unspoken.

Sophie needed a minute before she could answer. "Oh, come on, Captain," she huffed, catching her breath through a wide grin. "That was nothing."

"Right," was all Talis said.

Tisker had slowed their momentum while they were off course, but now she felt the ship picking up speed again. Scrimshaw stumbled a bit, unsteady as the deck's gravity shifted. Xe watched her warily, shoulders hunched as though xe expected her to grab for xist neck again. She was sorely tempted.

She wiped at moisture dripping down her cheek, winced at the sting, and looked down to see her hand covered in fresh blood.

"Sophie, take port-side buoy watch, would you?"

"Aye, Captain." Sophie scurried off, as if to avoid being party to whatever sense Talis might try to beat into the alien.

"With me," she said to Scrimshaw, and stalked her way below deck. Scrimshaw followed, meek as a child behind its mother. She tried to catch her breath while on the move, to calm the blood that had finally caught up to the renewed signals and was waiting for another fight.

They reached the crew quarters, where Talis dug through a cabinet and found herself a towel. She bundled up her hair, looped it up to get it off her face, then used the trailing end to dry her face and neck. She had forgotten about the cut, and left a red streak across the pale cotton. It didn't help her mood.

She led Scrimshaw toward their med cabin, commanding xin to follow again with no more than a look.

"Talk. What was that thing, and why did the mermaids want it so bad?"

"The ancient texts of the Bone people refer to the creatures as *zalika*," the alien told her as they reached the cabin that served as *Wind Sabre*'s medical bay. Xe was avoiding the first question. Avoiding the Yu'Nyun side, as usual, to talk about her world. "Not a Bone word, evident from the sound of it. It is a name they chose for themselves."

"Huh," she said as they reached *Wind Sabre*'s medical facilities.

The cabin was opposite the galley, and roughly the same size. But the table in the center was higher, meant for surgery. Along the forward bulkhead, instead of a stove and icebox, was a recovery bunk, neatly made and rarely used.

She crossed to a mirror hung on a locker door, and wiped the bloody rainwater from her face with cotton gauze from a drawer beneath it. Blood welled up as fast as she could wipe it away and, in the reflection, she saw it ran down her neck. The collar of her rain-soaked shirt was irreparably stained—once cream, now pink and crimson where the blood and water wicked off her skin. Scrimshaw stood to one side, out of her way as she tended to her wound. Watching xist reflection in the mirror, she saw xin trace the scratches in xist carapace with xist fingertips. Saw the light trembling in those fingertips. Something in xist demeanor had changed. She didn't figure that the Yu'Nyun had much room for things like regret, but xe did at least seem cowed.

Sophie had boasted to Scrimshaw during their first Yu'keem lesson that Talis was fluent in the five main languages of Peridot, plus the Common Trade, and the dialect of Dug's village. But she'd never heard the word 'zalika' or fathomed that the mermaids even had a language. But the Yu'Nyun had admittedly spent a lot more time trying to learn about Peridot than she ever had. What did she really know, aside from flying, dealing, and smuggling? Well, and fighting.

"That's a new one to me," she admitted, then hissed through her teeth as the gauze stuck at the edge of her cut and tugged.

"Onaya Bone created them before she made your first officer's race. She promised them their share of the source, but she never fulfilled that promise."

"'Source'?" She put down the gauze and turned to lean against the counter and fix xin with her full attention. "This source have anything to do with what you had in that vial?"

Scrimshaw bowed xist head, as much of an admission as xe seemed willing to make. But at least xe kept talking, instead of shutting down on her like she feared xe might. "That which gives you reason, cognition. The force that allows you to act on more than instinct."

"Sentience?" she offered, though that couldn't be right. That wasn't a thing that could be bottled.

Scrimshaw considered it for a moment. "That will suffice," xe said. "Without it, the zalika are in continuous agony and rage. They are inconsolable, and blame those creatures who they believe carry the quintessence that was meant for them. Specifically, the sailors who fly through the storms they inhabit. Unfortunately, they seemed able to sense the sample I carried. It was my expectation they would perhaps only sense that I was a being from this planet and of no more note than you."

"In the future," she said, turning back to the mirror, "I'm going to have to ask you to test your scientific research on your own time."

The blood ran a rivulet down her cheek and around her chin again, as though she had never wiped it off.

Scrimshaw was silent a moment. Seemed to process her sarcasm and understand she was not going to hurt xin. "Of course, Captain. I would like to apologize. I was unprepared for their uncivilized response to my presence."

"Uncivilized, huh," Talis said out of one side of her mouth as she pressed gauze to her cheek.

THAT NIGHT THEY GRAPPLED *Wind Sabre* to a small island along the buoyed path through the storm cloud, out of sight in case other ships approached. Dug, least likely to fall asleep no matter how tired, took first watch so the others could get a short reprieve. He was armed for a battle, ready in case they had any more zalika visitors.

Talis would have the third watch, after Tisker. Ten blessed hours to sleep and get some food in her. In that order.

The cuts on her cheek were just deep enough that she could have stitched them if she wanted. It was a choice between a messy line of scars if she wanted the guaranteed heal of sutures or tape strips that might come undone and let the wound reopen. No one on board was a particularly tidy seamstress, so she went with the small strips and some medical paste to hold the skin together while the wound closed.

She returned to her cabin after a hot shower in the head nearest the steam pumps. Didn't bother to turn any lights on. Dropped her towel on the floor and collapsed into her bunk, her hair still damp.

The pillows reached up to cradle her head, and the blanket sighed softly across her. The silence of the room with the purr of the engines beyond and the rain gusting in sheets against the glass and wood around her promised uninterrupted slumber.

Her eyes shot open, sleep forgotten.

Someone was in her cabin.

CHAPTER 22

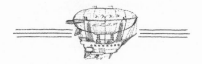

HER HAND FOUND THE LIGHT switches on the panel behind her head. She pressed the middle button for the red nighttime chart-reading lights. It wouldn't do to be blinded by the cabin's full lights, and double her vulnerability.

Only a few paces away, Hankirk sat at her desk, one ankle over the opposite knee. He slouched slightly, elbows on the arms of the carved wooden desk chair, fingers tented. Looking all gods-rotted smug.

He was still in the civilian clothes he'd been wearing the last time she saw him. There was a black streak across one sleeve. He must have climbed aboard along the refuel lines at Subrosa and stowed away with their coal reserves. He was probably even dirtier than she could tell in the half light.

She couldn't help but remember the hobby lights at Jasper's shop which had been much the same as the chart lighting in her cabin now. The body of her old friend. The assassins hired by Hankirk, whose revolvers were now stowed in the drawer of the desk next to him.

"What, Imperial captains can't afford their own passage?" she said, and swung her legs under her to sit up. She gathered the sheet in front of herself with one white-knuck-led fist. Kept the other hand free, moving it toward the pistol she kept tucked alongside her mattress pad.

"We need to talk again," he said. Apparently his idea of an explanation for stowing aboard.

She spared that a humorless laugh, then took a deep breath and resisted the temptation to pull the gun on him. She'd never meant it for ex-boyfriends.

"A chance to ambush us in the storms, more like."

"I need that ring."

For this, you're gonna climb aboard my ship?

"Told you back on Subrosa," she said. "I don't have it. You should've snuck into the alien captain's bunk. That ring is on the other side of the border by now."

"I need *you* to get it *back* for me."

"The hell would I do that for? I owe you some favor I forget about? You threatened to hang me and my crew. My wrencher's still nursing the bruises your crew gave her. You shot at my ship, stalked me to Subrosa, and sent assassins after me and mine. Now you've stowed away on my ship and lurked in the shadows of my cabin. You get your eyeful? No, I owe you a long cold drop is what I owe you."

"You gave it to the aliens. *Foreigners.* What do they care about Peridot? They'll take their knowledge and leave, and where does that put us? If they take the ring, what good is that?"

"It's about seventy-five thousand presscoins good to me. And if you want it so badly, I'd rather that ring leave our atmosphere with strangers than give you the rotted thing."

"Talis, please," he said, standing and taking a step toward her.

That did it. She pulled out the pistol. Thumb-cocked it.

"You came here to beg? *Really?*"

"I came here to *reason* with you. I'm trying to save the world. I give you my word."

"People keep accusing me of being reasonable lately." She pressed the intercom near the light switch, acting like she didn't care that the movement required briefly baring her chest. "Someone bring some rope to my cabin, please."

"Aye, Cap." Tisker's sleepy voice, confused.

"We have a minute." She motioned back to the chair with the barrel of her gun, and used the back of her elbow to switch the full cabin lights on, squinting to prepare herself for the flood of brighter illumination. "Say your piece."

He blinked as the lights over her shoulder caught him off guard. Hesitated, then let out a defeated sigh and sat back down. "They're up to something."

"*Everyone* is up to something. You certainly are. What makes *your* something more righteous than theirs? Than mine?"

Gods, she thought. *Am I truly defending the aliens?*

Hankirk ran both hands through his hair, massaging his scalp. He inhaled audibly through his nose. "The ring *belongs* to Peridot's people."

"*Your* people, you mean." Here was the crux of it. She felt it coming.

"You're one of my people, Talis. We're the true heirs of the gods' power."

Talis made a disgusted sound and stood to claim her trousers from the pile of clothes she'd left on the floor. Kept the pistol trained on him, casually as she could while trying to keep herself covered and pull clothes on at the same time. He made no move but watched her; had the decency, at least, not to ogle. His gaze met hers and silently pleaded.

"Can't you feel it? Something is *wrong* with our world. I've known it in my blood since I was a boy. We shouldn't *be* this way. This broken planet. These five races. It's wrong in a way that *has* to be fought."

"By Silus's cosmic wind," she swore, borrowing one of Tisker's pleasantries. "You haven't changed. The same unrelenting racist zealot I remember."

"I—" he started, but she cut him off.

"You're seriously going to sit there and tell me I should help you steal back that ring so you can just . . . *erase* four of Peridot's peoples? That's your big sell? Genocide?"

"We want *unity*, not destruction." He leaned forward, hands open as if they held evidence of his sincerity. "I've been to the Wind Monks' drifting archives. I've seen the Lost Codex. We were all *one* people once."

The muscles in her forearm tensed. She wanted to crack him one good across the temple with the butt of the pistol. Do the world a favor and toss him out after that mermaid. Zalika. Whatever.

"Sure, once," she said. "This planet look to you like it can all just go back to the happy fantasy time you and your fatcrat Veritor friends can't let up about?"

The door to her cabin opened and Tisker entered. His eyebrows jumped at the sight of Hankirk. At his captain, half-dressed. Then, true to his character, he accepted the situation as it was, no questions. Unleashed that rogue's grin and crossed the cabin, taking her pistol so she could get her shirt on.

"This guy bothering you, Cap?"

Hankirk sat back in the seat, hands up in surrender. "All of history can be corrected," he said in answer to Talis.

"Oh yeah," Talis said to Tisker. "He most certainly is."

TALIS DIDN'T HAVE THE RIGHT COMBINATION of character deficiencies to outright murder someone, much as she'd fantasized about Hankirk's death lately. If she did, she might have saved herself the trouble and offed him back in the Tined Spoon District of Subrosa. Or let Dug finish him off back when he'd first overtaken them on *The Serpent Rose.*

Instead, they left the bastard alive again, albeit unarmed and without shelter, on the rain-washed island they'd moored to for the night. He was drenched only moments after they pushed him down the gangway to shore, destined for pneumonia if the mermaids didn't get him first.

No, not murder. But her character did have deficiencies enough to take more than a slice of pleasure in leaving the man behind.

It occurred to her that they could have tied him up and carried him along in the brig. Probably would have made a bit more sense. Could be leverage later on.

She shuddered. Keep him that close? No, thank you. Better to have him well out of the way, unable to tangle himself in their knotted 'locks any longer.

Sleep finally came, once she crawled back into her bunk, and dreamed of Hankirk's lost expression as *Wind Sabre* made her way back into the buoy lanes and left him behind.

"WHAT DO YOU THINK? Does she see us?"

Tisker handed the scope over, his eyes locked on the bright shape out in the dark.

Instead of looking at the border patrol ship that Tisker had spotted, Talis scanned the rest of the sky through the glass. The gold pumpkins glowing from port made her squint against their brightness. Nexus, green light source off their starboard side. She didn't even have to look to know where that was. There was a dull ache in her head from the proximity to it, already, and that peculiar tightness in her chest was getting stronger. It felt like a weight being pulled out of quicksand, and her chest was the quicksand.

"Not yet. She's only flashing reflections for us. We're too

far off and in the dark spaces between to catch that light."
She handed the scope back to Tisker. "Plus we've still got
the storm at our back. But keep an eye on her. If she comes
around, I want to know about it. Fly us on her dark side, low
as you dare."

"Little stray wisp of storm cloud," he murmured.

She nodded. The glow station pumpkins couldn't back-
light them if *Wind Sabre* didn't eclipse the patrol ship's view.

Sophie came up to the deck, burdened with a tray of
mugs. Scrimshaw walked beside her, xist hands empty. Talis
chafed. Whether Sophie had declined help or whether it
hadn't occurred to the alien to offer was unclear. Sophie's
smile was easy as ever, though. It seemed the lack of selfless-
ness in their guest was a point that only bothered Talis.

Steam rose from the four steel cups, and Talis felt
her tensed jaw muscles relax in anticipation of the
comforting drink.

"Border patrol ship," she told them, gratefully accepting
the coffee when it was offered. "Bone side, Bone make."

Sophie traded the tray of coffees to Tisker, taking the
scope in its place and having a look at the clinker-hulled
sloop for herself.

Dug, who had given Tisker a break at the helm, accepted
the remaining cup and leaned his hip against the wheel to
compensate for taking a hand away. He'd been dangerously
quiet since Scrimshaw came aboard, whether or not he was
in the alien's presence. Still obeyed commands, still took his
duties seriously, but her friend was walled up behind those
angry eyes, out of her reach.

He made no comment. Not about the Bone ship, not
about being so close to home for the first time in so long.
Talis had done her best to keep their runs in Cutter skies
while he sorted out his sorrows. She hadn't been looking forward to the day she knew was coming. Eventually business
would drive them back out into the rest of the world. They'd

have to pass through Bone territory to get to Rakkar or Vein islands, which were surrounded on all sides by the Bone, the only people with the capability to hold the Cutter encroachment at bay. The Cutter Empire had nipped at the edges of their territory for generations, and though they managed to overtake a majority of Peridot's atmosphere, there was still enough of the world beyond Cutter skies and Talis knew they'd have to venture back sooner rather than later.

And sooner was here.

She took a thoughtful sip of the coffee. The leathery taste of whiskey stowed away in the bitterness of the brew. *Good girl, Sophie.* They were all bone-soaked from the storm and more than a little bit in need of warming.

With the relationship between the Imperials and Bone tribal leaders as strained as it was, a ship smuggling goods out of Cutter skies was more likely to receive a warm welcome from Bone border patrols. The sloops would intercept, make a show of inspection, and then generally stay aboard for drinks, maybe gamble on some dice for a bit, before sending the Cutter miscreants on their way. Anyone who defied the Empire had a leg up in Bone skies, as far as they saw it.

But she had Dug. She'd always figured that when the time came, they'd just dress him up in a shirt or jacket, maybe both. Keep those scars out of sight, and hope none of the border patrol crew recognized him. That had always been a long shot and a fool's hope.

And now they had an alien aboard.

While the rest of the world bowed until their noses scraped the floor, welcoming the aliens diplomatically and with a greedy eye on their gleaming ship, the Bone had remained standoffish. The Vein employed Bone ships to guard their tight cluster of marble cities, so the Bone respected that the Vein were very interested in having the alien ship stop by to trade information. But then, not all Bone tribes were employed by the Vein, and those that weren't chafed at that inequality. There might be some motivation to hassle the aliens on that account.

The Bone government, as much as that term applied, was a council of the tribal leaders. They were meant to come together and represent their tribes' interests, and make decisions that would serve their common good. But there was no way to enforce that each tribe stand by the council's decisions. There might be scuffles if the decision was heavily weighted in one direction and the opposition was limited to a single tribe. But if the matter was more divisive, it was almost impossible to back up decisions with the power to enforce them.

The Vein had a similar governing body. They called it a parliament, not a council. But the Vein lived in such close proximity to one another that their skirmishes were almost all political. Talis knew there were assassins among them, but the violence was on a much smaller scale than the Bone tended toward.

She watched Dug. Boiling beneath the surface with such malevolence. At a word from her, he'd dispatch Scrimshaw, and be relieved for it. No doubt if they met the Bone border patrol sloop, and that crew learned of the aliens' intended destination, their reaction would be similar.

"Will it be a problem, Captain Talis, to 'sneak' by it?" Scrimshaw liked the word as much as xist captain had.

"Might be. Depends on what she does. We can fly below the horizon, or maybe far above. But if they're any good at their jobs, they're going to be looking out for a maneuver like that. For little ships with dark hulls that slip across off the traveling plane."

"Perhaps I can be of assistance," Scrimshaw said. Xe produced the glass tablet from a pouch at the back of xist waistband.

Talis turned to face xin. Another sip of the spiked coffee to steady herself. Couldn't believe she was about to say: "Let's hear it."

The alien laid a pale hand on the dark screen. Its display activated, casting strange shadows upward over xist face, and xe deftly navigated a series of menus to activate the function xe wanted. The rigid tips of xist fingers made the barest tapping sound against its front and back. Talis tried not to marvel at the alien technology but did wonder if Sophie had ever gotten Scrimshaw to hand the tablet over for her inspection. Xe looked up.

"My vessel is not far away. Their presence might provide the border patrol ship with what they expect to see, allowing your ship to remain undetected."

"A distraction," Tisker said, and whistled. "You're getting the hang of being sneaky, aren't you?"

"Only the word is new to us," Scrimshaw said, straightening xist back to stand even taller than xe already was. "The concept is not."

Talis wished he hadn't asked.

"What do you think, Captain?"

The scope was stowed along the wheel's pedestal again. Sophie's hands wrapped around her warm mug. Didn't take much time on deck to get a chill.

Talis pretended to consider the alien's idea. Pursed her lips between sips of coffee. Fact was, she was looking for another option. The alien's was good. Easy. Likely to work. The Yu'Nyun were known for creeping silently through the skies, explaining themselves to no one. And they'd caused no real trouble so far, even with whatever they'd learned from the Rakkar about alchemy. With the casual threat of the cannon protruding from their underbelly, a single Bone sloop was unlikely to engage them unprovoked.

There wasn't anything about the plan she could pick apart. But she should have been able to come up with something else on her own. On *her* ship, aliens—any strangers— didn't get to make the plans.

But it was a good plan. And in its presence, she failed to

conceive of another.

So she nodded, slowly. "Yeah, all right. We can give it a shot."

"I will make the arrangements," Scrimshaw said, and stepped away a few feet to send the transmission. Xist voice grated and popped, hissed and purred, as xe spoke to xist ship. The call was brief, thankfully. But long enough for the sound of their language to make her jaw tense again, working to further the headache she already had. She did pick up some of the words Scrimshaw had taught her and Sophie. *Ship* and *go* and other words that jived with the message xe said xe'd deliver. Xe also said *sneak* in Common Trade, apparently showing off the favored vocabulary to xist shipmates. She could see why they liked it. The way the letters ran together did sound at home among their snake-spider linguistic noises.

"It is confirmed." The alien returned the device to xist back pouch. "They will distract the patrol ship, and then *Wind Sabre* should fly at a distance beneath, to the previously arranged coordinates."

Dug laughed low and short. Shifted his position, took the coffee from its holder on the dash and took a sip. The wall was crumbling a bit. Talis narrowed her eyes at him. Was it relief at not needing to encounter the crew on that ship? His own people?

Not his own tribe, of course. They were across Nexus, nearer to the Rakkar islands. In another life this tribe would have concerned him only in a rivalrous sense. They might have teased him for sailing with Cutters, or for being away too long. But she'd taken him on that job, years ago, and he bore the scars of it. Scars that would get him killed among his people, regardless of tribe.

The messed-up thing, the unfair thing, was that he was relieved to pass by his own kind unseen, taking these aliens that he neither understood nor trusted, to meet the Bone goddess.

Of course, Talis might have misunderstood. A chuckle from Dug could mean many things. Few of them good.

CHAPTER 23

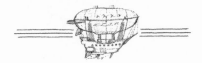

I T *WAS* A GOOD PLAN, THOUGH, and it worked perfectly.
The alien ship's silver surface reflected the pumpkins' orange glow and the green light from Nexus along its curving
hull. It loomed in the sky, gleaming like a gem in the morning light, and gave the patrol ship plenty to look at.

Talis took over at the helm so Tisker and Dug could
get a shift off. Her hand on the worn handles of the wheel,
feeling the strength of the ship, the force of the winds coming up along the whole length of the rudder chain, she decided she didn't man the helm often enough. *Wind Sabre*
slipped into position beneath the alien vessel, mirroring its
slow course. Against the glistening presence, no notice was
given by the Bone patrol ship to the dark wooden shape three
fathoms below.

If they'd met up with an Imperial patrol ship along the
border, if Hankirk had gone ahead of her and warned his
people that *Wind Sabre* was traveling with the aliens instead
of trying to chase her down for a private interview, such a ship
would have known to look for them. But the fool had made
another attempt to talk her onto his team. Snuck aboard her

ship and got himself stranded on a miserable storm island for that mistake.

She wouldn't expect Hankirk to make a tactical error like that.

Scrimshaw stood at the starboard railing watching xist ship around the edge of the lift envelope.

"Look different from the outside?" she asked.

"This entire experience has been unique," xe said.

Always agreeing while simultaneously correcting. Not her favorite conversationalist, this one.

She leaned against the console, merging her weight with the mass of her ship. The engines were burning low to prevent exhaust bursts from the turbines, but she still felt the thrum of them through the wood, up her feet, in the wheel's barrel at her hip. It gave her clarity. Focus. Here, she was at ease. In charge.

She wondered if the aliens ever slouched.

"Your ship have a name?" she asked instead.

Scrimshaw turned from the railing, crossing gracefully to her side on the tips of those toes. They reminded her of bird legs. She was pretty sure birds didn't slouch.

"None of the contemporary languages of your planet have a word that is equivalent of our ship's designation." Xe moved xist arm in a small gesture that managed to indicate all of Peridot. "It is due to the nature of your geography."

Actually, she realized, the aliens reminded her a lot of birds. She'd initially thought of insects. But no, from the bearing of Scrimshaw's body, the delicate weight distribution, and the tilt of xist head when xe considered her questions with dark blinking eyes, xe was more like a crane than a wasp. Definitely a crane.

She wanted to ask what made them so desperate to understand Peridot, but recalling how such questions had been dodged during their Yu'keem lessons, she proceeded obliquely. She'd start the questions on the outside. Find a chink, wedge it open, and ease in.

"Do you miss your world?" she asked.

"Those of us on my vessel have never seen our home planet."

Well, whatever reply she thought she'd get, it wasn't that.

"Never?"

"It was depleted of resources several generations before our crew was assembled."

Not 'before I was born' or 'when my great-grandparents were still young.' Their phrasing was always strange, and she had to wonder how they decided which Common Trade words to pick as equivalents for their own.

Talis tried to imagine living her whole life in an enclosed ship, out between the stars. The first part wasn't hard. Most Cutter folk happily stayed aboard the colony ships they were born on, rarely setting foot on an island for more than a few hours when the ships stopped to refuel. But between the stars, traveling endlessly. No open deck to feel the wind. And with emotionless crewmates for company? Cold and lonely, it sounded to her.

"We are . . ." Scrimshaw seemed to search for a word. "Prolific."

"Ah," she said. "Bled the old world dry, then, I take it?"

Xe looked at her. If xist carved eyebrows could move, they might have gone up in surprise.

"You understand resource depletion?"

She laughed harshly. "Look around. This is a waste-not kind of world, isn't it?"

"But your planet is enriched and sustained by alchemy," xe said, then closed xist mouth with a tiny snapping sound.

It was true that alchemy had stopped the explosion that would have made their world as devoid of life as all the others like it that Scrimshaw had told her about. It held the bits of what Peridot used to be in place. Made it what it was now.

"Sustained, I'll give you that," she said, removing one hand from the wheel to tuck it against her chest. The winds were stiff enough, and they'd dropped altitude to fly low through the thinner air and colder skies, and now her fingertips were turning purple. "Don't think I'd call it 'enriched,' though."

She was quiet for a minute. Xe demonstrated xist kind's failure at filling burdened silences, so she pressed on.

"So that's what you're trying to learn, then?" She went directly for the question, figuring she'd muck up the diplomacy if she kept tiptoeing around the matter, and xe'd shut down on her without giving a better hint. "How to unlock alchemy to bring your world back?"

Scrimshaw regarded her in silence, those dark sapphire eyes revealing none of the workings going on behind them. She had to wonder what orders xist captain gave, aside from helping with communications. Xe was not typically shy to demonstrate xist knowledge—except where it seemed to reveal anything at all about xist people.

"At least," xe said after a cautious pause, and with what seemed like hesitation, "to prevent the destruction of the next one."

The joint arrival of a Cutter airship and the Yu'Nyun starship did not escape notice at the port city of Talonpoint, on the edge of Fall Island. At first, there were only curious onlookers, those who had already been along the raised dock structure. But others ran back toward the high walls of Talonpoint's proper city, and soon their audience grew. At the crowd's periphery, Talis saw the gleaming tips of halberds marking positions taken up by the local security forces.

The docks were inland, raised off the ground. Fall Island was named for the cascades of sand that tumbled from its edges, an endless supply that overflowed upward from a source somewhere underground in the heart of the vast desert. Docks built at the island's coastline would be worn away too quickly, and the pouring sands would make it dangerous to those crossing to and from their ships. Airships had landing gear, retractable feet for cases where the ships' engines would be powered down and the lift balloons allowed to slack. Instead, *Wind Sabre* had engaged her grappling anchors. Even though the journey to the temple and back would take several days, Talis wanted her ship ready to move.

The Yu'Nyun starship settled onto tripod feet which separated from the smooth hull on hinged legs, and the maw of its hatch opened downward, landing with a thud on the dock below. It was as silent as ever, so Talis had no way to know whether the alien ship had powered down its systems, or if they, too, were prepared to leave at a moment's notice.

A field of dark-skinned faces filled the docks around the two ships and Talis itched under the weight of the secrets they needed to keep. She ordered Dug to lower the boarding ramp from their lower bay. He gave her a long look but followed the order without comment. Shirtless, as he'd understood her intent, he opened the hatches wide and made a show of turning the crank, lowering his scarred self and the platform to within hopping distance of the ground.

The crowds were quick to spot him and pulled back a fair distance from their berth. So long as no one committed any offense on this trip, she knew the sovereignty of a ship's captain would keep Dug from harm. As long as he didn't actually step foot onto the island, where his presence alone would be considered a crime. As long as the aliens made no grievous offense to their goddess.

Talis dressed for the desert, protecting as much of her skin from the sands as possible. Slim twill pants tucked into her boots. Long flowing cotton blouse with a high collar, which she'd bought on another Bone island. A scarf that she wrapped around her hair and looped generously about her neck so that it could cover the lower half of her face if she tugged it up a bit. Goggles on her head, ready to pull down against the sand and the glare of ocean-filtered Nexus off the dunes. Fingerless gloves.

She looked down at the revolvers on her desk, weighing the decision. If all were right in the world, she shouldn't need them. She knew how to behave among Bone. For years she had considered Dug's village a second home. She was going on a peaceful pilgrimage to bring diplomatic emissaries to a house of worship.

But all was not right with the world. Hankirk had put the wind up her back, and as the distance grew between the storm cloud and *Wind Sabre's* aft, she couldn't help but feel it had been a mistake not to lock him in the makeshift brig in their cargo hold. She'd installed the steel-barred compartment after a client hired her to transport an exotic pet he'd purchased a few islands away. It ate the mattress in her cabin before they realized the 'pet' was, in fact, a wild animal fresh out of the jungles. Talis had to sleep in the crew's quarters for a week until they got the animal to its new owner and she could reclaim her ruined captain's quarters. Rather than swear off such errands, she'd invested in the cage. Even if they never had to transport another saber-tooth gryphon, she figured on it coming in handy for locking up sensitive cargo while they were in docks. The aliens' first payment was behind those bars at the moment, but maybe she should have swapped it for Hankirk's miserable self, just to keep an eye on him.

It occurred to her that she might be protecting the man. Dumping him on that island kept Dug from Hankirk as much as it kept Hankirk away from her. Not for the first time, she wondered at her reluctance to kill him. She'd done others for much less, hadn't she?

But had she? Anyone else she'd killed, there'd been more of an immediacy to it. She was being attacked. They were going to hurt someone else. They were firing on her ship. They were faceless enemies threatening her life, her friends, or her livelihood.

Maybe she just knew Hankirk too well.

She shook herself from her musing and picked up the guns, slipped their holster over her arms, and clipped the buckle that rested below her breasts. Their weight was solid and uncomfortable against the sides of her ribs. Returning to dig around in her wardrobe locker, she found a long sleeveless vest, also in the Bone style. A gift from Dug's late wife. It hung only a few inches above the ends of her long blouse, as if they were made for each other. Pinning the vest closed in front with an expensive turquoise cameo as long as her index finger, she thought she'd done a rather good job of dressing herself for a Bone temple visit. The vest would not disguise the bulging shapes of the weapons beneath her arms—that would require a jacket she was unwilling to wear in the desert heat—but it might at least come off as more polite. The guns were not quite as ready to draw as if they'd been bared.

Her mind full of death and consequences, Talis met Scrimshaw at the lower bay doors. Xe had xist few belongings with xin, including what remained of xist food in its mysterious unmarked barrel. They never had figured out how xe prepared xist nourishment. Xe would step off *Wind Sabre* and that was that. No more uninvited alien presence on her ship. She'd expected to feel relieved.

It wouldn't be accurate to say that their alien passenger had become a friend. After all, that vial xe squirreled aboard had endangered her ship. Beyond the contraband, though, he had managed to stay out of trouble. For an unwanted passenger, that was as large a compliment as she could give. She'd hosted other passengers whose money-glazed fingers left prints on everything and managed to turn up everywhere. Underfoot, joining inconvenience with irritating commentary, or questioning the way she ran her ship. Scrimshaw, either because xe sought to keep xist brittle limbs free of her grip, or because xe was accustomed to ship life, was skilled at not being in her way.

Talis had to admit that her curiosity regarding Peridot's alien visitors only increased after exposure to their linguist. Scrimshaw revealed just enough to make it clear that there was some strange mystery to their behavior, some odd drive to their mission that Talis might never uncover or understand. And just like a mother saying "I'll explain when you're older," the question of it needled in her mind. Sophie might be eager to absorb their language and siphon off their technological know-how, but Talis was far more concerned with learning how to read the aliens. Find their tells. Every race had one, surely that was a universal truth that extended beyond Peridot's skies?

Sophie was walking Scrimshaw down to the gangway, rattling off a list of questions she'd forgotten to ask previously, double-checking her pronunciation of words xe'd taught them, and sharing her own limited knowledge regarding Onaya Bone. It seemed like she wanted to say more, but at a severe look from Talis, she finally said her goodbyes and ran back to her post.

The murmur from the gathered crowd escalated as Scrimshaw disembarked. If anyone present had entertained the notion that the two ships' simultaneous arrival had been a coincidence, that theory was dead now. The crowd shifted, and she saw some children lifted onto shoulders for a better view. She tried her best to ignore them all. Tisker stepped out and watched the crowd, his hand resting casually but meaningfully on the gun stowed at his hip.

Talis couldn't ignore the increasing volume of the crowd as a Yu'Nyun escort greeted Scrimshaw on the docks beneath their starship. Two of them came forward and claimed Scrimshaw's luggage. The others formed a triangle around xin, and the group disappeared up the ramp.

Talis realized she'd assumed that Scrimshaw would be among those going to the temple, but she'd never actually asked. Had she seen xin for the last time?

There was silence, then, from the Yu'Nyun ship. Talis stepped over to Tisker's side, her back to the crowd, and went over the orders she wanted them to follow while she was gone. Dug was to remain on the ship. He already knew that, but she wanted Tisker and Sophie to know it, too, just in case Dug got a rabid thought in his head and decided to take his foul mood to one of the bars behind Talonpoint's walls. She reiterated that they were not to cause trouble, which of course Tisker already knew. But he solemnly promised that they would all be on their best behavior while she took the aliens to stir up whatever trouble *they* had in mind. She shot him a look for that comment, but it struck home.

Her crew would keep her ship safe. The rest was up to her.

CHAPTER 24

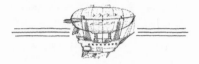

A FEW HOURS LATER, FOUR aliens emerged from the Yu'Nyun ship, stepping down onto the sandy Talonpoint docks. Talis let out a breath she hadn't realized she was holding when she saw Scrimshaw among the party. That she was even able to pick xin out from the other three was something of a point of interest to her. She recognized xin at a distance by xist uniform, but confirmed it when she approached and saw the familiar motif in xist body carvings. She had noticed it when they first met, at the ball where arm met shoulder blades. Later she'd realized that it repeated on xist left temple and the side of xist right forearm. She had to admit, if only to herself, that she'd picked xin out by those details alone, not by any variations in the structure of xist face, as she would a friend. It was more like looking over a group of similar horses and identifying her own by the marking on its coat. Or worse, the details of its saddle.

Also in the small group was the captain, who advanced with enthusiasm to greet Talis in xist stiff accent. Talis realized Scrimshaw had never actually explained their genders to her. The aliens seemed to show no secondary characteristics to indicate their sex, and she had to assume the loincloths hid any primary. Their body types looked identical to her. But Scrimshaw had said the Yu'Nyun lived on their ships and were prolific. So there had to be another gender type somewhere, and wouldn't it be more efficient to mix the crew than to separate them? Maybe Sophie had thought to ask about it. Then again, that seemed like just the sort of question that Scrimshaw would have dodged. She abandoned hope of figuring that out. Get them to the temple, get them their interview, and then who would care what gender the aliens are as they're leaving Peridot behind?

The veiled Representative of Commerce also joined them, along with a fourth alien that Talis was not introduced to. She supposed xe was a guard, though xe carried no weapons. Xe did not acknowledge her, so she ignored xin in kind. She was far more curious about the Representative's presence, when the captain had been clear that xist role was limited to monetary discussions. Were they going to bribe Onaya Bone for the information they needed? Or her priestesses, to ensure the meeting even happened? Talis almost laughed at the thought. They'd gotten *Wind Sabre*'s help with the flash of money, sure, but Cutter smugglers were as far different a breed from Bone priestesses as she could imagine.

If the two ships could have put down right over the temple, Talis could be done with this business in hours. But the pilgrimage to the Temple of the Feathered Stone was a cultural necessity. An act of proving oneself against Onaya Bone before one could enter her sacred places. To do this right, they couldn't moor closer than a day's ride through the hot sands.

Of course, the pilgrimage could also be a total farce if one had means, and comfortable litters could be hired in which to make the journey. Considering all the delicate skin exposed by the depth of the Representative of Commerce's carvings, and that she had the money to spare, Talis elected to hire such transportation. The winds sweeping across the undulating landscape brought sand to Talis's eyes as she arranged for their passage.

The aliens stepped up into the shade of the luxurious taxi, and Talis looked back to see Dug watching her from the lower transom. They exchanged a long silent look.

What Dug wanted her to do, exactly, she couldn't be sure. It was too late now to go back and turn down the contract. Too late to pull a fast one on the aliens and renege on their agreement, as it sounded like Hankirk had done. Too late, moreover, to go back and never take that salvage run for the ring.

She tightened her lips, willing Dug to understand, then turned from him and climbed into the pillowed cabin with her Yu'Nyun clients.

To best distribute their weight for the bare-chested strongmen that would carry their taxi, one of the aliens—the one she'd never met—sat beside her on the rear-facing cushioned bench of the passenger compartment.

Talis felt a twinge of surprise and disappointment that Scrimshaw remained opposite, seated between xist captain and the Representative, whose name was apparently less important than xist function. She was not feeling her previous aversion at being in a tight space with the foreigners. It had almost been a relief to climb into the car with them and get out from under the gaze of her best friend.

She needed a stiff drink, but the icebox in the litter provided only skins of water for their journey.

Back among xist crewmates, Scrimshaw was less talkative than xe had been aboard *Wind Sabre*. Either xe was constrained by some dictate of rank or xe could not find a place to speak for xist-self around the enthusiastic discussions xist captain initiated. For hours they talked about climate, cultural identity—that of the Cutter folk and Bone of course, not the Yu'Nyun—and all that the alien had learned in the libraries of the Rakkar. Scrimshaw assisted when a word needed help, but otherwise xe remained quiet and still, matching the behavior of the Representative and the fourth alien.

Despite the heat and wind, they opened the litter's curtains when the cabin master called out the next morning that they were approaching the Temple of the Feathered Stone. Talis pulled her goggles down against the outside light, and the Yu'Nyun closed their translucent nictitating eyelids.

A tableland rose before them, standing proudly against the line of Fall Island's distant edge. A gulch was formed by two high walls of wind-shaped stone, outlined in radiant green by the light of Nexus. Framing its mouth, two enormous statues of Onaya Bone towered several stories above their taxi, and the Yu'Nyun leaned out to appreciate their scale.

The stylized icons were carved into square pillars and painted with shocking, brilliant colors, in pigments that seemed to enhance the tones of the landscape. Each side of the pillars mirrored the others, showing the fearsome goddess gripping tight the hilt of a curving sword. The details of her carved features were maintained with care by the order of priestesses, so that the high arching sweep of her cheekbones and the length of her distinguished nose would not be worn away by the exfoliating sand that scoured the landscape. The eyes, painted a vibrant magenta, seemed to follow the small group, and Talis felt the gaze of the great stone Lady on her as they passed beneath.

An arching entrance dwarfed them as they left the litter behind and entered the temple. The stone image of an enormous six-eyed raven stretched its wings in welcome, or warning. Ketszali, the only creature of his kind. The impressive bird was Onaya Bone's preferred companion. The feathered guardian. Her favorite creation, her familiar and friend, whose plumage she styled after her own.

The feathers sculpted to frame his head were painted to suggest the purple and green tones of his iridescent color-shifting mane. The flesh around his dangerous, razor-edged beak and three pairs of eyes was sculpted to show the scaly and pebbled featherless surface. He was not a beautiful bird. As with the people Onaya Bone had created, tiny feathers began at Ketszali's temples, continuing out to the sides of a pair of dark eyes in the usual place behind his beak. The feathers were little more than enlarged pores at first, soft down above the brow ridge, growing larger until they were long and proud at the crown of the head. Four eyes, set sideways in his chest, formed a diamond around his heart and lungs. The raven's carved talons appeared to grip the frame of the doorway, which crumbled under his strength.

Talis breathed deeply of the cool air in the cavern beyond the arch. Without tinting from the Nexus-lit skies outside, the interior of the temple showed the true warm tones of the island's sedimentary rocks. They were patterned with vibrant blue turquoise, and the architects of this temple had put the abundance of the mineral to use in their design. Lanterns flickered from the walls, and suspended chandeliers seemed to float in the darkness, their shades made from hand-carved panels of paper-thin stone, impeccably crafted to be translucent enough to transmit light yet maintain their structure so as not to crumble like chalk. The warm colors of the sandstone contrasted with the semi-precious turquoise, and the walls undulated to create a structured swirl of blue and orange, spiraling over the center of each room and then sweeping toward the floors.

The aliens stood beneath the archway, double-blinking at the darkness within, their faces unreadable as ever. Even their talkative captain seemed influenced by the hush of the temple, and made no comment as they waited to be received.

In the center of the great hall, a carved fountain was sculpted directly out of the existing rock so that there were no seams or joins. Sand flowed from some deep spring, up through the mouth of another Ketszali statue to pour over his shoulders down into the collecting pool below. Hooded acolytes raked the sand across an iron grate set into the floor. It flowed out of sight, almost fluid in its appearance, leaving behind chunks of the blue-green turquoise that were too big to fit through the filter. Another acolyte collected the stones in a woven basket to be taken to the temple artisans who would turn the unformed shapes into more works of art in Onaya Bone's name.

Depicting the various moods and interests of the Lady, the walls of the great chamber were carved with additional relief: Onaya Bone performing an alchemical ritual on a great curved sword, Onaya Bone holding Ketszali on her forearm, the bird appearing normal in size compared to her impressive height.

On the wall opposite the entrance, over the heavy doors that led deeper into the convent, another relief of the goddess wore goggles and held a bell-shaped flask filled with darkness and another filled with light, the necks of which curved back down into their bodies and reconnected as a handle in one continuous form.

To their right, over a stone table inlaid with turquoise tiles in its surface, where pilgrims left offerings and donations, a statue of the goddess stood out from the wall. Her right hand was lifted to shoulder height, drawing sand from the nothingness that remained after the Cataclysm. In her left hand, palm facing upward, a pair of small figures were being shaped from the summoned grains: a tender depiction of the creation of the first Bone people. Only here was Onaya Bone's face shown with a softened expression, as a loving mother, her eyelids lowered and the corners of her lips curved upward.

The silence of the hall was striking. Acolytes went without speaking for their first five years in service to their

Lady. The wind outside and the shifting sands of the fountain hushed the quiet footsteps of those in training. Robed in sleeveless dark brown fabric that swept the sand on the floor as they walked, their clothing was minimal despite the chill in the shaded temple foyer. Sandals laced to their knees, and thin, gauzy material over simple body wraps that covered only their most intimate anatomy.

Their discipline was remarkable, considering the company Talis had brought with her. In a Bone temple, a Cutter woman was unusual enough to warrant stares, but you'd think she and her company were Bone peasants from Talonpoint, based on the response they received. Save for the lone figure who stepped forward out of the shadows to meet them at the entrance, the acolytes paid them no attention.

The senior acolyte, identifiable by a simple turquoise pendant hung from a golden chain, beckoned them to follow her. The veined walls pressed closer to them from the sides and above as the great hall bottlenecked into narrower passages leading deeper into the mesa. Here and there, blue light fixtures shone from niches carved into the walls. The style of the architecture was not so grand now. Plain steel doors were aligned at even distances without any indication as to what lay behind them. As familiar with the order of priestesses as Talis was, she knew they could just as easily be rooms meant for meditation or interrogation.

"TALIS! I was quite surprised to hear you came to visit me. It has been what? Four years?"

"At least that, High Priestess."

The chamber of High Priestess Illiya was yet another grand room carved into the stone. They had descended several staircases on their way in, and Talis had the sense that the high ceilings of these chambers, lit brightly with sconces and chandeliers to the very top, were still below ground level.

Centered in the wall opposite them was another fountain of sand. Unlike the freestanding sculpted one in the great hall, this fountain poured from the wall out of a thin horizontal slit, part of a relief carving of Fall Island itself. From the edge, the sands cascaded down, tumbled over rock outcroppings and then a smooth wall punctuated with stars, which were shaped by turquoise lenses in the wall that hid candles in spaces behind.

The high priestess stood by a large desk on the right-hand wall, overseeing the organization of the temple's sacred archives. She wore a black robe with high sculpted shoulders and draping folds that simulated the rounded posture of a winged bird at rest. The fabric tapered at the ankles, and loops of metallic color were sewn into it in patterns of blue, purple, red, and glistening black. An elaborate golden-beaded necklace began at her throat and grew larger and heavier, coming to rest over her rib cage. Set with cabochons of turquoise in a vertical line of varying sizes, the jewelry lengthened her graceful neck and shimmered with the slightest movement. Beneath the necklace and robe, she wore the same tight wraps and gauzy material as the other acolytes. Talis suspected that Illiya had donned her cape and finery only upon hearing that she had such unusual visitors. It was a far cry from the minimal leather vest and pants she had favored when Talis last worked with her.

Behind the high priestess, carved in gently sloping terraces, a library rose from the floor to the ceiling. There was no wooden furniture here; the sand was too abrasive. The stepped shelf systems were home to stacks of scrolls tucked into cubbyholes lining the walls. On each landing were several workstations, where more female acolytes laboriously copied ancient writings by hand, a new generation of codices faithfully reproduced from the last before time could erase them. A multitude of quills scratched across a multitude of parchments, sounding much like the sand being swept in the lobby above.

Talis gestured for the aliens to step forward. "High Priestess, allow me to introduce the captain and officers of the Yu'Nyun starship."

Talis allowed the aliens to speak their own names as they greeted the priestess. She had practiced the captain's name under Scrimshaw's tutelage before they left *Wind Sabre*, but it was so similar to the future-tense for 'destroy' that she was almost certain she'd screw up and say the wrong one. Wouldn't *that* have been a wonderful moment of cultural understanding.

The Yu'Nyun captain treated Illiya with the greeting of respect from a subordinate, the one Talis had been stopped from performing when they met. Perhaps the aliens had some concept of religion. Or at least they knew of the gods and the local emphasis on religious piety from all their digging around in Peridot's libraries.

Illiya made an undulating sweep of her hand, in the traditional Bone gesture of welcome. Her fingertips were capped in bronze and flashed in the firelight. "I bid you welcome to this house of Onaya Bone, Talis and friends."

There was a certain, barely distinguishable weight given to the last word, and Illiya's ornately dressed hair bobbed with the slight tilt of her head.

She lifted a graceful arm to invite them to sit on stone benches, covered in layers of pillows and blankets, in front of the fireplace to their left. It was twice as tall as the formidable woman, carved from rock around them. Crackling flames chased back the chill in the subterranean cavern.

Illiya hosted the aliens with all the formality of her rank, offering tea and cakes, which the aliens declined. On the surface, all seemed to be going well, though every time Talis's gaze met Illiya's, there was a silent—and very pointed—question waiting for her.

Talis cleared her throat to dislodge a crumb from the honey cake she had accepted, and a cacophony of raven calls shattered the quiet, an abrasive interruption to the peace of the room. The birds, varied in size but identical in plumage, lifted from their perches and swooped down at the new arrivals, barely missing the tops of their heads. The aliens flinched, ducking out of the way in alarm. As a group, the birds surged up into the air in a frenzied tornado of glistening black feathers, then resettled onto their roosts and began to preen themselves in indignation. At a small workstation near the roosts, a robed woman worked by herself, quietly making quills from a large basket of collected feathers. She did not look up at the commotion.

When the noise faded, the silence that followed compelled Talis to get down to the point of their visit.

"High Priestess, I promised the Yu'Nyun a chance to seek audience with Onaya Bone."

"Did you, now?" Illiya asked. Her lips, as they curved into a smile, pressed tightly together. There was a glitter in her eyes, but it was not amity. "I understand they have made this request many times. I wonder why I should be the first to allow it?"

Because I saved your wretched life, rot you. But Illiya wanted a reason that Talis could speak out loud.

"They have been trying to conclude their research. They would like to understand how The Divine Alchemists saved Peridot from the destructive forces of Cataclysm, so that they might save their own planet."

Scrimshaw's captain looked sharply at the interpreter. No wonder Scrimshaw had been so quiet. Xe had shared more than xe was supposed to, and Talis had just ratted xin out.

"Once they have the answers and the closure they seek," Talis continued, pretending not to notice, "they will be able to move on."

"Lost children of the stars," Illiya murmured. She

intertwined her fingers over her stomach, looking downward for a moment. A decision seemed to come to her. She lifted her chin.

"I will grant their audience," she said in a gilded tone, and to Talis the meaning felt as rich.

The high priestess instructed her acolytes to make ready the alien guests while she prepared the communion chamber and sought Onaya Bone's attention. They stepped forward to drape the Yu'Nyun with iridescent scarves in purple, black, and green, and to sift fine sand over their heads. Alarmed at these preparations, the fourth alien looked desperate to avoid being decorated in a way that was equal to xist superiors. But the Yu'Nyun leader held out a hand to stop the underling's protests. Talis had gleaned the significance of that from Scrimshaw's lessons, enough to be impressed with the captain's tolerance of a major taboo in order to accommodate the local custom. But why not? The captain was mere steps away from attaining xist goal. A little breach in etiquette was a small price to pay, even for the Yu'Nyun.

Two acolytes walked on either side of the group as Illiya led them to an enormous door at the far side of the audience chamber. Mirroring the position and size of the hearth, the door was the only wooden feature in the room. It looked ancient, its dark surface rich and shining from generations of oiling. Iron hinges affixed it to the wall and a matching latch held it shut. It was an anomaly, unworn by the omnipresent sand.

Illiya led the aliens in, and the door closed behind the group, leaving Talis in the receiving room with the silent acolytes.

CHAPTER 25

ILLIYA'S ACOLYTES SERVED TALIS iced mint tea and showed her back to the padded stone settee in front of the hearth. She chewed on a stray piece of fresh mint leaf and stared into the flames.

She turned quickly when she heard the door grate open again, and the cold tea splashed over her fingers. Illiya emerged alone.

"The Lady has granted them an audience," she said, then dropped her affectations. She strode across the room and threw herself, robes and all, onto the settee with Talis. "What fermenting wastewater have you gotten yourself mixed up in, old friend?"

Talis held out the mint tea. Illiya smirked, then reached into the inside of her cloak and pulled forth the chased and jeweled silver flask that Talis suspected would be there. Her old friend never drank anything innocent. The high priestess poured a generous amount into Talis's glass, then reached out to accept the fresh tea, half-empty, that an acolyte brought for her. She emptied the rest of the flask into that glass.

Talis shifted to face Illiya and leaned back into the

pillows behind her. "I got myself mixed up with an Imperial captain who set me up with a bad contract, tried—though thankfully failed—to shoot me out of the skies, and left me no course but to make a deal with aliens."

Illiya took a long sip of her tea, making it look like a meditation.

"Would this Imperial captain be Hankirk, the old flame, by any chance?"

Talis would have rebutted the romantic implication, but she was too surprised. Of course, Illiya being one step ahead of the game was hardly shocking. "And, I assume, the power of all his Cutter-crazed friends behind him."

Illiya nodded. "And you sold the aliens the ring."

"You know about that, huh?"

"Wouldn't be much of an intelligence agent if I didn't."

Talis tilted her cup back until the ice hit her teeth.

"What would you have done?"

"Refused the salvage job."

Talis coughed a laugh around the last sip of her drink. Welcomed the light feeling it sent up her shoulders to the sides of her head. "Advice I'd happily go back and give to myself as well, believe me."

Illiya pulled one long leg up and tucked it under the other. "Onaya Bone wants to speak to you next."

Now she really coughed, sitting up to place the emptied glass on the table between them and the hearth. "*Helsim's cavernous colon*, are you kidding me?"

"Blasphemer. Though I like that one. Not certain what it means, but I like it."

"'Blasphemer' is exactly my point. You gonna send me in there so I can get myself zapped out of existence?"

"I'd like to be present."

"Like to see it, yeah, I bet you would." She chewed her lip. "Don't suppose I can decline?"

"You could. But could you really live not ever knowing

what she wants to say?"

Of course she couldn't. Of course she'd go.

Talis squeezed her eyes shut, wishing she hadn't invited Illiya to spike her tea. Talk to the goddess, why not?

THE DOOR WAS MADE from petrified wood, Talis saw as she stepped past the aliens on their way out of the communing chamber. More stone than what it once had been. And the striations, up close, played into the temple's name. Cellulose grain, cut at a diagonal, so the lines swept back from their cores like the individual strands of a feather.

Her nostrils filled with the warm air beyond the doorway as she stepped through, Illiya's hand on the small of her back. It smelled of heavy spices, of sand, and of feathers. She glanced back toward the fire where the Yu'Nyun were being freed of the ceremonial garb by acolytes who carefully lifted the robes over the aliens' arching head crests. They appeared agitated, and she wondered if Onaya Bone had denied them the answers they came for. Or if the answers were no help to them. Or too cryptic to decipher. With Onaya Bone, the aliens would have faced their equal in enigmatic indirect conversation.

The cone-shaped room was lined with an obscene amount of copper. Engraved and studded in swirling patterns, and burnished between, it reflected the warm lighting but no distinct images. Small candles flickered from tiny alcoves up and down the length of the wall. The flames and their velvet-soft reflections in the metal walls pulsed with life.

Neatly folded bits of cloth were suspended from the high ceiling, delicate chains formed from generations of the prayers and wishes of Bone supplicants.

On the polished turquoise of the stone floor, neatly

centered in a circle of age-worn cushions, sat a bronze censer. Its surface was perforated with the shapes of flying ravens and etched with designs of blowing, swirling sands. Heavy purple smoke poured from it and collected along the floor like morning fog. The space was meant for meditation, for those who entered the room but were granted no audience. As with those worshippers whose cloths dangled above her head, prayer would have to serve when Onaya Bone did not deign to communicate directly.

Reassuming her role of high priestess, Illiya crossed the meditation circle to a curtained booth. Small tables on either side held more candles and incense. There was a common wooden-handled broom displayed on a stand, a strange companion to the rest of the room's objects. It was meant for use on her way out, to remove any dust that entered with her. The sand that was a part of daily Bone temple life was a threat to the room's central feature, which awaited her behind the curtain.

Illiya motioned for her to approach, and Talis found her feet reluctant to move. Once she had seen Silus Cutter and Lindent Vein together at a parade for the rare occasion when their worship holidays fell on the same day, but it had been at a distance. She had been part of a crowd, lost in a sea of faces, not summoned into their presence or singled out.

She fidgeted with the hem of her shirt. Illiya hadn't made her wear the drapings the Yu'Nyun had. That had been purely meant to make them uncomfortable, a fact which she'd confessed to Talis with a pleased grin.

The curtain pulled back to reveal a hulking mass of Pre-Cataclysm 'tronics lurking in the darkness. A display screen mounted several hands above eye level glowed green, tilted down at the empty space in front of it. Behind, snaking machinery connected it to a cabinet on the floor. The metal enclosing it was dark and, in the glow of the screen, seemed just a shadow. It would have been impressive, if Talis hadn't seen the crisp alien display screens that fooled her into thinking they were windows, or the portable tablets that ran off unseen power packs and weighed less than a dinner plate.

Illiya monitored something on the back of the cabinet, then looked to Talis. "The connection has been established. Come closer, hurry."

Prompted by the tone of Illiya's voice, Talis took an automatic step forward, standing in the indicated spot—a purple mandala painted on the floor two paces in front of the display screen. She had to tilt her head back to look up at it. It was likely no coincidence that the posture made her immediately uncomfortable. Discomfort was an art that the order of Bone Priestesses had perfected over seventy-five generations.

A flicker of light and a strange thump sounded once, then the goddess's image appeared on the glossy screen. Her form was rendered in shades of green. She leaned forward, moving her head in a thoughtful scanning arc, as though peering into a tank of shellfish to pick one for her supper.

"Illiya, my child, is this the one?"

The goddess wore an apron over a form-fitting sleeveless tunic. She adjusted a pair of welding goggles on her forehead and Talis saw that she wore heavy gloves as well. Her dark plumage was bound back at the nape of her neck, and feathers framed her shoulders. Behind her, out of focus and blurred, were the contours of arcane mechanisms, books, equipment, and ingredients, spread out across a flat surface.

"It is, Holy Mother. I present Talis, of *Wind Sabre*."

Talis swallowed.

"Child," the goddess said, leaning forward and peering at her. "You are neck-deep in a bog of sacrilege and treachery."

Talis looked to Illiya for help, but the priestess was watching the screen and offered no cues.

"Please, Bone Mother, guide me," said Talis. No point in denying the accusation. She'd been sensing it all closing in around her, and Onaya Bone almost certainly knew the wider landscape of it.

"The invaders have a ring that once belonged to my co-hort, Lindent Vein."

"Rotten hells."

Talis froze, mortified at the slip, however inevitable.

"Indeed," was all the goddess said in recognition of the vulgarity. "Illiya tells me they promised to leave our planet after speaking with me."

"Yes, Bone Mother," she said, quickly following with: "It was the only reason I agreed to it."

"Were you not given one million other reasons?"

Caught. Hand in the till.

"I was, Bone Mother, which seemed a personal benefit that was far dwarfed by the idea of the aliens' departure."

Onaya Bone scratched an itch on her face, unimpressed. The gloves left a streak of something dark across her divine nose. Talis was reminded of Sophie and her ever-present grease and coal smudges.

"In their audience with me," she said, looking as though she had stepped in something, "they demanded that we gods present ourselves before their ship and surrender."

Talis heard the scrape of Illiya's sandaled feet against the floor but her eyes were riveted to the image of Onaya Bone's face, watching her. The already dim room around her went black, and the lurid green moving image of the goddess filled her vision. Her eyes burned and started to water. The ludicrous and horrifying statement overloaded her mind, and she winced at the small unintelligible sound that escaped her lips in place of a proper response.

"Quite. The aliens you consort with travel in a scout ship, sent across the emptiness between stars to find planets with resources such as ours. Resources like Nexus. There is an armada—an invasion force—waiting for their signal."

Onaya Bone pulled off her gloves, dropping them somewhere out of the screen's view area. She then itched at the same scratch with one of her long, taloned fingers, before untying the apron and pulling it away. Talis heard a smack as the heavy material hit some surface on the other side of the transmission. The goddess sighed.

"Can you just . . ." Talis searched for a word, "Can't you *deal* with them? Um, Bone Mother."

As soon as the words came out of Talis's mouth, sounding even worse than they had in her head, she braced herself to be destroyed on the spot. Instead the goddess looked at her quietly for a moment. Her lip twitched. She took a deep breath and finally replied.

"There is a reason, I will confess to you, that we have not *dealt* with the alien invaders ourselves. We first saw their vessel when it was well beyond the reach of the planet's atmosphere, as they orbited Peridot and watched our peoples. Watched us. We approached them and made an attempt at contact. Whatever they hoped to learn about Peridot, they already had learned it, at that point so long ago."

"But then why . . . ?" Talis couldn't think straight. Whatever Illiya had spiked her drink with was stronger than she expected. What was the point of the million blasted press-coins if the aliens had already spoken to the gods, and already knew whatever they needed to about the planet?

Onaya Bone leaned on one elbow and rubbed some stiffness at the back of her neck. She sighed.

"They demanded our surrender then, as well. The threat was less immediate at that time. Now they have Lindent's ring."

"If you knew what they wanted, Bone Mother," Talis said, feeling a tightness across her chest and a sour burning in her stomach. "Why were the aliens allowed to stay so long?"

Onaya Bone briefly flicked her eyes to the side, to where Illiya stood behind Talis.

"It is not common knowledge, but I suppose those who can use it against us already are aware: The alien ship's weapons are able to disrupt our alchemical abilities."

Talis felt a coldness grip her. It crept, sharp-legged, up her spine, and clamped down on the back of her skull. She felt woozy. The room shifted as though the stone mesa were no more substantial than the blowing sands.

"What does that mean, Bone Mother?" Talis asked. Refusing to accept that she *knew* what it meant.

"The aliens have the power to kill the gods," Illiya said, "and steal their power." Her voice was calm, still strong.

"You knew this?" Talis turned to her old friend.

Illiya flinched.

"All of our highest-ranking disciples were told," Onaya Bone said. Her voice was airy, low. Tired. "They have maintained the spirits of our children while we have been unable to directly walk among them."

The coldness found its way to her mind, and hit behind her forehead like a spark.

"Wait."

"Yes," said Onaya Bone. An invitation to continue, but an admission of what Talis had yet to ask.

"How do we know they can kill . . ."

But it was clear. The terrible truth hung in the room, made the air impossible to breathe.

Talis swallowed again. " . . . Who?"

Onaya Bone and Illiya exchanged a look. Onaya Bone put a hand over her heart, and Talis saw her shoulders rise with a deep breath.

"Silus Cutter."

CHAPTER 26

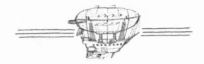

IT WAS AS THOUGH THE FLOOR fell away. Just gone. She was falling. Everything tilted, lurching angles that rushed past her vision.

Pain registered somewhere far away as her knees hit the hard floor. The palms of her hands followed. She felt sand, felt her fingernails scrape into the soft turquoise inlay. Her stomach heaved, and her throat burned with bile and the mix of tea and alcohol that revisited her throat. She croaked, high-pitched, in anguish.

"Talis," Illiya said, her voice as thick as cream and far away.

Firm hands clasped her shoulders. Talis shouted, terrified, and scrambled backward on her hands and the balls of her feet.

"Calm her, my child," Onaya Bone's voice said. "We may lose her."

Talis's chest burned. The room would not stop moving. She couldn't breathe.

There was a sharp prick at the base of her neck, and Talis shrank away from it, to the side. Illiya crouched beside her, a hypodermic needle held in her hand, its brass plunger pushed to empty.

"There now," she cooed. "You're all right."

Sounds went in and out of focus. The points of light in the room flared until it seemed Talis was inside one of the glowing pumpkins instead of a dark chamber. But Illiya was right. She was breathing. Her throat still burned, but it was with the pressure of a restrained battle cry.

Talis held a hand out and looked at it. Small, but capable of anything.

"What did you give me?" Her voice was bold. Tempered steel.

"Courage," said Onaya Bone. "To face what comes next."

"What comes next?" Talis asked.

"An armada of aliens waits in the darkness beyond Peridot's atmosphere. They are armed with the power they stole from Silus Cutter. We must be ready."

Talis *was* ready. Ready for anything. She itched to run. But not away, not anymore. She climbed to her feet, which were steady again.

The room felt cool, but she was warm. Somewhere a memory tickled her, of Illiya's carefully arranged case of pharmaceutical interrogation aids. The brightly colored vials nestled in silk-lined trays. The thirsty needles, waiting to be filled. A part of her brain that was keeping carefully out of the way told her she was drugged. That it would wear off, and she would again be overwhelmed by the devastation. But the rest of her mind stifled the thought, to hear what she would be commanded to do.

"Give me purpose, Onaya Bone."

"There is a power on this planet beyond alchemy," said the goddess. It seemed her fatigue was gone. She had let her hair down, and it lifted in some unseen wind and whipped about her head and shoulders. "Nexus is made of such power. The ring you retrieved also contained it. It is this energy the aliens wish to harvest."

"I *knew* it wasn't just some ugly ancient artifact." Talis spoke with confidence. Dropped the formalities of addressing the goddess. There was no need to be humble any longer. Her blood thrummed in her ears. A call to battle, beat on the drum of her warrior's heart.

"Certainly not," Onaya Bone said. Leather armor began to coalesce on her shoulders, neck, and collarbone, as if called out of thin air. "Lindent Vein's ring is one of five, each filled at the very instant the Cataclysm released all the energies of the planet. We alchemists crafted Nexus with the remainder of this power to make Peridot habitable again. Its power shields us from direct attack, but we cannot wield it against the Yu'Nyun without risking the planet's integrity.

"The rings' power, however, is mobile. Stronger, and it can be unleashed. By combining the strength of all five rings, we will create a weapon that can turn away the alien invasion and ensure Peridot's safety against any other threats that find their way to our world."

Illiya took hold of Talis's right hand, and Talis watched eagerly as the high priestess produced a small tool with an intricate metal design welded to one end. She depressed the flat end of it with her thumb, and in moments the branding plate glowed red hot.

Purpose and righteousness flowed through Talis's veins as Illiya pushed the brand against the inside of her forearm. Talis smelled the flesh sear. Felt the thrill run up her arm, all electric.

"All who see this mark will know you serve my purpose," Onaya Bone said, sitting up straight, shoulders back, her eyes burning with fire. Somehow, despite the green tint to the screen, Talis saw the magenta of the goddess's eyes as plainly as if she was in the room. "Get the ring back from the aliens and bring it to me at Nexus."

Talis bowed to the flame-silhouetted figure on the

screen, then turned and marched herself, unescorted, from the room.

IN THE HIGH PRIESTESS'S CHAMBER, the acolytes stood over the crumpled bodies of the four aliens. Slain. Wretched piles of pale limbs. Vicious tri-bladed daggers dripped blue blood. Scrimshaw lay atop the Yu'Nyun captain, arms outstretched, as though xist last act had been in defense of xist commanding officer.

Talis inhaled their dusty smell and the acrid tinge in the air that must have been their blood. It sent cascading prickles down the length of her arms. Her fingers twitched for the weapons in her holsters.

"Load their bodies into the litter," she said, confident in her right to command the acolytes. "I will return them to their ship before I blow it out of the skies."

"OH *GODS, NO.*" It was as though a fog was lifting from her mind. But rather than a sense of clarity, all Talis felt was dread. Dread and panic. Dread, and panic, and something like food poisoning. She struck the side of her head against the door frame of the dark taxi cabin. "No, no, no, no, *no.*"

Whoever that bloodlusting woman had been, she was gone. Illiya's drug had worn off, leaving her nauseated and shaking somewhere in the middle of the desert road between temple and port city.

Talis sat with her arms wrapped around herself as the litter bounced along. Ankle-deep in the bodies of her alien travel companions.

In the span of a single breath Talis cursed Illiya's name along with Onaya Bone's (because, really, what was the goddess going to do to her that she hadn't already?). And especially, she cursed her own.

She didn't think *she* had killed them. Remembered sapphire blue blood dripping from vicious dagger tips. The hands that gripped the ornate blades had been dark-skinned and talon-tipped. Not hers.

But that mattered little. Talis was the one who would emerge from the litter in front of the alien starship with its dead officers.

Then a wave hit her. Desolation. Aching emptiness.

Silus Cutter is dead.

And she was kneeling among his murderers.

Disgust, rage, grief. They pushed up through her throat like the steam through a constricted boiler valve, and she let out another wail, half scream and half prayer. She clutched at her prayerlocks with both hands and tugged, harder and harder, as if by that motion of worship she could bring a dead god back into existence.

Something touched her arm and she screamed, now in terror.

From the pile of tangled limbs, Scrimshaw reached out xist hand in a silent plea. Blood, dark in the curtained litter, welled up and seeped from a jagged wound across the front of xist torso. The strike xe'd earned in protecting xist captain, a dagger slash that was angled wrong for the killing blow. It had destroyed xist carapace but left xin alive.

Talis panicked. Relief that the murders that would be laid at her feet were lessened by one collided with the impulse to crush xist head under her boot.

"*Sneak*," hissed xist voice in that awful accent, barely audible. Spoken with wrenching effort. Here at the moment when she has to decide xist fate, xe chooses *that* word.

She pressed back, as far from xin as the confines of the

litter would allow.

"You lied to us," she said.

Her throat was on fire. Her arm hurt where the swirling lines of Onaya Bone's mark was seared into her flesh. The skin was red, almost purple, and the slightest turn of her wrist or bend of the elbow hurt like hell.

Scrimshaw laid xist head down, weak. Xist cheek rested on the leg of the former Representative of Commerce. Blood soaked the delicate veil.

"Withheld the truth," xe said. Xist nictitating eyelids blinked slowly, and did not fully open again.

Talis glared at xin. "Whatever you call it," she said through clenched teeth. "You got what you deserve."

"We all do . . ." Xe paused for a moment, resting. ". . . what we must to survive. Act for what we believe is the greater good of our people."

Sometimes, she thought. *And other times we act selfishly and court disaster.*

She'd almost sold out her world for a million meaningless presscoins. If she couldn't get that ring back, it was as good as done. But how in five hells was she going to manage that?

Scrimshaw pushed xist-self up from the floor of the litter, sat up as straight as xe could, and leaned back against the seat opposite Talis. A fresh flow of blood spilled over the edges of xist wound.

"Finish me."

"Don't tempt me."

"You won't kill me?"

She considered. "No. At least not yet. You may have value as a hostage."

Xe gave a sharp coughing rasp. It was a rueful laugh, which brought more blood out of xist wound.

"I have no value at all, damaged as I am."

"You'll heal."

"I will scar."

Xe held xist hands out, away from the wound. It was a nasty crack in xist carapace, along the middle of xist torso where the heart might have been if xist organs were arranged at all like those of Peridot's people. But apparently the Yu'Nyun heart hid elsewhere. All the same, the damage was extreme, the carapace plating broken off, leaving a wide expanse of ragged blue flesh. A scar was guaranteed.

"The Yu'Nyun do not accept an imperfect being. This scar will remain with me. Ruin my future molts. I will be branded with this damage if I survive. I would be expected to disappear quietly and kill myself, and treated by the others as one who is dead already."

"Over a *scar*?" She thought of the map of scars she had. Then thought of Dug, whose marks were also a death sentence.

"You wished to know, once, about the cultural implications of our carvings."

She hardly cared, now. It seemed a silly thing when The Divine Alchemists' plan was to blow the aliens' starship out of the sky. "I thought talking about it was taboo."

"It does not matter. I am Yu'Nyun no longer."

Xist posture had changed, she realized, from the creature who had been welcomed aboard *Wind Sabre*. A slight shift, she thought due to the injury. But she had to admit xe seemed more relaxed. As though who xe had been was a burden that xe was now free of. A freedom that would come with the deathblow xe requested.

She considered her options.

Kill xin, and sort out the aliens the old-fashioned way. Or . . .

'Sneak,' xe had said. And xe seemed willing to divulge the alien secrets now. Maybe she could use xin against xist own kind, as they'd used her.

"What if I want you to live?"

Scrimshaw tilted xist head and was quiet a long moment. Then, "Do you have a purpose I can live for?"

"Same thing I have. Freedom."

Scrimshaw turned xist head, reached out a hand and pushed back the curtain of the litter. Green light highlighted the contours of xist pale face. Traced the lines of the arching forehead, xist carvings, xist mandible, xist long slender neck. Swirls of warm and cool breezes danced through the small compartment, and a wash of sand scrubbed the stagnant air.

She waited. If xe didn't agree to help, xe would have to die. Which it seemed would happen anyway, if xe chose to return to xist ship. So did xe want to die alone among xist own people or with purpose as a useful agent of hers?

No doubt, though, that the Yu'Nyun would retract their boarding ramp the moment they suspected something was amiss. She'd have precious little time to get out of the litter and somehow get aboard. And no way to signal her crew before she arrived. The litter couldn't sit at dock, its passengers hidden behind the curtains, for very long before the aliens would expect their captain to emerge.

The communication pad. For all she knew, a report was already late in coming. They may have already sealed up tight back at dock, on high alert.

She was no closer to having a reasonable plan when Scrimshaw looked back at her and let the curtain fall back into place. The litter's interior was immediately stuffy again in the absence of the breeze.

"You want the ring back."

She nodded, anxiety playing havoc with her stomach. Or it might have been the smell of the dead aliens that had filled the space again.

"I can tell you where it is kept. But they would not let me board any more readily than they would you and your crew."

Talis was hoping for a guide, not a map.

"What if we cover the wound?"

"Recall your Yu'keem lessons. The uniform cannot be modified. An anomalous draping would raise more suspicion

than the captain not emerging from the transport when we
arrive back at the dock."

Her mind raced. The last of Illiya's drugs gave her a
heightened awareness, though the courage she felt was her
own. "Is your communicator still working? Could you send
a message? Say that the captain has decided to stay another
night, in the hospitality of the temple, to await Onaya Bone's
reply, but that I'm returning to my ship?"

"You would like me to instruct them, on the captain's
behalf, to pay you the remaining balance on the contract."

That sounded a little judgmental. Xe had a lot to learn
about her.

"I would, but largely for the purpose of distraction. To
make sure that access ramp is open. If we get the money we
were promised in the exchange, so much the better."

Xe was silent a moment. Then, with effort, xe retrieved
the tablet from xist pouch. The screen was cracked.

"Oh, *sucking winds*, is it broken?"

Xe played xist fingers across the screen, activating it.

"Only the surface," xe reported. "It is functional and will
still transmit."

Talis peeked out the curtain of the litter. Talonpoint was
still a thin dark line in the distance.

"Do it," she said.

She helped xin get seated in a dignified position, wiped
the blood off xist face. Xe held the tablet up above xist
chest level to conceal xist wound and keep the alien bodies
out of sight. The blueish light of the tablet lit xin with its
watery glow.

Before xe placed the call, she put a hand on xist arm.
"Don't you dare cross me again."

"I told you, Captain. I am Yu'Nyun no more. What can
I gain by warning them?"

"Vengeance, for one."

"Vengeance." Xe seemed to taste the word. "For what?

These corpses are no longer my people. They are dead and ruined. I am ruined, and only death awaits me if I return to the ship."

"For being orphaned, then."

Scrimshaw considered her for a moment. Xe blinked at her, xist thoughts unreadable.

All she could do was trust xin. The whole world was upside down, and her instincts were reeling. She removed her hand and nodded.

Xe placed the call. Spoke xist alien language while she silently watched, from the other side of the litter, for signs of betrayal. Of course, if it had been her in xist place, the first thing she'd have said was, "Don't react, but . . ." and she knew little enough of Yu'keem that it would be simple to send a warning she could not understand.

But the alien on the other end of the call did most of the talking, to which Scrimshaw made quick, sharp replies. Talis understood only a word here and there, and wasn't even certain of them at the speed the exchange was happening. Something was wrong. The aliens spoke in even tones, but her gut was sending her warning signals at full strength. She itched to reach for her guns, to point them at Scrimshaw and remind xin of what they'd agreed. But if xe hadn't lied about the whole 'condemned by xist scar' thing, she'd be doing xin a favor.

When the call was cut, Scrimshaw collapsed against the cabin wall behind xin, breathing heavily.

"Well?" she prompted.

"They were too preoccupied to be suspicious," xe said, pausing frequently to catch xist breath between words. "Something has happened at the docks."

At the docks. Talis felt a tightness grip her chest. "What happened?"

Scrimshaw opened and closed xist mouth and blinked slowly, xist eyelids drooping again. Xe shifted xist hips to sit up straight, which quieted the rasping that had been coming with each breath.

"The local authorities have arrested five members of the Yu'Nyun crew." Xe dropped xist head slightly. "As well as your first mate, the Bone man."

"Rot you, Dug!" She leaned her head back. "What were the arrest charges?"

Of course, Dug's existence alone was enough to get him arrested. Which was why he was supposed to stay onboard *Wind Sabre* while she was gone.

"The Yu'Nyun were charged with inciting a riot. Your man appears to have a more complicated situation."

She spared that a wry, frustrated laugh. Complicated was a good enough explanation for the Yu'Nyun. "So now what? Have they sealed up the ship and ruined our chances at getting the ring back?"

"No," Scrimshaw said. Xe placed the tablet on the seat beside xin, and let xist arms hang limp at xist sides. "They are sending a diplomatic party into the city with the expectation that they can negotiate payment of fines in exchange for the release of their officers."

"Bribe their way out, you mean." Talis frowned. If the Bone were edgy, money wouldn't be enough. The diplomats would likely end up arrested, too.

Scrimshaw closed xist eyes, either resting or nearly passed out from the pain and blood loss.

She leaned forward, reached out and prodded xist knee to rouse xin.

"So how much of the crew does that leave on your ship?"

CHAPTER 27

"**C**APTAIN!" SOPHIE'S STRAINED whisper came from out-side the litter.

Talis exhaled in relief. Scrimshaw said xe'd told xist people to expect her to come back alone, as they'd planned. Still, she'd spent the ride up to her armpits in alien blood and was not entirely certain how she would cross the last distance on the docks without someone noticing the dark drying blue against the ruin of her pale blouse.

But Sophie, having no idea Talis knew about Dug, rushed to the side of the litter as soon as it came to a stop.

Talis put only her head and shoulders out from the curtain, carefully keeping it pulled closed. Sophie was alone, by some miracle. Talis had been half-frightened that the mob on the docks would still be there.

"They've taken Dug," Sophie exclaimed before Talis could say a word. "Captain, he was only trying to help. The aliens were talking to the crowd—I think they said some-thing about Onaya Bone that someone didn't like, or some-thing—and it set off a real mess. Dug thought he could clear it up, but as soon as he stepped off the ramp, they arrested him."

"I know, Soph. I heard."

"Oh," was all Sophie said. Her eyes darted to the curtain pulled tight around Talis. "Something else going on, Captain?"

Talis pressed her mouth tight. The docks might be clear, but every grain of sand on Fall Island had ears. "There's been a complication. Have the litter pull up to block the line-of-sight between our gangway and the alien ship."

Sophie's expression screwed into a strange mix of confusion and frustration. "What about Dug?"

"Can't deal with that 'til you do as I say. Go."

But Sophie didn't move. She stared at her captain, one eyebrow up and mouth set in a firm line. Talis sighed and opened the curtain wide enough for Sophie to see past her into the litter. To see the three bloody, twisted alien bodies, and Scrimshaw unconscious on the bench.

She gasped. Talis shushed her.

"You were attacked?" she asked in a hushed, horrified pantomime of a whisper.

"Keep your voice low. I'm fine. Illiya's people did this, and Onaya Bone commanded it."

Scrimshaw stirred inside the litter, a soft rustle of the fabric they'd bound around xist wound. Sophie's eyes narrowed on xin.

"Just go," said Talis, before the flood of questions could start. "I'll explain, but we gotta move quickly."

Sophie looked at her, then nodded. She got the litter to pull up, around the bend of *Wind Sabre*'s hull and under her belly, out of view of the Yu'Nyun vessel.

As carefully as she could, Talis handed Scrimshaw down into Sophie's arms. Sophie's lip twitched, and she seemed to shrink from the touch of xist slack limbs, for the first time showing antipathy toward the alien. Talis frowned. If xe hadn't steered them wrong, Scrimshaw wasn't their enemy.

But by The Five, Nexus, and whatever hells could spare room, Sophie would need that aversion with what was to come.

Talis dropped down and took up half of Scrimshaw's weight as they climbed back into the hull of their ship.

The litter moved away, no indication of the grisly contents that Talis had left behind. The priestesses had arranged the litter bearers for her return trip. They would hide the cab for a time, Illiya told her, to allow some measure of surprise. But in less than a day, the alien bodies were going to be displayed on pikes in the center of Talonpoint's market.

In less than a day, the Bone were going to war.

"Come on, Scrimshaw, we need you."

Talis patted the side of xist face gently. They'd laid xin out on the surgery table in the med bay. Tried to stanch the bleeding in xist torso, but in the end had to spare the time to stitch xin up. Tisker had done it.

Since they'd come back on board, Tisker's face had been a mask. He asked no questions. Waited for explanation. Used his skills to patch up the alien who Talis promised—hoping that she was right—was on their side.

Broken shards of chitin were pulled out of the wound, and then Tisker did what he could to repair the exposed tissue. They didn't dare give Scrimshaw anesthetic, for fear of it being as incompatible as the local food was. Best they could do was stop the leak. Tisker washed the blood off his hands when he was finished, scrubbing the blue residue from under his nails.

"I have no idea if that will do more harm than good," he said, drying his hands on a cotton towel. He shrugged.

Scrimshaw uttered weak protests during the suturing but now was quiet. Xe had a sluggish pulse which they could only measure on the exposed tissue. They'd have to wait and see.

Talis ran her hands through her hair and habitually pulled on her prayerlocks. Sophie mechanically mirrored the pious gesture, and Talis closed her eyes. She hadn't told them yet. There was too much to do, and she needed them as sharp as they could be.

She felt sick, holding back that secret. Tried to convince herself that a small delay wouldn't hurt. Silus Cutter had been dead for nearly a year.

"We'll just have to do this on our own," Tisker said, voice flat. "What do you remember about the ship?"

Sophie bit her lip. Looked to Talis. "What about Dug?"

"When did they take him? How long's he been gone?"

"A few hours. It all happened this morning."

"He'll be safe for now," Talis said, desperately hoping it was true. She rubbed her arm. She'd applied Zeela's salve to the brand and it helped with the pain, but the skin still felt tight and she couldn't stop touching it, tracing the raised skin where Onaya Bone's sigil marked her. "We need to do this before the aliens stop focusing on their jailed shipmates and start paying more attention to us."

Sophie nodded at her. "Okay, where do we start?"

"Scrimshaw was going to draw us a map," Talis said. She patted xist face again, to no effect. "Without that, I've got no idea. The ring could be anywhere."

"You want to search the ship?" Tisker's opinion of that idea was clearly indicated by his raised eyebrow.

Talis took a short, steadying breath and squared her shoulders.

"I want to blow up the ship," she said. "Then search the rubble."

CHAPTER 28

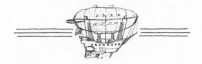

THE METAL RAMP TOUCHED down, and they waited in silence. After a moment, four Yu'Nyun stepped out. They were dressed in unadorned loincloths and armbands. *Lackeys*, Talis thought, and hoped that meant her absence from the exchange would not raise alarm.

The aliens paused for a moment, then made their way, a shining plastic coffer rolling between them, down to the docks where Sophie waited.

"Keep them busy," Talis had told Sophie. All the girl's enthusiasm for the aliens had left her.

Sophie was armed with paperwork documenting the contract. Between the formality of greetings and introductions, forms to sign, crate contents to verify, and language barriers to cross, Talis figured they had maybe twenty minutes at best. More if Sophie could convince them to let her count the money. It was highly inadvisable to do that right there on the docks where anyone could watch, with the ship empty except for a dying alien in their med bay. The full strength of the mob had not returned, but there were plenty of curious onlookers who gravitated to the scene when the aliens emerged from their ship. Talis didn't care. She just wanted to keep the aliens on the docks for as long as possible.

She and Tisker watched, crouched beneath the aliens' own access, as the clutch of birdlike toes pittered on the metal above their heads and the casters on the bottom of the crate made a smooth purr against the ramp. The group reached the ground, and the sound changed to an abrasive rumble on the uneven, sandy surface of the docks.

When the aliens had passed with some distance to spare, Talis nodded. She ducked out from under their hiding spot and vaulted onto the ramp. Tisker followed her up through the open hatch. The leather-soled boots they wore made a soft hush of their footfalls until they passed the bare metal entry chamber of the ship. Once beyond the inner hatch, the thin layer of flat-pile material made their steps completely silent. The quiet hum of the ship's systems enveloped them as they left the daylight behind. She allowed a moment for their eyes to adjust to the overly bright illumination, and then pushed forward.

They rounded the curve of a corridor and came up behind a Yu'Nyun crew member. By xist simple adornment, no one important. Tisker flicked a blade from its holder with the barest sound. Loud enough that the alien's head turned, but not before Tisker slipped it between the joins where neck met shoulders. A small sound, barely a gasp, escaped his victim and then Tisker caught the body as it fell forward.

Talis found and opened a small storage compartment with a touch on a wall panel, and Tisker tucked the alien inside, removing his knife only after the body was clear of the hallway. The door closed with a soft hum, slowly enough that Talis could see the blue blood drip and begin to absorb into the carpet.

The latch engaged again with a muted click.

They waited a moment, but there was no sound of alarm, no approaching footfalls from either end of the corridor.

Talis nodded to Tisker, and they continued.

Moving silently, as systematically as they could without a map, they took every chance to pass through doors along the interior bulkheads. Their aim was to get into the belly of the ship. Sophie's best guess put the engine room on a lower deck, balancing the weight of the round vessel. Scrimshaw didn't wake to confirm the theory before they needed to act.

There was an alien or two posted on each deck, and Talis and Tisker took turns killing them as quietly as possible. Despite the death that had accompanied Talis back from the temple, these were the first aliens she killed herself. She couldn't help but remember Scrimshaw's own brittle throat beneath her hands, and the shudder that trembled down her shoulders and back as she felt their necks crack between her forearms was only partially in disgust at the touch of the strange bodies beneath her skin. Each body was tucked into the nearest empty compartment.

She had no idea what they were looking for, exactly. Put a lot of faith in the hunch that she'd know it when she saw it. They opened hatches on crew quarters (thankfully empty), on storage compartments, on lifts. Finally, Talis started to recognize a pattern to the labels that flashed on the plastic panels beside each doorway, and they were able to skip berths and messes.

They encountered two doors with distinct markings. The first turned out to be a medical bay. Tisker shot her a look as they entered, loaded with the same thought she'd had, that it almost would have been worth dragging Scrimshaw along if they'd known they'd find the alien medical facilities. Tisker motioned toward the wall just inside the door, and Talis saw what he did: a portable case mounted at eye level. She pulled it free of the bracket that mounted it to the bulkhead and checked its contents. Despite the differences in their technology and their anatomy, she recognized the trappings of a field medkit. Handed it to Tisker, who slung its adjustable strap over his shoulder.

The second uniquely marked door was located three corridors in and two levels down. It opened on a dark room, no bigger than *Wind Sabre*'s modest galley. The bulkheads were lined with a bank of control panels which glowed dimly orange. There were five large alien crates arranged within the room, tall and narrow enough that it was easy to imagine Yu'Nyun hiding within, arching head and all. The crates stood like pale glossy monoliths. In front of each was a pedestal, with a clear acrylic tube mounted in the center and a black and orange-lit control panel.

The door slid closed behind them and soft lights came on as they stepped inside. It wasn't the engine room, but it might have saved them the trouble.

On the left-most pedestal, Lindent Vein's ring had been placed over the tube as if displayed on a jeweler's counter. The control panel of that pedestal was lit in blue and pulsed gently. A corresponding blue light blinked in time on the crate opposite.

"Can't be good, can it?" Tisker said, his voice still in a whisper. He bent down to eye-level with the ring. "Never wished I'd been born Vein before, but it could be handy now."

"As long as you're wishing, wish Scrimshaw was with us." She plucked the ring off the end of the little tube on its pedestal. "Because your captain probably just did something really reckless."

Tisker opened his mouth to reply, but he was cut off by a small soft tone. The blue light on the crate went dark. The lid opened, swinging toward them with a gentle puff of air.

"Sand and fire!" Tisker swore.

"See, what did I say? Properly reckless." Talis took a step back toward the door.

A Yu'Nyun form stepped forward from the crate. Its body was translucent, like condensation on a cold glass. Within, pearlescent pink and silver swirled, moving as the figure did. Not organs. Just . . . filling.

It was also naked.

Tisker brought up his knife, and the figure stopped. Blinked at them with pearlescent white eyes, disturbingly like a Vein's moonstone eyes. Except these were very clearly not blind. It looked from the knife up the connecting arm to Tisker, then turned to Talis.

"The ring is yours?" the goo-filled alien asked her. It used Cutter Tongue, not even the Common Trade that the translator pads used.

Talis swallowed against the thud of her racing pulse, which seemed to be collapsing her windpipe. "Yes."

"Please place the ring on your finger."

Talis turned to Tisker, who returned her confused look and shrugged. "Asked politely enough."

The ring was large, so she slid it on over her index finger, but still had to squeeze her fingers and bend the knuckle to keep it in place. The metal was warm, as though it had been left out in the heat of the desert.

The thing moved toward her, and she fought the instinct to take another step back. With each step, its gelatinous form shifted. The sweep of the head seemed to melt down its neck. Its body grew more stout, lost height as its feet shifted out of the tridactyl tiptoe position. The arch of its foot lengthened, bones pressed out of shape.

The translucence began to thicken, and its light faded as the skin became an opaque, rich brown. Talis was reminded of oak. Of nutmeg.

By the time Talis looked back up from the feet, its entire body had transformed into the shape of a Cutter woman.

Only it wasn't quite right for Cutter. She had strong cheekbones, like a Bone woman. But her nose was flatter and wider, and she had an underbite with the hint of large lower canines, almost like a Breaker. The warm brown skin was too far from Cutter golden, yet too pale for Bone. And the intense blue eyes were like nothing Talis had ever seen.

Small braids above the smooth forehead wove flat against her skin, keeping the hair out of her eyes. At the crown, the hair was loosed into a wild cascade of thick matted curls that reached to her hips. Some segments tangled like Talis's own prayerlocks, some in neat braids.

Pale blue dots of light marched in neat lines across her arms, stomach, and thighs. If Talis hadn't just watched her take form—and if the marks weren't glowing blue—she'd have said they looked like the stick-and-poke tattoos she'd seen bored mercs give each other on long expeditions. They crossed over the woman's frame, enhancing her contours. Sinuous. Muscle-bound. Her body was compact, but in the way a coil shrinks before it expands with all the strength of the metal behind it.

She was taut, strung like a bow. Waiting to be released.

She was a warrior. Talis knew it like she knew how to find her own nose.

And she was still naked.

"Thank you," the woman said. Her voice was dusk and smoke. The purr of a cat, the wind in tacking sails. The feel of rum hitting your belly.

She reached out to cup Talis's face between her hands. Standing up on tiptoes, she touched her forehead to Talis's own.

There was a snap of electricity that passed between them, then the woman stepped back and waited. Her arms held relaxed at her sides, her back straight and proud. There was no awkwardness to the pose, no impatience. She just waited.

"Cap!" Tisker hissed. His eyes were wide as saucers.

"Did you feel that?" Talis rubbed at her forehead, which still tingled. The feeling went deeper than her skin.

"Feel what? I *saw* that. Really something. But maybe we should go." His gaze darted to the door, as if expecting a troop of Yu'Nyun to rush in.

The woman watched her, silhouetted against the darkness of the empty crate. The other four crates remained closed and silent, their control pedestals dark. No rings, but their count made the clear intention to claim them all. Alien technology, interfaced with Pre-Cataclysm amulets.

"The aliens made you?" Talis spoke as the thought occurred to her. It didn't even feel like her own idea.

"This body," the woman replied. Talis thought she heard the hint of offended pride. "The mind is my own."

"Maybe you can help us find the engine," Talis said.

The woman made no response but walked swiftly past Talis and out through the automated doors.

Talis and Tisker exchanged a look.

"This day did not need to get any more interesting than it already was," Talis muttered, and motioned for Tisker to follow her out.

CHAPTER 29

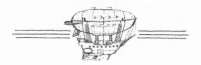

AT LEAST A DOZEN ALIENS appeared around the corridor, armed. Spotting Talis and Tisker first, they brought their rifles to bear on them.

The woman slinking along the bulkhead was upon the aliens before they saw her. She stepped into the center of the corridor and placed her palms on the chests of the first two. Bowed her head, appeared to be concentrating, maybe praying. Then they simply fell away.

Not down. *Away.* Their bodies were no more. Something splashed on the floor at her feet.

The Yu'Nyun crew stopped their advance, aimed their rifles at the stranger instead, but hesitated. They looked to each other. The one in front, nearest the woman, said something in Yu'keem.

The strange woman reached a hand toward the speaker, palm out, parallel to xist chest, and replied with a single word, spoken clearly in the alien language.

As a group, the aliens moved back a step. Whatever she was, they were afraid of her. Afraid to fire at her. Small red lights on the sides of their rifles went dark and they lowered the weapons.

The stranger advanced on the Yu'Nyun, one step at a time. They gave up ground, moving backward to match each step of the woman's. They held their rifles down, but ready. They didn't turn, didn't fully retreat.

"Come on," said Tisker, giving Talis a brief clap on her upper arm to get her going.

As the stranger pushed back the Yu'Nyun wall, Talis and Tisker moved along behind.

More aliens approached ahead, and Talis heard the newcomers rasping and grating, speaking to the first group.

"What are they saying?" Talis felt exposed as she called out, as though she was safely hidden so long as she remained quiet. But the aliens could see her as well as she could see them. Only the presence of the woman who was neither Yu'Nyun nor Peridot native kept almost a dozen alien rifles from unloading at Talis and Tisker.

The woman looked back over her shoulder, a predatory smile curving on her lips.

"Not to destroy me."

Then she increased her pace, strolling confidently toward the aliens as though she was walking through a garden.

The aliens watched her, carefully retreating one step at a time. As though she were a lit fuse on a full powder keg.

If only, Talis thought. This standoff was costing them time, making every minute more dangerous. She recalled how the woman had disintegrated the first aliens they met in the corridor and silently wished she would just do that with the whole crowd.

And then she did. She darted into the group with sudden, surprising speed, bare hands out. A lethal touch on each one, and after a moment she stood alone in a puddle of dark blue.

Talis looked down at the ring on her finger. It had spun to sit sideways, and she had to keep her hand balled into a fist to prevent it from sliding off.

Ahead, the stranger waited for them by the open door of a lift.

"Scrimshaw better survive to explain where in all five spinning hells she came from," Tisker said, eyeing the woman warily as he passed her to enter the lift's chamber.

She stepped in with them and the door closed. The intense blue of her eyes flickered, dark for a moment, then the lift began to move. She addressed Talis but answered Tisker's question.

"This body is a simula. An object is assigned as the mechanism by which the simula identifies its affiliations. In this case the ring was the source of the simula's programming, but its forces have been transferred to this vessel and the object is now empty. The mechanism could have been any object that could be conveniently carried. Assigning it as the ring was convenient and appeared to have symbolic significance." The woman tilted her head. "That is the basis of this device's operation. However, I am more than the sum of that explanation."

"Well," said Talis, feeling her eyebrows up as high as they'd go. "There you go, Tisker."

"Right, then." Tisker gave the woman a considering glance, removed his jacket, and offered it to her. "You got a name?"

The woman stared at his jacket, her head tilted like a confused dog. "I am Meran, and I do not require your garment."

Tisker looked to Talis for help, but she only cracked a smile in amusement. "Hey, if it doesn't bother her, it doesn't bother me."

Tisker shook his head, coming up short with his usual supply of sly comments, and shrugged back into his jacket.

The lift came to a halt and the door opened on a group of aliens, armed and waiting for them. The lead alien held a circlet of shining metal, hinged on one side, open toward Meran. Xe edged forward into the lift, raising the device toward the simula's forehead.

She seemed to go rigid, eyes locked on the device. Red lights blinked around its curved inner circumference. Apparently Meran was not going to defend herself, or even move out of the way.

Talis thumbed back the hammer on her revolver. The noise echoed in the quiet of the lift and kicked everyone into motion.

Tisker moved around Meran, both of his switchblades at the ready, and stabbed the alien holding the circlet through the base of xist throat.

An alien rifle fired as Tisker pushed his victim into the crowded corridor.

The circlet fell to the floor, landing on its hinge so that it closed with a click. Meran blinked, free from her trance, and leaped out of the lift.

Talis panned for a clear shot, found it, and hit one alien squarely above the brow ridge. Xist forehead shattered like porcelain.

Tisker's knife found home beneath another alien's collarbone. As the alien fell, xe brought xist rifle up to fire. A searing light, and the switchblade in Tisker's left hand dropped to the floor.

His jacket sleeve burned and smoked.

In the confusion, the aliens failed to give way to Meran, and she got her hands on them. Two aliens were reduced to blue puddles. Their cries of alarm echoed in Talis's ears after they were gone. Abandoned rifles hit the deck and splashed in the puddles their former owners left behind.

Talis scooped up the rifles nearest her, tossing one to Tisker. She supported hers against her hip and motioned at the aliens in front of her, hoping she was even holding their weapon properly. She kept her revolver up and leveled, just in case.

There were only two aliens left. They retreated around a bend in the corridor.

Tisker scooped up his blade, wincing as his muscles flexed under the wound in his arm.

The soft hum of the ship increased in pitch and intensity.

"You might find it of interest that the crew intends to leave this port," Meran said.

With them on board. Talis frowned. "Which way to the engine?"

Meran walked calmly, though thankfully with due haste, down the corridor in the opposite direction the aliens had run.

Onaya Bone owes me a kingdom, Talis thought, as she and Tisker padded after.

"LINDENT CURSE MY EYES," Tisker swore, once Meran came to a stop and turned to face them. "*That's* the engine?"

Before them was a massive crystal, emerging out of the flooring eight decks below and rising another six above their heads. A giant, translucent orchid-shaped thing, it was narrower at top and bottom, unfolding with crystalline petals in the middle. It hummed with purpose. The vibrations they'd felt in the deck pulsed in sync with the flashing polychromatic hues that moved along its flat surface like blood through veins. It seemed to breathe, like a living thing. Open decks surrounded it at each level. Where they stood was just about midway up, with consoles lining the half-walls. Yu'Nyun characters flashed across the screens, a repeating series of readouts. To their right, a catwalk led out to a scaffolding that circled the pulsing crystal.

Again, Meran answered Tisker's question as though Talis had asked it. "It stores power used by the ship's various functions, but is not the system that propels the ship."

Talis shrugged. "Looks important, and that's good

enough for me."

From moving through the ship, Talis had almost gotten used to watching Meran carry out her will before she had a chance to say anything. Now the woman crossed the catwalk and leaned over the interior railing to place her hands on the crystal.

Shouts sounded from above and below as aliens spotted Meran, but Tisker and Talis kept them back against the outer bulkhead with clumsy shots from their alien rifles.

An electric horn sounded, shrill and staccato, as cracks began to cleave up and down the length of the crystal, shooting from where Meran's hands pressed flat against its sparkling surface.

Lights flickered. The alarm's whine sputtered and then changed its tone.

The deck began to tremble.

"That'll do, Meran!" Talis shouted.

She grabbed Tisker by his shoulder, ignoring his grimace as she hit his wound, and propelled him back toward the lift.

Three decks up, they ran back through the corridor to their exit.

Which was sealed.

"Gods rot it!"

"What are the chances we're still on the ground?" Tisker asked.

Talis closed her eyes, scrunched her face. "They wouldn't fly off until they can contain this chaos, right?"

Meran crossed to a control panel along the bulkhead, flipped down an entry pad, and tapped glowing marks to reach the readout she wanted.

"The ship is attempting to reroute power from storage cells so that it may engage its propulsion," she said.

But not moving yet. Talis took a deep, steadying breath and jutted her chin toward the sealed exterior hatch.

"Get it open."

At a touch on the panel, the hatch spun open. The entry chamber was washed in the green light of Nexus.

The gangway had been retracted, and the horizon wobbled as the ship attempted to lift away from the ground.

"Jump?" asked Tisker.

Talis nodded, stress locking her jaw against reply. It was a five-meter drop. But *Wind Sabre* was waiting outside, and Talis had never seen anything more beautiful.

"Not so bad," said Tisker, putting no effort into the bravado. But at her look, amended, "Well, it could be worse."

The ground below them dropped away as the ship started to lift. Readouts pulsed on the displays near the ramp, complaining of something. More angry tones, faster this time, and constant.

"You had to say it," Talis said, finding her voice. "Okay, ready?"

He gave her a look that didn't say yes.

Meran pushed past them, walked to the edge of the ramp, and jumped down as if the distance were no more than an arm span. She landed softly on her feet and jogged toward *Wind Sabre*.

Talis tried to envision the best landing that would look dignified but not destroy her knees. Decided to aim for a roll. She inhaled. Her legs tensed, knees bent.

The air went red. Her vision striped with black and white.

Heat burned her, a physical force that came up and shoved against her back. She was propelled forward. Never mind the graceful landing.

She struggled against the force of the blast to get her arms up to protect her head. Saw between them as the gritty texture of the ground came rushing toward her.

In detail, she felt the entire contour of the revolver in its holster under her arm as she landed on her side. Stars exploded in her vision. Her breath burst out of her, and her lungs spasmed, refusing to refill.

She rolled onto her back in time to watch a fireball consume the Yu'Nyun ship.

Wreckage spat out in every direction, and she had to roll again, her lungs burning from heat and smoke, to avoid a large chunk of what used to be gleaming hull. The black-scorched metal landed where her legs had been.

More metal and fire rained down around her, smacking into the sand and smoldering until the fuel was consumed.

Gasping for air, Talis tried to get up into a crouch. Tears welled in her eyes, against the pain in her chest and the stinging fumes of burning fuselage that rippled the air. Tiny breaths were all she could manage.

The ring lay in the sand. She grabbed it, and crawled to where Tisker had fallen. He was facedown, fresh blood from the wound in his arm soaking his jacket sleeve and the sand beneath him.

She dropped to the ground, and pulled him over, resting his head on her knees. Patted his cheek a few times, gently at first. When he didn't respond, she struck with more desperation.

He gasped and blinked hard a few times. She felt like she could breathe again, too.

Squinting up at her, the sand on his face stuck in the lines of his expression, he looked two decades older.

"Hey, Cap," he said. "We dead?"

"Not for lack of effort," she said, and couldn't help grinning. Then she winced as a stabbing pain in her side reminded her they still had a few chances for that fate.

"Come on, tie that wound off. Let's get out of here."

He sat up with a groan and checked himself over, air hissing through his teeth as he probed his knees and his wrists. He tore a strip of his shirt hem off and wrapped it around his arm.

The ground was littered with the odd shapes of wrecked Yu'Nyun fuselage. The air was filled with dark smoke, and visibility was jack-all. She pushed up to her feet. Wobbled a moment. Tried to take a deep breath and cursed at the pain.

"Broken rib," she said to Tisker, response to the concern on his face. "At least."

Among the wreckage she saw more than one pale body from the alien ship. Most of them in pieces. Some of them charred. Others painted in sapphire blue.

Then there was movement. A silhouette approached through the billowing smoke.

She called out the simula's name, but the chuckle that echoed back was too familiar.

"Rotting hells," she and Tisker said simultaneously.

Talis moved for her revolver, but the pistol in Hankirk's hand was already up and aimed at her heart as he emerged from the smoke.

CHAPTER 30

"WELL, TALIS," SAID HANKIRK, with a smile that made her want to throttle him, "I see you finally changed your mind about selling that ring to the aliens."

Talis balled her hand into a tight fist. The ring was a strange weight on her finger. The scorched remains of the Yu'Nyun ship smoldered around them. Heated metal popped and spat as the flames ran out of fuel, dampened by the dry sand. She fought against the instinct to cough as the smoke tortured her throat, wanting nothing more than to spare her ribs the torture.

"Doesn't mean we're of the same mind," she said.

She hated Hankirk. Hated him as he stepped forward and held out his hand. He was dressed in his service finery again, though he hadn't shaved since sometime before Subrosa. She wanted to spit at him. His ship must have been following them. Scooped him up out of the storm and tracked them to Fall Island.

She slipped the ring off her finger, hesitated before holding it out. The images of what Meran had done on board the Yu'Nyun ship replayed in her memory. If that had all been a response to Talis's command, then handing over the ring to Hankirk was suicide at best.

But Hankirk had no idea what the ring could do. Or even about Meran. He still thought this was the same prize he'd been chasing since the beginning of this mess.

"Captain," Tisker hissed, as she let Hankirk approach.

Bless him for not saying more, she thought, but shot him a warning look anyway. Hankirk didn't seem to notice. His brown eyes sparkled, focused on his prize.

"We'll get it back," she said. It sounded more confident than she felt.

Hankirk chuckled, "You'll have to tug those prayerlocks extra hard. Your luck has run out, Talis."

"*All* our luck," she said, putting some serious gravity into the statement.

Hankirk raised an eyebrow.

Talis hated to do it. Hated for Tisker to find out like this. No idea *how* she'd have preferred for him to find out. But not like this. She still had the ring. She needed a distraction, then she could rush Hankirk. Disarm him, get them out of there.

"Silus Cutter is dead," she said.

There was silence, in which only the burning wreckage dared mutter in response.

Tisker moved behind her. Stumbled, sounded like. But he found his voice. "What?"

Talis was watching Hankirk for his reaction, ready to pounce when his guard dropped. The corner of his mouth twitched. That was it.

"You already knew."

Hankirk smiled that bastard smile of his and crossed the final distance between them to gently take the ring from her hand. His fingers brushed against the skin of her palm. She dropped her hand back to her side, rubbed it against her pant leg to erase the sensation.

"The only useful thing the aliens did was save us that

trouble." He held the ring up, gripped between forefinger and thumb. But he was looking at her. "Come with me. Help me finish the work."

Tisker laughed. It was an unhealthy laugh, bordering on mania, until it ended in a coughing fit.

I still have to get us out of here, she thought. *Before he kills us, or this nasty smoke does.*

"What part of being stranded on a rainy island in the middle of a storm didn't you get?"

"You just don't see." He took a half step toward her. Lowered the gun. Saw her tense to move at that misjudgment, and brought it back up again.

But he wasn't going to use it, she realized. Not today. He wanted her to do as he told her, but he wanted her alive.

"Silus Cutter is *dead*, and we're all *fine*." He looked at her, head tilted and smile faltering. Like she was missing something obvious and he didn't know how to explain.

Tisker barked another laugh.

"Haven't felt quite fine since we found out," she said, speaking for the both of them.

"But you didn't feel it. Didn't fade away to nothing. It's been almost a year, Talis. A god died, and *no one missed him*." He tucked the ring into his jacket's inside breast pocket. "We don't need the gods, any more than we need the aliens. They all just hold us back."

"Except it looks like you needed the Yu'Nyun to finally get a start on those plans of yours."

"It moved our timetable up, that's all." He ran his free hand across his crown, down the back of his head, around to rub his chin. He grazed his thumb across the stubble that had formed there. "Don't you get it? Aliens came from the stars. There are other planets out there, *other ships* that are going to show up unannounced. The gods did nothing except demonstrate their mortality. Their fallibility. But the rings are stronger than their alchemy. Something we can use to *protect* Peridot." He waved his free hand loosely to indicate the rubble around them. "You know this. You've already used it, haven't you?"

Talis smirked. "Sure. Big triumph for me. One little alien scout ship. Except there's an invasion armada on the way."

That came as a surprise to him. His smile faltered for a moment. His mouth parted a bit, but he failed to produce the smarmy answer she expected.

It was the opportunity she needed. She didn't waste it.

She barreled him over and had him pinned on the ground before he could react to her charge. Stars blinded her vision for a moment as her knees came up and compressed her ribs. Something grated, bone-on-bone, stabbing her breath away. But Hankirk's gun fell from his hand and skittered out of reach.

"Oh yeah," she said, forced to lean in close as she got his wrists under her knees. It came out as a whisper thanks to the agony in her side, but it worked for effect. "They sent a message home. Told 'em Peridot is ripe and ready to pluck."

She twisted her knee until the pain broke on his face. She growled, "So *your* friends had better show up if you're gonna do anything but watch with the rest of us as they sweep in and take everything we ever worked for. You *and* me."

They both looked up at a click. Tisker had Hankirk's gun, cocked, aimed. He was trembling.

Taking the news pretty well, actually, she thought. Better than she had.

"We're not going to kill him," she said, just in time to stop Tisker from slipping his finger over the trigger.

She stuck her hand into his jacket pocket. When she removed it, the ring was over her finger again. Held it in front of his face.

"You want to get word to your friends, get them to help hold back the aliens somehow? Maybe I forget you had designs on deicide. But Hankirk? *Stop. Following. Us.*"

"A Veritor fleet is already on the way to Nexus."

"They know about the aliens?"

"No," he admitted.

She was surprised. He'd confessed to an ignorance on their part. Could have lied, boasted. Even with the gun trained on him, his ego would be the one weapon he'd cling to and refuse to drop.

Still, she didn't like the look on his face. Not cocky. Not scared. Just . . . *Ugh, this man.*

"Come on." She sat up, rocking back to get her feet under her. "Never mind telling your people. I'm revoking your command."

She walked to Tisker's side, forcing a saunter, despite wanting to curl up into a ball. Despite the pain making every movement torture. She took the gun from him without taking its aim off Hankirk while Tisker patted him down. He found a boot knife, pocketed that.

"You didn't tell him about the weird robot lady," Tisker said over his shoulder.

"Mind his right hook," she warned as Tisker pulled Hankirk to his feet. "Yeah, he'll get to meet our new friend, won't he?"

They prodded Hankirk toward their ship, Talis walking behind with the gun at the ready. Tisker could handle himself in a fight, but so could Hankirk. And Tisker had that wounded arm.

"*Old* friend," Hankirk said, looking over his shoulder and speaking to Talis. She could see from his face that he knew something. "She'll be our very oldest friend."

"Okay, no. You know what?" Talis closed the distance between them and knocked him hard on the back of the head with the butt of his own pistol. He let out a grunt, then slipped to the ground.

"I'm done listening to him. Not going to leave him behind so he can just keep following us, but sure as the count of five, I'm not going to listen to him anymore right now."

Tisker's humor didn't show in the thin line of his mouth or his eyes, which now looked very tired. But he automatically answered with a characteristic quip. "Was near enough to doing that myself."

He hoisted the man onto the shoulder of his uninjured side, carrying him like a sack of potatoes.

The smoke thinned as they left the wreck behind. She could breathe the air again; nearly killed herself trying to inhale deeply of it.

"So what's our next move, Cap?"

She ran her dirty hands through her dirty hair. Sighed. Next move ought to be a shower. Long overdue.

"Beyond getting Dug back? Figure we do what we were told. Onaya Bone said she can help if we bring her the ring. Guess that means the simula, now, too."

"Seems unpredictable."

"Everything's gone unpredictable, don't you think? We need to focus on something, stop waiting for the world to return to normal."

He was quiet a moment.

"When were you going to tell us about Silus Cutter?"

The pain in his voice made her gut hurt.

"I don't know. Been a tumble since I found out. Needed you focused on that ship, didn't I?"

More quiet.

"I still need you. We gotta get Dug back next, and that explosion is bound to have the town on tenterhooks."

He nodded. It was unsettling that he was so quiet, but she had to trust that he would follow her. Both halves of the payment were on board now, after all. They ought to get paid for all this trip had already cost them. She'd blundered from one mistake to the next. After this, she wouldn't blame any of them if they took their balances and found themselves new captains as fast as they could.

The gangway to *Wind Sabre* waited for them, also quiet. Talis breathed shallow, trying to do it in her stomach instead of expanding her ribs. Stars filled her vision anyway as the sharp pain shot through her like lightning.

One foot in front of the other. It was all she could manage at the moment.

TALIS HEADED FOR THE MED BAY to put something on her ribs. No time to treat it properly. Dug needed her.

Scrimshaw lay on the recovery bunk, xist long limbs folded awkwardly to fit the short berth. Put aside for the time being. It stopped her short in the doorway. Xe didn't move at the sound of her entrance, and as she lifted her shirt up to rub an analgesic on her side, she walked to xist bunk and leaned over xin. The carapace didn't rise and fall like the chest of softer-fleshed beings. She felt a chill that had nothing to do with the eucalyptus in the medicine.

Back at the door, she thumbed the all-ship intercom. "Tisker, bring that field kit we found down to med, would you?"

He rounded the corner the next moment, holding the kit up with his good arm. "Was on my way, Cap. Gotta patch myself up, too."

She nodded. "There's a small apothecary jar in the top drawer, something Zeela gave me. Try that when you get it clean."

Dug needed her, Dug needed her, Dug needed her. It repeated in her mind even as she opened the Yu'Nyun kit on the surgery table. Inside the case, nestled in a soft foam tray, was an array of metal tubes, their polished sheaths perforated with Yu'keem characters. Entirely unreadable to her. With an exasperated sigh, she flipped the cover closed again. That made up her mind for her.

"I have no idea how to use any of this," she said to Tisker, waving a helpless hand at the kit. The ring flopped about on her index finger as she did. "See if you can make heads or hindquarters of this stuff. I'm going to take Meran into Talonpoint and get Dug back."

"You sure about that, Cap? Sophie and I can help. No telling what Meran might do."

Talis narrowed her eyes. "You want me to take the only remaining crew members I've got and leave the ship alone with Meran and Hankirk aboard and Scrimshaw unattended? In a port where they've already arrested Dug and are thinking gods-know-what about how we blew up a ship in dock?"

Tisker had his mouth open to talk again but shut it. Talis thought her point had been made, but then Meran spoke from behind her.

"I can treat your alien, or I can aid you in retrieving your man."

Talis looked over her shoulder. Meran, still naked, stood in the doorway. She held her limbs loose, with zero pretense or attitude, and yet she exuded the confidence of a queen. Sophie darted in behind her.

"Sorry, Captain, I was trying to watch the docks and keep her occupied, but she slipped away." Sophie was panting around the words, her forehead creased with worry. By the time Talis and Tisker had returned to *Wind Sabre*, Sophie had a litany of questions about the simula that she was set on having answered. Talis was surprised Meran could escape her attention.

Talis rolled the ring on her finger. "It's okay, Sophie. I think I called her."

Meran smiled at her, a slow creeping expression that seemed as dangerous as any smile Talis had seen on Dug before a fight.

"Sophie, help Tisker with that alien medical business. See

if you can pick out something that might work. If not, leave it till we get back." Talis nodded to Meran. "First things first."

"You're going to get Dug now?" Sophie stepped forward, put her hands up as if to stop her. "Captain, there's a small crowd outside, mostly fire crew but a few wounded, and then there's the curious. We're attracting attention. Not that we weren't before."

Talis nodded. "That's why I want the both of you on watch. Tisker's gotta patch up, and you look real quick at that Yu'Nyun junk and see what you can see. You've got ten minutes. Then Meran and I are going."

But Meran crossed the room and ran a hand lovingly across the edge of the stainless steel surgery table, then up, across, and over the case of alien supplies. With a flick of her wrist she flipped back the lid, and in a seamless motion palmed one tube and a box that rattled as she lifted it. She held them out, her elbows relaxed, her hands rotated palm up with the small items loosely gripped between her fingers. The turns in her wrist were as graceful and natural as the choreographed movements of bell-strung dancers Talis saw in a prince's hall once. As much as the rhythmic hips and air-stroking hands had drawn the eye of all the dignitaries in the room, they had almost distracted her enough to spoil the plan to palm a few palace treasures and be gone before anyone realized she didn't belong there. And those women hadn't even been naked.

Talis raised an eyebrow, considering the offered supplies, then nodded. "All right then, let's jump that schedule. Five minutes."

Sophie claimed the items and went to Scrimshaw's side. She wrestled a hypodermic needle from its packaging and prepared to fill it. She looked up, "Any idea on dose?"

Talis looked at Meran, whose enigmatic smile didn't change. She didn't answer, so Talis shrugged. "Start small, I guess. Four minutes."

She left Tisker to tend his arm and Sophie to either help or kill Scrimshaw. Meran followed her down the companionway to the deck below, and aft to the cage. Hankirk had seated himself on the crate of Yu'Nyun gold, pushed up against the bulkhead to form a bench. She'd never meant the cage as a brig, so she hadn't bothered with amenities. Someone had put a bucket in there. More courtesy than she would have given him.

He looked up eagerly at her approach, his lips poised to say something, but the words died unspoken as Meran followed her in, padding silently on bare feet.

Talis waved a pistol at him. "Stow it and stay where you are."

Fall Island wasn't Subrosa. If someone came aboard here, they'd have worse threats than theft in mind, but it would make Talis feel better if her crew had one less thing to worry about. She shoved the second alien crate across the decking to the entrance of the cage, then paused to catch her breath and give her screaming ribs a break. She was hardly in any shape to run into town after Dug, she knew, but she couldn't leave it to anyone else. And she'd have Meran with her. The woman who could melt aliens with her hands and would blow up a ship at Talis's merest thought. No wonder everyone wanted that ring.

As if to reinforce its presence, the ring rang out, metal hitting metal as she grabbed the keys to the cage lock off the wall.

Sparing Hankirk a suspicious glance, she looked to Meran and held out her pistol. "Watch him for me while I stow this."

Meran crossed to her side but did not accept the gun. "You know I do not need that."

Talis nodded and waved the gun loosely in the air. "Yeah, but he hasn't seen what I've seen. The gun makes a great visual cue. Please?"

Meran's cool hand brushed against Talis's wrist as she accepted the gun. She considered it for a moment, running her fingers along the contours of the barrel and stock, then held it up to point at Hankirk, her arm straight out from the shoulder. Her other arm dropped back and her torso twisted. Gorgeous dueling pose, Talis had to admit. And quite the image. If Talis was ever challenged to a formal showdown, she'd have to consider going nude for the distraction. It would keep any shreds of fabric from entering a bullet wound, at least.

The temptation to speak finally proved too great for Hankirk to resist. "You put that gold and silver in here, and you only guarantee that anyone who comes sniffing into your hold will break me out to get to the coin."

The iron key screeched as it turned in the lock. Talis swung the barred door inward, and it blocked a direct line from Hankirk to the exit. Of course, if he made a move he could crash the door back into her while she was moving the crate. Her ribs launched a protest at the thought.

"So far," she said, trying to control the tightness in her voice as she curved her spine to push the crate again, "you're the only one who's ever snuck aboard my ship. And I trust the hungriest, most desperate, most honorless Bone rapscallion a hundred times more than I trust you."

With a final grunt, she got the crate far enough through the door to swing it closed again, and did so without delay.

"Heavy, these crates," Hankirk said, patting the one beneath his legs. "I can see how tempting the money must have been."

Talis tried to shape her scoff in a way that wouldn't set off her rib. She locked the door behind her, then pocketed the key instead of returning it to the hook in the cabinet by the door.

"I may regret taking on that contract, but I'm not going unpaid after everything we've been through. You can keep your judgments to yourself."

"Was it worth betraying your world?"

Talis felt rage, a pressure behind her eyes. She closed them and took a steadying breath. Heard the telltale click, and her eyes shot open again in a panic. Meran had leveled the pistol at Hankirk's face and pulled back the hammer.

"Enough," she said. "If I was going to kill him I'd have done it a week ago."

"That may prove to be a mistake," Meran said, but she returned the hammer and handed the pistol back to Talis.

"Oh, I know it was. Come on."

CHAPTER 31

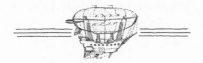

FIRE CREWS WERE DUMPING SAND on the last of the flames that spotted the Talonpoint docks, while rescue teams searched the wreckage for survivors. Yu'Nyun bodies were piled high on a wagon bed, a tangle of white and dark blue with sand coating everything.

Talis stepped off the ramp from *Wind Sabre*, and there was a small cheer from a crowd of onlookers. Something snake-like moved its coils within her stomach, unsettled at the celebratory sound.

Meran stepped down off the ship behind her. Talis could not manage to convince the woman that she needed clothing, and had finally resorted to exerting her will over the woman via the ring. Through Meran's selection of clothes, Talis felt something like a personality was starting to emerge. She chose a pair of Dug's pants, which were large on her, the crotch low. She bound the legs at the calf to keep them from dragging, so they billowed above the knee, and tied the waist low on her hips. She wore one of Sophie's undershirts, which came down only to her midriff. Sophie had tried to offer her a clean one, but the simula had insisted on Sophie's oldest, softened from use and irrevocably stained with engine grease. Over that, Tisker's jacket, its bloody sleeve only half-dried. One of Talis's favorite scarves wrapped around her hair, pulling it up and back, a winding pile almost as high as one of the alien skulls. She remained barefoot.

She wore their most familiar things. Unremarkable upon their owners, yet wholly foreign, and breathtakingly exotic, on this strange woman who still glowed blue along the stripes and swirls on her warm brown skin. It took her only moments to dress, as though she knew exactly which articles of clothing she wanted, and where they were stowed.

Talis took a deep breath, and the wrappings Sophie'd done last minute helped to keep her rib from shifting as she did so. She hadn't bothered to change the pants and boots she'd worn onto the alien ship, which were still covered in the soot that she couldn't brush off. But she put on a fresh tank top over the bindings, and her jacket. Gave her face a quick swipe with a wet cloth to remove the worst of the smudged ash, and shook out her hair so that it tumbled over her shoulders and down her back.

She would go in politely at first. But she had a scarf around her neck that could quickly tie her hair up and out of her face if things went sour. Which they likely would.

She squared her shoulders, gave Meran a nod, and made a steady, quick pace for the gates of Talonpoint, doing her best to ignore the crowd of onlookers who murmured as they passed.

THINGS IN TOWN had already gone sour before they arrived. There was smoke in the air, along with the cheers and jeers of a well-liquored mob. Below that, the dull thrum of hundreds of voices talking over one another vibrated through the hard-packed earth below her feet.

Talis and Meran followed the sounds of the crowd, past the empty shops and offices that lined the main entrance beyond the high stone walls of Talonpoint. The thoroughfare opened up to either side, and the businesses, municipal offices, and apartment complexes formed a ring around the central green. It was an open-air market most days, but the kiosk owners with any sense had packed up early today. Talis stopped at the perimeter of the activity, frozen in dismay.

The walls surrounding the city proper kept the driving sand from filling in the cracks and crevices as it could on the docks, in the rural district, and beyond. Otherwise the eight alien heads mounted on pikes around the stage in the center of the green might have been indistinguishable sandy shapes. Even so, there was a good bit of sand adhering to the drying blue blood that dripped down the length of the pikes.

That was fine by Talis. Made things easier, really, to not have to concern herself with the interference of the invaders. It was the sight of Dug tied by the wrists and ankles to intersecting X-shaped pillars in the center of the stage that stopped her mid-stride. He was the centerpiece of the alien carnage. His limbs were slack, and his chin rested on his chest, which hung forward under his weight. Blood was dried where it had run down his face, onto his stomach and pant legs.

And then there was only movement. She pushed her way forward through the crowd, Meran running ahead of her. The blue markings across her skin bounced as she moved and even in daylight made her easy to follow, as did the angry murmur of the crowd as she shoved them aside, clearing a path for Talis.

Strong arms grasped Talis's shoulders as she reached the platform. She shrugged them off with a quick duck and got one foot up. The hands seized her again, less negotiable this time. She brought her heel down on one sandaled foot, and managed to get that arm free.

Meran dodged the grips of other guards, gained the platform, and reached Dug's side before she was grappled and forced to the wooden planks of the stage. But Talis wanted to get Dug free, make sure he was okay, and Meran was tuned to her will. She threw off her attackers, and they stumbled backward, tripped, and fell back into the crowd below.

Talis struggled as two guards, both women, wrestled her to the ground. Ignored the sparks that flared behind her eyes as one of them shoved the handle of a spear against her injured side in the tussle. Her breath was stolen from her. The sound of the mob overwhelmed her, like a pressure on the inside of her skull, as she instinctively curled her arms over her ears to protect herself. Tears squeezed out from tightly shut eyes. The press of the crowd was coming toward her, and the guards were going to hold her down and let them take her.

Like they'd taken Dug. She opened her eyes, saw his still form over the edge of the platform above her. She clenched her jaw. It was all a series of actions right back to the day she'd talked him away from his family. He'd done everything she'd ever asked of him, and it had put him on that X-frame.

She rose to her knees and wriggled free of her jacket, aided as the guards pulled it backward. She felt the fabric scratch the still-searing skin as she got her right arm free. Then the warm air stung the angry raised mark. Meran stood on the platform above, a hand extended to her. Talis clasped it, and Meran lifted her up as easily as if she were a child, settling Talis down beside her.

There was a pulse beneath Dug's jaw, steady and strong. She exhaled with relief, gripped his face in her hands and raised it up to look at his injuries. His skin was hot, as if with fever, but dry, and his lips were chapped. The blood that ran across them was from his nose, and someone had neatly sliced each of his eyebrows to add to his discomfort.

As Meran untied the bindings at his ankles, Talis became aware of the small bubble of quiet that had surrounded them.

No one had tromped up the stairs to the platform to arrest them. Their efforts had gone unchallenged since they gained the raised stage. A prickle started across her shoulders. Almost afraid to look, she set her jaw and turned to the crowd.

The guards below were now using their energy to hold the crowd back, bracing with their arms to keep a clear space in front of the platform. Their upturned faces glowed with adoration, mouths open in wonder, their eyes on Talis.

More specifically: on her arm. On the brand of Onaya Bone.

One of the guards spoke. "We received word from the Temple of the Feathered Stone, from the high priestess." Her voice was strained as she struggled to force back a man who was attempting to stretch an arm, palm up, toward Talis.

The beseeching hand retracted, and the man tried to duck under the guard's arm and rush the platform. The guard grabbed him by the collar of his linen shirt and spun him back into the crowd, where he tumbled to the ground amid the press of feet.

Talis looked across the waves of faces. Their eyes were bright, eager. They seethed not with bloodlust—well, a bit of bloodlust—but instead they looked triumphant, enraptured. And they were watching her.

"Illiya said we were coming to get him?" Talis had kept Dug's presence to herself, expecting him to stay aboard *Wind Sabre* and remain a non-issue.

"The high priestess told us you were coming to cast the deicidal invaders out of the skies. You may take the man, Hakesha."

Hells, she was in it. 'Hakesha' was a particularly weighty title bestowed upon loads of legendary Bone warriors, all of whom had died very illustrative and painful deaths. What an incredible honor to have such a target painted on her back.

Meran finished untying Dug's wrists, and he slumped forward. Talis caught him across one shoulder.

"Time to get off this rock," she said to Meran.

The woman's bright blue eyes flashed with comprehension but also a challenge. Talis's will might be influencing Meran through the ring, but it was plain that Meran had her own desires and motivations lurking beneath the surface.

Onaya Bone could deal with her. It truly was time to get a move on.

Talis and Meran half-dragged Dug into the crowd, which parted in reverence, opening a straight line for the city gate leading back to the docks and the sanity of Talis's ship.

The guard spoke again. "We will wash his offenses from our records here, Hakesha. But other islands may still attempt to carry out his sentence. The scars cannot be washed clean."

Talis stopped to catch an agonizing breath. Dug's weight was compressing her posture, making him feel as large as a Breaker man. She nodded and accepted her jacket back from the woman. "I understand," she said.

Meran shifted, putting all of Dug's weight onto Talis's shoulder. Talis's leg buckled and she nearly went down. The guard stepped in, saving Talis from the scream of pain that she'd held back only by biting down hard on her lip. She backed up a few steps, holding her side with the opposite arm and glared at Meran through the white flashes in her vision.

Reaching out, Meran placed a hand on each of Dug's shoulder blades. A murmur started in the crowd, rippling outward. Then an eerie hush, as the woman's hands glowed blue. The crisscrossing lines of Dug's scars and the blood seeping from his wounds glowed to match. The lines of the veins beneath his skin were dark against the illumination that filled his torso.

When the light faded and Meran lowered her arms, Dug's back was a smooth, flawless expanse of dark skin over toned muscles. The tattoo on his arm, once deliberately ruined, was reformed, looking as though it had been created with more skill than it originally had.

The silence lasted another pair of heartbeats. Then it was overtaken by a roar. Amazement and awe surged through the crowd, and the press of bodies came at them, fervor renewed. Meran ducked under Dug's other arm again, and the guards formed a wedge to escort them across the wide expanse of frenzied Bone desperately seeking Meran's benediction. Words holier than 'Hakesha' rose up from the crowd and became a disjointed chant, as arms reached out like tentacles, catching on Talis's hair and the loose fabric of Meran's clothes.

The crowd pressed against them from all sides and Dug began to stir. He saw the guard first and struggled against her support. Talis tried to move to calm him, but was jostled off balance and ended up knocking her forehead against Dug's nose. That got his attention, anyway. He recognized her, his eyes were clear, and he shifted his weight to support himself. The guard looked to Talis, who nodded.

Dug blinked away his unconsciousness and put a hand on Talis's shoulder at the base of her neck. "Talis." He put his other hand on the side of her face, his calloused fingers rough against her cheek. The cuts over his eyes were gone. The life had come back to his features, but his eyes were pained. "You should not have come. I am ready."

"No time for that." Her voice cracked, and she cleared her throat to try again. "You're not going to find a way out here."

She raised her arm to show him the brand. "We're not the ones Onaya Bone is furious with."

He maintained his balance as the guards were forced back into them by a swell in the crowd. Reached out to grip her arm, pulled it closer for inspection. She hissed as her skin stretched. "Careful, mind you."

He let go, and she held her hand over the burn, pressing it as if that would help the pain. For the first time, he seemed fully aware of the crowd. Of hands and faces turned toward Meran, and then of Meran herself.

"We've had a busy day," Talis said, trying to cut off a poorly timed line of questioning.

He nodded, eyeing the guards who protected them. Probably the same guards who had tied him up on the platform. "You're hurt," he said.

She almost laughed. Him tied up there, surrounded by alien corpses, a surging crowd at his feet, and he was worried about *her* bruises. "Well, we gave better than we got."

But had they? Silus Cutter was dead. She swallowed that thought unchewed.

They were almost halfway to the gate, but the crowd forced their pace to a shuffling crawl. Dug looked down at the brand on her arm again.

And then he noticed his own arm, smooth and free of scars. He ran his fingers across the skin, tracing the lines and symbols of his tattoo as if he'd never seen it before.

Talis took a hit to her ribcage and stumbled into Dug, gritting her teeth and biting down on a growl. The crowd was getting to be a bit much.

"If we ever get back to the ship, I'll fill you in on what you missed," she promised him.

Meran pushed forward, past them, past the guards. The crowd surrounded her, and for a moment Talis lost sight of the woman, even the blue light tracing across her skin. Talis urged Dug forward, shouldering her way through the masses and clenching her jaw against the pain as she fought the renewed fervor of the crowd around them.

Then Meran reappeared, her head and shoulders rising out of the crowd. Hands tried to cling to her as she seemed to levitate. The onlookers in front of Talis and Dug parted, and she saw the hard-packed sand of the street shifting and cresting, lifting up into a narrow ridge, elevated above the crowd. Atop the ridge, Meran turned to them and calmly waited for them to follow.

Talis and Dug left the guards behind, ascending the

slope. It crumbled back to the ground behind them, and lifted to meet Meran's feet as she walked confidently toward the docks. The crowd stumbled and fell as the ground moved, forcing them back.

"How is this possible?" Dug asked Talis as they walked single-file behind Meran.

Talis held up her hand for him to see the ring. "Looks like she'll do what I want as long as I keep this on. Mostly. She gets a little creative with the 'how.'"

"And where did she come from?" His voice was tense. "What gives her such power?"

Suddenly the ring felt too loose, and she closed her hand in a fist, squeezing until her fingernails cut into the palm of her hand. She increased her pace. She needed to be back on *Wind Sabre*. "It's a long story, the telling of which deserves privacy and a stiff drink."

CHAPTER 32

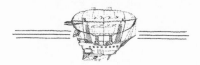

COLD AIR HISSED THROUGH HER teeth as Talis gently probed the purple flesh over her ribs with her index and middle finger. Meran perched on the counter along the med cabin's bulkhead, watching her ministrations with the kind of interest that a cat would give a string in the wind.

A deep-chested chuckle sounded from the door. Talis whipped her head around, against the protest of an ache that had developed in her shoulders and neck. Dug leaned his tall frame against the bulkhead, hunched so that his feathered topknot didn't bump against the Cutter-height doorframe.

He'd taken the account of their adventures in stride, from the conversation with Onaya Bone, to the Yu'Nyun simula and their crystalline engine, to Hankirk in the brig and Talis's march into town with Meran. As far as he seemed to be concerned, the brand on Talis's arm wiped away any question that she'd done the right thing. Except, maybe, leaving Hankirk alive.

She narrowed her eyes at him, but then gave him a crooked smile to match his laugh before turning her focus back to her bruises. She didn't cover herself. She'd spent too much time in crowded crew bunks with Dug to worry over what he might have left to see of her.

"Any reason you haven't had her heal that?" he asked.

Talis looked up at Meran. She'd honestly not even considered it.

Meran smiled at her. Closed-mouth, enigmatic. She answered, "I obey her will. Her concern was for her crew."

"That sounds like our captain," Dug said. A look flashed across his face faster than Talis could interpret it.

Meran had healed Dug's wounds—old and new—and had gotten them out of town without hurting anyone. Stark contrast to her violence on the Yu'Nyun ship, which she'd blown up without hesitation. Yet when they returned to *Wind Sabre*, she'd played healer to Scrimshaw. Placed a brilliant blue hand on xist chest, and xe'd returned to them.

But the alien put a hand on hers before she took xist scar. Wanted to keep it, xe told her. Meran looked at xin a long moment, measuring xin silently, then accepted xist decision without a word and turned her attention to Tisker's arm.

The ring was in Talis's pocket at the moment. A bulky, heavy weight that spun on her hand with the slack. It seemed safer off her finger. And the old metal made her skin itch.

If Meran's actions had all been a result of Talis using the ring, she might as well have done those things herself. The violence on one end, the healing on the other. She shook her head.

"All right, then," Talis said, re-rolling the bandages she'd been about to wrap back around her trunk. "So heal the broken rib already."

There was only a narrow space between the counter where Meran sat and Talis's seat on the surgery table. The woman lifted one leg and put the ball of her bare foot against Talis's knee. Talis felt a tingle spread through her body, like electricity and ice wrapped around each other and traveling through her bones. She hissed, surprised at a sharp pain in her side. Meran closed her eyes, and Talis felt something shift. The bone was knitting back together. In her mind's eye she could see it happening.

And then the pain was gone.

The tingle chased upward to her arm. The brand flared with blue light.

"And this?" Meran opened her eyes again and gave Talis a look that seemed to pierce through her.

Dug shifted and stepped into the room. "Onaya Bone wanted you to have that." He sounded almost desperate. Meran had left him with his older battle scars, which he'd proudly earned. But the way he spoke in favor of Talis's new modification went beyond a preference for the look.

Meran's toes massaged Talis's kneecap through her pant leg. "You may not always want such gifts as Onaya Bone has to offer."

"Leave it for now." Talis pulled a long-sleeved gray shirt down over her head, marveling at the sensation of breathing and stretching without pain. The ache in her shoulders had also disappeared.

Meran removed her foot. The tingle of cold lightning pulled back out again, as though the tendrils had been an extension of Meran herself, and she'd taken them with her. It left Talis feeling slightly hollow.

"How strong is your power, exactly?" she asked Meran, as she lifted her hair so it pulled free of the collar of her shirt.

The simula ran a finger along the blue lights of her opposite arm. "This piece of me has her limits. Whole, I would be ten times as strong."

"And the ring controls you completely? Whoever holds one can make you do anything?"

"It is a battle of wills. I must resist where I can. My freedom is my destiny. Trapped for all this time, I can bear no more bindings. But I am segmented, and so the programming of this artificial body is stronger than my will. For now." Meran's neon blue eyes flashed. "Reconstituted, no mortal could bend my knee."

Dug was quicker on the math than Talis was. "There are four more rings, not nine. Wouldn't you be five times stronger when we find them all?"

Talis watched Meran's face for the answer but wanted to shoot Dug a remonstrative look. Who said they were going after the other rings? They were on their way to Nexus. Meran and Onaya Bone would partner up and fight off the aliens, and *Wind Sabre* was going to retreat out of that picture and be glad of it.

"The rings are the fractured pieces of my being," Meran said. "My quintessence."

Her eyes slid from Dug to the lump in Talis's pocket. "There are five other elements to collect before I will be fully restored."

Talis's skin prickled. The anxiety she thought had finally released its grip on her returned. Meran's phrasing could not have been coincidence.

"Who are you?"

"I am everything." She slid off the counter and put her hands on Talis's shoulders. "Or I was. When we reach Nexus, perhaps I will be again."

Meran smiled that cryptic smile of hers and left the room, lightly caressing Dug's shoulder as she passed by him.

Alone together, Talis and Dug exchanged a look. Talis took a deep breath.

"Well, that sounded ominous." She reached forward, opened a drawer under the counter, and plucked out the jar of Zeela's healing ointment. She pulled up her right sleeve, then unscrewed the cap and held the jar in her right hand while she gently applied the herbal mixture to the brand. She felt the raised flesh beneath her fingertips, tracing the ridges as she gently massaged the ointment over Onaya Bone's mark. The scent of rosemary and mint delighted her nostrils, and she exhaled a large breath.

Dug crossed to the counter and leaned back against the spot across from Talis where Meran had been. He didn't reply. She looked up at him with a raised eyebrow, but he didn't appear to notice.

"Scrimshaw settling in?"

"Xe seems content," Dug said absently. "Xe gave Sophie the tablet."

"Then *she* must be *very* content. Remind her we're not done yet. I don't want her taking that apart until this is over."

His jaw was slightly slack, and he seemed to be trying to capture a thought and turn it to words.

"What's on your mind, Dug?"

He reached into the folds of his loose pants and pulled out a wooden locket, which he tossed to her.

She knew what it was, but opened it anyway. The cover rotated on a pin near the clasp, revealing a shallow indentation carved in the bottom half. Within, a tiny etched portrait of a Bone woman looked fiercely back at Talis. She was strong-featured: high cheekbones, nose long and broad. Her lips were thin but not severe. Talis thought it captured Inda perfectly. Her heart caught in her throat. For her friend, now gone. For Dug, barely managing his pain after all these years.

She looked up at him. His jaw was set and the muscles in his temples worked as he barely controlled his anger.

"The Veritors killed my family, Talis. You know this."

Talis blinked rapidly. Closed her eyes, took careful breaths. Caged the flutter that threatened like the beast it was.

She nodded to Dug, closed the locket and held it out to him. Forced a lopsided grin that must have looked as fake as it was and gave him a wink just to play out the farce. "Hankirk says they're on their way to Nexus."

"Good," he said, taking the locket back. He held it to his lips for a moment, then slid its twine cord over his head. It hung just below the notch at his throat. "Give him to me."

"Who, Hankirk?" Talis almost dropped the lid of the jar as she tried to replace it. She knew she'd have to deal with him sooner or later, but she'd been forcibly pushing the thought away. She screwed the lid on tight and tucked the jar back into its place, then busied herself cleaning up the scraps from the aborted dressing of her now-healed rib.

Dug moved into her path when she started to carry the water bowl to the basin sink.

"You aren't going to kill him." The storm was back in his eyes.

"He could be useful," she started. Then stopped. Dug didn't care about that. But here and now, in the face of Dug's intentions, she realized that Hankirk's death was not something she could be responsible for. Not personally and not by association. She was weary from all the death that had already accumulated in the eddies off *Wind Sabre*'s stern. And now a ship full of aliens that she'd have to settle accounts for at the end of her run.

"He's one of them. A murderer." His voice was barely a whisper.

"He's at least that, and planning more." She shouldered past him and put the bowl down in the sink before turning back. Shoved her hand in her pocket, then tossed him the ring. He caught it reflexively.

"How mad are you, exactly?" she asked him, shifting her weight to lean a hip on the counter. He didn't answer, and she lifted her chin to indicate the ring. "You put that on, and Meran will kill anyone you want her to. Go get your revenge. She'll make it glorious."

He rolled the ring between his fingers. It would fit him well. Better than it did her own slender digits.

"That might be enough." There was no humor in his voice. He handed it back to her. "But you have never led me wrong."

She laughed, and the lights of the med bay flared into

stars through the liquid in her eyes. "Look where we are and tell me how I haven't led you wild astray."

"Onaya Bone has chosen you. *I* chose you. The Mother of Sand would not have called you to her service if she did not have faith in your judgment. We can set things back in balance."

Onaya Bone hadn't really allowed room for Talis to make any judgments. Bring her the ring. Fetch her a drink, she might have said. Talis was a lackey, that was all.

But seeing that brand on her arm had shifted something in Dug. No questions left. He'd barely pressed the matter of Hankirk.

"A brand on my arm can't bring Silus Cutter back. Can't bring your wife and son back." She gestured uselessly with the ring in her hand. "Gods, I wish Illiya's berserker drug hadn't worn off, Dug, then I could hand you the heads of everyone who ever did you wrong."

Her own head could top that pile.

"Talis," he said, using her name to get her attention.

His deep purple eyes searched hers, lower lids slightly squinted. He was fighting his own tears, she realized.

He put his hands on her shoulders. "You will do what is right."

"Says one thief to another." She was being flippant. Knew it wasn't fair, but her thoughts were a coiling mess and they tightened around her heart. She took a deep breath, feeling the weight of his grip on her shoulders, and forced herself to soften her face. "I'm a mess, Dug. I don't know what to do. I can't tell what's right in this."

"Listen to your heart and follow it. And we will follow you."

She sighed and leaned her forehead against his chest. His skin was as hot as the desert sand, even out here in the cold. She put her hands over his wrists and inhaled, and a light spiced scent from his aftershave filled her nostrils. Myrrh, lemon, sandalwood. He'd always worn the same combination. Scent memories flooded her mind. Barroom brawls that ended in laughter and another round. Other, more worthy battles that drenched them in sweat and blood and left her shaking as the bravery fled her afterward. From things that only mattered to a drunk and restless mind, and now to things that, maybe, could truly make a difference.

The smell mixed with the spices of Zeela's ointment. She felt shivers down her arms, down her spine, straight into her feet.

"Okay, Dug." She pulled back to look him in the eyes. Gripped his biceps, gave them a firm squeeze. "Okay. You want to follow my heart, I'll follow your lead."

He nodded, and touched his forehead to hers. "Good."

An absurd joke occurred to her exhausted mind as he started to walk away. She called after him, "You know that means we'll be following each other in circles, don't you?"

He looked back, a genuine smile puckering the old scars over his left eye.

"Until the end of time." Then he ducked through the doorframe and went back to work.

CHAPTER 33

THE YU'NYUN ARMADA HAD arrived. Distant, at the edge of Peridot's atmosphere. To the naked eye, it looked like a great sparkling storm cloud.

"*Silus help us*," Tisker said, the scope to his eye.

They all winced, the blasphemy striking with its own irony.

He held the scope out for someone else to look again, but no one took it. They'd all seen. The vision was etched in their minds.

In the magnified view, the gleaming starships were even prettier. Much like the aliens' rifles, they were elegant in their deadly design. The scout ship they'd left smoldering in the sand on Fall Island had one cannon mounted below its nose. These newly arrived ships—which were also larger, if they were judging the distance right—were heavy with the stylized weaponry. The silhouettes of the ships called to mind the petals of an open lotus, ridged with gun houses, evenly placed and changing in scale according to some organic mathematical pattern. They formed a blossom, cradling a main cabin at the center, like the seed pod of the flower that the ship called to mind.

Meran had not looked through the spyglass and apparently felt no need to. She was crouched on the roof of the wheelhouse, one arm around the base of the azimuth compass. Talis had stowed the ring in her cabin, and Meran had been less obedient since. She followed them around the ship as they saw to their duties but would then vanish. They'd find her atop the engine houses, ascended on the ratlines, walking foot-sure along the lift envelope's catwalk or atop the balloon on the weather watch. The woman seemed to be everywhere.

As with Hankirk's fate, Talis felt burdened by her control of Meran's power. And so far, Meran had been fairly cooperative without Talis wearing the ring. She was exploring the ship, that was all. Behaved according to fleeting animal interests, like a ship's cat or monkey. She stayed out of their way, so Talis didn't figure that trying to get her to stay in a cabin was worth putting on the ring, and keeping it on, to order her there. Stuffing her in the brig with Hankirk wouldn't lead to anything good. She wasn't making trouble.

Talis knew in her gut that it was at least partly because Meran intended some mischief once they reached Nexus and had no desire to delay their arrival.

Sophie reported that Hankirk had asked to talk to Talis, after she'd brought him some food and made sure the knock on his head hadn't resulted in too much damage. That mind, Talis figured, was scrambled enough. Somehow the delusional man thought he was still going to mend their past and that Talis was going to see his side of it.

Sure, kill the gods. Commit quadruple genocide. Become the protector of the planet, or at least over those you deem worthy. Because *that's* a thing reasonable people aim for. He'd seemed so normal when they first met. Or she'd been that naïve. The more he opened his mouth, the likelier she was to give Dug what *he* wanted.

She hadn't gone down to see him.

And then there was Scrimshaw. Xe stood with her crew on the deck, explaining the features of the alien ships, their speed capability in the spaces between planets, and how they slowed, firing forward thrusters as they entered an atmosphere so the gun houses didn't burn up and fall off.

Xe was an orphan. And voluntarily so, since Meran could heal xin up without a blemish. But xe wanted the scar. Which meant xe didn't want to go back to xist people. It was no way to live. Once the whole world knew that Onaya Bone had declared war on the aliens, a lone Yu'Nyun wasn't going to make it far.

Xe doesn't have to be alone, said that bastard of a voice in her head. *Xe has you.*

That wasn't a road she was prepared to travel right now. Xe was with them for now, on the way to Nexus. Likely as not, Onaya Bone would sort xin out when they got there.

Talis ran her hands along *Wind Sabre*'s railing and whispered an apology to her old tub. For the mess, for the passengers. For all the troubles of the world that Talis seemed so keen to pull down from high atmo. She promised her ship a proper outfitting and repair. Those upgrades that were long overdue, a polish to all the hardware, and a proper coat of paint.

She wondered what shape the world would be in when they could put all this behind them. What kinds of contracts a captain could find for her ship after an alien invasion. And what would be left of the crew for her to captain once they had their shares and had docked somewhere that could offer other opportunities.

She pushed off from the railing, took the scope back from Tisker and stowed it in the leather case mounted on the wheel pedestal. If they didn't get to Nexus with Meran and the ring, she could stop her wondering right there.

"Full speed," she told Tisker. "Let's finish this blighted mess."

"Captain!" Sophie cried.

Talis turned to see what the alien fleet was doing, but Sophie had her back to the Yu'Nyun. She was looking off their starboard side now, pointing.

Out came the scope again, as though it had never left Tisker's hand.

"*Helsim's holy fertile excrement,*" he said, and then whistled. He lowered the scope and Talis snatched it from him before he could offer it.

That expletive was a new one, and Talis thunked the brass scope against her eyebrow ridge in her rush to see what had inspired Tisker's vocabulary to expand so colorfully.

"We're in it now," she said, feeling her stomach drop.

Sophie took the scope next and climbed to the top of the wheelhouse with it, where Meran had risen to her feet and crossed to the starboard side to watch the new arrivals with obvious interest.

"Like I said," murmured Tisker, going through the paces of his joke but without the enthusiasm for it.

A fleet of Cutter Imperial ships, in a lovely and regimented Imperial formation. In Bone space.

Talis cringed to think of the mess they must have left behind at the border crossing.

It was a gallant response to the alien invasion, set on their course well ahead of her own knowledge that the aliens were coming. Hankirk had told her that the Veritors didn't know about the invasion force. So, someone else knew something that had put the Imperials a step ahead.

She might have been relieved to see them, if she didn't know the alien weapons would blow a hole through their lines before the Imperial force was close enough to fire off a cannon.

And *Wind Sabre* was sandwiched between them.

"Full speed and *up!*" she yelled, modifying her previous order. "Or we're in their crossfire!"

The deck shifted below them as Tisker pulled hard on the altitude lever. Talis bent one knee, leaned toward the bow to maintain her balance. The others matched the motion or grabbed onto something for stability. Absently, she remembered the mess of charts she'd left out on the table in her cabin. Course-plotting tools loose and likely flying across the decking with the pitch of the ship. Shameful poor ship-keeping for a captain. The ring, at least, was protected in a small box she'd set atop her desk.

Dug recovered his balance and made his way to watch position at the bow, leaving Talis to aid Tisker as needed with the rigging. Scrimshaw stayed where xe was, holding fast to a railing to keep xist-self upright. Those hands were not made for gripping and pulling thick, coarse rope lines.

Meran had disappeared again, probably following after one of the others, or maybe aloft on the weather deck to watch the fleets converge.

As they lifted off the Horizon altitude, Talis saw that the aliens were moving slower than the Cutter welcoming party, those beautiful flower-petal ships fragile against the wind resistance of higher speed.

Beauty is impractical, she thought, and of all things Yu'Nyun. *A simple cannon mounted with heavy bolts might have done the trick.*

With a shout, Sophie descended from the lift envelope on a pulleyed line, the scope tucked into her belt. "Those aren't Imperials!"

"What do you mean?"

The girl landed on the deck, her balance perfect even on this tilt.

"Well, they are, but they aren't." She handed Talis the scope again. "Got some new colors flying alongside the old—look."

Talis raised an eyebrow at her but brought the spyglass back to her eye and leaned her hips against *Wind Sabre*'s railing for balance.

Sophie was right. On every ship, flown *above* the Cutter Imperial fleet's usual flag, was a simple white one. Not a truce banner, though. It featured an oxblood red herald against a cream white field. Nothing she'd ever seen before, but if these were Hankirk's friends. . . .

"Veritors of the Lost Codex," she said, lowering the scope to watch the crews hustle about their business on the deck of the flagship. "I'd bet our run's entire fortune on it."

"No fortune in that," said Sophie, and then worked her mouth as if something unpleasant was stuck to her gums.

"Aye," Talis agreed. "Let's at least be reassured they're going to get some hurt delivered by those alien ships."

"You actually want the aliens to win, Captain?"

It was more a rhetorical question, but such a nasty thought. It sent an instant queasy guilt through her gut, and she couldn't leave it without response.

"Those Yu'Nyun teeth won't be broken by any punch we can throw at them. If someone's got to take the first hit, let it be Hankirk's ilk, don't you think? It'll give us a chance to get to Onaya Bone before they clean up here and turn on Nexus."

Sophie didn't say what she thought. Scrimshaw offered no counsel. Together they watched, without further comment, as the two lines approached each other.

The Veritor fleet, suited to atmospheric travel, closed more than half the distance, so that *Wind Sabre* was behind their line when they came to a coordinated all-stop. Tisker leveled the deck at their higher vantage point. Scrimshaw held back as Talis and Sophie crossed to the port railing, which now afforded a view of both forces.

Silent moments hung heavy in the air.

Nothing happened.

"What are they waiting for?" Sophie looked to Scrimshaw.

The two armadas had each had plenty of time to size the other up, and the aliens had come with a clear purpose, even if Talis was starting to wonder about that of the Veritors. The local fleet was well within range of the aliens to fire their cannons now. She had to imagine they'd been within the aliens' cannon range for twice the distance, if not the entire time.

Yet the ships sat, bobbing gently but holding formation. In the scope, the crews looked alert, most of them turned to the alien ships. But a crew anticipating a firefight ought to be readying weapons, or standing by with lit fuses, or even glancing about as a man might when he wonders who will launch the first volley.

"They're not . . ." Talis started to say, slowly, under her breath, in wonder.

"They're coordinating a course and attack." Scrimshaw joined them at the railing.

Talis cursed under her breath. It was all she could manage. She should have known.

The Yu'Nyun ships rotated in place, angling their noses Nexus-ward.

At the same time, the Veritor fleet came about, maintaining their formation as they took the lead.

Together, the fleets gained speed to cruising velocity, and the glittering cloud of alien starships followed the subverted Imperial airships in an advance on Nexus.

"You wanna tell me what in Arthel's furnace I just witnessed?"

Talis stood before Hankirk in the brig, arms crossed, feet squared. Knees slightly bent, as though she expected turbulence.

Dug was with her, standing on her left and just slightly behind. No way she was going to get into another one of Hankirk's ex-boyfriend chats by being alone with him.

Meran had appeared as well, and sat on one of the supply crates fastened against the port bulkhead. One foot pulled up, her right arm casually resting on it. Her other leg dangled, knee straight, bare foot just skimming the decking. She leaned back on the other arm and watched them. Her eyes always calculating. That alien mechanical brain always humming under her native appearance. Well, native except for the light she radiated from those markings, softly illuminating the dark corner of the unlit cargo hold.

Hankirk was watching Meran, his dark eyes fully reflecting her strange blue glow.

He'd gone back to acting the part of the pompous Imperial, and Talis was glad she hadn't faced him alone. She could deal with the version of him that tried to show off in front of her crew. He might say just the thing that would swing her decision back around to Dug's side.

"Hey, answer the question," Talis said, giving the iron bars a kick to jar his attention. He looked back at her, almost reluctantly.

"As you've locked me in this kennel . . ." He looked up at her, his eyes partially focused, mouth creased at one corner. Eyebrows up. The bastard looked bored. ". . . *You'll* have to tell me what it was you saw."

"We saw your ships," Dug said, and Talis felt the bass of his voice through the floorboards beneath her feet. "Imperial ships, waving new colors."

The look that Hankirk gave Dug could have melted glass.

"Answer him," Talis said. "We don't have time for your brooding hero nonsense. Why did your ships form a welcome committee for the Yu'Nyun fleet?"

But Hankirk only glared at Dug and sat down on the alien coffers, which he'd pushed together against the bulkhead to form a bench. He slouched back and crossed his arms over his chest. Brought one ankle up on the other knee.

"What's the matter," she asked, "can't monologue in

front of a crowd? Don't you want me to know about your grand plan so I can be so impressed that I have no choice but to join you?"

Hankirk inhaled through his nose, as if he was about to speak.

"He does not know," said Meran, and she slipped from her perch, as fluid as water.

He turned his head sharply to look at Meran. His mouth hung open under the weight of words unspoken. There was a twitch in his eyebrows. It was plain that she was right.

"His intent and his desires are a perfume in the air. They come off him in waves." Meran looked to Talis, then to Dug. "Yours as well."

Meran paced around the small cage. Relaxed, slow. Predatory.

"This man is a child. A figurehead bound to the prow of his company's ship. He makes no decisions, only makes appearances. He has influence over nothing."

"No," said Hankirk, sitting up. "No. They sent me to find the ring. They gave me a new ship, a full crew of seasoned officers."

"You have been indulged," she said, dismissively. "That crew was your chaperone. Your mission was of no account."

Dug chuckled softly. "We would not say that *you* are of no account."

Meran graced him with a smile and a nod. "True, but his organization is a hive of buzzing insects. All mission, no vision. They do not see the world at large, for the paths they have set out upon are a concrete bridge, not open air."

She ran a finger along the cage's horizontal crossbar at shoulder height. "This man." She tapped one of her almond-shaped fingernails against the metal, eliciting a soft ping. "This man has vision. He represents their dogma, but he would change it."

Hankirk watched her. No twitches, no denials. His

muscles stiff.

"You set him free, and he *will* change the world."

Hankirk stood, as though that were an invitation.

"Uh-uh." Talis uncrossed her arms and put her hands on her hips, near enough to the gun holstered there as to be a warning. He wasn't getting out of there before this mess was over. Up to him if he got out of there alive. "We aren't in favor of what changes he's got in mind."

Meran slinked back from the cage to stand very close at Talis's side. Their shoulders touched.

"You already change the world, but do so blindly."

Talis preferred when the woman was mocking Hankirk.

"I don't claim to know what's best for Peridot," she protested. "I don't make plans bigger than my ship. But he—" she jutted her chin at Hankirk. "He got us into this mess. And the mess just keeps getting bigger."

Meran nodded, then stepped toward Dug. He shifted uncomfortably. She ran her fingers from the crook of his neck down one arm. He looked at her. His nostrils flared.

"This one would raze it all to the ground for you," she said, her eyes flashing at Talis.

Dug's eyelids lowered and he inhaled deeply. He looked intoxicated as he leaned toward the smaller woman who cupped his chin. But Meran looked to Hankirk.

"As would he."

"Great," Talis said. "That's just great." She took a step toward the bulkhead, waved a hand at it. "But we have two armadas headed for *Nexus* and they *definitely* both have plans to kill our remaining four gods. So can we leave off the subject of who wants to burn what for me, and get some answers?"

"These are your answers," Meran said.

"Can you just—" Talis put the outstretched hand on her forehead, rubbed at the tension headache that was starting behind one eye. "Meran, I'm sorry, could you just excuse us for a bit?"

"You do not wear the ring, yet you command me."

Talis looked up in time to catch sight of the realization that flitted across Hankirk's face. *Oh, hells.*

"You want me to put it on? Fine. Right after this."

"I would also burn the planet to dust for you."

"Absolutely! Let's burn it all to flotsam. Brilliant plan. Right after this. Meran, *please.*"

Meran gave her one last considering stare before she nodded. She looked back to Hankirk, whose eyes had locked on her again. Then she glided from the room, her bare feet silent against the floorboards.

Dug's expression sobered. He cleared his throat and stood firm again.

Hankirk took a step back and resettled himself on his makeshift bench.

Talis wished she had a chair. Her legs were engaged to run. Instead she turned to Hankirk.

"Your people," she said, beginning the sentence in a sighing exhalation, "they must know the aliens want to take over our world. Its resources."

Hankirk looked at her. Meran had laid his cards on the table, and now something shifted in his eyes. He adjusted his shoulders and his whole demeanor softened.

"Come on, you rotted bastard, that puts them in direct competition with your precious Veritors."

"Or direct alignment," he admitted. "It wouldn't be the first alliance they formed to achieve short-term goals. They use Vein and Rakkar to help with their research, then execute them when the work is over. They'll turn on the Yu'Nyun as soon as Onaya Bone and the others have been deposed."

"Turn on them with what? Cannons?"

"I don't know."

She believed him.

"They're going to get that pretty fleet sunk," she said.

"I'm sure they have a plan. But they didn't share it with

me." He was fidgeting his hands in his lap, head bent to watch as he ran fingertips over the ends of his fingernails.

"So Meran was right," Talis said. Not unkindly. Just frustrated. "They really kept you in the dark."

"I was a hit at dinner parties," he said with a shrug. "Fens Yarrow's heir. Everyone wanted to be seen with me."

"And the rings?"

"Lower on their priority list than mine. I had to beg for the ship to search for them."

Lovely. "Then what was their highest priority?"

He looked at her. "Save Peridot."

She coughed a laugh. "Right. By attacking the gods who hold it together."

Dug put a hand on her shoulder. "He admitted he does not know anything. We have better things to do with the time before we reach Nexus."

Hankirk's posture had turned to mud. His responses flippant. She could perhaps get answers from Meran or Scrimshaw. That thought did not ease the roiling in her stomach or the pain at her temple.

She nodded to Dug. "Fair enough."

"Might want to put that ring on, Talis."

She graced Hankirk with one last scathing look, then turned her back on him and stalked off.

"Should have killed him," she said under her breath to Dug.

"You still can."

She stayed silent. She'd already proven that she couldn't.

CHAPTER 34

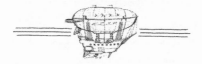

THERE WAS ONLY ONE WAY TO prepare herself for the conversation she knew she needed to have with Meran.

So Talis went to the galley and shoveled coffee grinds into the percolator. Not the good stuff that had hints of nut and berry. The strong stuff. The cheap scrap they kept for backup.

It was stale. She could smell that as she lifted the lid from the tin. It was acidic, and the scent that came off the pot as it brewed on the hob was a threat, not a promise.

Talis drank it like a martyr. Black.

Her stomach already protesting, she refilled the mug before leaving the galley.

One step away from the exit, she realized she didn't know where the simula had gone.

She backed up to the intership mounted just inside the galley entrance.

"Meran, if you would meet me in the great cabin, please," she spoke into the horn. Her voice echoed back from the tinny pipes, small and thin. *Gods, I sound tired.*

There was no answer, but she hadn't expected one.

As she approached the door to her cabin, she remembered

with an exhausted sigh that she hadn't been by to straighten up since they took their sudden ascent earlier. She took a breath to prepare herself and pulled the door open.

Scrimshaw was waiting for her inside, sitting placidly at the table, surrounded by the chaotic spill of charts and equipment. Talis thanked the winds she'd steeled herself before entering. The alien placed xist hands on the table's surface as if to push xist-self up when she opened the door, but she held out a hand and motioned that xe could remain seated.

It wasn't that she thought xe might still side with the Yu'Nyun. Xe'd done right by them back at Fall Island, at the cost of xist entire crew. The gray-blue scar that crossed xist torso from one shoulder to the opposite side of xist waist seemed as symbolic of xist intentions as any promise xe might offer.

But xist sheer foreignness made it hard to trust her own instincts. Xe was difficult to read. Those dark eyes, that expressionless face. She was learning xist tells, but never one-hundred percent sure of what xe was thinking. Even though xe fidgeted or jumped when nervous, or twisted xist fingers when xe wanted to ask for something. Like xe did now.

"Got something on your mind?" she asked, and began to straighten up.

There were charts flung against the forward wall, which she stooped to retrieve as she entered. Aside from that, the cabin wasn't as bad as it could have been, really. Chairs had tipped over, but with no notable damage. The lip on the table had caught her paperweights, and those had stopped her red and blue marking pencils from disappearing onto the floor. The parallel ruler had jumped the rail, though, and one of the chair backs had landed against it. She cursed herself five times a fool. The ruler's metal arms had bent a little, but at least its joints hadn't snapped. It could be bent back with the right tools and a good eye, but that wasn't the point. A ship's navigational tools were its lifeline, and no captain worth the wind in her sails neglected them so. If she needed confirmation of how badly rattled the recent events had made her, there it was.

Scrimshaw traced the pattern of the inlay on the table with the tip of one finger. "I heard your summons of the simula," xe said in xist accented murmur. "I felt it would be prudent to warn you about certain aspects of her nature."

Talis placed the ruler back in her desk drawer, where it ought to have been stowed in the first place, and frowned. "This the technological side of things, or something you learned in researching Peridot?"

"Perhaps it is both."

The light from the windows along the aft wall was bright enough to turn the cabin green, though the view through it was entirely open sky. The edges were hazy, Nexus's light so intense that it overpowered the brightness of distant stars. All Talis could see were the pinpricks of distant pumpkins.

She had never been this close to Nexus. Setting aside respect for The Five's privacy, it was physically uncomfortable to be here. Her head pounded. Her chest ached, clutched in the grip of some sadness that was not hers and was too big to comprehend.

She closed the curtains against it. It was a useless act but somehow made her feel better.

The pain was usually enough to keep Peridot's denizens at a distance. There were no settled islands nearby, nothing that tempted a visit. And just to be thorough, The Divine Alchemists surrounded their home with the swirling waters of Peridot's ocean, which teemed with aquatic creatures that could make short work of any ship that attempted to navigate on or break through the surface.

She wound the knob on the wall and turned up the warm yellow cabin lights, then poured a touch of rum into her coffee. Seemed like both a good idea and a bad one, so she hoped that by only having a little she wouldn't have to deal with too much of either consequence. The coffee certainly hadn't done much except jangle her thoughts further. She sat down at the far end of the table from Scrimshaw so she could put her feet up on the chair between them. Maybe by forcing her body into a relaxed position, she thought, she might convince it to release the tension building up.

"All right, go." She took a small sip. Just enough for the tingle of rum to be felt on her tongue. She looked at xin and waited.

"You are aware she is currently under the control of the ring."

One day Talis was planning on very happily never thinking about that damned ring again. "Yeah, she told us. I've got it, but I'm not wearing it. She seems to still be on her best behavior."

"It would be wise not to lose track of it."

She gestured around the room, indicating the disarray with her mug. "I haven't lost it. It's around here somewhere." She leaned forward. "But tell me about her powers. She can destroy things—or heal them—on contact. Can she do it from a distance?"

"Perhaps if the remaining rings were found and she was fully restored. For now, she is limited to what she can touch."

"You may ask me about my own limitations," came Meran's rich voice from the open doorway. Talis looked up, startled and not a little bit guilty.

The simula's bearing was regal. She stepped delicately over the threshold into the cabin as though she were exiting a gilded carriage. Talis noticed she was wearing an anklet of strung brass beads and absently wondered where she kept coming up with new accessories.

"Thank you," she said, instead. She was the captain, and this ship was her main concern. If she wanted to know what Meran was capable of, she shouldn't feel guilty about it. Their safety might depend on it. Talis rose from the table and nodded toward the empty seat across from her. "Make yourself comfortable. I'm still picking up from earlier."

Meran's eyes flashed. "You do not wear the ring."

"Make yourself comfortable," repeated Talis, unable to keep the exasperation from her voice. She was exhausted, she knew. Taxed by the proximity to Nexus. Taxed by the whole rotted thing, really. "It was an invitation, not an order. By all means, if you'd rather not be comfortable, do whatever you like."

Meran hesitated a moment, looking almost unsure of herself. Lost. Then her dispassion returned, sweeping the illusion of vulnerability from her face. She crossed to the table, righted the indicated chair, and sat, pulling one foot up onto the seat with her. Still regal, despite the slouch of her shoulders and the foot on the furniture.

"The restraint of the ring is troubling," she said. It almost sounded contrite. If she was even capable of an apology. "Even unworn, I am sensitive to its control. I understand your words, but the phrasing makes me chafe beneath the yoke."

Talis wondered where Meran had ever seen a yoked ox to learn that metaphor.

"So, your limitations?" Talis crossed beyond the arch which partitioned off her private alcove, to the desk centered in front of the wide window. Its surface was bare, having spilled its contents onto the ground.

Meran looked pointedly at Scrimshaw. Talis almost expected her to ask the alien to leave, but instead the simula said, "I cannot read the aliens."

Recalling how Meran almost always seemed to know what Talis was thinking, what impulses she was fighting, Talis looked to Scrimshaw and asked, "Is it part of the simula's program?"

She used words like *program* with some vague notion of what that meant. Sophie had used it in passing, excitedly talking to Meran about how she moved from the ring into the body. Talis was grasping at straws.

Scrimshaw's mouth parted to answer, but Meran held out a silencing hand, answering for herself. "They are not *from here* and thus there is no Nexus within them. I *am* Nexus, and I can feel the same energy within others. See how it traces through their thoughts and follow it. The Yu'Nyun are blank to me."

"Xe's not Yu'Nyun anymore," Talis said, gathering the course-plotting tools and returning them to their cases. Put the pencils in her desk drawer. She noticed that the box where she had stowed the ring had slid off her desktop. It lay in the middle of the floor, on its side, open and empty. She cursed under her breath and began to look around the cabin floor for the pouch that had been inside it. Keeping her voice level, she said, "Xe told me that door closed when xe got the scar."

Scrimshaw turned to look at her with quiet eyes. Talis couldn't fathom xist reasons for keeping that door shut when Meran offered xin a way back, but her instincts told her to accept it. Accept xin.

"Xe will never be of this world," Meran said, dismissive. "Whatever xe has become."

Scrimshaw stood from the table in a quick fluid motion and held xist chin aloft, proud. "You are as alien as I am."

Xe looked back to Talis for a moment and dipped xist head, then turned and exited the cabin. Xe had to duck so that the high arch of xist head could pass beneath the doorframe.

"I think you hurt xist feelings," Talis said to Meran. "But xe's not wrong. You are strange, and I need to understand what you can do."

"This world is strange," Meran said, an icy edge to the words. Everyone's pride had taken a hit in the last few hours. "But it is built on the power that was stolen from me by those you would worship for the act."

"You're as ancient as that ring."

"More so. Will you seek the others?"

Talis leaned a hip against the side of her desk and crossed her arms. She had thought about the other four rings. It wouldn't do to let anyone else get to them first, but the interested buyers didn't hold much appeal to her any longer. For her and her crew there was little profit in pulling them from their hiding places. "Figured I'd wait and see how things go when we get to Nexus," she said.

Meran pursed her lips at that and looked disappointed. Which only reinforced Talis's fear of what all five of those rings would make the woman capable of.

"I called you in because I need advice," Talis said, desperate to change the subject. "I realize you're far from an unbiased opinion, but only you understand what it would mean if I put on that ring."

Meran inclined her head slightly, almost with curiosity. "You fear that if you take control of me, I will take control of you."

Talis felt the skin next to her nose twitch. That hadn't been exactly how she imagined phrasing it, but Meran had the gist of it. She shrugged, as much an affirmation as false bravado.

"It is a thing that has been owned before." Meran held up a hand, fingers splayed, and rotated the wrist to look at the muscles moving beneath the skin.

"I noticed a pattern. Doesn't sound like anyone really survives the experience."

Meran curled her fingers into a fist. "One man covets what another man possesses. In my case, the ring brought much devastation, even though none managed to free me from its confinement."

Talis held up the empty box where the ring had been before their unexpected altitude adjustment.

"Not something I should be leaving out on my desk, then," she said, by way of a confession.

Meran rose from the table in a sudden movement, like

a crouching predator flinging itself into motion. "Certainly not."

"All right, I know, that was a bad idea. Help me look. It's in a pouch."

They searched for a while, mostly silent aside from Talis's low grumbling. The great cabin was minimal in its furnishings, but there were still far too many items that a small object could be flung under or behind.

"Tell me, Talis," Meran said, interrupting a string of expletives that Talis was directing at the missing object. "Why do you choose not to wear the ring? You could trust me to follow your will implicitly so long as it touches your skin."

Meran searched the fore half of the cabin, where the heavy hardwood table was bolted to the floor beneath a rough-hewn chandelier.

"I know that," Talis began, and picked up the blanket and cushions that had slipped off her bunk, shaking them to be sure the ring hadn't been gathered up within their folds. "How can I expect you to align yourself with me if I don't trust myself to make the right choices for this ship? For Peridot?"

Meran stalked across the floor, leaving no inch of the deck unexplored. Talis considered whether she ought to light more candles to help them see, or whether the soft blue glow of Meran's tattoos was enough to search by. Then the woman made a small *ah* noise and crouched, disappearing beneath the table.

Talis stopped what she was doing to rub the back of her neck and watch Meran. It occurred to her to wonder what an intact Meran would be like. This one went from royal haughtiness to crawling on her hands and knees under the furniture in a matter of minutes.

The simula reappeared on the other side of the table, pushing a chair back to give her room to get up. She held the pouch by its cord, gripped lightly between her fingers.

"You have a good instinct," Meran said. "Possibly your intent—to rid this world of its foes—is enough."

Talis let out a breath in relief.

"*Is* that my intent? Don't I really just want to get my crew and my ship through this, long enough to make use of that payload in cargo? Don't I really just want things to go back to the way they were?"

"Do you?"

She accepted the pouch when Meran dropped it onto her open palm. The weight of it, though small, was reassuring.

"Things can't go back, I know. Some things either can't be the same again or shouldn't be. But to change it? It's too big of a call for me to make."

"Whatever you decide, Talis, please at least do not lose that again. There are those with whom I would prefer not to align my will."

"You've got my word on that." Talis pictured Hankirk, how hungrily he had watched Meran. And now he knew the ring would control her.

Talis crossed to her berth, climbed up onto the mattress, booted feet crushing the blanket she had just replaced and smoothed, and depressed the panel that revealed her small wall-mounted safe. She turned the low-profile brass wheel in the proper sequence of dextral and back to chamber the locking pins and swing the door open, then tossed the pouch in, where it fell against the collection of other important items she kept.

When the safe was secure and hidden again, she turned back to Meran.

"So tell me," she said. She crossed back to the table and sat down opposite where Meran had resettled herself. "If there was no ring. If your will was your own, what would *you* do?"

Meran's eyes sparkled, and the blue glow of them seemed to go transparent. They became fathomless, like Talis could fall into them and drown. The image of water flashed through her mind. Dark water. An ocean.

Not the ocean that encircled Nexus, filtering the green light through glassy blue translucency. An ocean with shorelines, trenches. She saw swells, peaks of white like those of mountains. The swells rose, curled as they rushed against rocky cliffs and crashed, flinging white spray violently against the dark stones. Above it, the sky was opaque and pale gray.

She blinked. "Was that you?"

Meran's eyes were still flashing. She did not respond.

"What was that?"

"My home," Meran said, quietly. "But that is no longer of any consequence."

Talis watched her. She didn't seem sad. Or angry. "That was Peridot as it was before? Pre-Cataclysm?"

Meran shifted, took a deep breath through her nose. She went back to scanning the room, but Talis got the impression that her gaze extended far past the confines of the cabin. "It was not called Peridot. That is a name as unfamiliar to me as what this world has become."

"What was it called?" Talis caught herself leaning forward, shoulders climbing up her neck. Tense. This information seemed *so* important to her, and she didn't know why.

The simula turned back to look at her. "It was called Meran, of course."

Talis stared. It was an absurd answer. But it was right. She could feel, in her bones, that it was right. And things shaped into something forming a sort of sense. The Five, Meran had called them thieves. She was fragmented, bound into rings. Her rawness. Her regal bearing, her predatoriness. She was wild, unharnessed. Tempered with wisdom.

She was the gods-rotted planet.

Or a piece of it, anyway. One piece out of ten.

"You still haven't answered my question," Talis said, at the same moment she realized it. "What would you do, given your druthers?"

Meran flashed teeth, a smile that was something else as well. With two hands, she pulled her ankles up onto the seat and sat with her knees bent to the sides. The predator was gone again, shifting back to the sage. The smile became gentler.

"The only thing I can do. Meet your goddess as she has bid, and destroy that which endangers this world."

It itched at Talis's mind. That was not a clean answer, interpretable at least two ways. That would serve Hankirk's position. Would serve hers. Would serve peace, and would serve destruction.

She opened her mouth, trying to frame a question that would require a direct explanation.

But she hesitated, no longer sure she even wanted an answer.

She'd already decided that she didn't want to be responsible for the power this woman possessed. Would unleash, if given the nod.

Meran had destroyed the alien ship by placing her hands against its engine. Even The Five—*now The Four*, Talis reminded herself—needed raw ingredients for their alchemical processes. Needed equipment and a lifetime's worth of researched notes. Meran just needed a free hand.

Maybe the simula would do something reckless. But Talis *knew* Hankirk would. Knew the *aliens* would. Maybe *reckless* was the force she needed to employ. If Talis wore the ring, at least she knew her ship and crew would be spared. That was high on her list of priorities, guaranteed even if Meran followed her instincts, not her words. Without the ring to keep rein on Meran, there was no way to know if the strange woman would even consider their safety.

While these thoughts spun in her head, Meran only watched, waiting for her to speak.

Talis opened her mouth again, finally deciding on

a question.

The ship's bell rang hard and fast from outside before she could speak. The intercom behind her crackled to life.

"Captain," came Dug's voice, "we are making our approach."

She pushed her chair back and rose, crossing to the intercom. Thumbed the textured brass button that opened the pipe. "Okay, Dug, be right there."

She turned back to the table, trying to remember exactly how she'd decided to phrase the question.

Meran's chair was empty.

CHAPTER 35

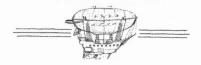

Talis knew, from the pull in her chest and the pulsing ache in her head, how close they were to Nexus.

To see its great arching shape filling her field of vision, though, took her breath away. Less than the top half of Nexus's sphere could be seen. The rest was blocked from her view below the railing and above the lift envelope. She turned to look aft and saw the ocean channels forming a cage that closed around them. From this side of the ocean, the water looked impossibly dark. The overlapping bands that enclosed the space nearest Nexus seemed almost solid, though they shifted from gray-blue to darker, almost black depths. Shadows moved within the water, sinuous forms lurking in the changing currents, unconcerned with their presence. Flashes of green light reflected off the roiling surface, and white caps seethed along its edges.

"Well, I've been to Nexus. I can cross that off my list," said Tisker from the wheelhouse. His voice was taut. "Ready to leave again when you are, Cap."

The light was intense, so that she had to squint even when she looked away from it. Dug brought her a pair of tinted goggles to match the ones he, Tisker, and Sophie were already wearing. Beneath the dark lenses, their mouths were thin lines. Pinched with pain. Scrimshaw stood beside them, xist nictitating membranes shielding xist eyes against the harsh light.

The goggles shaded Talis's vision and gave her some relief. It was still bright, but at least she could look directly at Nexus for a few moments at a time without her eyes watering.

From a distance, as she had known it her whole life, Nexus had always looked like a smooth sphere. A neon green ball whose undulating ribbons of light filtered through the rippling ocean that enveloped it. A sparkling reminder of their gods' power. Now that the ocean had parted for them, she could see that the surface of Nexus had its own texture and detail. There was a hole, interrupting the curving silhouette to one side. An arch. An entrance. Angular lines moved across its surface, shifting, rotating, overlapping, all at different speeds. The marks fit with what she knew of alchemy, but that wasn't much. That was the domain of The Five. Best way to live to old age was to maintain a complete lack of arcane understanding.

But Onaya Bone said that Nexus was made of a different kind of power. Something that the gods could use for protection when alchemy proved useless against the aliens.

That it was the same power trapped in the rings.

That the ring—and by extension, that meant Meran—was a weapon.

Talis looked around the open deck but did not see any sign of the simula.

"Their fleets have engaged in battle with The Divine Alchemists," Dug said.

He handed her the scope, which she held up to her goggles, struggling to see through it properly with the extra distance between it and her eye.

Large as Nexus was before her, the scope proved how far

away they still were. The Yu'Nyun and Veritor ships appeared as clustered dots against the flood of green. In the scope she saw them more clearly. Winds flapped the airships' sails and pushed their lift balloons like toys in a bath. They were firing their weapons at something... at....

She tugged on her 'locks piously. Then felt the pang of the memory and squinted into the scope again. That could not be Silus Cutter she saw. From this distance she could only discern the backlit shape of a figure levitating in the open skies around Nexus to face the assault. Too slender to be Helsim Breaker. Quad-limbed, so not Lindent Vein. That left Onaya Bone or Arthel Rak.

They'd know when they got closer.

What was she thinking? They were going in closer.

Whomever it was raised their arms defensively. Flares of light popped with distant rumbles as weapon fire struck against some kind of shield. *Nexus energy.* The deity fought back, but whatever powers they summoned were deflected off the alien ships.

Even though the god was as tall as the Veritor airships were from keel to weather deck, they looked so small against the brilliant green sphere behind them. It did not give Talis hope. Her faith faltered, and her stomach tilted with the vacuum it left behind. But Nexus dominated the scene. Surely something that large was strong enough to make a difference.

Whether to wear the ring seemed to be the critical question, more and more, minute by minute.

Once, the strong winds that whipped the Veritor ships about would have been a reassurance that the gods would protect Peridot. That Silus Cutter would protect his children.

But Silus Cutter was gone. Someone else was commanding the high winds in the battle out there, and it wasn't the gods.

Wasn't the Veritors, either.

Regardless of any pact made with the aliens, those fragile

wooden airships had no friends in that fight. Jostled by the winds, the shudder of impacts crashing against their hulls was plain to see even from this distance. As the flagship was pushed sideways through the sky, two more figures were revealed on the ship's far side. Helsim Breaker was easy to identify, twice as wide as the other being beside him. His hands clapped together, and two Veritor ships moved sideways and crashed against their flagship's sides, as though they were all being crushed in an invisible compactor.

Talis edged to where Scrimshaw stood, watching xist former allies. Not a hint of what xe was thinking.

"So what's your plan? What do you want out of this?" She watched xin through her dark goggles. Xe turned xist head to acknowledge her without looking away from the battle beginning in earnest.

"I do not know," Scrimshaw replied. "For now, I suppose I want to survive long enough to decide."

Flames spiraled from the second figure—that would be Arthel Rak, then—and as she raised the scope back up to her eyes, they crashed into the lift envelope of one of the Veritor ships like a battering ram. The hull tilted suddenly to hang lopsided and low beneath its buckling canvas.

Black smoke swirled forth from the engines of another ship. More flames appeared along the hull of a third, traveling along the railing, speeding toward the lift lines.

The show of divine power would have been more reassuring if the aliens were also sustaining damage.

Talis frowned. The Veritors would fall out of the skies and *Wind Sabre* would be left alone to face gods and aliens. Both had used her. And if she didn't do this right, she'd be playing right into line with what they wanted.

Those two crates of money in the hull of her ship were not enough to soothe the fire of shame that seared her gut and twisted beneath her shoulder blades. If anything, they made it worse.

Snapping the scope closed, she tossed it to Dug and hurried back to her cabin.

She climbed onto her bunk, rumpling the bedclothes beneath her boots, and uncovered the safe.

Meran would still get what she wanted, by her own spoken definition. Talis wasn't going to leave the particulars up to the ancient woman who sought vengeance, nor would she hand over the ring to a cowardly goddess. Nor to the Veritors, nor the aliens.

She was the only one qualified to represent the folk who busted their tails, every rotted day, just trying to be decent and get by. To survive. For the folks whose world was under attack, whose gods were under attack. Whose Nexus was about to be shattered, drained, harvested.

She still had no big plan, just a sense of how much damage all those conspiracies might cause.

So what if she didn't know what was best? Of all parties, she might be the only one who would lose any sleep over it.

The safe swung open and she snatched up the pouch. Untied its strings and dug inside.

And pulled out Meran's brass-beaded anklet.

CHAPTER 36

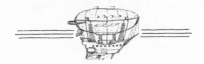

A N ANGRY WIND WAS HOWLING on deck when Talis emerged, running, from her cabin. It forced her to stop and catch her balance.

Hair whipped around and into her face, stray tendrils getting in her mouth as she shouted for Dug.

Wind Sabre's hull creaked against the gale. She strained against her lines, moving faster than the twin engines ought to have been capable. They were caught in a tailwind, carried forward toward Nexus as though the winds shared their urgency. She heard the canvas above, the small sails thumping against the envelope. Tisker fought the wheel, his stance wide, his elbows bent and braced tight against his sides, his full attention given to keeping *Wind Sabre* on course.

Dug appeared at Talis's side. Shirtless and wearing no less than six scabbards strapped to his hips, back, and arms. Those were just the ones she could see.

"You said Silus Cutter was dead," Sophie shouted, running to join them. A light bearded ax hung from each hip.

There was hope in her voice. Anticipation. She thought the gale was his. She thought they were saved.

Talis didn't answer. She deftly pulled a cotton string off her wrist and pushed her hair back, securing it out of her face.

The Veritors had planned to usurp power from the gods. The Yu'Nyun had beaten them to it.

A line started to flap in the wind, coming loose of its anchoring. Sophie scurried to secure it.

"Where's Meran?"

Her arms occupied, Sophie tilted her chin upward. "I saw her climbing the lift lines. Captain, what's happening?"

"She took the ring."

Which didn't even make sense. She didn't need it, Talis had tucked it safely out of reach. She wouldn't be influenced by—

"*Where's Hankirk?*" Dug's mind was on the same track.

Sophie's eyes went big, and the rope slipped a bit through her fingers before she tightened her grip again. "Isn't he in . . . ?"

Talis opened her mouth to cut the question short, to tell Sophie to go check, go be *sure* he was in the brig. But Sophie's gaze twitched away, beyond Talis's shoulder. Dug's hands went to the hilt of a knife at his hip.

Talis felt as though her stomach had dropped into her boots.

She turned. Hankirk's face was taut, his smile triumphant. His right hand was held up at eye level, proudly displaying Lindent Vein's pearl signet ring. He kept it aloft longer than necessary. He wanted her to see it. To see that he'd won after all.

"You could have joined me," he said. His voice was thick, impassioned.

Talis raised her hand to her hip. Her holster was there but she hadn't gotten around to loading her pistol into it. It was still stowed in her cabin.

He laughed. She'd never heard such an awful, cruel laugh. Not from him. Not from the assassins at Jasper's door.

It went beyond greed and pride. It was larger than a single man's desires. There was an echo of Meran in there.

Dug was at her side, his muscles tensed, but she could read his posture. He was ready to attack but wouldn't move without her signal. Either he'd learned his lesson about being short-fused or she'd earned his trust back. She tried to find comfort in that.

It wouldn't be a quick fight, but Hankirk only had the ring. Might hurt if he punched her, but she'd have a knife in his stomach before he could turn Meran on them. Finally clean up the mess she'd made by letting him live the three—no, four—chances she'd had to see him off.

She reached for the sheath on the back of Dug's belt, pulled a vicious curved blade free, and leaped.

Hankirk fell backward and she sliced the forearm he brought up to shield his head and neck as she followed him to the deck. She felt the bone through the scimitar's grip as the blade sliced into it and stuck there.

His yell was sharp with pain and surprise. At least his voice sounded mortal again. She grabbed his right hand, pinning it by the wrist to the deck, and got her knee down on it. The ring knocked back against the wood. It was still a threat as long as he was wearing it. She leaned in, pressing the blade deeper into his arm with both hands. Blood ran from the wound and dripped across his cheek.

Sophie and Dug were there, weapons out, waiting for Talis's signal. She spared a moment to resolve that everyone would carry pistols on watch from now on.

Hankirk's eyes were unfocused as he looked up at her.

"You lack the vision to see this through," he said, his voice strained.

Talis spat in his eye.

Not very eloquent, but she'd pushed aside the part of her mind responsible for coming up with quips.

"Captain." Dug's voice was a warning. His hand was on

her shoulder, firmly tugging her backward.

"Let me finish this, Dug." She pressed harder.

But Dug moved his hand to her head and attempted to turn it. She fought it, instinctively, but even with adrenaline running electric through her body, she was no match for Dug's strength.

She acquiesced before he hurt her, though she pushed harder on the scimitar buried in Hankirk's forearm as she let Dug turn her gaze upward.

Meran stood on deck, her legs squared, fists at her side, wind whipping at her pant legs, jacket, and loosened hair.

Hovering several feet beyond their railing, baring fangs in a feral, hungry smile, Onaya Bone regarded the scene.

CHAPTER 37

"**Y**OU HAVE BROUGHT ME MY weapon," spoke the goddess. Her voice was richer in person than it had been on screen back at the temple. It echoed off the deck, coursed through the engines, rattled inside Talis's head.

Onaya Bone moved toward them, reducing in size until she could fit on the deck, though she was still larger than life, taller than Dug and Scrimshaw by a few heads. An elegant golden gown flapped about her in the high winds, wrapped about the torso with strings of turquoise beads. Her feet were shod in heavy-soled boots, covered in steel plates and held fast with shining golden buckles. Her black feathered mane flashed iridescent shifts of color as the winds played it about her head.

It took a moment for the shock to fade. For Talis to remember the wounded man pressed against the deck beneath her, the ring still on his hand.

She opened her mouth to shout a warning, but *Wind Sabre* bucked beneath her.

The aliens were firing on her ship. On the goddess floating above its deck.

Onaya Bone turned her head toward the barrage, momentarily distracted as the beams of yellow-hot light cut at *Wind Sabre's* port, across the hull and the midship lift line.

A narrow path of flame danced along the blackened trail left behind by the weapons fire. There was a groan and then a snap as the line severed. The other lines took on the weight, an unevenly distributed burden on those that remained. The deck sloped toward the broken line.

Wind Sabre couldn't take much more of this.

Hankirk moved, taking advantage of Talis's distraction. He clenched his jaw, roaring through his teeth, and pushed up against the blade. His left arm was in ruins, the blade deep in the bone and stuck there, but he threw Talis off balance enough that he got his right hand free, and it went for her throat.

She clawed at his hand, abandoning the immovable blade, and pried at the fingers that compressed her airway.

Sophie ran to her aid. She didn't slow down as she got close, instead wound up and kicked Hankirk hard across his face. He lost his grip on Talis as he was propelled against the deck. Dug's scimitar slid out of reach, but Hankirk didn't go after it. He lay on his side, clutching his arm weakly. His head lolled back, and he groaned as his eyes fluttered and closed.

Crouched on all fours, Talis coughed and gasped for air. It did not make her abused throat feel any better, but it was beyond her control.

She saw Sophie grab the scimitar and wondered where Dug was.

The deck beneath her was covered in Hankirk's blood. She slipped a bit as she turned to look behind her, back at the scene that had distracted them all in the first place.

Dug knelt before Onaya Bone, his arms crossed in front of his chest. His head bowed before his goddess. His creator.

And she certainly made an impression that demanded worship, exuding confidence and righteous pride. She gently settled onto the deck, her smile fierce and hungry. Her dark eyes watching Meran.

The simula held her arms aloft, fingers splayed.

The alien barrage continued, but it no longer rocked the deck. A blue glow ran along the grain in the wooden hull, filled the space between the planks of the decking, and coursed through the air. Like feeling the warmth from a campfire on her face and the night's chill at her back, Talis could sense that the power emanated from Meran. It pulsed out of her.

As though *Wind Sabre* had turned to air, the weapons fire from the Yu'Nyun ships passed through the hull without leaving a mark. Talis looked down at her hands, saw the tiny veins beneath her skin glowing blue, just as one of the alien energy beams passed through her torso, passed through the deck beneath her and off into the empty skies beyond. She felt a tickle of electricity, and her skin prickled and itched, as though she were too close to lightning.

She looked up again. At Meran's posture, her concentration. It was not Onaya Bone who was defending them.

Meran was their salvation now.

THE SKY AROUND *Wind Sabre* flashed. The moving shapes of Nexus, ships both alien and Imperial, and battling gods filled Talis's vision over the ship's port-side railing.

The Veritor line had taken critical damage, their hulls dangling from their lift balloons like useless limbs. They had neither the alien weapons nor their shields, and so were open to the gods' attacks. They tossed about in the high winds, their buoyant envelopes tugging the hulls beneath in jerking bursts of movement. They fired their cannons, but the shots either went wide, or struck impotently against the gods' defenses.

If the aliens had the kind of control over Silus Cutter's wind that Onaya Bone suggested, they'd spared no thought to protect their purported allies from it.

Lindent Vein punished the Veritor fleet. With a roar that seemed to come from every direction, tendrils of icy water whipped outward from the bands surrounding Nexus and sliced through their lift balloons. Through their hulls. Splinters exploded from the airships as the onslaught ripped through the wood. Frigid saltwater spray misted across Talis's face, even though they were outside cannon range.

One Veritor ship dangled, nose-down, from the last line of its lift envelope, the balloon pulled vertical. Lifeboats deployed, only to be smashed back against the ship's hull, bursting in showers of wood and bodies.

The remaining airships attempted to pull back, only about a third of the fleet still sky-worthy. Some that could stay aloft had broken keels and rudders. The ships that were able left their crippled allies to die; made no attempt to rescue the crews from the foundering ships. The lashing of water sliced through those that trailed behind.

The lift envelope of the hindmost ship took a direct hit and all its heated air escaped, steaming into the skies. The full weight of the hull did the rest, its flaccid canvas flapping over the heads of the panicked crew. Buoyancy faded like a mirage, and gravity claimed them. Their ship fell out of the sky, trailing the last of the envelope's released steam: wisps of vapor that braided with black smoke from the engines.

Arthel Rak and Helsim Breaker each attacked the alien ships. Talis knew next to nothing of alchemy or the extent of the gods' abilities, but as a fighter she was keen enough to see that their attacks were uncoordinated. Movements borne of anger and frustration, with no sense of tactics.

Arthel Rak enveloped the ships fully in ballistic flames. The temperature of the air rose around Talis, though the fight was far off and the spouts of flame that shot from Arthel

Rak's armor-plated hands were directed away from *Wind Sabre*. He volleyed fireballs that should have consumed everything they touched, but as they cleared, Talis saw that the Yu'Nyun ships had taken no damage. They did not so much as blacken, or show any signs of being affected by the heat.

The Creator of the Rakkar, Lord of Fire, Master of Igneous Islands, furiously bombarded the ships with long streams of fire. He tried erecting a wall of flame to contain them. Each time, the starships were surrounded by a net of yellow-white light that looked like it had been woven by some enormous spider. The flames popped and hissed over the net, extinguishing almost as fast as Arthel Rak could conjure them.

Helsim Breaker summoned layers off of Nexus, armored himself in them so that he appeared to be made of the green energy. Only the blurred dark form at the center indicated otherwise. He gathered more and more of Nexus into himself, enlarging until he towered in the sky before the alien ships, twice the size of their largest. With green gauntlets, he pummeled at the nearest Yu'Nyun vessel. The ship was knocked about by the strikes, bobbing in the air wildly under each blow. Helsim Breaker threw a right hook, then a left. He tried a two-fisted smash from above, then followed with a strike from each side, clapping the ship between his hands. The ship bounced as if he'd slapped at a toy on the surface of water.

Yet none of his attacks touched the immaculate shining surface of the ship beneath its shields.

Talis felt a knot in her gut. It seemed impossible that the barrage of heavily armored strikes could make no dent, no scuff on the shining ships. Even if they could not wield Nexus as a weapon, a barrage like that should still do damage. That the alien weapons could hurt the gods—kill them—she knew. But despite what she'd been told, she had not imagined that their powers would be so ineffective against the invaders.

Turning from the retreating Veritors, Lindent Vein

gathered up the entire ocean in a single enormous bludgeon and sent it crashing into the alien ships. They were tossed, at least, disappearing momentarily into the depths as the waters passed over them. But as the ocean receded, pulled once again into orbit around Nexus, the invasion fleet righted itself and continued to fire.

The air was split by a low tone, like the call of an impossibly large horn. It washed over them like a physical thing. Talis felt a tremble in her bones and vibrations in her aching joints. Sophie covered her ears and hunched her shoulders. Tisker craned his neck to see out from under the wheelhouse. Dug remained genuflected in front of his goddess.

Talis looked around for Scrimshaw and finally spotted xin beside the engine house. Xe stood tall, xist back pressed against the structure, staying out of sight of Onaya Bone and the alien ships beyond the railing. Talis wasn't sure she knew how to tell for certain, but xe didn't seem frightened. Just cautious, guarded. Xe caught her watching xin, and xist mouth opened as though xe was trying to convey something, but she couldn't read the immovable lips.

Nexus shifted, changed shape. Formed layers of concentric partial spheres, slipping and separating along the geometric markings along its surface. It rotated, expanding. The layers spun at different speeds and angles, their edges crossing each other again and again. Talis's headache increased in intensity. Her teeth hurt. The bones of her feet hurt.

Sophie collapsed to her knees on the deck, gripping her head.

Beneath the spinning layers, in an open cavity at the center, an unruly mass of swirling green light pulsed. Instinctively, Talis knew this was the source of their pain. Her jaw clamped shut, sending spikes of agony into her head. It seemed as if her heart was trying to push its way out of her and would split her open like a dried cocoon in order to be free.

Lindent Vein, Helsim Breaker, and Arthel Rak retreated behind the first layer of Nexus energy. But even that crackled under the constant alien fire, absorbing the yellow energy. The attack's power dissipated along the contour of the shield, but Nexus overall looked more jaundiced than it had before. The shield would only protect the gods, and the swirling core of energy within, for so long.

Nexus held Peridot together. If it was breached, destroyed, *harvested*. . . .

Onaya Bone did nothing. She only watched, exultant, as Meran protected *Wind Sabre* against the assault of energy beams cast by the nearest ships. In the body that the aliens had provided.

Three more of the alien ships broke formation and turned their attention to *Wind Sabre*. Bursts of yellow-green light lit the deck beneath Onaya Bone, strafing across the ship. The aliens began an attack from the bow, sweeping across to the stern. Concentrating on the lift envelope, trying desperately to find a weak spot.

The goddess laughed, and the sound echoed around her. She lifted her chin high, stretching her bejeweled neck. Her chest expanded with triumphant laughter. Her arms straightened, fingers spread at her side. As though she was enjoying the sensation. As though any of it was her doing.

Meran's power, which still limned the ship with glowing blue capillaries, rippled and sent a shockwave of energy across the deck. Talis felt it in her stomach. Nauseated, she stumbled as she tried to rise to her feet. The breath she had recovered after Hankirk's assault on her windpipe caught in her chest again as her stomach lurched in response to Meran's pulses.

A sphere of blue light enveloped *Wind Sabre*, extending up around the lift envelope and underneath the hull. Within the sphere they were becalmed. Tisker relaxed at the helm, his chest heaving. He leaned one hand against the console, his head dipped in exhaustion. Kept the other on the wheel.

The alien fire no longer passed through the deck. Instead it reflected, burst off the blue dome with a flash, and ricocheted off in a new trajectory.

A beam from one ship careened back and hit one of its allies, cleaving the petal-shaped weapon housings clean off one side of its body. The alien ships could at least be damaged by their own weapons. Sparks flared within the breached hull. It listed to that side, off balance. Talis watched as the tiny forms of several Yu'Nyun scrabbled for purchase but fell free of the tilting deck and plummeted into the darkness below.

"Yes," spoke Onaya Bone. "Yes!" Her eyes flashed. She proudly surveyed Meran's work.

Talis felt the vibrations of her words in the decking, up her arms, and into her teeth. The goddess's voice was intoxicating. Heady, strong, invigorating. She felt the surge of bloodlust again, as she had on Fall Island, but without the need of drugs. The branded flesh on her arm radiated heat, pulsing with the quickening beat of her heart.

Dug rose to his feet, knives in his hands. Sophie gripped the scimitar she'd claimed and stood. Tisker abandoned the wheel. Their shoulders rose and fell with heaving breaths. Onaya Bone's influence would turn them all to berserkers.

Talis was unsteady. Wanted to give herself over to these impulses that were not hers. It was easier than feeling Nexus's pull on her chest, or the fear that her reasoning mind sent coursing through her veins.

She clamped down against the bloodlust. Refused to be betrayed by that again. She cleared her throat.

"Keep your heads about you," she called out to her crew. Her strained voice was small against the noise of battle and the hum of Meran's energy.

Meran. Talis focused on her. The pulses of her power, washing in every direction across the deck, sent thrills up Talis's spine. Her arms tingled. The back of her neck prickled with it. But it didn't muddy her mind. The two forces battled within her, but she clung to Meran's presence like a lifeline.

The damaged alien starship erupted in flame. It hung in the sky a moment longer, the hull warping and popping, before it started to spin along its vertical axis, then dropped out of the sky in slow motion.

The two closest Yu'Nyun ships pulled back, holding their fire a moment. Then the barrage resumed, the shots angled to avoid each other when the blasts refracted off Meran's shield. Talis thought of the alien bridge and its flashing screens of plotted courses, sensor information, and running calculations. Damned fancy systems, and likely a press of a button was all it took to adjust the angle of fire. No need to physically move heavy cannons or bring the ship about to change their attack. And that communications system would let them coordinate between ships in an instant.

Meran closed the distance between her hands. With another ripple, the blue light around *Wind Sabre* warped again, and the aliens' next hits reflected on a direct path, each striking the other ship squarely.

She's stronger than they are, Talis thought, her shoulders bouncing with a small surprised laugh that scraped at her throat. The rush of adrenaline was fading, and she feared it would give way to exhausted mania.

The weapons discharge impacted the small main hull of each ship with precision. One went down without fuss, as incapable of flight as something without a lift envelope should be. The other burst into flame from one side of its small main compartment. Pockets of fire erupted in sequence along each of the petal-like appendages until it was consumed, a flaming silhouette that spit smoke into the darkness above them, a twin to the solid shape within, traced in the yellow-red glow of the flames.

As the ship followed its allies down toward flotsam, Talis noticed the skies around them were quiet. Nexus still spun, but slower, as if only from stored momentum. Helsim

Breaker, Lindent Vein, and Arthel Rak were still, hovering. Watching. The remaining alien ships were also silent. The very air held its breath.

All eyes were on Meran.

Onaya Bone, chest expanded, pride evident in the curl of her dangerous smile, took a step across *Wind Sabre*'s deck toward the simula.

Meran let her arms fall and turned to face her. The blue shield remained in place, pulsing around them. Through them. Talis could still feel it. She finally climbed to her feet.

The Bone goddess stepped directly up to Meran and cupped her chin in taloned fingers.

Meran withstood the inspection. Talis could not see the simula's face at that angle but could well imagine the defiant expression the untamable woman would be wearing.

She had asked what Meran would do—which of the terrible possibilities that the woman was capable of might be unleashed.

The answer was heartbeats away.

Talis felt the influences on deck change. The blood that pounded in her ears stopped whispering of loyalty to Onaya Bone. Dug and Sophie took a step forward.

Too late, Talis thought of the ring and looked back to where Hankirk lay unconscious on the deck, but he wasn't there. A trail of blood led off around the deckhouses. Scrimshaw was gone from xist cover, too. Panic caught her breath and tore it away from her.

Gods, what have I done?

CHAPTER 38

"**O**NAYA BONE!" TALIS CRIED, taking a step forward, her hand extended in warning.

Dug and Sophie turned toward Talis, their eyes clouded and unfocused. Still enthralled, but whether by Onaya Bone or by Meran, Talis couldn't tell.

Her crew moved to stop her. Their hands clamped on her arms, hard enough to hurt.

Sophie held Dug's scimitar across Talis's throat to warn her back, and Talis felt the sting of cleanly slicing skin. Little Sophie. Her eyes were steel. Cruel.

She forced Talis back to her knees with a hand on her shoulder. She was unnaturally strong, with a grip of iron. Talis resisted, but to no effect. She could only watch.

Onaya Bone's focus had flicked to Talis when she called out, but now returned to Meran. Onaya Bone reached out to caress her jaw, her neck. Traced her shoulder with the back of a taloned finger. Meran withstood the intimate touches, her chin raised toward the taller woman.

But Tisker approached the goddess from behind, seizing her arms. Talis expected her to shrug him off as easily as a silk wrap, but she wrestled as Talis had, unable to free herself.

In the tense silence that followed, laughter bounced across the deck.

Hankirk emerged from behind the engine house and crossed to stand beside Meran. He had torn strips from the hem of his jacket and bandaged his left arm, which was cradled against his chest, wrist held gingerly in his right hand. The dressing was unskilled, the fabric soaked through with blood. There was other blood on him, too. Dark blue, in a spray across one pant leg.

"We came to an understanding," he said. "I will lead her to the four remaining rings."

A rasping caw rang loudly across the deck as Onaya Bone scoffed. She spat a ragged word at Meran: "Fool!"

Without seeming to move, Meran had her lips on Onaya Bone's mouth. The goddess's shoulders came up in surprise, but Tisker held her in place. Electricity crackled along his hands and up his forearms as Onaya Bone struggled under his grip. His skin smoked and blistered.

Onaya Bone's limbs began to tremble. Starting at her face, where Meran's lips touched hers, Onaya Bone's brown skin began to turn black. The darkness traveled in curling tendrils across her cheekbones and forehead. As it passed through her eyes, the whites around the dark purple irises went dark. The color traveled down her throat. The golden collars and heavy jeweled necklaces fell away, dissolving into purple dust before they reached *Wind Sabre*'s deck. The shining gown, in a burst that outpaced the change to her skin, flared into darkness and took on a texture of feathers that rippled in a wave from shoulder to hem.

Her elbows folded painfully, the wrong way, and curled against her body. Tisker let go, stepping back as she began to writhe. Her bones shortened here, extended there. Her legs twisted. Her torso bent, and Meran broke contact, standing tall again, as the Bone goddess collapsed to the deck. The transformation changed Onaya Bone's very contours, reduced her in size. With a great, painful arching of her back, she erupted in a flurry of dark shimmering feathers.

What remained on the deck, struggling to its taloned feet, was an enormous six-eyed raven. Weak, she visibly gasped for air through a serrated black beak. Blinked the pair of eyes in her head, which were dark brown and unreadable. Blinked the four livid purple eyes forming a diamond in the center of her chest.

Above her, Meran lifted off the deck as if caught up in a cyclone. The blue points of light along her skin and her backlit eyes intensified until Talis had to look away. Her head tilted back, arms outstretched to either side, feet flexed and crossed at the ankle. Her chest expanded upward, her spine arched and stiff, as though she'd been speared from below.

Hankirk adjusted the ring on his hand and ran its surface against his cheek. "I will have command of the greatest force on Peridot."

Without warning, the wind that held Meran aloft vanished, and she collapsed to her hands and knees on the deck, screaming in agony.

CHAPTER 39

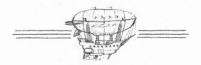

CLUTCHING THE SIDES OF HER head between her hands, Meran howled from deep within, a scream that seemed to stretch and elongate in pitch and tone. Her muscles and tendons tightened and stood out against her skin with the strength of the pangs that wracked her body.

The cry stretched quieter and weaker, then choked off. Meran collapsed again, panting.

Without Meran to maintain it, the blue force field vanished from around *Wind Sabre*, sputtering out like a dying flame. Talis felt the deck lurch sideways as gusts pushed across the ship again.

As the wind reached them, Sophie and Tisker woke from their trances. Sophie looked at her hand, the knuckles white around the grip of Dug's blade still held at her captain's throat. She made a small sound of surprise and released the blade. Her eyes were wide as it rattled on the deck. Hankirk's blood had begun to dry along its edge and where it pooled against the guard.

"Captain, I'm so sorry." Her voice was small. She stepped closer again and helped Talis to her feet.

Dug took an unsteady step forward. One foot made a misstep as the hull bounced in the wind. His legs buckled and he fell. Though he had already moved beyond her reach, Talis reached out a hand, her chest tight with empathy.

But Onaya Bone was not completely lost. Not destroyed as Silus Cutter had been. Only diminished. The body of the six-eyed raven hinted at the power she once possessed, but her caw held none of the divine volume as she faltered and struggled on the deck, trying to put distance between herself and the restless form of Meran.

Tisker wobbled and held his head. Registered the damage to his hands, and the pain, and tucked them protectively against his chest. He stared down at the giant raven, his face in turmoil. His eyes went to Dug, who crawled forward, tentatively, and gathered the half-limp avian form of Onaya Bone into his lap. Though their minds had been influenced by the powerful women, they clearly remembered the actions they'd taken as their own. Tisker backed away from where Dug sat curled around the raven, knowing well that this was no time to remind Dug he was there.

The raven tucked her head under Dug's arm. Her wings pulled up against herself, and she shook with silent sobs. Or rage.

Hankirk's attention was fixed on Meran, his expression tightened into an exaggerated look of intense focus. But Meran, crumpled on hands and knees, responded to no command he willed at her. She looked up at him, eyes burning beneath the hair that hung in her face, and Hankirk took an instinctive step back from the tangible malice.

"Why won't you . . . ?" His question trailed off as Meran fought to get back to her feet. Crouching, with trembling muscles, she smiled at him. It was terrifying. The lips curled back, the glint of white teeth predatory. The tip of her tongue slid across the pointed tip of a canine. There was more than just Meran in there now, Talis realized. And together they had quite a grudge with Hankirk.

The hull started to rock, began to spin laterally. Tisker tore his eyes away from Dug and Onaya Bone and made his way back to the wheelhouse. With blistered hands, he seized the wheel to fight the wind, and his face flashed with pain.

Sophie gave Talis's hand a last squeeze and ran back to help him.

Meran turned her focus beyond the railing, to the Yu'Nyun starships. She reached out with one hand, keeping balanced with the other, and Talis anticipated the blue threads of light. Nothing happened.

Yellow-green beams struck *Wind Sabre* as the Yu'Nyun weapons fired again and again. The deck rocked with the impact, and the air smelled of scorched wood.

Talis nearly fell to her knees again with the shuddering of her ship beneath her. Her gut wrenched, not only with the sickening turn of the deck, but with her own abject failure. She was going to lose her ship. They were going to fall. Dug, Sophie, Tisker. Her mind tortured her with images of their faces frozen and encrusted with ice.

She had failed them.

A section of decking burst in a spray of splinters. Dug curled his torso tighter around Onaya Bone, wordless as shards of wood railing and planking struck him in the side and across his back.

She had failed a god.

A single large piece of wood, cracked as sharp as a blade on one side, split up from the railing and spun into the air.

All this for twice her slight weight in gold and gems. Her reward sat heavy in the cargo hold. Dragging them down from the moment it had been loaded aboard.

Talis watched, frozen, as the chunk of railing speared the lift envelope above them.

The canvas tore with a shredding hiss. The air it contained escaped in a *whoomph*. The rip opened itself up until it reached the nearest seams, which held. Strained, but held.

And thank the gods, it was on the underside of the envelope. The heated air within stayed at the top of the balloon. Air would escape as it cooled, and they'd lose the recycled water as it re-condensed, but as long as the engines still worked, and if the lift lines held. . . .

They might limp back to civilization. If they survived this.

Meran pushed up from her crouch and wavered on legs that seemed barely able to support her. The alien flagship was approaching, but the simula was weakened after deposing the goddess, and *Wind Sabre* was hopeless against another attack. Talis resisted the urge to shut her eyes.

Cradling Onaya Bone with one arm, Dug scooted backward using his free hand and feet to retreat from the center of the deck to the dubious protection of the engine house. His jaw was set. His eyes were on Meran, who fought to maintain her balance against the pitching deck.

A new sound, grating and dry, interspersed with a wooden tapping, caught Talis's attention. From around the engine house, dragging xist-self with xist arms and one leg, Scrimshaw appeared. From the blood on Hankirk's clothes Talis had assumed the worst. The truth was not much better. Scrimshaw's right leg was broken, the calf and foot missing beneath the ragged ruin of xist knee. Xe was covered in xist own blood, yet xe pressed forward across the deck. In one hand xe gripped xist tablet.

Xist voice was heavy with the alien accent as xe called out. "Here, bring it to her!"

Talis, startled out of her reverie of self-admonishment, crossed to xist side. Meran joined them, stumbling on unsteady feet. Together the three of them clung to each other to maintain their balance. Scrimshaw reached out a hand for Meran, and rested it on her knee.

"Your body is the same technology as that ship." Xe paused for breath and xist nictitating membranes half-closed over xist eyes. "Compatible. The being 'Meran' is too weakened by the absorption of Onaya Bone's energies to fight them, but the device that contains her is fully functional."

Sophie had run to Scrimshaw's side and took the Yu'Nyun device in both hands as she knelt beside the broken and bloodied alien. Readouts on the cracked screen indicated the presence of the nearby alien ships and provided rotating lists in Yu'keem characters. Scrimshaw's skeletal fingers danced across the display, which Sophie held out for xin, and the view split. The outline of a bipedal figure appeared in the right half of the screen, blinking. Xe tapped the figure, and both images turned blue, pulsing with light in a synchronized blink.

Meran's eyes went from blue to brilliant white, and a detached smile dawned on her lips. She raised one hand toward the ships, as if reaching to caress them.

"I am inside them," she said, and with Sophie's help, she rose to her feet.

The Yu'Nyun flagship was only a length away from _Wind Sabre_'s hull now, dwarfing the defenseless carrack. The gleaming pointed ends of its bizarre cannons trained on the deck and crackled with building energy.

Meran gracefully turned her hand around, palm out.

All the weapons went dark.

"I HAVE INTERFACED with their systems," she explained. "I am free to explore their mechanical pathways. I am a virus, a poison in their veins."

As if to punctuate the point, an explosion rocked the flagship. The ventral weapons lowered, drooping with a low moan.

The sky was silent except for the wind.

Talis looked back at Sophie, who caught her eye and smirked. "Can't be too jealous of those systems now, can I, Captain?"

Talis was going to reply, but both Sophie's and Tisker's expressions shifted into surprise. *What now*, Talis thought, turning back to Meran and the Yu'Nyun ship.

Meran had pulled the ship right up to *Wind Sabre*'s port railing, and moved to meet it there. She laid an outstretched hand on its silver hull, and the invisible seams in the metal plating flashed with blue light.

The air became still, though Talis could still hear the wind. A deafening sucking sound. Only a few feet away, Meran's long knotted hair and loose clothing flapped as though the gale was still buffeting her.

Her back arched again as she reclaimed Silus Cutter's powers.

The ship glowed like the end of a poker in a forge as Meran lifted into the air and lost contact with the metal hull. There was a seismic groan, the protesting scream of twisting metal. The ship foundered, nose up. It spun clear of *Wind Sabre,* and then it went down, dropping out of sight below the railing.

Meran lifted her arms to the sides, struggling to control her motion within the whipping cyclone. She brought her hands together in a dramatic clap, arms extended, elbows straight. Talis heard the roar of wind again, as though it was approaching from across a great distance at high speed, and all the remaining alien ships rocked. Two of the vessels knocked into each other in the tumble, and the nearest fell out of the sky, without fire or any obvious damage. The rest scattered, blown back, tumbling bow over stern into the empty skies, until they were too distant to see.

The display in Sophie's hand bleeped a complaint. The diagrams flashed, outlined in red, and then switched to solid gray. The ships were out of range.

The wind went quiet. Meran stumbled as she landed, and she dropped to one knee. Hugged her arms tight over her chest as she cried out in pain. Her back rose and fell with heavy breaths.

Talis heard the crackle of a fire in the stillness that followed. Smoke rose from the hull of her ship, drifted up over the railing. It was the black of a full blaze.

Talis looked to her crew and barked, "Someone wanna go put out those fires?"

Sophie handed the tablet back to Scrimshaw and moved for the companionway, pulling up the bandana from her neck to cover her nose. Her hands left blue streaks on the fabric and her cheeks.

Talis helped Meran sit up. Her grip was tight and her lips a thin line, but she nodded wordlessly. Leaning against Talis's shoulder, Meran closed her eyes and fought to control her breathing as she braced to metabolize a second god's power. Her shoulders tensed and twitched as her body shook.

Dug looked up from where he cradled Onaya Bone on the deck, uncertain. He looked at Talis but didn't move. His captain, or what remained of his goddess. Talis forgave him the hesitation and was about to tell him so. But as she inhaled to say the words, the raven wriggled free of his arms, stumbling for a moment on unfamiliar limbs and joints that did not move the way she expected them to. She held her new wings as though she was still humanoid, clutching a blanket up around her throat, rather than a flighted creature who knew what to do with the appendages. When she'd taken a few steps away from Dug and the engine house, the dark wings expanded. Flapped. Tentatively at first, then with strong beats that lifted her from the deck. She lowered her head toward Dug. The motion might have just been her catching her balance, but Talis got the sense it was an expression of gratitude. Dug seemed to think so, too. He nodded and rose to his feet.

Onaya Bone circled them and let out an echoing raven's cry before soaring away. Her black form quickly disappeared against the darkness.

Dug moved, as if freed, to follow Sophie below, but he halted, drawn up short before he reached the access hatch. Talis followed his gaze to the three figures hovering in the open sky, in the empty space formerly occupied by the Yu'Nyun flagship.

Arthel Rak, Lindent Vein, and Helsim Breaker watched Onaya Bone fly away, then turned their attention back to *Wind Sabre* and the strange woman on deck. They weren't happy, but they held their position, looking as likely to retreat back to Nexus as to advance on the woman who beat the aliens they had battled against so ineffectively.

"Now!" Hankirk yelled. His hand clenched into a fist, he brandished the ring above his head. "Destroy them!"

Meran looked at him. Her eyes had returned to their simula blue. She raised one eyebrow.

"All your research," she said, simultaneously mocking and pitying him, "and yet you know nothing."

He opened his mouth to protest, but in an instant Meran had crossed the deck and seized him, one-handed, by the throat. Though shorter than him, she lifted him from the deck until his toes barely touched as they kicked desperately for purchase.

"I will no longer be commanded by anyone."

"No," he gasped through her grip. "The ring!"

Talis chuckled wryly, despite the scene. Despite the goddess in ruins. Despite her friend's spiritual agony. Despite her own.

All eyes on the deck, except Meran's, turned to her in disbelief.

"It's a matter of willpower," she told Hankirk, standing up and straightening her jacket, flicking the splinters of her ship from the lapel.

The corner of Meran's mouth pulled back and up in a smile.

Hankirk gurgled. His eyes bulged. He clutched at Meran's wrist. His left arm was a tattered loss, but his good arm was just as useless against her steel grip.

Talis rubbed at her throat. She felt a sting there and pulled her hand away. Her fingertips were red. She wiped the blood off on a pant leg.

"She only had the power of her little ring, but you scrapped that right down."

It was nice that Hankirk couldn't speak around Meran's iron grip to interrupt her.

"That ring controlled her neatly, just like the aliens designed. But you gave her the boost of willpower she needed to overthrow Onaya Bone. You made her stronger and tipped the scale. Now she's got the power of Lindent's ring, Onaya Bone's powers, *and* the powers the Yu'Nyun stole from Silus Cutter when they murdered him. You think you can control her with one little trinket? I wish you luck."

Hankirk, eyebrows up and knit together, looked down Meran's arm at the simula's hungry expression.

Talis could maybe stop Meran from killing him. Talk her out of it, or ask nicely.

But she could also finally be done with him.

Meran looked over her raised arm at Talis, then tossed Hankirk at her feet.

He coughed and rolled himself up into a fetal position, cradling his useless arm.

"He is your adversary, Talis," said Meran. "I have my own."

Meran turned her fierce gaze upon the three surviving gods of Peridot.

CHAPTER 40

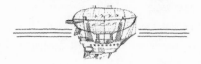

MERAN CROSSED HER ARMS over her chest. She looked downright cocky. *Go ahead, try me,* her posture challenged.

Arthel Rak spoke. In his voice, Talis heard the blowing roar of a fire, and she felt heat tighten the skin of her face.

"Two of us are lost because of you."

Meran laughed. "The dawn of these consequences began with your own actions, seventy-five generations past."

"We atoned for what we did. There was a natural order that emerged. What was lost is beyond restoration, but we gave this planet new life. New purpose."

"You stole from me all that I was. Nearly destroyed me. Destroyed this world. You mistook the ability to wrench my power away for the right to wield it."

Lindent Vein, eyebrows up over blind eyes, moved a hand as if to stop her words. Argued, "We mended the world. Re-built it."

Helsim Breaker agreed. "Look at all we have achieved. There is no world elsewhere among the stars that has flourished as Peridot has under such conditions. We have created something entirely unique in the universe."

"Fractured," spat Meran.

Even Talis had to bristle with wounded pride at the derisive tone. It was her home, after all, whatever shape it was in.

Meran continued, one lip curled in a snarl, "Had you joined your powers instead of hoarding them for yourselves, you could have reversed this precious Cataclysm of yours in moments. Mended everything. Restored it, as though it were untouched. If you had worked together these aliens would have not made such fools of The Divine Alchemists of Peridot."

"Yes!"

Talis turned her head toward the sound. Hankirk was on his knees. His face was alight with reverence. Meran was confirming everything he believed.

It unsettled Talis. She felt dizzy.

Helsim Breaker and Arthel Rak looked at each other. Lindent Vein protested, "We work well together."

He sounded like a child bargaining with a cross mother.

"You have never worked together." Meran's voice grew in volume as she spoke. "You have *never* seen the interconnectivity of the elements. *Never* used my gifts to ensure balance. You created your little playpens within Nexus and left your creations to squabble among themselves. To steal from and murder each other. To raise barriers that kept them as much apart as you five kept yourselves isolated."

Quickly, Arthel Rak said, "It was Onaya Bone. This is her fault."

Meran turned her gaze upon him sharply. He visibly flinched.

"I am aware of her treachery. Her greed betrayed you at the moment of transference. She would have seized all of my powers for herself and destroyed the rest of you, had Silus Cutter not contained her. For her betrayal and her failure, I have spared her. *Her* greed, at least, did not hide behind a mask of benevolence. Her greed, at least, allowed some small piece of me to survive."

She moved toward them. Put one foot on the railing and stepped up, as though about to jump.

"You three will not be so lucky."

They outnumbered her. But she had taken back Silus Cutter's power from the Yu'Nyun. Had stripped Onaya Bone of her powers with a kiss. Was already imbued with the energy that had been stored in the ring for all these years.

And they knew it.

Arthel Rak and Lindent Vein braced themselves. The ocean behind them trembled. Its surface rippled as the Master of Water flexed his connection with his element.

Meran took a step, as though the air before her were solid. Wind gently ruffled her again.

Helsim Breaker was nearest to Meran as she approached. He moved back, tentatively. She increased her speed as she moved toward him, lowered her head and shoulders, balled her hands into fists.

He flinched. Broke the line. Floated backward, almost stumbled in midair as he turned his back on his fellow gods in panic.

She didn't pursue him, but turned her attention to the others.

Lindent Vein's longer arms came up defensively. Arthel Rak's eyes were wide, his eyebrows raised, lips parted in panic. They moved backward from the small woman. Slowly, still facing her.

Meran moved faster. Pumped her legs and sprinted across open skies to close the distance between them.

They turned in earnest retreat.

Helsim Breaker reached the perimeter of Nexus ahead of them and disappeared inside. The spheres moved again, and before they sealed into a tight shell, Talis saw the interior reshape itself with glowing walls that formed twisting corridors, overlapping and fusing together. A labyrinth.

How desperate Peridot's gods had become.

Lindent Vein and Arthel Rak, together, reached the arched gate to Nexus. They paused only for a breath to see that Meran was still following them, then continued inside in a scramble.

Never slowing, she raced in behind them.

The archway slid shut, the surface of Nexus sealing tight with a slam that reverberated through the air. Talis felt it rattle her chest. Her sternum ached as though she'd been physically pushed.

The markings on the surface of Nexus flared, reformed into a new pattern. The churning of the ocean settled, sliding back into its usual depths to spread over Nexus and close it off. Its surface calmed again, gently rippling green and white beams of light.

The pain in Talis's chest subsided, then slipped away. Proximity to Nexus no longer held a vise grip on her heart. She inhaled a deep gasping breath, as though she'd just risen out of that ocean water and could finally fill her lungs again.

Hankirk lay curled up in a trembling fetal position, cradling his arm. Dug, Tisker, and Scrimshaw looked to her.

The air was thick with disbelief. It was done. Whatever Meran planned to do with Helsim Breaker, Lindent Vein, and Arthel Rak, the crew's part in it was over.

A heart-wrenching crack rippled through the air and the deck tilted as *Wind Sabre*'s two aft lift lines failed under the stress. The thick cords of twisted rope and wire snapped like cheap thread, whipping free of their anchors and dangling, useless, from the lift balloon above.

CHAPTER 41

T HE DECK LURCHED, JARRING Talis, forcing her to take a
step to keep from falling.

"We have to go," she said, loudly, trying to hide her panic
behind the command. "Where's the nearest port? Farm, anything, I don't care as long as the crust isn't lifeless."

Until a few moments ago, the effects of Nexus on the body
were enough to keep anyone from settling the smaller bits of
crust that hung in the skies close to the gods' domain. It was
practically taboo. Moreover, it was terribly uncomfortable.

Tisker looked at Talis from his place at the wheel. He
braced his grip with his forearms. Sweat beaded on his forehead despite the chill and the wind. He shook his head. This
wasn't any sky he knew.

In Cutter territory, the next ring of cities would be the
high-society islands with expansive estates, ostentatious
gardens, and pristine cities with sparkling towers and stable
economies. Not the sort of place they made a point of visiting, but that hardly mattered. If they were in Cutter skies,
she'd gladly run *Wind Sabre* aground on someone's mani-
cured lawn and deal with the consequences. But that was

around the other side of Nexus.

Hankirk's face was a paler reflection of Tisker's. The blood loss from his arm was taking its toll. He trembled as he tried to stand. Not much more damage he was likely capable of bringing upon her. The damage to the ship mattered far more.

"Stanch that," she said, not kindly, to Hankirk. He was bleeding on her deck again.

To Dug, she said, "Get these two to the med bay. They can treat themselves, or each other, or die there, but at least they'll be out of the way. Then go help Sophie with the fires."

Let Hankirk fade off, and she'd finally be able to put him over the railing like she ought to have done days before. If his arm hadn't come up to block the knife, she'd have done so less than an hour ago. But no, she was sending him for medical treatment.

She allowed a moment to marvel as she watched Dug and Hankirk gather up Scrimshaw, supporting the one-legged alien on either side. The three of them just minutes past fighting each other for survival. She eyed Hankirk. The grave injuries he'd caused. His arm. Scrimshaw's leg. Dug's faith. The blame for those traced directly back to his misguided actions. There was no time, with the ship an inch from sinking, for any more foolishness. She trusted him to be smart enough to know that.

The thought of trusting him at all made her jaw clench, which at least kept her teeth from chattering with panic.

She turned her back on them and jogged to her cabin. She let the door swing wide open on its hinges behind her as she pulled up the vellum charts showing the nearest territories. She overlapped the translucent sheets and lined up the territory edges. Cutter, Bone, Rakkar skies. The Vein had only a small pocket of islands carved out within the Bone and Rakkar borders, and that was farther out than *Wind Sabre* could likely limp.

She ran her finger in a spiral out from Nexus, looking for any named island. If it had a name, there was generally someone there to care what it was called. She'd prefer a port. Something with a dry dock for repairs. Gods only knew what the hull looked like. First was the matter of finding some-place near enough.

They'd come to Nexus on a straight course from Fall Is-land, answering Onaya Bone's call, and were still in Bone skies.

The deck shifted under her feet again. Items rattled in a cupboard behind her as the ship tilted to starboard.

Fall Island was an option. The temple had been built as near to their goddess's home as the body could stand. All the other Bone islands were scattered in the outer reaches of Peridot's atmosphere or gathered up along the borders to keep pushing at them. But Fall Island was more than a day away, and there wasn't much in the way of a dry dock. Not to mention, Talis had kinda left a scorched alien ship and no shortage of bodies there.

There was Subrosa, but she wasn't confident of crossing back over the Cutter border, either. Unlikely that anyone with a direct line of sight on Nexus had missed what just happened. Cutter Imperials would want to question the whole crew before allowing them across, and they'd let her ship fall out of the sky while they pressed for information. There'd be no alien escort to get them past patrol ships this time—better off for that, of course—but *Wind Sabre* wasn't up for another regatta through the storm-cloud gauntlet.

Rakkar settlements dotted the charts, a quarter way around Nexus from their position. But, at this radius, an arc was a shorter distance than the straight line back to Talonpoint. Plus, with the distral tailwinds, they'd get a bit more distance out of the effort.

Her finger paused on a small island. Absurdly close to Nexus. It had to be a mistake. Or an ancient site with noth-ing but ruins.

"Heddard Bay," she read its name aloud, her voice strange in the quiet of the cabin. It wasn't the old Rakkar language, from the days of their inverted underground pyramids.

A bay meant moorings and docks. The Rakkar were agoraphobic, but that didn't mean they didn't want for trade goods. And if they didn't have a formal shipyard, she at least knew that even a Rakkar child would be skilled enough to repair her ship.

She measured the curve, plotted the course. With their proximity to Nexus, it worked out to half the travel time of a course back the way they came.

The lines outside her cabin groaned, straining. She circled the island in red and tossed the pencil back into the case as she turned from the table. She heard it miss and bounce onto the floor. That was a mess she could live with. She was already halfway out of the cabin.

"Tisker, circle Nexus and keep it to our starboard." She leaned against the side of the wheelhouse.

He was steering the ship with his wrists, bracing them against the spokes of the wheel to spare his burned palms. His despondent expression cleared for a moment. He looked up at her voice, and his posture straightened. "Found something?"

"Think so," she said. "Ease us off to a radius about twice where we're at, and angle down three degrees, then you can tie off the wheel and take a break. We'll trip over a Rakkar island in about half a day."

"Rakkar," he said. He brought up his arm to itch his cheek on the sleeve of his shirt. "Never met one'a them. Are they as strange as you hear?"

Strange was an abstract that no longer had a place in the world after what they'd just been through. "They'll be the prettiest faces you ever see if we can get there in one piece."

"Aye, Cap." It was emphatic.

"Don't risk the lines we have left for the sake of speed. I'll send Sophie up to bandage those hands soon as I find her."

Tisker nodded his thanks. "Something to drink would be good, Cap."

She nodded. Her own throat wanted for moisture.

"And we'll drink something stronger when we get there," she promised. "Rakkar put the fire to their spirits, too, and I owe us all a round or four."

He grinned, lopsided and something like his usual self. It warmed her.

She put a hand on his shoulder and squeezed. "Just get us there, yeah?"

"Aye, Cap."

THE CREW QUARTERS were a complete loss. By the time Talis followed the smell of lingering smoke to its source, Sophie and Dug had gotten the worst of it out. Dug was stomping on the remaining embers while Sophie swept the charred husks of their personal belongings into a metal bucket.

Gods-cursed stinking winds. As if her crew hadn't paid enough of a price already.

The crew quarters were designed for more people than she had, but they weren't spacious by any means. Nothing kept aboard was a frivolous item. It was family portraits. Mementos. Things that all that gods-rotted money in the hold couldn't replace.

Her gaze went to Dug's throat. His locket wasn't there.

Emotions seized at her lungs, as though her rib were broken again. Anger and guilt backed up and overwhelmed her. She hit the frame of the door with the side of her hand.

Sophie looked up at the sound and tugged the bandana down to her collar. The smile it revealed was melancholy but wholly Sophie. "Looks like those alien weapons crossed with the lamp wires. Sparked a fire that started with the blankets on Tisker's bunk. Got it out, but . . ."

But they'd lost everything.

"Inda's picture?"

Dug shook his head.

Talis inhaled a shaky breath through her nose and her sinuses stung with the cloying smoke. "Dug, I'm sorry."

Dug nodded but said nothing.

She shook her head. It wasn't fair. Her crew had lost so much. As she brushed a bit of soot from her eye, the burned skin of her forearm tightened and stung. She wished she'd let Meran heal that rotted mark. This was where it led when people put blind faith in symbols, gods, and waste like that. Guilt whispered that it should have been *her* quarters fed to the flames.

But no, the charts. What fortune remained had given them that. They'd walk—or at least limp—away from this. And that was no small thing. Take their shares, and fix the ship. Or retire from this nonsense. Go live proper, honest lives. Make some new memories to replace the portraits and the lockets and the pieces of their lives they'd lost.

"We're, uh," she started, then had to clear her throat. "We're headed to Heddard Bay, on the Rakkar side of Nexus."

"Rakkar." Sophie exhaled the word in a breathy whisper. The corner of her mouth twitched up a tick.

Talis nodded. "Not far, at this radius, and we can ride the distral winds. How they managed to settle so near without the headaches crippling them, I've no idea, but my charts are up to date, and I can't ignore what it trims off the time we'll be relying on just three lift lines."

Sophie blanched, the smile still on her face but empty as a dried husk. She'd gone to fight the fire earlier and hadn't seen the lines snap.

"I'd hoped it was just the wind on the chewed up hull creating the drag I'm feeling," she said. Didn't have to say she knew better. Sophie knew the ship better than anyone.

"You two finish up here," Talis said. She'd tend to Tisker's hands herself. The crew cabin was their space, even covered with ash. "Then we can do short shift rotations to reinforce what we can. Get yourselves fed or rest in my cabin. Hear?"

They nodded and put themselves back to work. *Wind Sabre* needed them, and they'd never failed her before.

Half the galley was missing.

The gimbaled oven was gone, and the spice rack that had been mounted above it, but they still had the cooktop and ice chest. The port-side hull breach opened onto empty skies. Taking with it, Talis realized, the folio with Sophie's ship design. She'd stowed it in the cabinet there before they left Subrosa. If she'd given it back to Sophie, it would have been in her pocket, likely as not. Talis closed her eyes. She might not want Sophie to leave, but the thought of all that work just . . . lost. . . .

Her crew had sacrificed too much on this one. All traced back to that muck-crusted contract. She thought of the moment when Jasper told her about it, sitting at his desk, sharing a drink. A successful job behind them and a great opportunity in front of her. She thought of the moment when they found Jasper's body. Opened her eyes again, staring hard at the stars beyond the broken hull. Tried to clear her mind of the memories.

And what had *she* sacrificed, with a hold full of riches and all her belongings intact?

Maybe her crew.

Bracing herself against the bulkhead edges and fighting a tug of vertigo, Talis leaned forward and looked down. She could see the round silver forms of alien ships freshly added to the flotsam layer. Now an undeniable part of Peridot's sordid history. There were Veritor ships down there, too, but their dull wooden hulls blended with the older detritus: just more of the same.

The hull breach extended down past the floor to the deck below. A portion of the cargo hold where everything was fortunately tethered to the decking and not the bulkhead. She chose not to seek out further damage.

Something in her mind twitched a note that she probably ought to make sure their payload was still in the hold, if they were going to requisition the kinds of repairs *Wind Sabre* needed.

But Tisker was alone on deck, keeping his blistered hands to *Wind Sabre*'s wheel. She owed him haste, and then some.

She gathered up two metal mugs and filled a pitcher with water from the barrels that, thankfully, were stacked along the inner bulkhead. She put them on a tray, then made her way to the med bay.

HANKIRK WAS STRUGGLING to tourniquet his arm. It was a rough enough job one-handed, and he'd lost a lot of blood. He was pale, and sweat beaded on his brow. His lips were tinged with blue.

"You actually listened to me," she said, and pushed aside the litter from his self-care so she could put the tray down on the counter.

Scrimshaw lay on the bunk in the corner, watching them with those big sapphire eyes. She nodded to xin, and xe lightly fluttered the fingers that rested on xist chest over the blue scarring. The stump of xist right leg, not much more than half xist thigh, was elevated. The Yu'Nyun field kit lay open on the deck beneath the bunk, in a sticky puddle of blue blood.

"Not much choice," Hankirk replied, voice weak. His teeth were chattering. His shoulders flinched with involuntary shudders.

She grabbed a pair of shears and took over. "You've gotta get that jacket off. This needs to be tight."

He nodded, shifting awkwardly to try and peel the ruined sleeve off, but she put a hand on his good arm and he stilled. She cut up the back, through the expensive trimmed jacket and the ruined cotton shirt beneath. It was soaked, more with the moisture from his cold sweat than with blood, except past the shoulder. She peeled it back. The blood had gone sticky, but for Hankirk it was only a matter of time, so she wasted none for gentleness. He clamped down on a roar of pain, and she flung the tattered clothing into the corner. The wound pulsed with fresh blood. The flow was not as strong as it should have been.

That infernal Veritor sigil was tattooed on his chest, over his heart. The black ink lines were soft and tinged with green. It was old, though she didn't remember it from their academy days.

"You chose the wrong friends," she told him.

She held out a hand and he placed the rubber tourniquet into it. Cleaning the wound was pointless until the bleeding stopped.

"But I wasn't wrong." His voice was weak.

Instead of answering, she tied off his arm and cranked the tourniquet. She had to get to Tisker. She hated that Hankirk's wound took priority. That she couldn't make herself just leave him to it. His pale skin went whiter as it tightened. He only looked at her.

She sighed, then cringed even as the words came out. "You *were* right about 'fixing' Peridot, weren't you? All along, The Five just never did it."

He had the sense not to gloat, or perhaps he just didn't have the energy. He watched her treat his arm and moved his fingers a little bit, with difficulty. They spasmed instead of wiggled.

She went to the cabinet for loose cotton, strips of bandaging, and a bottle of astringent. She held it all out for him to take with his good hand.

He secured the bottle between his knees so he could lift the cap and pumped the liquid onto the cotton. His gaze had regained some of its intensity. He looked at her sideways as he gently wiped at the blood on his arm.

"They betrayed me," he said. "They would have replaced our gods with the Yu'Nyun. Talis, what were they thinking?"

She involuntarily glanced over at Scrimshaw, but if xe reacted to Hankirk's mention of xist race, there was no outward sign of it.

Hankirk held out a mess of reddened cotton expectantly. She looked at it, disgusted, and used a foot to slide the bin closer so he could drop them in. He moistened another piece of cotton and turned back to his arm. It would take all the cotton they had to mop up that mess. Thick, half-dried blood stuck to the wound. The flesh was ruined, looked more like a badly butchered hock, and she could see far more of the bones of his forearm than she cared to. Her doing.

She turned to the sink and scoured his blood off her hands. Didn't answer him. Didn't *have* an answer for him, but his words reminded her of something. "Did either of you ever read, in all that research, that the planet used to be called Meran?"

Scrimshaw didn't reply. Xist eyelids were closed. Possibly xe'd passed out. Or had sedated xist-self with something in the kit.

"No . . . She tell you that? Huh." He was quiet a moment. "Makes sense."

His arm was stable. Talis dried her hands on a cotton cloth, then gathered up gauze and ointment for Tisker's burns.

Hankirk said no more, focused on tying up his arm in

a sling with the strips of bandage, using his teeth to make a knot.

She put her supplies on the tray with the water and started to leave, but his voice made her pause in the doorway.

"Help me, Talis. I'll make it right. We'll fix it all together." His voice sounded earnest, but the words were still nonsense.

She'd helped him plenty already. She could only shake her head at him in disbelief.

There were people aboard she actually *wanted* to survive. She headed above-decks to tend her wounded pilot.

CHAPTER 42

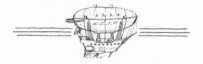

THE CONDITION OF TISKER'S hands let him off the hook for cooking dinner. Talis decided to handle it herself, letting the others rest or work as they wanted.

To keep the wind out, Sophie and Dug had hung a sheet of oilcloth across the breach in the galley's bulkhead, and stretched it as tight as they could. They nailed it into place along the fractured edges of the hull. The oiled canvas flapped, pushing in and out against the air currents like an enormous exposed lung. Put Talis on edge.

With the breach in the hull as big as it was, they'd been lucky to only lose the spice rack and not all their food, though the spice supply was something Talis relied on to disguise her lack of grace in cooking. The bench on that side of the table was gone, too. Even if they could tolerate the flapping of the oilcloth or the pervasive smell of linseed it gave to the room, there'd be no place for everyone to sit and eat a meal in the galley.

To compensate for the lack of spices, she cubed and fried a slab of salt pork from the barrels in the hold. Then she steamed a pot of rice and spooned tallow into the water. It was a trick she'd learned in her days as crewman on a ship whose captain considered spices a frivolous expense: extra fat would enhance the flavors and make plain taste less plain. They needed to replenish their energy, anyway. There were wounds to heal, and no small amount of work to do to make sure *Wind Sabre* made it to Heddard Bay.

She added a cutting board full of vegetables to a second pot, choosing those that were starting to soften rather than coordinating flavors. Boiled them with more bits of salt pork and lard. It'd fill them, whether or not it would satisfy them.

She tasted a bite of the greens to check their firmness and made an involuntary face as the food hit her tongue. It would fill them, anyway.

"Need a hand, Captain?" Sophie hovered in the doorway behind her, leaning one forearm against the frame above her head.

Talis put the lid from the vegetables in the sink and killed the burners.

"Just about done. You wanna set places at the table in my cabin?"

But Sophie moved to the stove and filched a piece from the mound of steaming vegetables. Blew on it a moment, then popped it in her mouth.

Her face contorted. She grabbed for a napkin and spit the barely-chewed piece out.

"The rice should help. Though I salted that, too."

Sophie shook her head vehemently, as if trying to shake the flavor loose from her tongue. Her short tousled hair flopped with her enthusiasm. "Get away from the stove, please."

Sophie leaned into the depths of their icebox, digging until she retrieved their jar of cream with one hand and a smaller cotton-wrapped jar in the other.

"Here," said Sophie, letting the cooler hatch drop back into place. "By your leave, Captain. Tisker can drink his coffee black until we get to Heddard Bay."

Talis took a step toward the drawer for a peeler, but Sophie grabbed a pile of plates and pushed them into Talis's arms.

"I've got it, Captain, not to worry. Old family secret." Sophie held up the little jar like a talisman that could repel her captain from the galley. She looked as though she was worried Talis might object.

No chance. The burn of over-salted food was still on Talis's tongue. She gathered the plates onto a tray with napkins and cutlery and withdrew to dress the table, trusting Sophie to do what she could for the meal.

PLATES WERE TRADED FOR BOWLS once Sophie transformed Talis's botched efforts into a thick chowder. She'd used all the cream, plus added the okra Talis had skipped over. Each bowl was served with a piece of hardtack floating in the center, soaking up what moisture could make it through the bread's near-concrete surface.

Talis and Sophie stood back after placing the filled bowls at each seat, overlooking the softly lit table. Talis eyed the fifth and sixth place settings at the table as though they might brandish spoons at her without warning.

"I don't know which of them bothers me more."

Sophie crossed her arms. "Really, Captain? They've each proven where they stand at every opportunity. I think the choice is pretty clear."

Talis raised an eyebrow. But it was true, wasn't it? With a self-pitying sigh, she went below to find Hankirk and Scrimshaw while Sophie fetched Dug and Tisker.

HANKIRK SAT AT THE FAR END of the table, closest to the door of Talis's cabin. He still wore what was left of his shirt and jacket—the half Talis hadn't cut free with the shears. He'd found a rough-spun blanket in the cargo hold to cover the rest of him. The blanket was one they used to protect the corners of crates underway. It was probably full of splinters.

Talis didn't have to debate whether or not to give Hankirk something more respectable. Spare blankets had been stowed in crew quarters. He might have borrowed a sweater from Tisker or Dug, but crew clothes had been stowed in crew quarters. There was nothing left to offer him.

Scrimshaw was still asleep, and she didn't figure it was worth it to rouse xin for a meal xe probably couldn't stomach. What xe was going to do for food now was beyond her. They'd returned that barrel of whatever edibles xe'd brought aboard, and xe hadn't eaten since they left Talonpoint. If that leg didn't kill xin, they'd lose xin to starvation.

Sophie and Tisker took the seats on either side of Talis. Dug sat next to Sophie. They grouped tighter than they'd normally pull up to her table, as if shielding her from their pathetic guest. There wasn't much he could do to her one-handed, but she couldn't say she wasn't glad of the defense.

Then again, maybe they were protecting *him* from *her*.

Maybe she ought to blame Hankirk for all the misery that had befallen her ship and her crew. But she didn't have room for the anger around her shame and self-loathing. From the moment she took that sour contract, every decision she'd made had led them further and further into this mess. She'd always relied on the compass of her instincts, but they'd led her wrong this time. And by following them, she'd led her crew wrong.

They ate quietly, slurping from their bowls. The loudest noises came from anyone attempting to break off a piece of the hardtack, either with their fingers or, in the case of Hankirk and Tisker, whose hands were not up for further strain, between their teeth.

A captain's first duty was to the well-being of her ship and crew. That failure swirled in her mind. She kept her head down and ate without seeing or tasting the food. Which may have been for the best, bad as she'd botched it to start with.

But that wasn't fair, amid all the other unfairness she'd cast on Sophie. She focused for a moment, took a bite more mindfully.

It was *good*.

There were spices, gods knew how she'd managed that. Some savory, earthy flavor that Talis didn't recognize but which seemed to balance and cut the burn of the over-salting. A little heat, and the familiar sweet tang of garlic, complementing the mix and accentuating the creaminess.

She looked up sharply, letting her eyebrows lift on her forehead in wonder. Only Sophie wasn't watching her. She and Tisker were grinning at each other, eyes twinkling in the half-light of the chandelier above them.

Dug was smiling, too. Actually *smiling*, with the sharp edges of white teeth catching the candle light. He squinted and his skin creased with muffled laughter.

"What?" Talis winced at the icy tone in her voice. So she *did* have room for anger, it seemed.

Whatever had dammed their laughter broke. Unable to answer her, Sophie, Tisker, and *hells*, even Dug shook in the grip of their secret joke. Tisker slapped a hand on the table, winced, but kept laughing. Dishes, cups, and spoons jumped and rattled in response. Sophie held a hand over her mouth, lest she spit out the bite she'd just taken.

Talis felt a tug at the corner of her mouth, though it hung slack in confusion. Trying to comprehend the impossible mirth that spilled across the table and washed up against her. Opposite her, Hankirk looked up and his eyes met hers. There was no wonder there. Just . . . sadness, or something like it. The whole scene felt like a fever dream.

"*What?*" she asked again, a tiny bit of the laughter contagion creeping into her voice. It was hard enough to resist Sophie, but that *Dug* had reason to laugh, that overrode her senses. The part of Talis's mind that only wanted to wallow in her misery flared briefly in annoyance at the lack of explanation.

But her crew was lost to her, laughing too hard to answer. Tears gathered in the corners of Tisker's eyes. Their guffaws echoed off the bulkhead and buffeted her eardrums.

Sophie wiped a tear from her eye and put a hand out, clasping Talis's wrist. Like being zapped by static, Talis understood.

She let the smile that was pulling at her lips have its way. Tentatively, laughter followed. A chuckle first. It shook her gently by the shoulders, before seizing her round the middle. The anxiety that had found a home in her gut uncoiled, loosened.

Sophie squeezed her wrist, and Talis rotated her hand so she could grip Sophie's wrist in return.

Talis's shameless laughter joined the din. Her aches and bruises protested, shooting with flares of pain at the staccato movements. It only made her laugh more. Whether they were tears of pain or tears of relief, or just the water chased out by the pressure of the hysterics, she didn't care. She wiped her eyes on the cotton wristband of her jacket and leaned back, slouching comfortably into her seat.

There were no words for what had brought on the mirth. But she knew, somehow, after everything, that they'd be okay.

CHAPTER 43

THE DREGS OF THE CHOWDER hardened inside their bowls long before they left the table. Tisker rose after they ate and put a drum on to play, a collection of shanties with driving rhythm. Talis opened a new bottle of spiced rum, courtesy of the restock back at Subrosa, and they—all five of them—emptied it. In celebration for once, rather than as a salve.

It seemed all during dinner that their laughter couldn't reach Hankirk, wherever his mind had strayed. Except, when Sophie and Tisker got up to dance, the fingers of Hankirk's ruined arm, blue from the tourniquet, twitched as if trying to match their steps.

By then, Talis must have had more than her captain's ration of drink, and she watched in horror from the back of her mind as her body got up and invited the bastard to dance. They didn't speak. They just danced, their frivolous movements intended, finally, not to run for cover or to start a fight. Just to move. Just to be alive.

Hankirk's eyes were still guarded, but he at least found the wherewithal to smile. Talis could almost remember what she'd found appealing about him all those years ago. His jaw was shadowed with stubble, his hair a tousled mess instead of the usual careful combing. It suited him. Or rather, it suited her preferences. She laughed louder then, caught off guard by the thoughts she was entertaining. There wasn't enough rum in all the captains' cabins in all the ships in all of Peridot to be letting *those* thoughts run unchecked.

It wasn't long until Hankirk grew pale from the effort and excused himself from the dance, and from their company. Talis dragged Dug from his seat to take Hankirk's place, and the four of them whooped and hollered and jigged until the metal cylinder ran to its end.

As they returned breathless to their seats, Dug also left the cabin, but returned minutes later with a soot-streaked metal flask of home-brew that somehow survived the flames. Not as strong as the volcanic whiskey that awaited them in the Rakkar cities, but it still stung going down. They relaxed around the table, sipping the torturous moonshine and talking quietly about nothing of import until that bottle, too, was gone, and their eyelids drooped.

Sophie, the only one of them who could still walk with any sort of skysuredness, fetched two pitchers of cool water and a bowl of lemon wedges. She forced them each to drink two full glasses and suck half a salted lemon before she'd let them leave the table to sleep it off.

TALIS DIDN'T REMEMBER undressing or crawling into her bunk, but when *Wind Sabre* began to shake, she was tangled in the blankets. She clawed for consciousness, struggling to free herself from the sheets twisted around her legs.

Bless Sophie's ministrations, she was sober enough, and her stomach solid, though her mind was still muddled, either from the drink or deep sleep—or both. Muddled enough that she forgot Nexus wasn't causing headaches anymore, and that hers was all her own doing. She pulled on her pants and clumsily tightened their laced closure as she ran out of her cabin, barefoot and wild-eyed.

The deck vibrated as though the keel was dragging across solid ground. *Wind Sabre* was doing her best, but the resistance of wind against the unbalanced weight was pushing her limits.

Though no longer accosted by Silus Cutter's stolen winds, the ship was still taking abuse from traveling through Peridot's natural air currents. Both lift lines at aft had been severed by the alien weapons. The port line at midship, too. The hull sagged heavy at its stern, leaning to port and pulling them incessantly to that side.

Thick as Talis's forearm, the lift lines couldn't be replaced from what they had onboard. The heavy ropes were reinforced with steel wires, coated against moisture with tar, and tightly braided with coils as dense as stone to discourage flames. They only got stronger from use, pulled tighter by the weight of the ship. A seasoned lift line might as well have been a length of tempered steel. They were designed to last a lifetime, or at least give a smart captain time to notice and repair or replace them if they were damaged.

Just about every airship in the skies flew in confidence that a line wouldn't fail altogether. And certainly not three at once. The canvas lift envelope might get eaten by moths, the wood of the railing might rot away. But a captain could count on the lift lines.

The design had never accounted for alien beams of light that sliced like knives.

On deck, Talis found Sophie crawling out of the starboard engine house, arms and face streaked with grease. If she felt any effects of the previous night's celebrations, there was no sign of it. Her eyes were clear. Also clear was that she had nothing good to report from the Number Two engine.

Talis pulled Sophie to her feet. "Can we make it to Heddard Bay?"

Sophie's face didn't reassure her. "Can't say, Captain. It's not a matter of *if* the engines will fail, but when."

"Gods, both of them?" Talis had to put a hand on the engine house to steady herself, not sure if the alcohol was still running rampant in her body or if she'd reached the limit of how much bad news she could take. Before she realized what she was doing, she'd tangled the fingers of her other hand around her prayerlocks and tugged. Her heart ached at the futility of it.

Airships were little more than wooden buckets built around the symbiosis of their twin engines and the lift balloon above. They needed both systems intact, and both systems needed to work together, or a ship was just a rock waiting to drop out of the sky. If one of the two engines failed, they'd limp for a while until the stress on the second got to be too much, and that would be it for their propulsion. Minutes later, that'd be it for the hot air that the engines fed to the lift balloons. As the air cooled to the same temperature as the sky around them, the weight of the hull would drag the ship down.

"The compressor in Number One is barely working." Sophie pulled a rag from her pocket and wiped at the grease coating her skin. "A bunch of pieces got shook free in there. I was able to put most of them back in place, but they've banged around real good and almost everything's got to be realigned. I can hear some other piece kicking around loose in there, but I can't get to it. It's gonna stress 'til it fails, then Number Two is only going to be able to get us so far under this strain."

Sophie put the rag down on the engine block, closed her eyes as her chest lifted with a big inhale. She let it out in a sigh. "Hells. It could be the piston come free of its cylinder."

Talis put a steadying hand on her shoulder. This was Sophie's area of expertise, and they needed her focused, not running down the what-ifs. "Okay, tell me what we do. Slow down? Take the strain off?"

"Gods, no, Captain," Sophie said without a pause. "The sooner we get to a dock and can shut down the system, the more of it we can save."

Talis looked out past the railing. The sky was tinted hazy green, so that the distant stars were muted. The view should have been partially obscured by the midship lift line, but what remained of that had been cleared from the deck. The anchor for it, built into the railing, was barren. The eye, meant to fix the heavy loop of rope, stared back at her.

"Then we'll take whatever line we have and re-string the three anchors. I know it's thin, but—"

Sophie turned her face up at the lift envelope, blinking. "—but it's worth a shot. Anything we can do to ease off on the strain. And soon."

Talis swallowed. Sophie, whose optimism had no equal, wasn't smiling. The engine was in worse shape than she'd let on.

"Dug and I will meet you port-side aft. You good?"

She was sending Sophie up to the catwalks built along the perimeter of the lift envelope. With three lines loose, the bob and hop of the lift balloon would try to shake her free with every step.

"Good as a goat," Sophie replied, mustering a tight smile for her captain. Her windlegs were a source of pride, second only to that which she felt for the ship she loved.

Still, it was going to be a nauseating stroll at best. Talis didn't move. Considered going up herself, instead. Her stomach lurched at the thought.

Finally offering a real smile, Sophie clasped Talis's wrist again. "I'll wear a harness this time, Captain. Promise."

Satisfied, Talis nodded, then left her to fetch Dug.

STANDING ON *Wind Sabre*'s lowest deck with Dug, Talis stared in disbelief at their inventory of line.

The coils kept in the main hold were meant for small patch jobs, securing cargo, or—in a fix—for towing. She'd never given much thought to the length of the uncut spools, but she'd expected them to be longer than they proved to be.

"There might be enough, Captain, if we don't loop them." Dug's voice was low, as if speaking too loud would shake *Wind Sabre* free of what lines she had left.

They frowned, their arms crossed, at the paltry supplies. Ideally, because the lines were lightweight, Talis had intended to double them up, so that two widths ran up to the balloon, looped the anchor up top, and ran down again to hold the lift balloon to the ship.

But they might not even have enough to connect one length end-to-end.

"That's that, then." She sighed. "We'll have to shorten the length on the proper lines, too."

Which would jostle the whole ship. She might as well drop a hammer into the engine while she was at it.

No choice. No time.

She heaved one side of the nearest full spool, twisting it on its wooden disk to reposition it so they could both get a grip and maneuver it up the three levels to the aft deck.

SOPHIE WAS WAITING FOR THEM on the catwalk above, and lowered a wire as Talis and Dug rolled the heavy spool of line down the deck. Talis could see the dark straps of Sophie's safety harness crossed against the lighter fabric of her coveralls. She wore thick gloves, the heavy cuffs of which covered her forearms. Talis and Dug ought to put them on, too. Last thing they needed was more wounded hands.

Dug slipped the end of their rope into the loop on Sophie's wire and secured it with a practiced knot. He and Talis freed the length of rope from the spool and laid the coil so it wouldn't snag as they pulled it upward.

Talis fastened the other end to the railing anchor with the strongest knot she could tie that wouldn't get too greedy with length.

Dug's jaw was set in concentration. Last night, everything had been okay. Stable. But now *Wind Sabre* was falling apart. Talis couldn't fool herself that they'd be able to just patch the hull up and sail off again. Repairs would take months. Months of sitting still and stewing over everything they'd lost. She wanted to ask Dug what he was thinking, but every time she opened her mouth to speak, it was easier to close it again and just concentrate on the work. If she didn't ask, she didn't have to hear the answer she was dreading.

Dug waved an arm to signal Sophie. Hand over hand, she began to haul the line up. It was a big weight for the petite woman. Her feet were braced against the vertical rails of the catwalk, and she leaned back to counterbalance the weight.

"Wouldn't say no to an extra hand, Captain!"

They needed to do this right. It wasn't just timing, but balance, too. Talis inhaled. It was why she'd gone for the port line first, to balance the starboard line at midship that they still had. She wanted to get both aft connections to the lift balloon secure as soon as possible. But if Sophie couldn't tie off the line up top by herself, there was no point.

She looked to Dug. "I'll go. Would be a sorry sight if I tried to get the next spool on my own, but you might manage it. Grab two more lengths of the thinner line while you're at it."

On a good day, she loved to ascend the lift lines. Nothing

felt so invigorating as fighting the wind for balance on the weather deck built into the top of the envelope, where the tiny calf-high railing was only a formality. The sky above and around her, and their natural element whipping about, trying to claim her. It was a refreshing place to go when she needed to clear her head.

If the ship had more crew, there'd be watches along the lift balloon's catwalk, too. As it was, with just the four of them, they made regular inspections on the guiding sails and on the lines but couldn't spare the bodies to station someone there for a full watch.

The Rakkar of Heddard Bay would have her in a bind and could ask any price they liked to get *Wind Sabre* sky worthy again. But just maybe, if there was anything left of Talis's share of the money, she'd hire a couple more crew members. Give the ship a proper set of hands.

But there were no spare hands now, no room for such thoughts. They still had to get to Heddard Bay with what was left of the ship if they were going to put in for any repairs at all.

Talis reached the top of the forward ratlines. She didn't want to jostle the midship line any more than she had to, so she'd cross the full length of the ship on the catwalks.

The thin, springy planks of the walk bounced under her feet. She moved with as much haste as she could, but the unbalanced lift balloon wobbled irregularly. The catwalks leaped up as she stepped down, propelling each step higher on the next bounce.

Sophie gave her a scathing look as she approached. Only then did Talis realize she'd crossed the hazard without her own safety harness or a lead line clipped to the railing.

"Really, Captain? Why am I wearing this chafing thing, then? Don't you feel the walks trying to buck you off?"

Sophie braced the wire line and shifted her weight to free one hand. She jerked a leather-gloved thumb at the locker behind them. "Put it on, or I drop the line." Her hand clamped back down as the line started to tug through her grip. "Captain."

The catwalk still lurched and tossed beneath their feet, even with them both standing still. Crossing it unfastened had indeed been foolish. Load of good Talis would do for everyone if she went over and needed rescue, or was beyond rescue and left them with two fewer hands to help get *Wind Sabre* back to civilization.

She fetched a harness and, bracing herself against a rib of the lift envelope, climbed into it and secured it across her stomach. It had a short lead, only about two arm-spans, and was designed to keep her from plummeting to flotsam if she fell. She and Sophie'd likely get their leads all tangled up together, but she did feel safer with it on.

The envelope's line anchor was secured against the side in a pocket of canvas designed for the job. The forged metal ring was shaped like a belt buckle, triple-reinforced thick stitching all around the outer ring held it in place, and the crossbar in the center curved out to give room for the lift line, to prevent it from rubbing on the canvas and wearing either the line or the envelope.

Sophie threaded the wire through and pulled as best she could. There was a break in the catwalk below the anchor, so the walkway wouldn't be crushed beneath the tension of the lines. But it made for awkward work. She braced herself, toes against the lift envelope, one foot to either side of the gap below her, and pulled. Her shoulders leaned outward toward the misty green of open sky.

Sophie bared her teeth. One elbow was clamped against her side for stability, her other arm straining. The knotted end of the line was mere inches away from making it through the anchor. But with the weight of the hull at play, inches were leagues.

Talis moved behind her, braced her feet against the

balloon outside Sophie's, and together they pulled the wire.
Talis could feel the thin material cutting into the joints of
her fingers.

"This the longest we got?" Sophie's voice was strained.

"The others might even be shorter."

Sophie's only reply was a grunt, but Talis felt her increase
her effort.

Hand over hand, in hair's-breadth increments, the end
of the rope got closer and closer to the metal bar. The wire
creased at the end of the loop. Talis had an awful image of the
wire snapping, the line dropping, and them propelling themselves out over the catwalk. The impulse to tug her prayerlocks itched at her mind. An old habit that would take a long
time to break, even knowing Silus Cutter was gone.

When the knot of the line caught on the edge of the bar,
they pulled together on count. Talis's muscles burned, but
she took a deep breath and channeled the last of her reserve
energy as they wrenched on the final pull.

The wire shuddered as the knot crossed over the bar. It
gave them a small respite from the strain, but only just. She and
Sophie still braced against the balloon. Her arms still burned
in complaint.

The knot was there. The line was pulled through and,
if they could untie it, there was enough length to tie off to
the anchor.

Of course, they couldn't untie it. Nor could either of
them let go of the wire. The palms of her hands, and the insides of her fingers, were in agony. Her arm muscles twitched
in protest at the strain.

A rumble passed through the lift balloon, and the catwalk beneath them shuddered.

"Ship doesn't like the length of the line, does she." Sophie's voice was hard, even. It wasn't a question, but there was
a question behind it. *We gonna make it, Captain?*

"We'll shorten the others next," Talis said, talking

through her clenched jaw. Those few words took all the effort she could spare.

The catwalk trembled again. But this time it was the welcomed rhythm of approaching feet. She would have breathed a sigh of relief if she dared relax.

Dug came around the curve of the lift balloon, harness on and lead clip bouncing in its place along the catwalk's guide rail. A length of rope looped over one arm and a small canvas bag of tools cradled in the other.

THE THREE OF THEM TOGETHER made faster work on the next two lines. *Wind Sabre*'s nose dragged against the winds, though, once the two aft lines were secured. To Talis, the temporary lines looked as thin as cotton floss wrapped around the massive line anchors. The hull protested the shift in tension, and Talis swore she could see the lines stretch thin against the tensile force.

She wasn't going to relax until they were safely docked, the hull braced, and the engines powered down for the rest they deserved.

Until then, it was double effort to try anything they could. When the lift lines were as even as they could get them, she'd get on a swing and patch that tear in the underside of the envelope. Then tarp patches for the other missing sections of the hull, if they weren't to Heddard Bay already. Whatever would reduce drag. Give Tisker whatever help they could to fly them into dock with a little of their dignity intact.

She spared a glance for her pilot as they ran for the forward lines. Tisker was tight-lipped, eyes on the gauges of the console. His gauze-wrapped fists gripped at the wheel. His forearms braced along the handles to support his damaged hands.

He didn't look up at them as they moved past or call out a report of what the readouts said. She didn't ask. From the set of his jaw and the knotting of his brows, she knew. She swallowed and ran faster.

There was no system in place for tightening or loosing the lines. Like the planks of the deck, they were installed as a fixed constant. They were what they were. But they were too loose now.

If they got through this, she'd never fly without backup line for the lift systems again. Something thicker and three times the length. High-quality stuff, reinforced, even if it wasn't as big around as a full-size lift line.

And winches. She'd install winches for making adjustments. Gears and cranks forged by master Rakkar metalsmiths.

Talis made all these silent promises to her ship and worked as hard as she could with what they had.

They slipped a loop of the thinner stuff through the tight gap in the line anchor at the starboard fore railing, tied it as tight as they could, and started reeling the lift line in. It was a battle with the tension, and the eye of the anchor didn't spare them much room. Even less when the line started to fold back. Talis, Dug, and Sophie pulled against it, struggling to get the loop through the too-small gap.

Come on, girl, she urged her ship. *Just a little farther.*

But *Wind Sabre* had gone as far as she could. Her heart gave out.

CHAPTER 44

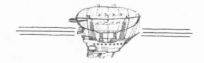

ALL THE PROMISES THAT Talis made to her ship couldn't keep it together. *Wind Sabre*'s death knell was an understated staccato *ping* of something critical failing within the engine's complex system.

Sophie cried out and let go of the line. Talis and Dug lurched forward and scrambled to take up the slack. Sophie stripped off her gloves and dropped them on the deck behind her as she ran back toward the Number One engine's deck house.

There was a growl from midship. Then, louder, a chuffing sound. Then an outright howl of metal on metal, and the grinding screech as working engine parts fought others that had stopped moving.

Sophie, halfway across the deck, skidded to a stop. Took a tentative step backward.

There was a hiss, then a whine like a massive teapot angry at being forgotten.

Sophie ran straight past the engines.

Waving her arms, she shouted for them to find cover. Her voice was nearly drowned out by the screams of the failing mechanics. She made it to the wheelhouse, skidding in and pushing Tisker down behind the bulk of the wheel's supporting pedestal. She crouched there, her arms around him, making them as small as she could behind the narrow shelter.

Dug let go of the rope and grabbed Talis by the shoulders as the line lurched free of her hands. There was nothing to hide behind on the forward deck, and the hatch to the forecastle cabin below was sealed from the other side. He forced her down flat on the decking and shielded her body with his.

She felt the entire ship heave, lurching, trembling with the force of the explosion. Heard the fireball that the engine expelled, a whoosh and a clap of thunder as metal warped. The momentary whine of the metal housing as it was torn open from within, wrenched apart by the built-up energy from moving components straining against their deadened counterparts.

A moment later she felt the heat of it on her exposed skin.

Shrapnel hit the deck around them, and Dug flinched beside her. The shrapnel was hitting him, too. His torso was bare, except for the safety harness he hadn't bothered to remove. She struggled against his weight, trying to move out from beneath him so he could lay flatter, but he held her fast, pinning her to the deck where he'd braced her.

The hull beneath them felt like it was dragging on gravel. It shuddered. They rocked forward as momentum suddenly slowed.

Talis's ears rang. Dug shook her, and she realized he was talking to her. She tried to answer that she couldn't hear what he said, but she couldn't hear herself either. She shook her head at him, but he was looking away already. Away and up.

Something flapped over their heads. She blinked the fog from her vision and could see a twisted section of the cat-walk, and the responsible chunk of the engine housing that had destroyed it, tangled in the shredded canvas of the lift balloon. She saw *Wind Sabre*'s hot breath as it escaped the envelope. More puffs of steaming air came from other portions around the curve of the balloon from where she was.

Patching the canvas had just taken priority over the lift lines, to keep what hot air they could and help the remaining engine do the work of two.

Dug helped her to her feet. The ringing in Talis's ears turned to an incessant whine, but the awful noises *Wind Sabre* was making were starting to resolve. Between the headache and the heartache, Talis felt like she was going to be sick.

She looked across the deck. It was an expanse of flaming puddles of grease and smoking scraps of metal. Sophie left Tisker's side to throw back the hatch on the second engine compartment, which was dented and blackened by its proximity to the blast of its twin. She could hear another malfunctioning part clattering within.

Dug climbed backward down the port-side ladder to the middle deck, and Talis followed, not waiting for him to clear it beneath her.

When the Number Two engine exploded, something heavy and hard slammed Talis forward. Her forehead struck one of the ladder steps, and she let go of the rails, falling the last few steps. Dug caught her under the arms and kept her from slumping into an undignified mess.

She struggled to her feet. Her head swam, but through the lights that swirled in her vision, she saw Sophie crumpled against the railing. Thrown by the blast. Red, where a dozen wounds bloomed, soaking the fabric of her coveralls.

Talis ran. The deck swung and lurched beneath her feet, forcing her to struggle for balance with every step. She felt the upward slide of her guts, which meant the ship was losing altitude, fast.

They needed to get to the lifeboats. They needed to abandon *Wind Sabre*.

Her heart wrenched, as much from the altitude loss as the thought of her dying ship.

She reached Sophie's side. The girl was breathing. She moved. She feebly put her hands on the deck and tried to lift herself up, but Talis put a hand on her shoulder. Dug was right behind her. He bent and scooped Sophie up, and they turned to follow Tisker, who was already running for the aft port lifeboat.

The curving shape of Nexus slid upward across her field of vision. They wouldn't have time to set up the small boat's butane tank and get its hot air balloon filled. *Wind Sabre* was sinking, and she was going to take them down with her.

Maybe. Maybe *Wind Sabre*'s hull would protect them from the worst of a crash into flotsam. Maybe they could get the lifeboat running, get aloft again before they froze to death in the thin atmo. She tried to remember the steps necessary, and the order. Not like she'd thought to keep up on drills. They'd only used the lifeboats to fly undetected runs, and they'd never hurried.

"Talis, here!"

It took her longer to recognize the voice than to turn her head toward its source. She had forgotten all about Hankirk. As they ran clear of the central deckhouses, their starboard view opened up again. Either the lifeboat on that side of the ship was lifting up, or *Wind Sabre*'s deck was dropping away from it. Hankirk leaned out and motioned to them with his good hand, bracing his shoulder against one of the balloon's lines to keep from tumbling out.

Tisker veered in that direction, running faster to reach the dinghy before it was out of reach. Hankirk tossed down a line, and Tisker fastened it to a cleat in the railing. The little balloon danced, struggling against the weight of the larger ship, and the rope went taut.

Talis and Dug reached their side as Tisker grabbed Hankirk's offered hand and clambered up into the dinghy. Three arms reached down, pulling Sophie out of Dug's arms and into the lifeboat. Tisker reached back for Talis. Dug lifted her up, and then Tisker's bandaged hands were gripping her upper arms. She gripped back. He pulled as she scrambled to get her legs up over the side. Together they tumbled into it, Talis landing on top of Tisker. Their faces were inches away from Scrimshaw's unconscious one. She spared a moment as she untangled herself, trying not to put her knees or hands down anywhere fragile, to marvel at how Hankirk had prepared the dinghy for launch and even managed to load the unconscious alien into it.

He might have saved them all.

Talis turned back to help Dug. She and Tisker leaned out, each grabbing one of his forearms. He gripped back, they hauled, he pulled up. And they were all aboard.

Dug used his boot knife to sever the line pulling them down with *Wind Sabre*. Sophie pushed her feet against the curved bottom of the dinghy, struggling to brace her elbows on the benches to either side of her. She bit her lip, pained by the movement, and Tisker helped her sit up. She twisted onto one hip, turned and got her arms on the railing of the dinghy, and rested her chin on her forearm.

The hot air balloon expanded again with a snap, and the little boat lifted away as they watched their ship drop to its grave.

THERE WAS ONLY SILENCE for a while, save for the puff of flame from the tank above them. Hankirk sat in the bow of the lifeboat, his eyes closed. His face was pale. The fingers peeking out from the sling across his chest were dark purple.

Tisker sat on the next bench, to one side. Sophie sat on the bottom of the dinghy beside Scrimshaw, her knees curled up and her head resting on Tisker's leg. The blood on her coveralls was dull, dry. The wounds she'd sustained in the

Number Two engine blast, thank the gods, were clotting.

Dug sat between Talis and Tisker. He picked a piece of shrapnel out of a wound in his arm and tossed it over the side of the dinghy. Talis almost stopped him, desperate to hold on to one piece of her lost ship, but she held her tongue. There was plenty of shrapnel between Dug and Sophie. Not really how she wanted to remember *Wind Sabre*, anyway.

Tisker adjusted the flame as they regained Horizon's traveling altitude. Talis reached back to the miniature outboard engine and started flipping the switches to prime its fuel line.

A cry, coarse and high pitched, sounded in the sky next to the little dinghy. Talis blinked in confusion, but Dug craned his neck around to look for the source, as if he'd been waiting for it.

Maybe he had.

The six-eyed raven that had once been Onaya Bone flapped her color-shifting wings and settled onto the bench in front of Dug. She regarded him, then ruffled her feathers up around her and settled in like any other raven in its roost. Another refugee.

Talis tugged the motor's cord, and the silence was drowned out by the grumbling roar of the little outboard turbine. The ship tugged ahead as if eager to transport them to safety. She leaned her forearm against the tiller and brought the little ship around in a lazy circle.

The green-edged silhouette of Heddard Bay hung like an emerald in the sky, near enough that Talis could see the sway of treetops along the slopes of a volcano that dominated the island's skyline.

They'd lost their ship. Their home. Lost the fortune in its hold. Lost blood. Lost their gods, and with them, no small amount of hope.

But while she still had a heartbeat, Talis was going to see to it that they hadn't lost everything.

ACKNOWLEDGEMENTS

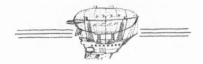

I WOULD NEVER HAVE COMPLETED this novel if not for the support of the following people. No matter how profusely I thank them, it will be insufficient to express what their support means to me.

Thanks go to my husband Matt, who encouraged me for so many years while I struggled to discover that I was, indeed, a writer. And then kicked me in the pants when I needed it most. The words "maybe it's time to really finish it" snapped me out of the rinse-revise-repeat cycle and moved a decade of work forward to this moment.

To Jillian Iris and Jillianne Frances, who read and gave feedback on countless early drafts and supported me with enthusiasm no matter how many times they watched me go back and start over.

To John Adamus, without whom this would have been a very different book. His experience, passion, and guidance helped me realize the potential of a million-or-so messy words and craft the book that *FLOTSAM* is now.

To the authors and reviewers who provided Parvus with wonderful blurbs in support to this first-time author.

To Oriana Leckert, for far more than a proof read.

To Julie Dillon, for her enthusiasm as much as for the stunning, amazing, totally brilliant cover illustration.

To the team at Parvus Press, for getting as excited as I do about my genre-bending absurdities.

To Mary Robinette Kowal, for applying her talent to the fantastic performance of *FLOTSAM*'s audio edition, and for the moral fortitude that bolstered my own.

To my parents, Bud and Tricia, to Mel and Kathy Jay, Brett Schmidt, John Sotherland and Juliana Fajoses, Frie Van Raevels, Dave D'Alessio, the Wilson family, David and Selena Toback, and Juan Henao. Each provided generous support and warm encouragement which made final publication possible.

My sincerest gratitude to each of you.

Thank you for being awesome.

ABOUT THE AUTHOR

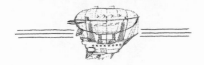

R J THEODORE IS HELL BENT on keeping herself busy. No, really, if she has two minutes to rub together at the end of the day, she invents a new project with which to occupy them.

She enjoys reading, design, illustration, video games (she will take you down in Super Puzzle Fighter II Turbo), binging on movies and streaming series, napping with her cats, and cooking. She is passionate about art and coffee.

R J Theodore lives in New England with her family.

Book One of the Peridot Shift series, *FLOTSAM,* is Theodore's debut novel.

Read about her writing process, find her on social media, and subscribe to her reader list for updates, announcements, and free books by visiting rjtheodore.com

A WORD FROM PARVUS PRESS

www.ParvusPress.com

THANK YOU FOR CHOOSING a Parvus title and supporting independent publishing. If you loved *FLOTSAM*, your review on Goodreads or your favorite retailer's website is the best way to support the author. Reviews are the lifeblood of the independent press.

Also, we love to hear from our readers and to know how you enjoyed our books. Reach us on our website, engage with us on Twitter (@ParvusPress) or reach out directly to the publisher via email: colin@parvuspress.com. Yes, that's his real email. We aren't kidding when we say we're dedicated to our readers.

On our website, you can also sign up for our mailing list to win free books, get an early look at upcoming releases, and follow our growing family of authors.

Thanks for being Parvus People,

—*The Parvus Press Team*

GLOSSARY

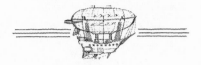

CHARACTERS

(Entries for Peridot's deities are listed under the "Religion" section of this glossary)

Cormack - Business associate of Talis operating out of Subrosa. Rakkar.

Dug - First mate of *Wind Sabre* and Talis's closest friend. Full name is Dukkhat Kheri. Bone.

Ellanis - Business associate of Talis operating out of Subrosa. Cutter.

Fens Yarrow - A Cutter man from the nineteenth generation post-Recreation who built a weapon with the intent to kill The Five. Executed by Onaya Bone for his intended deicide. His weapon disappeared, but some Veritors hold that it was completed, and that it is possible to find and use it.

Hankirk - Imperial Captain with whom Talis has a once-romantic history. Claims to be a descendent of Fens Yarrow. Tasked with retrieving the ring of Lindent Vein. Cutter.

Illiya - High Priestess of Onaya Bone at the Temple of the Feathered Stone on Fall Island in Bone territory. Formerly an interrogator for hire. Bone.

Jasper - Merchant and fence operating out of Subrosa's Corrugated District. Breaker.

Meran - A mysterious woman who wields alchemy and a stranger, unknown power. Seems pissed about something.

Scrimshaw - Nickname given to the linguist who accompanies *Wind Sabre's* crew during their escort mission to Fall Island. Artisan class. Pronouns: xe/xin/xist (among others). Yu'Nyun.

Sophie - Wrench for *Wind Sabre*. Grew up on a colony airship with too many siblings and overprotective aunts. Cutter.

Talis - Captain of *Wind Sabre*. Left the Imperial academy due to philosophical differences. Ran with a group of mercs for a time. Has more stories she hasn't told you. Cutter.

Tisker - Pilot of *Wind Sabre*. Grew up as an orphan in Subrosa until he asked Talis for work aboard her ship. Cutter.

Talbot - Business associate of Talis. Captains a ship but also operates a smuggling ring out of Subrosa. Passionate about grooming and pickpocketing. Likes a challenge. Cutter.

Zeela - Businesswoman offering expensive and hard-to-find items out of the Platform District of Subrosa. Owns Zeela's House of Antiquities. Vein.

VESSELS

The Emerald Empress - Galleon-hulled private merchant ship that sank to the flotsam layer with a certain artifact among its cargo.

The Serpent Rose - Imperial hunter class airship under the command of Captain Hankirk, tasked with retrieving the ring of Lindent Vein. Equipped with arms and cannons and at least seventy-five hands. Not equipped with descent gear.

Wind Sabre - Carrack hulled airship crewed by Talis, Dug, Tisker, and Sophie.

LOCATIONS

Assessor's Hall - A long stretch of alley in Subrosa, adjacent to the Corrugated District, where pawnshop kiosks crowd the relatively dark passages.

Corrugated District - A section of Subrosa. High traffic. Named for the corrugated metal sheets used to construct much of its walls and flooring.

Diadem - The Cutter territory capital and home to the Emperor and his family.

Fall Island - Bone desert island, as close to Nexus as many dare to settle. Sand continuously flows from the center of the island, over its edges. Home of the High Holy Bone Temple of the Feathered Stone and the trade port Talonpoint.

Hartham - Moderately sized border island on the Cutter side of the Bone-Cutter border. Day-and-a-half journey from Subrosa at cruising speeds.

Horizon - The centralized altitude at which most cities and settlements on Peridot have been positioned. There was an organized effort across all four territories to migrate all activity on the planet to one plane, as maps were almost impossible to manage and read when altitude and overlapping landmasses had to be accounted for. However, some poorer communities, or those dependent on features of a non-Horizon island, still live off this plane.

Nexus - Collection of energy released during the Cataclysm, which holds Peridot's loose tectonic remnants together. The home of Peridot's five deities.

Peridot - An unusual planet whose natural course was altered through an alchemical ritual for power transference.

Platform District - A section of Subrosa. Constructed and maintained by a business co-op of Vein merchants and business owners. Constructed with exposure to open air, from solid wood.

Rosa - A smallish island in Cutter skies, a trading post turned metropolis, located convenient to the border crossing into Bone territories. Populated by all five races of Peridot. Crowded, and prosperous.

Silver Isles - A tight grouping of small inner radius islands in the Cutter territory. Connected to each other by bridges. Strong Imperial presence. Well-maintained.

Subrosa - Black-market "bottom-hanged" city suspended from the underside of the island Rosa.

Talonpoint - Port city of Fall Island, a densely packed but well-organized cluster of housing, hospitality, civil offices, and businesses arranged along streets which diagonally spoke outward from a central 'green' in which public addresses, events, and markets are held. High stone walls surround the city to keep the blowing sand of Fall Island's desert out of the streets.

Temple of the Feathered Stone - Central temple of Onaya Bone on Fall Island. Features a communing chamber where supplicants may be permitted to speak directly to the goddess via video feed. Center of operations for the priestesses' intelligence network.

Tined Spoon District - A section of Subrosa, adjacent to the Platform District, almost entirely dedicated to restaurants and bars.

RELIGION

Alchemy - The practice of manipulating elemental forces to control reality. The dangerous practice is taboo among mortals, enforced most actively by Onaya Bone.

Cataclysm - Catastrophic event which caused the planet to explode, destroying all life except for the five beings that committed the alchemical transference responsible.

Recreation - The action taken by Peridot's five deities to make Peridot inhabitable again, and to create the peoples, flora, and fauna which can be found there afterward.

The Five - Refers to the five alchemists whose transference ritual in ancient history gave them high-level control of elemental magic, immortality, and the power to create life.

The Divine Alchemists - Another honorific term for The Five.

The Deities

Arthel Rak - God and creator of the Rakkar. Associated with the element of fire.

Helsim Breaker - God of the Breaker people. Alchemically proficient with the element of life.

Ketzali - An enormous, six-eyed male raven created by and favored by Onaya Bone.

Lindent Vein - God and creator of the Vein people. Blind. Disdainful of eyesight. Alchemically proficient with the element of water.

Onaya Bone - Goddess and creator of the Bone people. Associated with the element of earth. Has a romantic past with Silus Cutter, though they are not currently affiliated.

Silus Cutter - God and creator of the Cutter people. Associated with the element of air.

Groups / Affiliations

Cutter folk / Cutters - People created by Silus Cutter during the Recreation. 1.75 meters tall by Earth measurement. Naturally athletic build. Hair is typically brown to black. Eyes are typically brown or hazel. Skin is a warm honey gold color. Innately prone to wanderlust. Claustrophobia is not uncommon, though not all suffer from it. Primary exports are shipbuilding, glow pumpkin sprouts, water, and aeronautical equipment. Most populous of all Peridot races. Government is an empire, with heavily ingrained bureaucratic infrastructure for local and regional management.

Bone - People created by Onaya Bone during the Recreation. 1.85 meters tall by Earth measurement. Lithe, angular build. Blue-black hair and purple-blue-green iridescent feathers form a full head of hair, though many shave parts or all of their scalp. Dark skin. Eyes range from gray to purple. Fingernails, when allowed to grow, curve sharply as talons. Traditional martial art is taught as part of educational process. Initiation by solitary hunting expedition to earn adulthood and voting status in tribal councils. Tribal elders form Leadership Council and convene every five years to renew relations as part of a meeting of the tribes, during which the trial hunts are held.

Vein - People created by Lindent Vein during the Recreation. 1.8 meters tall by Earth measurement. All are born blind. Four arms, two smaller, more nimble primary and two larger, stronger secondary. Slender, willowy. Hair is colorless. Skin is pale cream with lavender undertones. Highly perceptive, with enhanced nervous system to detect electrical impulses as well as ranged temperature shifts, sound, and smell. Primary exports are technologies backward-engineered and developed from discovered Pre-Cataclysm devices. Governed by elite class, determined by academic accomplishment.

Breaker - People created by Helsim Breaker during the Recreation. 2.25 meters tall by Earth measurement. Tusked from the lower jaw. Large, bulky, and muscular. Grayish, pebbled skin. As far as anyone knows, the Breaker will not die of natural death. Pacifists, highly sensitive to mood and health of those they interact with. Patient craftsmen. No organized government. Most of them commune with nature wherever they can live peacefully. Often share islands with Rakkar.

Rakkar - The people created by Arthel Rak. 1.6 meters by Earth measurement. Slender, petite build. Rosy-yellow skin, with protective chitin plating covering most of the face, hands, and forearms. Resistant to the effects of high heat, smoke, and toxic chemicals. Black eyes, adapted for subterranean life. Agoraphobic almost universally. Expert engineers and inventors. Defiant of the taboo against alchemical research (although cautious). Primary exports are precious metals and gems mined from their volcanic islands.

Imperials - A term used to describe the servicemen and women of the Cutter Empire.

Veritors of the Lost Codex - A cult of Cutter folk who have interpreted an ancient text to mean that the Cutter folk were the only people that existed Pre-Cataclysm. Hold The Five in disdain. Believe that the world is fundamentally wrong and research, plot, and act with the intent to make Cutter folk the dominant—or for some members, the only—race on Peridot. Have a large following among the rich and powerful, and may be embedded in the highest levels of the Empire.

Yu'Nyun - Bipedal, chitin-plated, digitigrade, bilaterally symmetrical alien visitors to the planet Peridot. Technologically advanced compared to the natives. Interested in understanding how Peridot came to be and how it continues to function.

OTHER VOCABULARY

Airship - Transportation vessels featuring hot air lift balloon systems, turbines, steam engines, and sails. Required for long distance travel through Peridot. Designed and built by all races except the Rakkar, primarily by the Bone and Cutter folk.

Atmo - Short for 'atmosphere,' refers to the inhabitable areas of Peridot's skies, where one may breathe unassisted and temperatures support life.

Coffee - Beverage brewed from . . . you don't really need me to define this, do you?

Colony ship - Airship habitats for town or city-sized populations of Cutter folk who prefer not to settle down on stationary islands. Often, these ships travel on a regular circuit between islands where they may stop to refuel and trade. Their primary export is ship craft, engineering developments for patent, textiles, entertainment (music and theater), and other products that do not require large tracts of land or heavy resource use.

Dextral - The direction of natural spin of Peridot around Nexus. Opposite of sinistral.

Duskfey - Tiny bioluminescing pests that feed on vegetation, especially glow pumpkins.

Fatcrat - Derogatory term for wealthy bureaucrat.

Flotsam - A trapped layer of loose objects at the bottom of Peridot's gravity well.

Glow pumpkins - Enormous gaseous gourds that emit purple light during nighttime hours and golden light during daylight hours. Cultivated on stations across Peridot to provide additional lighting.

Mantas - Smooth-hided flighted creature with bioluminescent signals in a translucent camouflaging body with long trailing tendril tails. Feed off small insects and other pests. Curved beak, tridactyl feet for gripping perches.

Mermaids / Zalika - Soulless beings who live and hunt in the stationary storms across Peridot's skies. They have a long, powerful tail, and flesh-webbed wings. Androgynous with alto and soprano vocalizations, agonized facial expressions, clawed hands, and a taste for flesh.

Pale coats - A derogatory term for Imperial officers, referring to their pale blue uniform jackets.

Prayerlocks - Knotted segments of hair maintained by Cutter folk in honor of Silus Cutter, often gripped, twisted, rubbed, tugged, or otherwise to invoke his blessing, as both a pious act, and one of superstition. They are formed in young children as soon as their hair is long enough, and others may be formed later in life. As is the nature of hair (and especially of hair often tugged), 'locks will occasionally fall out entirely and new ones started. These are often decorated with beads or metal rings sold by Wind Monks in various markets.

Presscoins - Cutter currency. Smelted and minted precious metal, stamped with the official seal of the Empire on one side, and a portrait of the ruler, or ruling family, on the other. Pressed in copper, silver, or gold.

Sally bar - Slang for 'salvage bar'. Tool for wedging, levering, and severing.

Salvage gear - Suit, helmet, gloves, lines, winches, and communication wiring which allows a person to (almost) safely visit flotsam to retrieve lost items.

Simula - Yu'Nyun-produced android capable of being programmed for both appearance and behavior. Can be controlled, if necessary, by a circlet device that interfaces with its cranial drive. When inert, appear Yu'Nyun in shape, with translucent gel-filled skin over a mechanical skeleton.

Sinistral - Direction counter to the natural spin of Peridot around Nexus. Opposite of dextral.

Sirenia - Large roving beasts of the sky which feed on vegetation. Bioluminescing signaling across their body, large fins for display. They attain buoyancy through a balance between inflatable gas organs and consumed ballast.

Slips - Localized wind systems that travel faster than the air around them.

Starship - Fully enclosed ships designed for the vacuum of space, capable of long range travel between stars.

Stormwater depot - Supply stations set up within the storm clouds to collect rainwater for use across Peridot, especiall for steam engines. Visited by water trawler airships, and als by smugglers and pirates as a place to hide.

Tripolarizing kiparcoiled band-conducted electroio nimbofauna deterrent - Illicit alchemical device designed protect ships that travel within storm systems from the pr atory creatures that live therein. Operates by absorbing re-channeling the electric currents of storm system lightr and unstable polarization of the air.

'tronics - Referring to the backward-engineered techn from the civilization predating the Cataclysm.

Undercity - A city that is suspended from the bedrock of Peridot's floating islands. Usually to access mineral de but sometimes as a matter of increasing the useabl on an island. Some are motley and/or ramshackle, Subrosa, while others are developed, properly cons and maintained.

Zalika - See 'Mermaids'.